IN THE COURT OF THE DEADLY QUEEN

"Why is he about to die?" demanded Nemone. "And how is he about to die?"

"He is to die because he came here in the dead of night to assassinate your majesty," explained Tomos; "the manner of his death rests of course in the hands of our gracious Queen."

Nemone's dark eyes, veiled behind long lashes, appraised the ape-man, lingering upon his bronzed skin and the rolling contours of his muscles, then rose to the handsome face until her eyes met his. "Why did you not kneel?" she asked.

"Why should I kneel to you who they have said will have me killed?" demanded Tarzan. "Why should I kneel to you who are not my Queen? Why should I, Tarzan of the Apes, who kneels to no one, kneel to you . . . ?"

By Edgar Rice Burroughs
Published by Ballantine Books:

THE TARZAN SERIES
Tarzan of the Apes (#1)
The Return of Tarzan (#2)
The Beasts of Tarzan (#3)
The Son of Tarzan (#4)
Tarzan and the Jewels of Opar (#5)
Jungle Tales of Tarzan (#6)
Tarzan the Untamed (#7)
Tarzan the Terrible (#8)
Tarzan and the Golden Lion (#9)
Tarzan and the Ant Men (#10)
Tarzan, Lord of the Jungle (#11)
Tarzan and the Lost Empire (#12)
Tarzan at the Earth's Core (#13)
Tarzan the Invincible (#14)
Tarzan Triumphant (#15)
Tarzan and the City of Gold (#16)
Tarzan and the Lion Man (#17)
Tarzan and the Leopard Men (#18)
Tarzan's Quest (#19)
Tarzan and the Forbidden City (#20)
Tarzan the Magnificent (#21)
Tarzan and the Foreign Legion (#22)
Tarzan and the Madman (#23)
Tarzan and the Castaways (#24)

COMPLETE AND UNABRIDGED!

And be sure to look for all 11 books of the *Mars* series and all 6
books of the *Pellucidar* series, also published by Ballantine!

By Edgar Rice Burroughs and Joe R. Lansdale:
TARZAN: THE LOST ADVENTURE

TARZAN TRIUMPHANT

Edgar Rice Burroughs

TARZAN AND THE CITY OF GOLD

A Del Rey® Book

BALLANTINE BOOKS • NEW YORK

A Del Rey® Book
Published by Ballantine Books

Tarzan Triumphant copyright © 1931, 1932 by Edgar Rice Burroughs, Inc.
Tarzan and the City of Gold copyright © 1932, 1959 by Frank A. Munsey Co.

Tarzan Triumphant was originally published serially in *The Blue Book Magazine* from October 1931 to March 1932 under the title "The Triumph of Tarzan."
Tarzan and the City of Gold was originally published serially in *Argosy* magazine from March 12 to April 16, 1932.

http://www.randomhouse.com

Library of Congress Catalog Card Number: 97-91948

ISBN 0-345-41641-4

This authorized edition published by arrangement with Edgar Rice Burroughs, Inc.

Manufactured in the United States of America

First Edition: November 1997

10 9 8 7 6 5 4 3 2 1

Contents

TARZAN
TRIUMPHANT

Contents

Prologue

TIME IS THE warp of the tapestry which is life. It is eternal, constant, unchanging. But the woof is gathered together from the four corners of the earth and the twenty-eight seas and out of the air and the minds of men by that master artist, Fate, as she weaves the design that is never finished.

A thread from here, a thread from there, another from out of the past that has waited years for the companion thread without which the picture must be incomplete.

But Fate is patient. She waits a hundred or a thousand years to bring together two strands of thread whose union is essential to the fabrication of her tapestry, to the composition of the design that was without beginning and is without end.

A matter of some one thousand eight hundred sixty-five years ago (scholars do not agree as to the exact year), Paul of Tarsus suffered martyrdom at Rome.

That a tragedy so remote should seriously affect the lives and destinies of an English aviatrix and an American professor of geology, neither of whom was conscious of the existence of the other at the time this narrative begins—when it does begin, which is not yet, since Paul of Tarsus is merely by way of prologue—may seem remarkable to us, but not to Fate, who has been patiently waiting these nearly two thousand years for these very events I am about to chronicle.

But there is a link between Paul and these two young people. It is Angustus the Ephesian. Angustus was a young man of moods and epilepsy, a nephew of the house of Onesiphorus. Numbered was he among the early converts to the new faith when Paul of Tarsus first visited the ancient Ionian city of Ephesus.

Inclined to fanaticism, from early childhood an epileptic, and worshipping the apostle as the representative of the Master of earth, it is not strange that news of the martyrdom of Paul should have so affected Angustus as to seriously imperil his mental balance.

Conjuring delusions of persecution, he fled Ephesus, taking ship for Alexandria; and here we might leave him, wrapped in his robe, huddled, sick and frightened, on the deck of the little vessel, were it not for the fact that at the Island of Rhodes, where the ship touched, Angustus, going ashore, acquired in some manner (whether by conversion or purchase we know not) a fair-haired slave girl from some far northern barbarian tribe.

And here we bid Angustus and the days of the Caesars adieu, and not without some regrets upon my part for I can well imagine adventure, if not romance, in the flight of Angustus and the fair-haired slave girl down into Africa from the storied port of Alexandria, through Memphis and Thebae into the great unknown.

1

Gathering the Threads

As far as I know the first Earl of Whimsey has nothing to do with this story, and so we are not particularly interested in the fact that it was not so much the fine grade of whiskey that he manufactured that won him his earldom as the generous contribution he made to the Liberal party at the time that it was in power a number of years ago.

Being merely a simple historian and no prophet, I cannot say whether we shall see the Earl of Whimsey again or not. But if we do not find the Earl particularly interesting, I can assure you that the same may not be said of his fair daughter, Lady Barbara Collis.

The African sun, still an hour high, was hidden from the face of the earth by solid cloud banks that enveloped the loftier peaks of the mysterious, impenetrable fastnesses of the forbidding Ghenzi Mountain range that frowned perpetually upon a thousand valleys little known to man.

From far above this seeming solitude, out of the heart of the densely banked clouds, there came to whatever ears there might be to hear a strange and terrifying droning, suggesting the presence of a preposterous Gargantuan bumblebee circling far above the jagged peaks of Ghenzi. At times it grew in volume until it attained terrifying proportions; and then gradually it diminished until it was only a suggestion of a sound, only to grow once again in volume and to again retreat.

For a long time, invisible and mysterious, it had been

describing its great circles deep in the concealing vapors that hid it from the earth and hid the earth from it.

Lady Barbara Collis was worried. Her petrol was running low. At the crucial moment her compass had failed her, and she had been flying blind through the clouds looking for an opening for what now seemed an eternity of hours to her.

She had known that she must cross a lofty range of mountains, and she had kept at a considerable altitude above the clouds for this purpose; but presently they had risen to such heights that she could not surmount them; and, foolishly, rather than turn back and give up her projected nonstop flight from Cairo to the Cape, she had risked all in one effort to penetrate them.

For an hour Lady Barbara had been indulging in considerable high-powered thinking, intermingled with the regret that she had not started thinking a little more heavily before she had taken off, as she had, against the explicit command of her sire. To say that she was terrified in the sense that fear had impaired any of her faculties would not be true. However, she was a girl of keen intelligence, fully competent to understand the grave danger of her situation; and when there loomed suddenly close to the tip of her left wing a granite escarpment that was lost immediately above and below her in the all enveloping vapor, it is no reflection upon her courage that she involuntarily caught her breath in a quick gasp and simultaneously turned the nose of her ship upwards until her altimeter registered an altitude that she knew must be far higher than the loftiest peak that reared its head above any part of Africa.

Rising in a wide spiral, she was soon miles away from that terrifying menace that had seemingly leaped out of the clouds to seize her. Yet even so, her plight was still as utterly hopeless as it well could be. Her fuel was practically exhausted. To attempt to drop below the cloud banks, now that she knew positively that she was among lofty mountains, would be utter madness; and so she did the only thing that remained to her.

Alone in the cold wet clouds, far above an unknown country, Lady Barbara Collis breathed a little prayer as she bailed out. With the utmost meticulosity she counted ten before she jerked the rip cord of her chute.

At that same instant Fate was reaching out to gather other threads—far-flung threads—for this tiny fragment of her tapestry.

Kabariga, chief of the Bangalo people of Bungalo, knelt before Tarzan of the Apes many weary marches to the south of the Ghenzi Mountains.

In Moscow, Leon Stabutch entered the office of Stalin, the dictator of Red Russia.

Ignorant of the very existence of Kabariga, the black chief, or of Leon Stabutch or Lady Barbara Collis, Lafayette Smith, A.M., Ph.D., Sc.D., professor of geology at the Phil Sheridan Military Academy, boarded a steamship in the harbor of New York.

Mr. Smith was a quiet, modest, scholarly looking young man with horn-rimmed spectacles, which he wore not because of any defect of eyesight but in the belief that they added a certain dignity and semblance of age to his appearance. That his spectacles were fitted with plain glass was known only to himself and his optician.

Graduated from college at seventeen the young man had devoted four additional years to acquiring further degrees, during which time he optimistically expected the stamp of dignified maturity to make itself evident in his face and bearing; but, to his intense dismay, his appearance seemed quite as youthful at twenty-one as it had at seventeen.

Lafe Smith's great handicap to the immediate fulfillment of his ambition (to occupy the chair of geology in some university of standing) lay in his possession of the unusual combination of brilliant intellect and retentive memory with robust health and a splendid physique. Do what he might he could not look sufficiently mature and scholarly to impress any college board. He tried whiskers, but the result was humiliating; and then he conceived the idea of horn-rimmed spectacles and pared his ambition down, temporarily, from a university to a prep school.

For a school year, now, he had been an instructor in an inconspicuous western military academy, and now he was about to achieve another of his cherished ambitions—he was going to Africa to study the great rift valleys of the Dark Continent, concerning the formation of which there are so many theories propounded and acclaimed by acknowledged authorities on the subject as to leave the layman with the impression that a fundamental requisite to success in the science of geology is identical to that required by weather forecasters.

But be that as it may, Lafayette Smith was on his way to Africa with the financial backing of a wealthy father and the wide experience that might be gained from a number of weekend field excursions into the back pastures of accommodating farmers, plus considerable ability as a tennis player and a swimmer.

We may leave him now, with his notebooks and sea sickness, in the hands of Fate, who is leading him inexorably toward sinister situations from which no amount of geological knowledge nor swimming nor tennis ability may extricate him.

When it is two hours before noon in New York it is an hour before sunset in Moscow and so it was that as Lafe Smith boarded the liner in the morning, Leon Stabutch, at the same moment, was closeted with Stalin late in the afternoon.

"That is all," said Stalin; "you understand?"

"Perfectly," replied Stabutch. "Peter Zveri shall be avenged, and the obstacle that thwarted our plans in Africa shall be removed."

"The latter is most essential," emphasized Stalin, "but do not belittle the abilities of your obstacle. He may be, as you have said, naught but an ape-man; but he utterly routed a well organized Red expedition that might have accomplished much in Abyssinia and Egypt but for his interference. And," he added, "I may tell you, comrade, that we contemplate another attempt; but it will not be made until we have a report from you that—the obstacle has been removed."

Stabutch swelled his great chest. "Have I ever failed?" he asked.

Stalin rose and laid a hand upon the other's shoulder. "Red Russia does not look to the OGPU for failures," he said. Only his lips smiled as he spoke.

That same night Leon Stabutch left Moscow. He thought that he left secretly and alone, but Fate was at his side in the compartment of the railway carriage.

As Lady Barbara Collis bailed out in the clouds above the Ghenzi range, and Lafayette Smith trod the gangplank leading aboard the liner, and Stabutch stood before Stalin, Tarzan, with knitted brows, looked down upon the black kneeling at his feet.

"Rise!" he commanded, and then; "Who are you and why have you sought Tarzan of the Apes?"

"I am Kabariga, O Great Bwana," replied the black. "I am chief of the Bangalo people of Bungalo. I come to the Great Bwana because my people suffer much sorrow and great fear and our neighbors, who are related to the Gallas, have told us that you are the friend of those who suffer wrongs at the hands of bad men."

"And what wrongs have your people suffered?" demanded Tarzan, "and at whose hands?"

"For long we lived at peace with all men," explained Kabariga; "we did not make war upon our neighbors. We wished only to plant and harvest in security. But one day there came into our country from Abyssinia a band of *shiftas* who had been driven from their own country. They raided some of our villages, stealing our grain, our goats, and our people, and these they sold into slavery in far countries.

"They do not take everything; they destroy nothing; but they do not go away out of our country. They remain in a village they have built in inaccessible mountains, and when they need more provisions or slaves they come again to other villages of my people.

"And so they permit us to live and plant and harvest that they may continue to take toll of us."

"But why do you come to me?" demanded the ape-man. "I do not interfere among tribes beyond the boundaries of my own country, unless they commit some depredation against my own people."

"I come to you, Great Bwana," replied the black chief, "because you are a white man and these *shiftas* are led by a white man. It is known among all men that you are the enemy of bad white men."

"That," said Tarzan, "is different. I will return with you to your country."

And thus Fate, enlisting the services of the black chief, Kabariga, led Tarzan of the Apes out of his own country, toward the north. Nor did many of his own people know whither he had gone nor why—not even little Nkima, the close friend and confidant of the ape-man.

2

The Land of Midian

ABRAHAM, THE SON of Abraham, stood at the foot of the towering cliff that is the wall of the mighty crater of a long-extinct volcano. Behind and above him were the dwellings of his people, carved from the soft volcanic ash that rose from the bottom of the crater partway up the encircling cliffs; and clustered about him were the men and women and children of his tribe.

One and all, they stood with faces raised toward the heavens, upon each countenance reflected the particular emotion that the occasion evoked—wonder, questioning, fear, and always rapt, tense listening, for from the low clouds hanging but a few hundred feet above the rim of the great crater, the floor of which stretched away for fully five miles to its opposite side, came a strange, ominous droning sound, the like of which not one of them had ever heard before.

The sound grew in volume until it seemed to hover just above them, filling all the heavens with its terrifying threat; and then it diminished gradually until it was only a suggestion of a sound that might have been no more than a persistent memory rumbling in their heads; and when they thought that it had gone it grew again in volume until once more it thundered down upon them where they stood in terror or in ecstasy, as each interpreted the significance of the phenomenon.

And upon the opposite side of the crater a similar group,

actuated by identical fears and questionings, clustered about Elija, the son of Noah.

In the first group a woman turned to Abraham, the son of Abraham. "What is it, Father?" she asked. "I am afraid."

"Those who trust in the Lord," replied the man, "know no fear. You have revealed the wickedness of your heresy, woman."

The face of the questioner blenched and now, indeed, did she tremble. "Oh, Father, you know that I am no heretic!" she cried piteously.

"Silence, Martha!" commanded Abraham. "Perhaps this is the Lord Himself, come again to earth as was prophesied in the days of Paul, to judge us all." His voice was high and shrill, and he trembled as he spoke.

A half-grown child, upon the outskirts of the assemblage, fell to the ground, where he writhed, foaming at the mouth. A woman screamed and fainted.

"Oh, Lord, if it is indeed Thee, Thy chosen people await to receive Thy blessing and Thy commands," prayed Abraham; "but," he added, "if it is not Thee, we beseech that Thou savest us whole from harm."

"Perhaps it is Gabriel!" suggested another of the long-bearded men.

"And the sound of his trump," wailed a woman—"the trump of doom!"

"Silence!" shrilled Abraham, and the woman shrank back in fear.

Unnoticed, the youth floundered and gasped for breath as, with eyes set as in death, he struggled in the throes of agony; and then another lurched and fell and he, too, writhed and foamed.

And now they were dropping on all sides—some in convulsions and others in deathlike faints—until a dozen or more sprawled upon the ground, where their pitiable condition elicited no attention from their fellows unless a stricken one chanced to fall against a neighbor or upon his feet, in which case the latter merely stepped aside without vouchsafing so much as a glance at the poor unfortunate.

With few exceptions those who suffered the violent strokes were men and boys, while it was the women who merely fainted; but whether man, woman, or child, whether writhing in convulsions or lying quietly in coma, no one paid the slightest attention to any of them. As to whether this seeming indifference was customary, or merely induced by the excitement and apprehension of the moment, as they stood with eyes, ears, and minds focused on the clouds above them, only a closer acquaintance with these strange people may enlighten us.

Once more the terrifying sound, swollen to hideous proportions, swept toward them; it seemed to stop above them for a moment and then—

Out of the clouds floated a strange apparition—a terrifying thing—a great, white thing above, below which there swung to and fro a tiny figure. At sight of it, dropping gently toward them, a dozen of the watchers collapsed, frothing, in convulsions.

Abraham, the son of Abraham, dropped to his knees, raising his hands in supplication toward the heavens. His people, those of them who were still upon their feet, followed his example. From his lips issued a torrent of strange sounds—a prayer perhaps, but if so not in the same language as that in which he had previously spoken to his people nor in any language known to man, and as he prayed, his followers knelt in terrified silence.

Closer and closer floated the mysterious apparition until, at length, expectant eyes recognized in the figure floating beneath the small, white cloud the outlines of a human form.

A great cry arose as recognition spread—a cry that was a mingling of terror-born wail and ecstatic hosanna. Abraham was among the last to recognize the form of the dangling figure for what it was, or, perhaps, among the last to admit the testimony of his eyes. When he did he toppled to the ground, his muscles twitching and jerking his whole body into horrid contortions, his eyes rolled upward and set as in death, his breath expelled in painful gasps between lips flecked with foam.

Abraham, the son of Abraham, never an Adonis, was at this moment anything but a pretty sight; but no one seemed to notice him any more than they had the score or more of lesser creatures who had succumbed to the nervous excitation of the experiences of the past half hour.

Some five hundred people, men, women, and children, of which thirty, perhaps, lay quietly or writhed in convulsions upon the ground, formed the group of watchers toward which Lady Barbara Collis gently floated. As she landed in, if the truth must be told (and we historians are proverbially truthful, except when we are chronicling the lives of our national heroes, or living rulers within whose grasp we may be, or of enemy peoples with whom our country has been at war, and upon other occasions)—but, as I was recording, as Lady Barbara landed in an awkward sprawl within a hundred yards of the assemblage all those who had remained standing up to this time went down upon their knees.

Hastily scrambling to her feet, the girl disengaged the harness of her parachute and stood gazing in perplexity upon the scene about her. A quick glance had revealed the towering cliffs that formed the encircling walls of the gigantic crater, though at the time she did not suspect the true nature of the valley spreading before her. It was the people who claimed her surprised attention.

They were white! In the heart of Africa she had landed in the midst of a settlement of whites. But this thought did not wholly reassure her. There was something strange and unreal about these prone and kneeling figures; but at least they did not appear ferocious or unfriendly—their attitudes, in fact, were quite the opposite, and she saw no evidence of weapons among them.

She approached them, and, as she did so, many of them began to wail and press their faces against the ground, while other raised their hands in supplication—some toward the heavens and others toward her.

She was close enough now to see their features and her heart sank within her, for she had never conceived the existence of an entire village of people of such unprepossessing appearance, and Lady Barbara was one of those who are strongly impressed by externals.

The men were particularly repulsive. Their long hair and

beards seemed as little acquainted with soap, water, and combs as with shears and razors.

There were two features that impressed her most strongly and unfavorably—the huge noses and receding chins of practically the entire company. The noses were so large as to constitute a deformity, while in many of those before her, chins were almost nonexistent.

And then she saw two things that had diametrically opposite effects upon her—the score of epileptics writhing upon the ground and a singularly beautiful, golden-haired girl who had risen from the prostrate herd and was slowly approaching her, a questioning look in her large gray eyes.

Lady Barbara Collis looked the girl full in the eyes and smiled, and when Lady Barbara smiled stone crumbled before the radiant vision of her face—or so a poetic and enthralled admirer had once stated in her hearing. The fact that he lisped, however, had prejudiced her against his testimony.

The girl returned the smile with one almost as gorgeous, but quickly she erased it from her features, at the same time glancing furtively about her as though fearful that someone had detected her in the commission of a crime; but when Lady Barbara extended both her hands toward her, she came forward and placed her own within the grasp of the English girl's.

"Where am I?" asked Lady Barbara. "What country is this? Who are these people?"

The girl shook her head. "Who are you?" she asked. "Are you an angel that the Lord God of Hosts has sent to His chosen people?"

It was now the turn of Lady Barbara to shake her head to evidence her inability to understand the language of the other.

An old man with a long white beard arose and came toward them, having seen that the apparition from Heaven had not struck the girl dead for her temerity.

"Get thee gone, Jezebel!" cried the old man to the girl. "How durst thou address this Heavenly visitor?"

The girl stepped back, dropping her head; and though Lady Barbara had understood no word that the man spoke, his tone and gesture, together with the action of the girl, told her what had transpired between them.

She thought quickly. She had realized the impression that her miraculous appearance had made upon these seemingly ignorant people, and she guessed that their subsequent attitude toward her would be governed largely by the impression of her first acts; and being English, she held to the English tradition of impressing upon lesser people the authority of her breed. It would never do, therefore, to let this unkempt patriarch order the girl from her if Lady Barbara chose to retain her; and, after glancing at the faces about her, she was quite sure that if she must choose a companion from among them the fair-haired beauty would be her nominee.

With an imperious gesture, and a sinking heart, she stepped forward and took the girl by the arm, and, as the latter turned a surprised glance upon her, drew her to her side.

"Remain with me," she said, although she knew her words were unintelligible to the girl.

"What did she say, Jezebel?" demanded the old man.

The girl was about to reply that she did not know, but something stopped her. Perhaps the very strangeness of the question gave her pause, for it must have been obvious to the old man that the stranger spoke in a tongue unknown to him and, therefore, unknown to any of them.

She thought quickly, now. Why should he ask such a question unless he might entertain a belief that she might have understood? She recalled the smile that the stranger had brought to her lips without her volition, and she recalled, too, that the old man had noted it.

The girl called Jezebel knew the price of a smile in the land of Midian, where any expression of happiness is an acknowledgment of sin; and so, being a bright girl among a people who were almost uniformly stupid, she evolved a ready answer in the hope that it might save her from punishment.

She looked the ancient one straight in the eye. "She said, Jobab," she replied, "that she cometh from Heaven with a message for the chosen people and that she will deliver the message through me and through no other."

Now much of this statement had been suggested to Jezebel by the remarks of the elders and the apostles as they had watched the strange apparition descending from the clouds and had sought to find some explanation for the phenomenon. In fact, Jobab himself had volunteered the very essence of this theory and was, therefore, the more ready to acknowledge belief in the girl's statement.

Lady Barbara stood with an arm about the slim shoulders of the golden-haired Jezebel, her shocked gaze encompassing the scene before her—the degraded, unkempt people huddled stupidly before her, the inert forms of those who had fainted, the writhing contortions of the epileptics. With aversion she appraised the countenance of Jobab, noting the watery eyes, the huge monstrosity of his nose, the long, filthy beard that but half concealed his weak chin. With difficulty she stemmed the involuntary shudder that was her natural nervous reaction to the sight before her.

Jobab stood staring at her, an expression of awe on his stupid, almost imbecile face. From the crowd behind him several other old men approached, almost fearfully, halting just behind him. Jobab looked back over his shoulder. "Where is Abraham, the son of Abraham?" he demanded.

"He still communeth with Jehovah," replied one of the ancients.

"Perhaps even now Jehovah revealeth to him the purpose of this visitation," suggested another hopefully.

"She hath brought a message," said Jobab, "and she will deliver it only through the girl called Jezebel. I wish Abraham, the son of Abraham, was through communing with Jehovah," he added; but Abraham, the son of Abraham, still writhed upon the ground, foaming at the mouth.

"Verily," said another old man, "if this be indeed a messenger from Jehovah let us not stand thus idly staring, lest we arouse the anger of Jehovah, that he bring a plague upon us, even of flies or of lice."

"Thou speaketh true words, Timothy," agreed Jobab, and, turning to the crowd behind them; "Get thee hence quickly and fetch offerings that may be good in the sight of Jehovah, each in accordance with his ability."

Stupidly the assemblage turned away toward the caves and hovels that constituted the village, leaving the small knot of ancients facing Lady Barbara and the golden Jezebel and, upon the ground, the stricken ones, some of whom were evidencing symptoms of recovery from their seizures.

Once again a feeling of revulsion gripped the English girl as she noted the features and carriages of the villagers. Almost without exception they were disfigured by enormous noses and chins so small and receding that in many instances the chin seemed to be lacking entirely. When they walked they ordinarily leaned forward, giving the impression that they were upon the verge of pitching headlong upon their faces.

Occasionally among them appeared an individual whose countenance suggested a much higher mentality than that possessed by the general run of the villagers, and without exception these had blond hair, while the hair of all the others was black.

So striking was this phenomenon that Lady Barbara could not but note it almost in her first brief survey of these strange creatures, yet she was never to discover an indisputable explanation, for there was none to tell her of Angustus and the fair-haired slave girl from some barbarian horde of the north, none who knew that Angustus had had a large nose, a weak chin, and epilepsy, none to guess the splendid mind and the radiant health of that little slave girl, dead now for almost nineteen centuries, whose blood, even now, arose occasionally above the horrid decadence of all those long years of enforced inbreeding to produce such a creature as Jezebel in an effort, however futile, to stem the tide of degeneracy.

Lady Barbara wondered now why the people had gone to their dwellings—what did it portend? She looked at the old men who had remained behind; but their stupid, almost imbecile faces revealed nothing. Then she turned to the girl. How she wished that they might understand one another. She was positive that the girl was actively friendly, but she could not be so sure of these others. Everything about them repelled her, and she found it impossible to have confidence in their intentions toward her.

But how different was the girl! She, too, doubtless, was an alien among them; and that fact gave the English girl hope, for she had seen nothing to indicate that the golden-haired one was being threatened or mistreated; and at least she was alive and uninjured. Yet, she must be of another breed. Her simple, and scant, apparel, fabricated apparently from vegetable fibre, was clean, as were those parts of her body exposed to view, while the garments of all the others, especially the old men, were filthy beyond words, as were their hair and beards and every portion of their bodies not concealed by the mean garments that scarce half covered their nakedness.

As the old men whispered among themselves, Lady Barbara turned slowly to look about her in all directions. She saw precipitous cliffs completely hemming a small circular valley, near the center of which was a lake. Nowhere could she see any indication of a break in the encircling walls that rose hundreds of feet above the floor of the valley; and yet she felt that there must be an entrance from the outer world, else how had these people gained entrance?

Her survey suggested that the valley lay at the bottom of the crater of a great volcano, long extinct, and if that were true the path to the outer world must cross the summit of those lofty walls; yet these appeared, insofar as she could see, utterly unscalable. But how account for the presence of these people? The problem vexed her, but she knew that it must remain unsolved until she had determined the attitude of the villagers and discovered whether she were to be a guest or a prisoner.

Now the villagers were returning, and she saw that many of them carried articles in their hands. They came slowly, timidly nearer her, exhorted by the ancients, until at her feet they deposited the burdens they had carried—bowls of cooked food, raw vegetables and fruits, fish, and pieces of the fibre cloth such as that from which their crude garments were fabricated, the homely offerings of a simple people.

As they approached her many of them displayed symptoms of great nervousness and several sank to the ground, victims of the convulsive paroxysms that marked the seizures to which so many of them appeared to be subject.

To Lady Barbara it appeared that these simple folk were either bringing gifts attesting their hospitality or were offering their wares, in barter, to the stranger within their gates; nor did the truth once occur to her at the moment—that the villagers were, in fact, making votive offerings to one they believed the messenger of God, or even, perhaps, a goddess in her own right. When, after depositing their offerings at her feet, they turned and hastened away, the simple faces of some evidencing fear caused her to abandon the idea that the goods were offered for sale; and she determined that, if not gifts of hospitality, they might easily be considered as tribute to appease the wrath of a potential enemy.

Abraham, the son of Abraham, had regained consciousness. Slowly he raised himself to a sitting position and looked about him. He was very weak. He always was after these seizures. It required a minute or two before he could collect his wits and recall the events immediately preceding the attack. He saw the last of those bringing offerings to Lady Barbara deposit them at her feet. He saw the stranger. And then he recalled the strange droning that had come out of the heavens and the apparition that he had seen floating down toward them.

Abraham, the son of Abraham, arose. It was Jobab, among the ancients, who saw him first. "Hallelujah!" he exclaimed. "Abraham, the son of Abraham, walketh no longer with Jehovah. He hath returned to our midst. Let us pray!" Whereupon the entire assemblage, with the exception of Lady Barbara and the girl called Jezebel, dropped to its knees. Among them, Abraham, the son of Abraham, moved slowly, as though in a trance, toward the stranger, his mind still lethargic from the effects of his seizure. About him arose a strange, weird babel as the ancients prayed aloud without concord or harmony, interrupted by occasional cries of "Hallelujah" and "Amen."

Tall and thin, with a long gray beard still flecked with foam and saliva, his scant robe ragged and filthy, Abraham, the son of Abraham, presented a most repulsive appearance to the eyes of the English girl as, at last, he stopped before her.

Now his mind was clearing rapidly, and as he halted he seemed to note the presence of the girl, Jezebel, for the first time. "What doest thou here, wanton?" he demanded. "Why are thou not upon thy knees praying with the others?"

Lady Barbara was watching the two closely. She noted the stern and accusing attitude and tones of the man, and she saw the appealing glance that the girl cast toward her. Instantly she threw an arm about the latter's shoulders. "Remain here!" she said, for she feared that the man was ordering the girl to leave her.

If Jezebel did not understand the words of the strange, heavenly visitor, she could not mistake the detaining gesture; and, anyway, she did not wish to join the others in prayer. Perhaps it was only that she might cling a few brief minutes longer to the position of importance to which the incident had elevated her out of a lifetime of degradation and contempt to which her strange inheritance of beauty had condemned her.

And so, nerved by the pressure of the arm about her, she faced Abraham, the son of Abraham, resolutely, although, withal, a trifle fearfully, since who knew better than she what a terrible man Abraham, the son of Abraham, might become when crossed by anyone.

"Answer me, thou—thou—" Abraham, the son of Abraham, could not find an epithet sufficiently excoriating to meet the emergency.

"Let not thy anger blind thee to the will of Jehovah," warned the girl.

"What meanest thou?" he demanded.

"Canst thou not see that His messenger hath chosen me to be her mouthpiece?"

"What sacrilege is this, woman?"

"It is no sacrilege," she replied sturdily. "It is the will of Jehovah, and if thou believest me not, ask Jobab, the apostle."

Abraham, the son of Abraham, turned to where the ancients prayed. "Jobab!" he cried in a voice that arose above the din of prayer.

Instantly the devotions ceased with a loud "Amen!" from Jobab. The old men arose, their example being followed by those others of the villagers who were not held earthbound by epilepsy; and Jobab, the apostle, approached the three who were now the goal of every eye.

"What transpired while I walked with Jehovah?" demanded Abraham, the son of Abraham.

"There came this messenger from heaven," replied Jobab, "and we did her honor, and the people brought offerings, each according to his ability, and laid them at her feet, and she did not seem displeased—nor either did she seem pleased," he added. "And more than this we knew not what to do."

"But this daughter of Satan!" cried Abraham, the son of Abraham. "What of her?"

"Verily I say unto you that she speaks with the tongue of Jehovah," replied Jobab, "for He hath chosen her to be the mouthpiece of His messenger."

"Jehovah be praised," said Abraham, the son of Abraham; "the ways of the Almighty passeth understanding." He turned now to Jezebel, but when he spoke there was a new note in his tones—a conciliatory note—and, perhaps, not a little of fear in his eyes. "Beseech the messenger to look upon us poor servants of Jehovah with mercy and forgiveness; beg of her that she open her mouth to us poor sinners and divulge her wishes. We await her message, trembling and fearful in the knowledge of our unworthiness."

Jezebel turned to Lady Barbara.

"But wait!" cried Abraham, the son of Abraham, as a sudden questioning doubt assailed his weak mind. "How can you converse with her? You speak only the language of the land of Midian. Verily, if thou canst speak with her, why may not I, the Prophet of Paul, the son of Jehovah?"

Jezebel had a brain worth fifty such brains as that possessed by the Prophet of Paul; and now she used it to advantage, though, if the truth were known, not without some misgivings as to the outcome of her rash proposal, for, although she had a bright and resourceful mind, she was nonetheless the ignorant child of an ignorant and superstitious people.

"Thou hast a tongue, Prophet," she said. "Speak thou then to the messenger of Jehovah, and if she answers thee in the language of the land of Midian thou canst understand her as well as I."

"That," said Abraham, the son of Abraham, "is scarce less than an inspiration."

"A miracle!" exclaimed Jobab. "Jehovah must have put the words in her mouth."

"I shall address the messenger," said the Prophet. "O angel of light!" he cried, turning toward Lady Barbara, "look with compassion upon an old man, upon Abraham, the son of Abraham, the Prophet of Paul, the son of Jehovah, and deign to make known to him the wishes of Him who sent you to us."

Lady Barbara shook her head. "There is something that one does when one is embarrassed," she said. "I have read it repeatedly in the advertising sections of American periodicals, but I haven't that brand. However, any port in a storm," and she extracted a gold cigarette case from a pocket of her jacket and lighted one of the cigarettes.

"What didst she say, Jezebel?" demanded the Prophet— "and, in the name of Paul, what miracle is this? 'Out of his nostrils goeth smoke' is said of the behemoth of holy writ. What can be the meaning of this?"

"It is a warning," said Jezebel, "because thou didst doubt my words."

"Nay, nay," exclaimed Abraham, the son of Abraham, "I doubted thee not. Tell her that I did not doubt thee, and then tell me what she said."

"She said," replied Jezebel, "that Jehovah is not pleased with thee or thy people. He is angry because thou so mistreat Jezebel. His anger is terrible because thou dost make her work beyond her strength, nor give her the best food, and that thou dost punish her when she would laugh and be happy."

"Tell her," said the Prophet, "that we knew not that thou wert overworked and that we shall make amends. Tell her that we lovest thee and thou shalt have the best of food. Speak to her, O Jezebel, and ask if she has further commands for her poor servants."

Jezebel looked into the eyes of the English girl, and upon her countenance rested an expression of angelic guilelessness, while from her lips issued a stream of meaningless jargon which was as unintelligible to Jezebel as to Lady Barbara or the listening villagers of the land of Midian.

"My dear child," said Lady Barbara, when Jezebel eventually achieved a period, "what you say is as Greek to me, but you are very beautiful and your voice is musical. I am sorry that you can understand me no better than I understand you."

"What saith she?" demanded Abraham, the son of Abraham.

"She says that she is tired and hungry and that she wishes the offerings brought by the people to be taken to a cave—a clean cave—and that I accompany her and that she be left in peace, as she is tired and would rest; and she wishes no one but Jezebel to be with her."

Abraham, the son of Abraham, turned to Jobab. "Send women to make clean the cave next to mine," he commanded, "and have others carry the offerings to the cave, as well as clean grasses for a bed."

"For two beds," Jezebel corrected him.

"Yea, even for two beds," agreed the Prophet, hastily.

And so Lady Barbara and Jezebel were installed in a well renovated cave near the bottom of the cliff, with food enough to feed a numerous company. The English girl stood at the entrance to her strange, new abode looking out across the valley as she sought to evolve some plan whereby she might get word of her predicament and her whereabouts to the outside world. In another twenty-four hours she knew the apprehension of her friends and her family would be aroused and soon many an English plane would be roaring over the Cape to Cairo route in search of her, and, as she pondered her unfortunate situation, the girl called Jezebel lay in luxurious idleness upon her bed of fresh grasses and ate from a pile of fruit near her head, the while a happy smile of contentment illumed her lovely countenance.

The shadows of night were already falling, and Lady Barbara turned back into the cave with but a single practical idea evolved from all her thinking—that she must find the means to communicate with these people, nor could she escape the conviction that only by learning their language might this be accomplished.

As darkness came and chill night air replaced the heat of the day, Jezebel kindled a fire at the mouth of the cave. Near it the two girls sat upon a soft cushion of grass, the firelight playing upon their faces, and there the Lady Barbara commenced the long and tedious task of mastering a new language. The first step consisted in making Jezebel understand what she desired to accomplish, but she was agreeably astonished at the celerity with which the girl grasped the idea. Soon she was pointing to various objects, calling them by their English names and Jezebel was naming them in the language of the land of Midian.

Lady Barbara would repeat the word in the Midian language several times until she had mastered the pronunciation, and she noticed that, similarly, Jezebel was repeating its English equivalent. Thus was Jezebel acquiring an English vocabulary while she taught the Midian to her guest.

An hour passed while they occupied their time with their task. The village lay quiet about them. Faintly, from the distant lake, came the subdued chorus of the frogs. Occasionally a goat bleated somewhere out in the darkness. Faraway, upon the opposite side of the valley, shone tiny, flickering lights— the cooking fires of another village, thought Lady Barbara.

A man, bearing a lighted torch, appeared suddenly, coming from a nearby cave. In low, monotonous tones he voiced a chant. Another man, another torch, another voice joined him. And then came others until a procession wound down toward the level ground below the caves.

Gradually the voices rose. A child screamed. Lady Barbara saw it now—a small child being dragged along by an old man.

Now the procession encircled a large boulder and halted, but the chanting did not cease, nor did the screaming of the child. Tall among the others Lady Barbara recognized the figure of the man who had last interrogated her. Abraham, the son of Abraham, the Prophet, stood behind the boulder that rose waist high in front of him. He raised his open palm and the chanting ceased. The child had ceased to scream, but its broken sobs came clearly to the ears of the two girls.

Abraham, the son of Abraham, commenced to speak, his eyes raised toward the heavens. His voice came monotonously across the little span of darkness. His grotesque features were lighted by the flickering torches that played as well upon the equally repulsive faces of his congregation.

Unaccountably, the entire scene assumed an aspect of menace in the eyes of the English girl. Apparently it was only the simple religious service of a simple people and yet, to Barbara Collis, there was something terrible about it, something that seemed fraught with horror.

She glanced at Jezebel. The girl was sitting cross-legged, her elbows on her knees, her chin supported in the palms of her hands, staring straight ahead. There was no smile now upon her lips.

Suddenly the air was rent by a childish scream of fear and horror that brought the Lady Barbara's gaze back to the scene below. She saw the child, struggling and fighting, dragged to the top of the boulder; she saw Abraham, the son of Abraham, raise a hand above his head; she saw the torchlight play upon a knife; and then she turned away and hid her face in her hands.

3

The "Gunner"

DANNY "GUNNER" PATRICK stretched luxuriously in his deck chair. He was at peace with the world—temporarily, at least. In his clothes were 20 g securely hidden. Beneath his left armpit, also securely hidden, snuggled a .45 in a specially designed holster. "Gunner" Patrick did not expect to have to use it for a long, long time perhaps; but it was just as well to be prepared. "Gunner" hailed from Chicago where people in his circle of society believe in preparedness.

He had never been a Big Shot, and if he had been content to remain more or less obscure he might have gone along about his business for some time until there arrived the allotted moment when, like many of his late friends and acquaintances, he should be elected to stop his quota of machine gun bullets; but Danny Patrick was ambitious. For years he had been the right hand, and that means the pistol hand, of a Big Shot. He had seen his patron grow rich—"lousy rich," according to Danny's notion—and he had become envious.

So Danny double-crossed the Big Shot, went over to the other side, which, incidentally, boasted a bigger and better Big Shot, and was a party to the hijacking of several truckloads of booze belonging to his former employer.

Unfortunately, on the occasion of the hijacking of the last truck, one of his former pals in the service of the double-crossee recognized him; and Danny, knowing that he had been recognized, sought, quite pardonably, to eliminate this damaging evidence; but his unwilling target eluded him and before he could rectify his ballistic errors the police came.

It is true that they obligingly formed an escort to convoy the truck safely to the warehouse of the bigger and better Big Shot, but the witness to Danny's perfidy escaped.

Now Danny "Gunner" Patrick knew the temper of his erstwhile patron—and who better? Many of the Big Shot's enemies, and several of his friends, had Danny taken for a ride. He knew the power of the Big Shot, and he feared him. Danny did not want to go for a ride himself, but he knew that if he remained in dear old Chi he would go the way of all good gunmen much too soon to suit his plans.

And so, with the 20 g that had been the price of his perfidy, he had slipped quietly out of town; and, being wise in his day and generation, he had also slipped quietly out of the country, another thread to be woven into Fate's tapestry.

He knew that the Big Shot was slipping (that was one reason he had deserted him); and he also knew that, sooner or later, the Big Shot would have a grand funeral with truckloads of flowers and, at least, a ten thousand dollar casket. So Danny would dally in foreign climes until after the funeral.

Just where he would dally he did not know, for Danny was shy of geographic lore; but he knew he was going at least as far as England, which he also knew to be somewhere in London.

So now he lolled in the sun, at peace with the world that immediately surrounded him; or almost at peace, for there rankled in his youthful breast various snubs that had been aimed in his direction by the few fellow passengers he had accosted. Danny was at a loss to understand why he was *persona non grata*. He was good-looking. His clothes had been designed by one of Chicago's most exclusive tailors—they were quiet and in good taste. These things Danny knew, and he also knew that no one aboard ship had any inkling of his profession. Why then, after a few minutes conversation, did they invariably lose interest in him and thereafter look through him as though he did not exist? The "Gunner" was both puzzled and peeved.

It was the third day out, and Danny was already fed up on ocean travel. He almost wished that he were back in Chicago where he knew he could find congenial spirits with whom to foregather, but not quite. Better a temporary isolation above ground than a permanent one below.

A young man whom he had not before noticed among the passengers came and sat down in the chair next to his. He looked over at Danny and smiled. "Good morning," he said. "Lovely weather we're having."

Danny's cold, blue eyes surveyed the stranger. "Are we?" he replied in a tone as cold as his gaze; then he resumed his previous occupation of staring out across the rail at the illimitable expanse of rolling sea.

Lafayette Smith smiled, opened a book, settled himself more comfortably in his chair, and proceeded to forget all about his discourteous neighbor.

Later that day Danny saw the young man at the swimming pool and was impressed by one of the few things that Danny could really understand—proficiency in a physical sport. The young man far outshone the other passengers both in swimming and diving, and his sun-bronzed body evidenced long hours in a bathing suit.

The following morning when Danny came on deck he found that the young man had preceded him. "Good morning," said Danny pleasantly as he dropped into his chair. "Nice morning."

The young man looked up from his book. "Is it?" he asked and let his eyes fall again to the printed page.

Danny laughed. "Right back at me, eh?" he exclaimed. "You see I thought youse was one of them high-hat guys. Then I seen you in the tank. You sure can dive, buddy."

Lafayette Smith, A.M., Ph.D., Sc.D., let his book drop slowly to his lap as he turned to survey his neighbor. Presently a smile stole across his face—a good-natured, friendly smile. "Thanks," he said. "You see it is because I like it so well. A fellow who's spent as much time at it as I have ever since I was a little shaver would have to be an awful dub not to be fairly proficient."

"Yeah," agreed Danny. "It's your racket, I suppose."

Lafayette Smith looked about the deck around his chair. He thought, at first, that Danny was referring to a tennis racquet, as that would be the thing that the word would connote to the mind of so ardent a tennis enthusiast as he. Then he caught the intended meaning and smiled. "I am not a professional swimmer, if that is what you mean," he said.

"Pleasure trip?" inquired Danny.

"Well, I hope it will be," replied the other, "but it is largely what might be called a business trip, too. Scientific investigation. I am a geologist."

"Yeah? I never heard of that racket before."

"It is not exactly a racket," said Smith. "There is not enough money in it to raise it to the importance and dignity of a racket."

"Oh, well, I know a lot of little rackets that pay good—especially if a fellow goes it alone and doesn't have to split with a mob. Going to England?"

"I shall be in London a couple of days only," replied Smith.

"I thought maybe you was goin' to England."

Lafayette Smith looked puzzled. "I am," he said.

"Oh, you're goin' there from London?"

Was the young man trying to kid him? Very good! "Yes," he said, "If I can get permission from King George to do so I shall visit England while I am in London."

"Say, does that guy live in England? He's the fellow Big Bill was goin' to punch in the snoot. Geeze, but there is one big bag of hot wind."

"Who, King George?"

"No, I don't know him—I mean Thompson."

"I don't know either of them," admitted Smith; "but I've heard of King George."

"You ain't never heard of Big Bill Thompson, mayor of Chicago?"

"Oh, yes; but there are so many Thompsons—I didn't know to which one you referred."

"Do you have to get next to King George to get to England?" demanded Danny, and something in the earnestness of his tone assured Smith that the young man had not been kidding him.

"No," he replied. "You see London is the capital of England. When you are in London you are, of course, in England."

"Geeze!" exclaimed Danny. "I sure was all wet, wasn't I; but you see," he added confidentially, "I ain't never been out of America before."

"Are you making a protracted stay in England?"

"A what?"

"Are you going to remain in England for some time?"

"I'll see how I like it," replied Danny.

"I think you'll like London," Smith told him.

"I don't have to stay there," Danny confided; "I can go where I please. Where are you goin'?"

"To Africa."

"What sort of a burgh is it? I don't think I'd like bein' bossed by a lot of savages, though a lot of 'em is regular, at that. I knew some Negro cops in Chi that never looked to frame a guy."

"You wouldn't be bothered by any policeman where I'm going," Smith assured him; "there are none."

"Geeze! You don't say? But get me right, mister, I ain't worried about no cops—they ain't got nothin' on me. Though I sure would like to go somewhere where I wouldn't never see none of their ugly mugs. You know, mister," he added confidentially, "I just can't like a cop."

This young man puzzled Lafayette Smith the while he amused him. Being a scholar, and having pursued scholarly ways in a quiet university town, Smith was only aware of the strange underworld of America's great cities to such a sketchy extent as might result from a cursory and disinterested perusal of the daily press. He could not catalog his new acquaintance by any firsthand knowledge. He had never talked with exactly such a type before. Outwardly, the young man might be the undergraduate son of a cultured family, but when he spoke one had to revise this first impression.

"Say," exclaimed Danny, after a short silence; "I know

about this here Africa, now. I seen a moving pitcher once—lions and elephants and a lot of foolish lookin' deer with funny monickers. So that's where you're goin'? Huntin', I suppose?"

"Not for animals, but for rocks," explained Smith.

"Geeze! Who ain't huntin' for rocks?" demanded Danny. "I know guys would croak their best friends for a rock."

"Not the sort I'm going to look for," Smith assured him.

"You don't mean diamonds then?"

"No, just rock formations that will teach me more about the structure of the earth."

"And you can't cash in on them after you find them?"

"No."

"Geeze, that's a funny racket. You know a lot about this here Africa, don't you?"

"Only what I've read in books," replied Smith.

"I had a book once," said Danny, with almost a verbal swagger.

"Yes?" said Smith politely. "Was it about Africa?"

"I don't know. I never read it. Say, I been thinkin'," he added. "Why don't I go to this here Africa? That pitcher I seen looked like they wasn't many people there, and I sure would like to get away from people for a while—I'm fed up on 'em. How big a place is Africa?"

"Almost four times as large as the United States."

"Geeze! An' no cops?"

"Not where I'm going, nor very many people. Perhaps I shall see no one but the members of my safari for weeks at a time."

"Safari?"

"My people—porters, soldiers, servants."

"Oh, your mob."

"It may be."

"What say I go with you, mister? I don't understand your racket and I don't want to, but I won't demand no cut-in whatever it is. Like the old dame that attended the funeral, I just want to go along for the ride—only I'll pay my way."

Lafayette Smith wondered. There was something about this young man he liked, and he certainly found him interesting as a type. Then, too, there was an indefinable something in his manner and in those cold, blue eyes that suggested he might be a good companion in an emergency. Furthermore, Lafayette Smith had recently been thinking that long weeks in the interior without the companionship of another white man might prove intolerable. Yet he hesitated. He knew nothing about the man. He might be a fugitive from justice. He might be anything. Well, what of it? He had about made up his mind.

"If it's expenses that's worrying you," said Danny, noting the other's hesitation, "forget 'em. I'll pay my share and then some, if you say so."

"I wasn't thinking of that, though the trip will be expensive—not much more for two, though, than for one."

"How much?"

"Frankly, I don't know, but I have been assuming that five thousand dollars should cover everything, though I may be wrong."

Danny Patrick reached into his trousers' pocket and brought forth a great roll of bills—50's and 100's. He counted out three thousand dollars. "Here's three g to bind the bargain," he said, "and there's more where that came from. I ain't no piker. I'll pay my share and part of yours, too."

"No," said Smith, motioning the proferred bills aside. "It is not that. You see we don't know anything about each other. We might not get along together."

"You know as much about me as I do about you," replied Danny, "and I'm game to take a chance. Maybe the less we know the better. Anyhow, I'm goin' to this here Africa, and if you're goin' too, we might as well go together. It'll cut down expenses, and two white fellows is got a better chance than one alone. Do we stick or do we split?"

Lafayette Smith laughed. Here, perhaps, was the making of an adventure, and in his scholarly heart he had long held the secret hope that some day he might go adventuring. "We stick," he said.

"Gimme five!" exclaimed "Gunner" Patrick, extending his hand.

"Five what?" asked Lafayette Smith, A.M., Ph.D., Sc.D.

4

Gathering the Strands

WEEKS ROLLED BY. Trains rattled and chugged. Steamships plowed. Black feet padded well-worn trails. Three safaris, headed by white men from far separated parts of the earth, moved slowly along different trails that led toward the wild fastnesses of the Ghenzis. None knew of the presence of the others, nor were their missions in any way related.

From the West came Lafayette Smith and "Gunner" Patrick; from the South, an English big game hunter, Lord Passmore; from the East, Leon Stabutch.

The Russian had been having trouble with his men. They had enlisted with enthusiasm, but their eagerness to proceed had waned as they penetrated more deeply into strange and unknown country. Recently they had talked with men of a village beside which they had camped, and these men had told them terrifying tales of the great band of *shiftas*, led by a white man, that was terrorizing the country toward which they were marching, killing and raping as they collected slaves to be sold in the north.

Stabutch had halted for the noonday rest upon the southern slopes of the foothills of the Ghenzis. To the north rose the lofty peaks of the main range; to the south, below them, they could see forest and jungle stretching away into the distance; about them were rolling hills, sparsely timbered, and between the hills and the forest an open, grassy plain where herds of antelope and zebra could be seen grazing.

36

The Russian called his head man to him. "What's the matter with those fellows?" he asked, nodding toward the porters, who were gathered, squatting, in a circle, jabbering in low voices.

"They are afraid, Bwana," replied the black.

"Afraid of what?" demanded Stabutch, though he well knew.

"Afraid of the *shiftas*, Bwana. Three more deserted last night."

"We didn't need them anyway," snapped Stabutch; "the loads are getting lighter."

"More will run away," said the head man. "They are all afraid."

"They had better be afraid of me," blustered Stabutch. "If any more men desert I'll—I'll—"

"They are not afraid of you, Bwana," the head man told him, candidly. "They are afraid of the *shiftas* and the white man who is their chief. They do not want to be sold into slavery, far from their own country."

"Don't tell me you believe in that cock-and-bull story, you black rascal," snapped Stabutch. "It's just an excuse to turn back. They want to get home so they can loaf, the lazy dogs. And I guess you're as bad as the rest of them. Who said you were a head man, anyway? If you were worth a kopeck you'd straighten those fellows out in no time; and we wouldn't have any more talk about turning back, nor any more desertions, either."

"Yes, Bwana," replied the black; but what he thought was his own business.

"Now, listen to me," growled Stabutch, but that to which he would have had the head man listen was never voiced.

The interruption came from one of the porters, who leaped suddenly to his feet, voicing a low cry of warning pregnant with terror. "Look!" he cried, pointing toward the west. "The *shiftas!*"

Silhouetted against the sky, a group of mounted men had reined in their horses upon the summit of a low hill a mile away. The distance was too great to permit the excited watchers in the Russian's camp to distinguish details, but the very presence of a body of horsemen was all the assurance that the blacks needed to convince them that it was composed of members of the *shifta* band of which they had heard terrifying rumors that had filled their simple breasts with steadily increasing dread during the past several days. The white robes fluttering in the breeze at the summit of the distant hill, the barrels of rifles and the shafts of spears that, even at a distance, were sufficiently suggestive of their true nature to permit of no doubt, but served to definitely crystallize the conjectures of the members of Stabutch's safari and augment their panic.

They were standing now, every eye turned toward the menace of that bristling hilltop. Suddenly one of the men ran toward the loads that had been discarded during the noonday halt, calling something back over his shoulder to his fellows. Instantly there was a break for the loads.

"What are they doing?" cried Stabutch. "Stop them!"

The head man and the askaris ran quickly toward the porters, many of whom already had shouldered their loads and were starting on the back trail. The head man sought to stop them, but one, a great, burly fellow, felled him with a single blow. Then another, glancing back toward the west, voiced a shrill cry of terror. "Look!" he cried. "They come!"

Those who heard him turned to see the horsemen, their robes fluttering backward in the breeze, reining down the hillside toward them at a gallop.

It was enough. As one man, porters, askaris, and the head man, they turned and fled. Those who had shouldered loads threw them to the ground lest their weight retard the runner's speed.

Stabutch was alone. For an instant he hesitated on the verge of flight, but almost immediately he realized the futility of attempted escape.

With loud yells the horsemen were bearing down upon his camp; and presently, seeing him standing there alone, they drew rein before him. Hard faced, villainous appearing, they presented such an appearance of evil as might have caused the stoutest heart to quail.

Their leader was addressing Stabutch in a strange tongue,

but his attitude was so definitely menacing that the Russian had little need of knowledge of the other's language to interpret the threat reflected in the speaker's tones and scowling face; but he dissembled his fears and met the men with a cool equanimity that impressed them with the thought that the stranger must be sure of his power. Perhaps he was but the advance guard of a larger body of white men!

The *shiftas* looked about them uneasily as this thought was voiced by one of their number, for they well knew the temper and the arms of white men and feared both. Yet, notwithstanding their doubts, they could still appreciate the booty of the camp, as they cast covetous and appraising eyes upon the abandoned loads of the departed porters, most of whom were still in view as they scurried toward the jungle.

Failing to make himself understood by the white man, the leader of the *shiftas* fell into a heated argument with several of his henchmen and when one, sitting, stirrup to stirrup, beside him, raised his rifle and aimed it at Stabutch the leader struck the weapon up and berated his fellow angrily. Then he issued several orders, with the result that, while two of the band remained to guard Stabutch, the others dismounted and loaded the packs on several of the horses.

A half hour later the *shiftas* rode back in the direction from which they had come, taking with them all of the Russian's belongings and him, also, disarmed and a prisoner.

And, as they rode away, keen gray eyes watched them from the concealing verdure of the jungle—eyes that had been watching every turn of events in the camp of the Russian since Stabutch had called the halt for the disastrous noonday rest.

Though the distance from the jungle to the camp was considerable, nothing had escaped the keen eyes of the watcher reclining at ease in the fork of a great tree just at the edge of the plain. What his mental reactions to the happenings he had witnessed none might have guessed by any changing expression upon his stern, emotionless countenance.

He watched the retreating figures of the *shiftas* until they had disappeared from view, and then he sprang lightly to his feet and swung off through the jungle in the opposite direction—in the direction taken by the fleeing members of Stabutch's safari.

Goloba, the head man, trod fearfully the gloomy trails of the jungle; and with him were a considerable number of the other members of Stabutch's safari, all equally fearful lest the *shiftas* pursue them.

The first panic of their terror had abated; and as the minutes sped, with no sign of pursuit, they took greater heart, though there grew in the breast of Goloba another fear to replace that which was fading—it was the fear of the trusted lieutenant who has deserted his bwana. It was something that Goloba would have to explain one day, and even now he was formulating his excuse.

"They rode upon us, firing their rifles," he said. "There were many of them—at least a hundred." No one disputed him. "We fought bravely in defense of the bwana, but we were few and could not repulse them." He paused and looked at those walking near him. He saw that they nodded their heads in assent. "And then I saw the bwana fall and so, to escape being taken and sold into slavery, we ran away."

"Yes," said one walking at his side, "it is all as Goloba has said. I myself—" but he got no further. The figure of a bronzed white man, naked but for a loincloth, dropped from the foliage of the trees into the trail a dozen paces ahead of them. As one man they halted, surprise and fear writ large upon their faces.

"Which is the head man?" demanded the stranger in their own dialect, and every eye turned upon Goloba.

"I am," replied the black leader.

"Why did you desert your bwana?"

Goloba was about to reply when the thought occurred to him that here was only a single, primitively armed white without companions, without a safari—a poor creature, indeed, in the jungle—lower than the meanest black.

"Who are you, to question Goloba, the head man?" he demanded, sneeringly. "Get out of my way," and he started forward along the trail toward the stranger.

But the white man did not move. He merely spoke, in low,

even tones. "Goloba should know better," he said, "than to speak thus to any white man."

The black hesitated. He was not quite sure of himself, but yet he ventured to hold his ground. "Great bwanas do not go naked and alone through the forests, like the low Bagesu. Where is your safari?"

"Tarzan of the Apes needs no safari," replied the white man.

Goloba was stunned. He had never seen Tarzan of the Apes, for he came from a country far from Tarzan's stamping ground, but he had heard tales of the great bwana—tales that had lost nothing in the telling.

"You are Tarzan?" he asked.

The white man nodded, and Goloba sank, fearfully, to his knees. "Have mercy, great bwana!" he begged. "Goloba did not know."

"Now, answer my question," said Tarzan. "Why did you desert your bwana?"

"We were attacked by a band of *shiftas*," replied Goloba. "They rode upon us, firing their rifles. There were at least a hundred of them. We fought bravely—"

"Stop!" commanded Tarzan. "I saw all that transpired. No shots were fired. You ran away before you knew whether the horsemen were enemies or friends. Speak now, but speak true words."

"We knew that they were enemies," said Goloba, "for we had been warned by villagers, near whom we had camped, that these *shiftas* would attack us and sell into slavery all whom they captured."

"What more did the villagers tell you?" asked the ape-man.

"That the *shiftas* are led by a white man."

"That is what I wished to know," said Tarzan.

"And now may Goloba and his people go?" asked the black. "We fear that the *shiftas* may be pursuing us."

"They are not," Tarzan assured him. "I saw them ride away toward the west, taking your bwana with them. It is of him I would know more. Who is he? What does he here?"

"He is from a country far in the north," replied Goloba. "He called it Russa."

"Yes," said Tarzan. "I know the country. Why did he come here?"

"I do not know," replied Goloba. "It was not to hunt. He did not hunt, except for food."

"Did he speak ever of Tarzan?" demanded the ape-man.

"Yes," replied Goloba. "Often he asked about Tarzan. At every village he asked when they had seen Tarzan and where he was; but none knew."

"That is all," said the ape-man. "You may go."

5

When the Lion Charged

LORD PASSMORE WAS camped in a natural clearing on the bank of a small river a few miles south of the jungle's northern fringe. His stalwart porters and askaris squatted over their cooking fires laughing and joking among themselves. It was two hours past sunset; and Lord Passmore, faultlessly attired in dinner clothes, was dining, his native boy, standing behind his chair, ready to anticipate his every need.

A tall, well-built Negro approached the fly beneath which Lord Passmore's camp table had been placed. "You sent for me, Bwana?" he asked.

Lord Passmore glanced up into the intelligent eyes of the handsome black. There was just the faintest shadow of a smile lurking about the corners of the patrician mouth of the white man. "Have you anything to report?" he asked.

"No, Bwana," replied the black. "Neither to the east nor to the west were there signs of game. Perhaps the bwana had better luck."

"Yes," replied Passmore, "I was more fortunate. To the north I saw signs of game. Tomorrow, perhaps, we shall have better hunting. Tomorrow I shall—" He broke off abruptly. Both men were suddenly alert, straining their ears to a faint sound that rose above the nocturnal voices of the jungle for a few brief seconds.

The black looked questioningly at his master. "You heard it, Bwana?" he asked. The white nodded. "What was it, Bwana?"

"It sounded deucedly like a machine gun," replied Passmore. "It came from south of us; but who the devil would be firing a machine gun here? and why at night?"

"I do not know, Bwana," replied the head man. "Shall I go and find out?"

"No," said the Englishman. "Perhaps tomorrow. We shall see. Go now, and get your sleep."

"Yes, Bwana; good night."

"Good night—and warn the askari on sentry duty to be watchful."

"Yes, Bwana." The black bowed very low and backed from beneath the fly. Then he moved silently away, the flickering flames of the cook fires reflecting golden highlights from his smooth brown skin, beneath which played the mighty muscles of a giant.

"This," remarked "Gunner" Patrick, "is the life. I ain't seen a cop for weeks."

Lafayette Smith smiled. "If cops are the only things you fear, Danny, your mind and your nerves can be at rest for several weeks more."

"What give you the idea I was afraid of cops?" demanded Danny. "I ain't never seen the cop I was afraid of. They're a bunch of punks. Anyhow, they ain't got nothin' on me. What a guy's got to look out for though is they might frame a guy. But, geeze, out here a guy don't have to worry about nothin'." He settled back easily in his camp chair and exhaled a slowly spiraling column of cigarette smoke that rose lazily in the soft night air of the jungle. "Geeze," he remarked after a brief silence, "I didn't know a guy could feel so peaceful. Say, do you know that this is the first time in years I ain't packed a rod?"

"A what?"

"A rod, iron, a gat—you know—a gun."

"Why didn't you say so in the first place?" laughed Smith. "Why don't you try talking English once in a while?"

"Geeze!" exclaimed Danny. "You're a great guy to talk about a guy talkin' English. What's that you pulled on me the other day when we was crossin' that open rollin' country? I learned that by heart—'a country of low relief in an advanced stage of mature dissection'—an' you talk about me talkin' English! You and your thrust faults and escarpments, your calderas and solfataras—geeze!"

"Well, you're learning, Danny."

"Learnin' what? Every racket has its own lingo. What good is your line to me? But every guy wants to know what a rod is—if he knows what's good for his health."

"From what Ogonyo tells me it may be just as well to continue 'packing your rod,' " said Smith.

"How come?"

"He says we're getting into lion country. We may even find them near here. They don't often frequent jungles, but we're only about a day's march to more open terrain."

"Whatever that is. Talk English. Geeze! What was that?" A series of coughing grunts rose from somewhere in the solid black wall of jungle that surrounded the camp, to be followed by a thunderous roar that shook the earth.

"Simba!" cried one of the blacks, and immediately a half dozen men hastened to add fuel to the fires.

"Gunner" Patrick leaped to his feet and ran into the tent, emerging a moment later with a Thompson submachine gun. "T'ell with a rod," he said. "When I get that baby on the spot I want a typewriter."

"Are you going to take him for a ride?" inquired Lafayette Smith, whose education had progressed noticeably in the weeks he had spent in the society of Danny "Gunner" Patrick.

"No," admitted Danny, "unless he tries to muscle in on my racket."

Once again the rumbling roar of the lion shattered the quiet of the outer darkness. This time it sounded so close that both men started nervously.

"He appears to be harboring the thought," commented Smith.

"What thought?" demanded the "Gunner."

"About muscling in."

"The smokes got the same hunch," said Danny. "Look at 'em."

The porters were palpably terrified and were huddled close to the fires, the askaris fingering the triggers of their rifles. The "Gunner" walked over to where they stood straining their eyes out into the impenetrable darkness.

"Where is he?" he asked Ogonyo, the head man. "Have you seen him?"

"Over there," said Ogonyo. "It looks like something moving over there, Bwana."

Danny peered into the darkness. He could see nothing, but now he thought he heard a rustling of foliage beyond the fires. He dropped to one knee and aimed the machine gun in the direction of the sound. There was a burst of flame and the sudden rat-a-tat-tat of the weapon as he squeezed the trigger. For a moment the ringing ears of the watchers heard nothing, and then, as their auditory nerves returned to normal, to the keenest ears among them came the sound of crashing among the bushes, diminishing in the distance.

"I guess I nicked him," said Danny to Smith, who had walked over and was standing behind him.

"You didn't kill him," said Smith. "You must have wounded him."

"Simba is not wounded, Bwana," said Ogonyo.

"How do you know?" demanded Danny. "You can't see nothin' out there."

"If you had wounded him he would have charged," explained the head man. "He ran away. It was the noise that frightened him."

"Do you think he will come back?" asked Smith.

"I do not know, Bwana," replied the Negro. "No one knows what Simba will do."

"Of course he won't come back," said Danny. "The old typewriter scared him stiff. I'm goin' to turn in."

Numa, the lion, was old and hungry. He had been hunting in the open country; but his muscles, while still mighty, were not what they had been in his prime. When he reared to seize Pacco, the zebra, or Wappi, the antelope, he was always just a trifle slower than he had been in the past; and his prey eluded him. So Numa, the lion, had wandered into the jungle where the scent of man had attracted him to the camp. The beast fires of the blacks blinded him; but, beyond them, his still keen scent told him there was flesh and blood, and Numa, the lion, was ravenous.

Slowly his hunger was overcoming his inherent urge to avoid the man-things; little by little it drew him closer to the hated fires. Crouched almost upon his belly he moved forward a few inches at a time. In another moment he would charge—and then came the sudden burst of flame, the shattering crash of the machine gun, the shriek of bullets above his head.

The startling suddenness with which this unexpected tumult broke the fear-laden silence of the camp and the jungle snapped the taut nerves of the great cat, and his reaction was quite as natural as it was involuntary. Wheeling in his tracks, he bounded away into the forest.

The ears of Numa, the lion, were not the only jungle ears upon which the discord of "Gunner" Patrick's typewriter impinged, for that seeming solitude of impenetrable darkness harbored a myriad life. For an instant it was motionless, startled into immobility; and then it moved on again upon the multitudinous concerns of its varied existence. Some, concerned by the strangeness of the noise, moved farther from the vicinity of the camp of the man-things; but there was at least one that curiosity attracted to closer investigation.

Gradually the camp was settling down for the night. The two bwanas had retired to the seclusion of their tent. The porters had partially overcome their nervousness, and most of them had lain down to sleep. A few watched the beast fires near which two askaris stood on guard, one on either side of the camp.

Numa stood with low-hung head out there, somewhere, in the night. The tattoo of the machine gun had not appeased his appetite, but it had added to his nervous irritability—and to his caution. No longer did he rumble forth his coughing protests against the emptiness of his belly as he watched the flames of the beast fires that now fed the flood of his anger until it submerged his fears.

And as the camp drifted gradually into sleep the tawny body of the carnivore slunk slowly closer to the dancing circle of the beast fires' light. The yellow-green eyes stared in savage fixity at an unsuspecting askari leaning sleepily upon his rifle.

The man yawned and shifted his position. He noted the condition of the fire. It needed new fuel, and the man turned to the pile of branches and dead wood behind him. As he stooped to gather what he required, his back toward the jungle, Numa charged.

The great lion wished to strike swiftly and silently; but something within him, the mark of the ages of charging forebears that had preceded him, raised a low, ominous growl in his throat.

The victim heard and so did "Gunner" Patrick, lying sleepless on his cot. As the askari wheeled to the menace of that awesome warning, "the "Gunner" leaped to his feet, seizing the Thompson as he sprang into the open just as Numa rose, towering, above the black. A scream of terror burst from the lips of the doomed man in the instant that the lion's talons buried themselves in his shoulders. Then the giant jaws closed upon his face.

The scream, fraught with the terror of utter hopelessness, awakened the camp. Men, startled into terrified consciousness, sprang to their feet, most of them in time to see Numa, half carrying, half dragging his victim, bounding off into the darkness.

The "Gunner" was the first to see all this and the only one to act. Without waiting to kneel he raised the machine gun to his shoulder. That his bullets must indubitably find the man if they found the lion was of no moment to Danny Patrick, intimate of sudden and violent death. He might have argued that the man was already dead, but he did not waste a thought upon a possibility which was, in any event, of no consequence, so do environment and habitude warp or dull the sensibilities of man.

The lion was still discernible in the darkness when Danny squeezed the trigger of his beloved typewriter, and this time he did not miss—perhaps unfortunately, for a wounded lion is as dangerous an engine of destruction as an all-wise Providence can create.

Aroused by the deafening noise of the weapon, enraged by

the wound inflicted by the single slug that entered his body, apprehending that he was to be robbed of his prey, and bent upon swift and savage reprisal, Numa dropped the askari, wheeled about, and charged straight for Danny Patrick.

The "Gunner" was kneeling, now, to take better aim. Lafayette Smith stood just behind him, armed only with a nickel plated .32 caliber pistol that some friend had given him years before. A great tree spread above the two men—a sanctuary that Lafayette Smith, at least, should have sought, but his mind was not upon flight, for, in truth, Lafayette was assailed by no fear for his own welfare or that of his companion. He was excited, but not afraid, since he could conceive of no disaster, in the form of man or beast, overwhelming one under the protection of Danny Patrick and his submachine gun. And even in the remote contingency that they should fail, was not he, himself, adequately armed? He grasped the grip of his shiny toy more tightly and with a renewed sensation of security.

The porters, huddled in small groups, stood wide-eyed awaiting the outcome of the event, which was accomplished in a few brief seconds from the instant that one of Danny's slugs struck the fleeing carnivore.

And now as the lion came toward him, not in bounds, but rather in a low gliding rush of incredible speed, several things, surprising things, occurred almost simultaneously. And if there was the element of surprise, there was also, for Danny, at least one cause for embarrassment.

As the lion had wheeled Danny had again squeezed the trigger. The mechanism of the piece was set for a continuous discharge of bullets as long as Danny continued to squeeze and the remainder of the one hundred rounds in the drum lasted; but there was only a brief spurt of fire, and then the gun jammed.

How may one record in slow moving words the thoughts and happenings of a second and impart to the narration any suggestion of the speed and action of the instant?

Did the "Gunner" seek, frantically, to remove the empty cartridge that had caused the jam? Did terror enter his heart, causing his fingers to tremble and bungle? What did Lafayette Smith do? Or rather, what did he contemplate doing? since he had no opportunity to do aught but stand there, a silent observer of events. I do not know.

Before either could formulate a plan wherewith to meet the emergency, a bronzed white man, naked but for a G-string, dropped from the branches of the tree above them directly into the path of the charging lion. In the man's hand was a heavy spear, and as he alighted silently upon the soft mold he was already braced to receive the shock of the lion's charge upon the point of his weapon.

The impact of Numa's heavy body would have hurled a lesser man to earth; but this one kept his feet, and the well placed thrust drove into the carnivore's chest a full two feet, while in the same instant the man stepped aside. Numa, intercepted before the completion of his charge, had not yet reared to seize his intended victim. Now, surprised and thwarted by this new enemy, while the other was almost within his grasp, he was momentarily confused; and in that brief moment the strange man-thing leaped upon his back. A giant arm encircled his throat, legs of steel locked around his shrunken waist, and a stout blade was driven into his side.

Spellbound, Smith and Patrick and their men stood staring incredulously at the sight before them. They saw Numa turn quickly to seize his tormentor. They saw him leap and bound and throw himself to the ground in an effort to dislodge his opponent. They saw the free hand of the man repeatedly drive home the point of his knife in the tawny side of the raging lion.

From the tangled mass of man and lion there issued frightful snarls and growls, the most terrifying element of which came to the two travelers with the discovery that these bestial sounds issued not alone from the savage throat of the lion but from that of the man as well.

The battle was brief, for the already sorely wounded animal had received the spear thrust directly through its heart, only its remarkable tenacity of life having permitted it to live for the few seconds that intervened between the death blow and the collapse.

As Numa slumped suddenly to his side, the man leaped clear. For a moment he stood looking down upon the death throes of his vanquished foe, while Smith and Patrick remained in awestruck contemplation of the savage, primordial scene; and then he stepped closer; and, placing one foot upon the carcass of his kill, he raised his face to the heavens and gave tongue to a cry so hideous that the Negroes dropped to the ground in terror while the two whites felt the hair rise upon their scalps.

Once again upon the jungle fell the silence and the paralysis of momentary terror. Then faintly, from the far distance, came an answering challenge. Somewhere out there in the black void of night a bull ape, awakened, had answered the victory cry of his fellow. More faintly, and from a greater distance, came the rumbling roar of a lion.

The stranger stooped and seized the haft of his spear. He placed a foot against Numa's shoulder and withdrew the weapon from the carcass. Then he turned toward the two white men. It was the first intimation he had given that he had been aware of their presence.

"Geeze!" exclaimed "Gunner" Patrick, beyond which his vocabulary failed to meet the situation.

The stranger surveyed them coolly. "Who are you?" he asked. "What are you doing here?"

That he spoke English was both a surprise and a relief to Lafayette Smith. Suddenly he seemed less terrifying. "I am a geologist," he explained. "My name is Smith—Lafayette Smith—and my companion is Mr. Patrick. I am here to conduct some field research work—purely a scientific expedition."

The stranger pointed to the machine gun. "Is that part of the regular field equipment of a geologist?" he asked.

"No," replied Smith, "and I'm sure I don't know why Mr. Patrick insisted on bringing it along."

"I wasn't takin' no chances in a country full of strange characters," said the "Gunner." "Say, a broad I meets on the boat tells me some of these guys eats people."

"It would come in handy, perhaps, for hunting," suggested the stranger. "A herd of antelope would make an excellent target for a weapon of that sort."

"Geeze!" exclaimed the "Gunner," "wot do you think I am, mister, a butcher? I packs this for insurance only. It sure wasn't worth the premium this time though." He added disgustedly, "jammed on me right when I needed it the most. But say, you were there all right. I gotta hand it to you. You're regular, Mister, and if I can ever return the favor—" He made an expansive gesture that completed the sentence and promised all that the most exacting might demand of a reciprocatory nature.

The giant nodded. "Don't use it for hunting," he said, and then, turning to Smith, "Where are you going to conduct your research?"

Suddenly a comprehending light shone in the eyes of the "Gunner," and a pained expression settled definitely upon his face. "Geeze!" he exclaimed disgustedly to Smith. "I might have known it was too good to be true."

"What?" asked Lafayette.

"What I said about there not bein' no cops here."

"Where are you going?" asked the stranger, again.

"We are going to the Ghenzi Mountains now," replied Smith.

"Say, who the hell are you, anyhow?" demanded the "Gunner," "and what business is it of yours where we go?"

The stranger ignored him and turned again toward Smith. "Be very careful in the Ghenzi country," he said. "There is a band of slave raiders working there at present, I understand. If your men learn of it they may desert you."

"Thanks," replied Smith. "It is very kind of you to warn us. I should like to know to whom we are indebted," but the stranger was gone.

As mysteriously and silently as he had appeared, he swung again into the tree above and disappeared. The two whites looked at one another in amazement.

"Geeze," said Danny.

"I fully endorse your statement," said Smith.

"Say, Ogonyo," demanded the "Gunner," "who was that bozo? You or any of your men know?"

"Yes, Bwana," replied the head man, "that was Tarzan of the Apes."

6

The Waters of Chinnereth

Lady Barbara Collis walked slowly along the dusty path leading from the Midian village down to the lake that lay in the bottom of the ancient crater which formed the valley of the Land of Midian. At her right walked Abraham, the son of Abraham, and at her left the golden-haired Jezebel. Behind them came the apostles, surrounding a young girl whose sullen countenance was enlivened occasionally by the fearful glances she cast upon the old men who formed her escort or her guard. Following the apostles marched the remainder of the villagers, headed by the elders. Other than these general divisions of the cortege, loosely observed, there was no attempt to maintain a semblance of orderly formation. They moved like sheep, now huddled together, now spewing beyond the limits of the narrow path to spread out on either side, some forging ahead for a few yards only to drop back again.

Lady Barbara was apprehensive. She had learned many things in the long weeks of her virtual captivity among this strange religious sect. Among other things she had learned their language, and the mastery of it had opened to her enquiring mind many avenues of information previously closed. And now she was learning, or she believed she was, that Abraham, the son of Abraham, was nursing in his bosom a growing skepticism of her divinity.

Her first night in Midian had witnessed her introduction to the cruel customs and rites of this degenerate descendant of the earliest Christian Church, and as she acquired a working knowledge of the language of the land and gained an appreciation of the exalted origin the leaders of the people attributed to her, and her position of spokesman for their god, she had used her influence to discourage, and even to prohibit, the more terrible and degrading practices of their religion.

While recollection of the supernatural aspects of her descent from the clouds remained clear in the weak mind of Abraham, the son of Abraham, Lady Barbara had been successful in her campaign against brutality; but daily association with this celestial visitor had tended to dissipate the awe that had at first overwhelmed the prophet of Paul, the son of Jehovah. The interdictions of his heavenly guest were all contrary to the desires of Abraham, the son of Abraham, and to the word of Jehovah as it had been interpreted by the prophets beyond the memory of man. Such were the foundations of the prophet's increasing skepticism, nor was the changing attitude of the old man toward her unrecognized by the English girl.

Today he had ignored her and was even forcing her to accompany them and witness the proof of his apostasy. What would come next? She had had not only ocular proof of the fanatical blood frenzy of the terrible old man, but she had listened for hours to detailed descriptions of orgies of frightfulness from the lips of Jezebel. Yes, Lady Barbara Collis was apprehensive, and not without reason; but she determined to make a last effort to reassert her waning authority.

"Think well Abraham, the son of Abraham," she said to the man walking at her side, "of the wrath of Jehovah when he sees that you have disobeyed him."

"I walk in the path of the prophets," replied the old man. "Always we have punished those who defied the laws of Jehovah, and Jehovah has rewarded us. Why should he be wroth now? The girl must pay the price of her iniquity."

"But she only smiled," argued Lady Barbara.

"A sin in the eyes of Jehovah," replied Abraham, the son of Abraham. "Laughter is carnal, and smiles lead to laughter, which gives pleasure; and all pleasures are the lures of the devil. They are wicked."

"Do not say any more," said Jezebel, in English. "You will only anger him, and when he is angry he is terrible."

"What sayest thou, woman?" demanded Abraham, the son of Abraham.

"I was praying to Jehovah in the language of Heaven," replied the girl.

The Prophet let his scowling gaze rest upon her. "Thou doest well to pray, woman. Jehovah looks not with pleasure upon thee."

"Then I shall continue praying," replied the girl meekly, and to Lady Barbara, in English; "The old devil is already planning my punishment. He has always hated me, just as they always hate us poor creatures who are not created in the same image as they."

The remarkable difference in physical appearance and mentality that set Jezebel apart from the other Midians was an inexplicable phenomenon that had constantly puzzled Lady Barbara and would continue to puzzle her, since she could not know of the little fair-haired slave girl whose virile personality still sought to express itself beyond a grave nineteen centuries old. How greatly Jezebel's mentality surpassed that of her imbecile fellows had been demonstrated to Lady Barbara by the surprising facility with which the girl had learned to speak English while she was teaching Lady Barbara the language of the Midians. How often and how sincerely had she thanked a kindly Providence for Jezebel!

The procession had now arrived at the shore of the lake, which legend asserted to be bottomless, and had halted where a few flat lava rocks of great size overhung the waters. The apostles took their places with Abraham, the son of Abraham, upon one of the rocks, the girl in their midst; and then a half dozen younger men came forward at a signal from Jobab. One of their number carried a fibre net, and two others brought a heavy piece of lava. Quickly they threw the net over the now terrified and screaming girl and secured the lava rock to it.

Abraham, the son of Abraham, raised his hands above his head, and at the signal all knelt. He commenced to pray in that now familiar gibberish that was not Midian, nor, according to

Jezebel, any language whatsoever, for she insisted that the Prophet and the Apostles, to whose sole use it was restricted, could not understand it themselves. The girl, kneeling, was weeping softly now, sometimes choking down a muffled sob, while the young men held the net securely.

Suddenly Abraham, the son of Abraham, abandoned the ecclesiastical tongue and spoke in the language of his people. "For as she has sinned so shall she suffer," he cried. "It is the will of Jehovah, in his infinite mercy, that she shall not be consumed by fire, but that she shall be immersed three times in the waters of Chinnereth that her sins may be washed from her. Let us pray that they may be not too grievous, since otherwise she shall not survive." He nodded to the six young men, who seemed well schooled in their parts.

Four of them seized the net and raised it between them, while the remaining two held the ends of long fibre ropes that were attached to it. As the four commenced to swing the body of the girl pendulumlike between them, her screams and pleas for mercy rose above the silent waters of Chinnereth in a diapason of horror, mingled with which were the shrieks and groans of those who, excited beyond the capacity of their nervous systems, were falling to the ground in the throes of epileptic seizures.

To and fro, with increasing rapidity, the young men swung their terror-crazed burden. Suddenly one of them collapsed to sink, writhing and foaming, to the surface of the great block of lava upon which they stood, dropping the soft body of the girl heavily to the hard rocks. As Jobab signaled to another young man to take the place of him who had fallen, an apostle screamed and dropped in his tracks.

But no one gave heed to those who had succumbed, and a moment later the girl was swinging to and fro out over the waters of Chinnereth, back over the hard face of the lava.

"In the name of Jehovah! In the name of Jehovah!" chanted Abraham, the son of Abraham, to the cadence of the swinging sack. "In the name of Jehovah! In the name of his son—" there was a pause, and as the body of the girl swung again out over the water—"Paul!"

It was the signal. The four young men released their holds upon the net, and the body of the girl shot downward toward the dark waters of the lake. There was a splash. The screaming ceased. The waters closed in above the victim of cruel fanaticism, leaving only a widening circle of retreating wavelets and two fibre ropes extending upward to the altar of castigation.

For a few seconds there was silence and immobility, except for the groans and contortions of the now greatly increased numbers of the victims of the Nemesis of the Midians. Then Abraham, the son of Abraham, spoke again to the six executioners, who immediately laid hold of the two ropes and hauled the girl upward until she swung, dripping and choking, just above the surface of the water.

For a brief interval they held her there; and then, at a word from the Prophet, they dropped her again beneath the waters.

"You murderer!" cried Lady Barbara, no longer able to control her anger. "Order that poor creature drawn ashore before she is drowned."

Abraham, the son of Abraham, turned eyes upon the English girl that almost froze her with horror—the wild, staring eyes of a maniac; piercing pupils rimmed round with white. "Silence, blasphemer!" screamed the man. "Last night I walked with Jehovah, and He told me that you would be next."

"Oh, please," whispered Jezebel, tugging at Lady Barbara's sleeve. "Do not anger him more or you are lost."

The Prophet turned again to the six young men, and again, at his command, the victim was drawn above the surface of the lake. Fascinated by the horror of the situation, Lady Barbara had stepped to the edge of the rock, and, looking down, saw the poor creature limp but still gasping in an effort to regain her breath. She was not dead, but another immersion must surely prove fatal.

"Oh, please," she begged, turning to the Prophet, "in the name of merciful God, do not let them lower her again!"

Without a word of reply Abraham, the son of Abraham, gave the signal; and for the third time the now unconscious girl was dropped into the lake. The English girl sank to her knees in an attitude of prayer, and raising her eyes to heaven plead fervently to her Maker to move the heart of Abraham, the son of Abraham, to compassion, or out of the fullness of His own love to save the victim of these misguided creatures from what seemed now certain death. For a full minute she had prayed, and still the girl was left beneath the waters. Then the Prophet commanded that she be raised.

"If she is now pure in the eyes of Jehovah," he cried, "she will emerge alive. If she be dead, it is the will of Jehovah. I have but walked in the paths of the Prophets."

The six young men raised the sagging net to the surface of the rocks where they rolled the limp form of the girl from it close to where Lady Barbara knelt in prayer. And now the Prophet appeared to notice the attitude and the pleading voice of the English girl for the first time.

"What doest thou?" he demanded.

"I pray to a God whose power and mercy are beyond your understanding," she replied. "I pray for the life of this poor child."

"There is the answer to your prayer," sneered the Prophet contemptuously, indicating the still body of the girl. "She is dead, and Jehovah has revealed to all who may have doubted that Abraham, the son of Abraham, is His prophet and that thou art an impostor."

"We are lost," whispered Jezebel.

Lady Barbara thought as much herself; but she thought quickly, for the emergency was critical. Rising, she faced the Prophet. "Yes, she is dead," she replied, "but Jehovah can resurrect her."

"He can, but He will not," said Abraham, the son of Abraham.

"Not for you, for He is angry with him who dares to call himself His prophet and yet disobeys His commands." She stepped quickly to the side of the lifeless body. "But for me He will resurrect her. Come Jezebel and help me!"

Now Lady Barbara, in common with most modern, athletically inclined young women, was familiar with the ordinary methods for resuscitating the drowned; and she fell to work upon the victim of the Prophet's homicidal mania with a will born not only of compassion, but of vital necessity. She issued curt orders to Jezebel from time to time, orders which broke but did not terminate a constant flow of words which she voiced in chantlike measures. She started with "The Charge of the Light Brigade," but after two stanzas her memory failed and she had recourse to Mother Goose, snatches from the verse in *Alice In Wonderland*, Kipling, Omar Khayyam; and, as the girl after ten minutes of heartbreaking effort commenced to show signs of Life, Lady Barbara closed with excerpts from Lincoln's Gettysburg Address.

Crowded about them were the Prophet, the Apostles, the Elders, and the six executioners, while beyond these the villagers pressed as close as they dared to witness the miracle if such it were to be.

" 'And that government of the people, by the people, and for the people shall not perish from the earth,' " chanted Lady Barbara, rising to her feet. "Lay the child in the net," she commanded, turning to the wide-eyed young men who had cast her into the lake, "and carry her tenderly back to the cave of her parents. Come Jezebel!" To Abraham, the son of Abraham, she vouchsafed not even a glance.

That night the two girls sat at the entrance of their cave looking out across the uncharted valley of Midian. A full moon silvered the crest of the lofty escarpment of the crater's northern rim. In the middle distance the silent waters of Chinnereth lay like a burnished shield.

"It is beautiful," sighed Jezebel.

"But, oh, how horrible, because of man," replied Lady Barbara, with a shudder.

"At night, when I am alone, and can see only the beautiful things, I try to forget man," said the golden one. "Is there so much cruelty and wickedness in the land from which you come, Barbara?"

"There are cruelty and wickedness everywhere where men are, but in my land it is not so bad as here where the church rules and cruelty is the sole business of the church."

"They say the men over there are very cruel," said Jezebel,

pointing across the valley; "but they are beautiful—not like our people."

"You have seen them?"

"Yes. Sometimes they come searching for their strayed goats, but not often. Then they chase us into our caves, and we roll rocks down on them to keep them from coming up and killing us. They steal our goats at such times; and if they catch any of our men they kill them, too. If I were alone I would let them catch me for they are very beautiful, and I do not think they would kill me. I think they would like me."

"I don't doubt it," agreed Lady Barbara, "but if I were you I would not let them catch me."

"Why not? What have I to hope for here? Perhaps some day I shall be caught smiling or singing; and then I shall be killed, and you have not seen all of the ways in which the Prophet can destroy sinners. If I am not killed I shall certainly be taken to his cave by some horrible old man; and there, all my life, I shall be a slave to him and his other women; and the old women are more cruel to such as I than even the men. No, if I were not afraid of what lies between I should run away and go to the land of the North Midians."

"Perhaps your life will be happier and safer here with me since we showed Abraham, the son of Abraham, that we are more powerful than he; and when the time comes that my people find me, or I discover an avenue of escape, you shall come away with me, Jezebel; though I don't know that you will be much safer in England than you are here."

"Why?" demanded the girl.

"You are too beautiful ever to have perfect safety or perfect happiness."

"You think I am beautiful? I always thought so, too. I saw myself when I looked into the lake or into a vessel of water; and I thought that I was beautiful, although I did not look like the other girls of the land of Midian. Yet you are beautiful and I do not look like you. Have you never been safe or happy, Barbara?"

The English girl laughed. "I am not *too* beautiful, Jezebel," she explained.

A footfall on the steep pathway leading to the cave caught their attention. "Someone comes," said Jezebel.

"It is late," said Lady Barbara. "No one should be coming now to our cave."

"Perhaps it is a man from North Midian," suggested Jezebel. "Is my hair arranged prettily?"

"We had better be rolling a rock into position than thinking about our hair," said Lady Barbara, with a short laugh.

"Ah, but they are such beautiful men!" sighed Jezebel.

Lady Barbara drew a small knife from one of her pockets and opened the blade. "I do not like 'beautiful' men," she said.

The approaching footfalls were coming slowly nearer; but the two young women, sitting just within the entrance to their cave, could not see the steep pathway along which the nocturnal visitor was approaching. Presently a shadow fell across their threshold and an instant later a tall old man stepped into view. It was Abraham, the son of Abraham.

Lady Barbara rose to her feet and faced the Prophet. "What brings you to my cave at this time of night?" she demanded. "What is it, of such importance, that could not wait until morning? Why do you disturb me now?"

For a long moment the old man stood glaring at her. "I have walked with Jehovah in the moonlight," he said, presently; "and Jehovah hath spoken in the ear of Abraham, the son of Abraham, Prophet of Paul, the son of Jehovah."

"And you have come to make your peace with me as Jehovah directed?"

"Such are not the commands of Jehovah," replied the Prophet. "Rather He is wroth with thee who didst seek to deceive the Prophet of His son."

"You must have been walking with someone else," snapped Lady Barbara.

"Nay. I walked with Jehovah," insisted Abraham, the son of Abraham. "Thou hast deceived me. With trickery, perhaps even with sorcery, thou didst bring to life her who was dead by the will of Jehovah; and Jehovah is wroth."

"You heard my prayers, and you witnessed the miracle of the resurrection," Lady Barbara reminded him. "Thinkest thou that I am more powerful than Jehovah? It was Jehovah who raised the dead child."

"Thou speakest even as Jehovah prophesied," said the Prophet. "And He spoke in my ear and commanded that I should prove thee false, that all men might see thy iniquity."

"Interesting, if true," commented Lady Barbara, "but not true."

"Thou darest question the word of the Prophet?" cried the man angrily. "But tomorrow thou shalt have the opportunity to prove thy boasts. Tomorrow Jehovah shall judge thee. Tomorrow thou shalt be cast into the waters of Chinnereth in a weighted net, nor will there be cords attached whereby it may be drawn above the surface."

7

The Slave Raider

LEON STABUTCH, MOUNTED behind one of his captors, riding to an unknown fate, was warrantably perturbed. He had been close to death at the hands of one of the band already, and from their appearance and their attitude toward him it was not difficult for him to imagine that they would require but the slightest pretext to destroy him.

What their intentions might be was highly problematical, though he could conceive of but one motive which might inspire such as they to preserve him. But if ransom were their aim he could not conjecture any method by which these semi-savages might contact with his friends or superiors in Russia. He was forced to admit that his prospects appeared most discouraging.

The *shiftas* were forced to move slowly because of the packs some of their horses were carrying since the looting of the Russian's camp. Nor could they have ridden much more rapidly, under any circumstances, on the trail that they entered shortly following their capture of Stabutch.

Entering a narrow, rocky canyon the trail wound steeply upward to debouch at last upon a small, level mesa, at the upper end of which Stabutch saw what, at a distance, appeared to be a palisaded village nestling close beneath a rocky cliff that bounded the mesa in that direction.

This evidently was the destination of his captors, who were doubtless members of the very band the mere rumor of which had filled his men with terror. Stabutch was only sorry that the balance of the story, postulating the existence of a white leader, was evidently erroneous, since he would have anticipated less difficulty in arranging the terms and collection of a ransom with a European than with these ignorant savages.

As they neared the village Stabutch discovered that their approach had been made beneath the scrutiny of lookouts posted behind the palisade, whose heads and shoulders were now plainly visible above the crude though substantial rampart.

And presently these sentries were shouting greetings and queries to the members of the returning band as the village gate swung slowly open and the savage horsemen entered the enclosure with their captive, who was soon the center of a throng of men, women, and children, curious and questioning—a savage throng of surly blacks.

Although there was nothing actively menacing in the attitude of the savages there was a definite unfriendliness in their demeanor that cast a further gloom of apprehension upon the already depressed spirits of the Russian; and as the cavalcade entered the central compound, about which the huts were grouped, he experienced a sensation of utter hopelessness.

It was at this moment that he saw a short, bearded white man emerge from one of the squalid dwellings; and instantly the depression that had seized him was, partially at least, relieved.

The *shiftas* were dismounting, and now he was roughly dragged from the animal which had borne him from his camp and pushed unceremoniously toward the white man, who stood before the doorway from whence he had appeared surveying the prisoner sullenly, while he listened to the report of the leader of the returning band.

There was no smile upon the face of the bearded man as he addressed Stabutch after the black *shifta* had completed his report. The Russian recognized that the language employed by the stranger was Italian, a tongue which he could neither speak nor understand, and this he explained in Russian; but the bearded one only shrugged and shook his head. Then Stabutch tried English.

"That is better," said the other brokenly. "I understand

English a little. Who are you? What was the language you first spoke to me? From what country do you come?"

"I am a scientist," replied Stabutch. "I spoke to you in Russian."

"Is Russia your country?"

"Yes."

The man eyed him intently for some time, as though attempting to read the innermost secrets of his mind, before he spoke again. Stabutch noted the squat, powerful build of the stranger, the cruel lips, only partially concealed by the heavy, black beard, and the hard, crafty eyes, and guessed that he might have fared as well at the hands of the blacks.

"You say you are a Russian," said the man. "Red or white?"

Stabutch wished that he might know how to answer this question. He was aware that the Red Russians were not well beloved by all peoples; and that the majority of Italians were trained to hate them, and yet there was something in the personality of this stranger that suggested that he might be more favorably inclined to a Red than to a White Russian. Furthermore, to admit that he was a Red might assure the other that a ransom could be obtained more surely than from a White, whose organization was admittedly weak and poverty stricken. For these reasons Stabutch decided to tell the truth.

"I am a Red," he said.

The other considered him intently and in silence for a moment; then he made a gesture that would have passed unnoticed by any but a Red Communist. Leon Stabutch breathed an inaudible sigh of relief, but his facial expression gave no indication of recognition of this secret sign as he answered it in accordance with the ritual of his organization, while the other watched him closely.

"Your name, comrade?" inquired the bearded one in an altered tone.

"Leon Stabutch," replied the Russian; "and yours, comrade?"

"Dominic Capietro. Come, we will talk inside. I have a bottle there wherewith we may toast the cause and become better acquainted."

"Lead on, comrade," said Stabutch; "I feel the need of something to quiet my nerves. I have had a bad few hours."

"I apologize for the inconvenience to which my men have put you," replied Capietro, leading the way into the hut; "but all shall be made right again. Be seated. As you see, I lead the simple life; but what imperial throne may compare in grandeur with the bosom of Mother Earth!"

"None, comrade," agreed Stabutch, noting the entire absence of chairs, or even stools, that the other's speech had already suggested and condoned. "Especially," he added, "when enjoyed beneath a friendly roof."

Capietro rummaged in an old duffle bag and at last withdrew a bottle which he uncorked and handed to Stabutch. "Golden goblets are for royal tyrants, Comrade Stabutch," he declaimed, "but not for such as we, eh?"

Stabutch raised the bottle to his lips and took a draught of the fiery liquid, and as it burned its way to his stomach and the fumes rose to his head the last of his fears and doubts vanished. "Tell me now," he said, as he passed the bottle back to his host, "why I was seized, who you are, and what is to become of me?"

"My head man told me that he found you alone, deserted by your safari, and not knowing whether you were friend or enemy he brought you here to me. You are lucky, comrade, that Dongo chanced to be in charge of the scouting party today. Another might have killed you first and inquired later. They are a pack of murderers and thieves, these good men of mine. They have been oppressed by cruel masters, they have felt the heel of the tyrant upon their necks, and their hands are against all men. You cannot blame them.

"But they are good men. They serve me well. They are the manpower, I am the brains; and we divide the profits of our operations equally—half to the manpower, half to the brains," and Capietro grinned.

"And your operations?" asked Stabutch.

Capietro scowled; then his face cleared. "You are a comrade, but let me tell you that it is not always safe to be inquisitive."

Stabutch shrugged. "Tell me nothing," he said. "I do not care. It is none of my business."

"Good," exclaimed the Italian, "and why you are here in Africa is none of my business, unless you care to tell me. Let us drink again."

While the conversation that ensued, punctuated by numerous drinks, carefully eschewed personalities, the question of the other's occupation was uppermost in the mind of each; and as the natural effects of the liquor tended to disarm their suspicions and urge confidence it also stimulated the curiosity of the two, each of whom was now mellow and genial in his cups.

It was Capietro who broke first beneath the strain of an overpowering curiosity. They were sitting side by side upon a disreputably filthy rug, two empty bottles and a newly opened one before them. "Comrade," he cried, throwing an arm about the shoulders of the Russian affectionately, "I like you. Dominic Capietro does not like many men. This is his motto: Like few men and love all women," whereat he laughed loudly.

"Let's drink to that," suggested Stabutch, joining in the laughter. " 'Like few men and love all women.' That is the idea!"

"I knew the minute I saw you that you were a man after my own heart, comrade," continued Capietro, "and why should there be secrets between comrades?"

"Certainly, why?" agreed Stabutch.

"So I shall tell you why I am here with this filthy band of thieving cutthroats. I was a soldier in the Italian army. My regiment was stationed in Eritrea. I was fomenting discord and mutiny, as a good Communist should, when some dog of a Fascist reported me to the commanding officer. I was arrested. Doubtless, I should have been shot, but I escaped and made my way to Abyssinia, where Italians are none too well liked; but when it was known that I was a deserter I was treated well.

"After a while I obtained employment with a powerful ras to train his soldiers along European lines. There I became proficient in Amharic, the official language of the country, and also learned to speak that of the Gallas, who constituted the bulk of the population of the principality of the ras for whom I worked.

Naturally, being averse to any form of monarchistic government, I commenced at once to instill the glorious ideals of Communism into the breasts of the retainers of the old ras; but once again I was frustrated by an informer, and only by chance did I escape with my life.

"This time, however, I succeeded in enticing a number of men to accompany me. We stole horses and weapons from the ras and rode south where we joined a band of *shiftas*, or rather, I should say, absorbed them.

"This organized body of raiders and thieves made an excellent force with which to levy tribute upon chance travelers and caravans, but the returns were small and so we drifted down into this remote country of the Ghenzi where we can ply a lucrative trade in black ivory."

"Black ivory? I never knew there was such a thing."

Capietro laughed. "Two-legged ivory," he explained.

Stabutch whistled. "Oh," he said, "I think I understand. You are a slave raider; but where is there any market for slaves, other than the wage slaves of capitalistic countries?"

"You would be surprised, comrade. There are still many markets, including the mandates and protectorates of several highly civilized signatories to world court conventions aimed at the abolition of human slavery. Yes, I am a slave raider—rather a remarkable vocation for a university graduate and the former editor of a successful newspaper."

"And you prefer this?"

"I have no alternative, and I must live. At least I think I must live—a most common form of rationalization. You see, my newspaper was anti-Fascist. And now, comrade, about yourself—what 'scientific' research is the Soviet government undertaking in Africa?"

"Let us call it anthroplogy," replied Stabutch. "I am looking for a man."

"There are many men in Africa and much nearer the coast than the Ghenzi country. You have traveled far inland looking for a man."

"The man I look for I expected to find somewhere south of the Ghenzies," replied Stabutch.

"Perhaps I can aid you. I know many men, at least by name and reputation, in this part of the world," suggested the Italian.

Stabutch, had he been entirely sober, would have hesitated to give this information to a total stranger, but alcohol induces thoughtless confidences. "I search for an Englishman known as Tarzan of the Apes," he explained.

Capietro's eyes narrowed. "A friend of yours?" he asked.

"I know of no one I would rather see," replied Stabutch.

"You say he is here in the Ghenzi country?"

"I do not know. None of the natives I have questioned knew his whereabouts."

"His country is far south of the Ghenzies," said Capietro.

"Ah, you know of him, then?"

"Yes. Who does not? But what business have you with Tarzan of the Apes?"

"I have come from Moscow to kill him," blurted Stabutch, and in the same instant regretted his rash admission.

Capietro relaxed. "I am relieved," he said.

"Why?" demanded the Russian.

"I feared he was a friend of yours," explained the Italian. "In which case we could not be friends; but if you have come to kill him you shall have nothing but my best wishes and heartiest support."

Stabutch's relief was almost a thing of substance, so considerable and genuine was it. "You, too, have a grievance against him?" he asked.

"He is a constant threat against my little operations in black ivory," replied Capietro. "I should feel much safer if he were out of the way."

"Then perhaps you will help me, comrade?" enquired Stabutch eagerly.

"I have lost no ape-man," replied Capietro, "and if he leaves me alone I shall never look for him. That adventure, comrade, you will not have to share with me."

"But you have taken away my means of carrying out my plans. I cannot seek Tarzan without a safari," complained Stabutch.

"That is right," admitted the raider; "but perhaps the mistake of my men may be rectified. Your equipment and goods are safe. They will be returned to you, and, as for men, who better could find them for you than Dominic Capietro, who deals in men?"

The safari of Lord Passmore moved northward, skirting the western foothills of the Ghenzi Mountains. His stalwart porters marched almost with the precision of trained soldiers, at least in that proper distances were maintained and there were no stragglers. A hundred yards in advance were three askaris and behind these came Lord Passmore, his gun bearer, and his head man. At the head and rear of the column of porters was a detachment of askaris—well-armed, efficient appearing men. The whole entourage suggested intelligent organization and experienced supervision. Evidence of willingly observed discipline was apparent, a discipline that seemed to be respected by all with the possible exception of Isaza, Lord Passmore's "boy," who was also his cook.

Isaza marched where his fancy dictated, laughing and joking with first one and then another of the members of the safari—the personification of good nature that pervaded the whole party and that was constantly manifested by the laughter and singing of the men. It was evident that Lord Passmore was an experienced African traveler and that he knew what treatment to accord his followers.

How different, indeed, this well-ordered safari, from another that struggled up the steep slopes of the Ghenzies a few miles to the east. Here the column was strung out for fully a mile, the askaris straggling along among the porters, while the two white men whom they accompanied forged far ahead with a single boy and a gun bearer.

"Geeze," remarked the "Gunner," "you sure picked on a lousy racket! I could of stayed home and climbed up the front of the Sherman Hotel, if I had of wanted to climb, and always been within a spit of eats and drinks."

"Oh, no you couldn't," said Lafayette Smith.

"Why not? Who'd a stopped me?"

"Your friends, the cops."

"That's right; but don't call 'em my friends—the lousy bums. But wherinel do you think you're going?"

"I think I perceive in this mountain range evidences of upthrust by horizontal compression," replied Lafayette Smith, "and I wish to examine the surface indications more closely than it is possible to do from a distance. Therefore, we must go to the mountains, since they will not come to us."

"And what does it get you?" demanded "Gunner" Patrick. "Not a buck. It's a bum racket."

Lafayette Smith laughed good-naturedly. They were crossing a meadowland through which a mountain stream wound. Surrounding it was a forest. "This would make a good camp," he said, "from which to work for a few days. You can hunt, and I'll have a look at the formations in the vicinity. Then we'll move on."

"It's jake with me," replied the "Gunner." "I'm fed up on climbing."

"Suppose you remain with the safari and get camp made," suggested Smith. "I'll go on up a little farther with my boy and see what I can see. It's early yet."

"Oke," assented the "Gunner." "I'll park the mob up near them trees. Don't get lost, and say, you better take my protection guy with you," he added, nodding in the direction of his gun bearer.

"I'm not going to hunt," replied Smith. "I won't need him."

"Then take my rod here." The "Gunner" started to unbuckle his pistol belt. "You might need it."

"Thanks, I have one," replied Smith, tapping his .32.

"Geeze, you don't call that thing a rod, do you?" demanded the "Gunner," contemptuously.

"It's all I need. I'm looking for rocks, not trouble. Come on Obambi," and he motioned his boy to follow him as he started up the slope toward the higher mountains.

"Geeze," muttered the "Gunner," "I seen pipies what ain't as much of a nut as that guy; but," he added, "he's a regular guy at that. You can't help likin' him." Then he turned his attention to the selection of a campsite.

Lafayette Smith entered the forest beyond the meadowland;

and here the going became more difficult, for the ground rose rapidly; and the underbrush was thick. He fought his way upward, Obambi at his heels; and at last he reached higher elevation, where the forest growth was much thinner because of the rocky nature of the ground and the absence of topsoil. Here he paused to examine the formation, but only to move on again, this time at right angles to his original direction.

Thus, stopping occasionally to investigate, he moved erratically upward until he achieved the summit of a ridge from which he had a view of miles of rugged mountains in the distance. The canyon that lay before him, separating him from the next ridge, aroused his interest. The formation of the opposite wall, he decided, would bear closer investigation.

Obambi had flung himself to the ground when Smith halted. Obambi appeared exhausted. He was not. He was merely disgusted. To him the bwana was mad, quite mad. Upon no other premises could Obambi explain the senseless climbing, with an occasional pause to examine rocks. Obambi was positive that they might have discovered plenty of rocks at the foot of the mountains had they but searched for them. And then, too, this bwana did not hunt. He supposed all bwanas came to Africa to hunt. This one, being so different, must be mad.

Smith glanced at his boy. It was too bad, he thought, to make Obambi do all this climbing unnecessarily. Certainly there was no way in which the boy might assist him, while seeing him in a constant state of exhaustion reacted unfavorably on Smith. Better by far be alone. He turned to the boy. "Go back to camp, Obambi," he said. "I do not need you here."

Obambi looked at him in surprise. Now he knew the bwana was very mad. However, it would be much more pleasant in camp than climbing about in these mountains. He rose to his feet. "The bwana does not need me?" he asked. "Perhaps he will need me." Obambi's conscience was already troubling him. He knew that he should not leave his bwana alone.

"No, I shan't need you, Obambi," Smith assured him. "You run along back to camp. I'll come in pretty soon."

"Yes, Bwana," and Obambi turned back down the mountainside.

Lafayette Smith clambered down into the canyon, which was deeper than he had supposed, and then worked his way up the opposite side that proved to be even more precipitous than it had appeared from the summit of the ridge. However, he found so much to interest him that he considered it well worth the effort, and so deeply absorbed was he that he gave no heed to the passage of time.

It was not until he reached the top of the far side of the canyon that he noted the diminishing light that presaged the approach of night. Even then he was not greatly concerned; but he realized that it would be quite dark before he could hope to recross the canyon, and it occurred to him that by following up the ridge on which he stood he could reach the head of the canyon where it joined the ridge from which he had descended into it, thus saving him a long, arduous climb and shortening the time, if not the distance, back to camp.

As he trudged upward along the ridge, night fell; but still he kept on, though now he could only grope his way slowly, nor did it occur to him for several hours that he was hopelessly lost.

8

The Baboons

A NEW DAY HAD dawned, and Africa greeted the age-old miracle of Kudu emerging from his lair behind the eastern hills and smiled. With the exception of a few stragglers the creatures of the night had vanished, surrendering the world to their diurnal fellows.

Tongani, the baboon, perched upon his sentinel rock, surveyed the scene and, perhaps, not without appreciation of the beauties; for who are we to say that God touched so many countless of his works with beauty yet gave to but one of these the power of appreciation?

Below the sentinel fed the tribe of Zugash, the king; fierce tongani shes with their balus clinging to their backs, if very young, while others played about, imitating their elders in their constant search for food; surly, vicious bulls; old Zugash himself, the surliest and most vicious.

The keen, close-set eyes of the sentinel, constantly upon the alert downwind, perceived something moving among the little hills below. It was the top of a man's head. Presently the whole head came into view; and the sentinel saw that it belonged to a tarmangani; but as yet he sounded no alarm, for the tarmangani was still a long way off and might not be coming in the direction of the tribe. The sentinel would watch yet a little longer and make sure, for it was senseless to interrupt the feeding of the tribe if no danger threatened.

Now the tarmangani was in full view. Tongani wished that

he might have the evidence of his keen nose as well as his eyes; then there would be no doubt, for, like many animals, the tonganis preferred to submit all evidence to their sensitive nostrils before accepting the verdict of their eyes; but the wind was in the wrong direction.

Perhaps, too, Tongani was puzzled, for this was such a tarmangani as he had never before seen—a tarmangani who walked almost as naked as Tongani himself. But for the white skin he might have thought him a gomangani. This being a tarmangani, the sentinel looked for the feared thunder stick; and because he saw none he waited before giving the alarm. But presently he saw that the creature was coming directly toward the tribe.

The tarmangani had long been aware of the presence of the baboons, being downwind from them where their strong scent was borne to his keen nostrils. Also, he had seen the sentinel at almost the same instant that the sentinel had seen him; yet he continued upward, swinging along in easy strides that suggested the power and savage independence of Numa, the lion.

Suddenly Tongani, the baboon, sprang to his feet, uttering a sharp bark, and instantly the tribe awoke to action, swarming up the low cliffs at the foot of which they had been feeding. Here they turned and faced the intruder, barking their defiance as they ran excitedly to and fro.

When they saw that the creature was alone and bore no thunder stick they were more angry than frightened, and they scolded noisily at this interruption of their feeding. Zugash and several of the other larger bulls even clambered partway down the cliff to frighten him away; but in this they only succeeded in increasing their own anger, for the tarmangani continued upward toward them.

Zugash, the king, was now beside himself with rage. He stormed and threatened. "Go away!" he barked. "I am Zugash. I kill!"

And now the stranger halted at the foot of the cliff and surveyed him. "I am Tarzan of the Apes," he said. "Tarzan does not come to the stamping grounds of the tongani to kill. He comes as a friend."

Silence fell upon the tribe of Zugash; the silence of stunning surprise. Never before had they heard either tarmangani or gomangani speak the language of the ape-people. They had never heard of Tarzan of the Apes, whose country was far to the south; but nevertheless they were impressed by his ability to understand them and speak to them. However, he was a stranger, and so Zugash ordered him away again.

"Tarzan does not wish to remain with the tongani," replied the ape-man; "he desires only to pass them in peace."

"Go away!" growled Zugash. "I kill. I am Zugash."

Tarzan swung up the cliff quite as easily as had the baboons. It was his answer to Zugash, the king. None was there who better knew the strength, the courage, the ferocity of the tongani than he, yet he knew, too, that he might be in this country for some time and that, if he were to survive, he must establish himself definitely in the minds of all lesser creatures as one who walked without fear and whom it was well to let alone.

Barking furiously, the baboons retreated; and Tarzan gained the summit of the cliff, where he saw that the shes and balus had scattered, many of them going farther up into the hills, while the adult bulls remained to contest the way.

As Tarzan paused, just beyond the summit of the cliff, he found himself the center of a circle of snarling bulls against the combined strength and ferocity of which he would be helpless. To another than himself his position might have appeared precarious almost to the point of hopelessness; but Tarzan knew the wild peoples of his savage world too well to expect an unprovoked attack, or a killing for the love of killing such as only man, among all the creatures of the world, habitually commits. Neither was he unaware of the danger of his position should a bull, more nervous or suspicious than his fellows, mistake Tarzan's intentions or misinterpret some trivial act or gesture as a threat against the safety of the tribe.

But he knew that only an accident might precipitate a charge and that if he gave them no cause to attack him they would gladly let him proceed upon his way unmolested. However, he had hoped to achieve friendly relations with the tongani, whose knowledge of the country and its inhabitants might prove of inestimable value to him. Better, too, that the tribe of Zugash be allies than enemies. And so he assayed once more to win their confidence.

"Tell me, Zugash," he said, addressing the bristling king baboon, "if there be many tarmangani in your country. Tarzan hunts for a bad tarmangani who has many gomangani with him. They are bad men. They kill. With thunder sticks they kill. They will kill the tongani. Tarzan has come to drive them from your country."

But Zugash only growled and placed the back of his head against the ground in challenge. The other males moved restlessly sideways, their shoulders high, their tails bent in crooked curves. Now some of the younger bulls rested the backs of their heads upon the ground, imitating the challenge of their king.

Zugash, grimacing at Tarzan, raised and lowered his brows rapidly, exposing the white skin about his eyes. Thus did the savage old king seek to turn the heart of his antagonist to water by the frightfulness of his mien; but Tarzan only shrugged indifferently and moved on again as though convinced that the baboons would not accept his overtures of friendship.

Straight toward the challenging bulls that stood in his path he walked, without haste and apparently without concern; but his eyes were narrowed and watchful, his every sense on the alert. One bull, stiff legged and arrogant, moved grudgingly aside; but another stood his ground. Here, the ape-man knew the real test would come that should decide the issue.

The two were close now, face-to-face, when suddenly there burst from the lips of the man-beast a savage growl, and simultaneously he charged. With an answering growl and a catlike leap the baboon bounded aside; and Tarzan passed beyond the rim of the circle, victor in the game of bluff which is played by every order of living thing sufficiently advanced in the scale of intelligence to possess an imagination.

Seeing that the man-thing did not follow upward after the shes and balus, the bulls contented themselves with barking insults after him and aiming uncomplimentary gestures at his retreating figure; but such were not the acts that menaced safety, and the ape-man ignored them.

Purposely he had turned away from the shes and their young, with the intention of passing around them, rather than precipitate a genuine attack by seeming to threaten them. And thus his way took him to the edge of a shallow ravine into which, unknown either to Tarzan or the tongani, a young mother had fled with her tiny balu.

Tarzan was still in full view of the tribe of Zugash, though he alone could see into the ravine, when suddenly three things occurred that shattered the peace that seemed again descending upon the scene. A vagrant air current wafted upward from the thick verdure below him the scent of Sheeta, the panther; a baboon voiced a scream of terror; and, looking down, the ape-man saw the young she, her balu clinging to her back, fleeing upward toward him with savage Sheeta in pursuit.

As Tarzan, reacting instantly to the necessity of the moment, leaped downward with back thrown spear hand, the bulls of Zugash raced forward in answer to the note of terror in the voice of the young mother.

From his position above the actors in this sudden tragedy of the wilds the ape-man could see the panther over the head of the baboon and realizing that the beast must reach his victim before succor could arrive he hurled his spear in the forlorn hope of stopping the carnivore, if only for a moment.

The cast was one that only a practiced hand might have dared attempt, for the danger to the baboon was almost as great as that which threatened the panther should the aim of the ape-man not be perfect.

Zugash and his bulls, bounding forward at an awkward gallop, reached the edge of the ravine just in time to see the heavy spear hurtle past the head of the she by a margin of inches only and bury itself in the breast of Sheeta. Then they were down the slope, a snarling, snapping pack, and with them went an English viscount, to fall upon a surprised, pain-maddened panther.

The baboons leaped in to snap at their hereditary foe and leaped out again, and the man-beast, as quick and agile as they, leaped and struck with his hunting knife, while the frenzied cat lunged this way and that, first at one tormentor and then at another.

Twice those powerful, raking talons reached their mark and two bulls sprawled, torn and bloody, upon the ground; but the bronzed hide of the ape-man ever eluded the rage of the wounded cat.

Short was the furious battle, ferocious the growls and snarls of the combatants, prodigious the leaps and bounds of the excited shes hovering in the background; and then Sheeta, rearing high upon his hind feet, struck savagely at Tarzan and, in the same instant, plunged to earth dead, slain by the spear point puncturing his heart.

Instantly the great tarmangani, who had once been king of the great apes, leaped close and placed a foot upon the carcass of his kill. He raised his face toward Kudu, the sun; and from his lips broke the horrid challenge of the bull ape that has killed.

For a moment silence fell upon the forest, the mountain, and the jungle. Awed, the baboons ceased their restless movement and their din. Tarzan stooped and drew the spear from the quivering body of Sheeta, while the tongani watched him with a new interest.

Then Zugash approached. This time he did not rest the back of his head against the ground in challenge. "The bulls of the tribe of Zugash are the friends of Tarzan of the Apes," he said.

"Tarzan is the friend of the bulls of the tribe of Zugash," responded the ape-man.

"We have seen a tarmangani," said Zugash. "He has many gomangani. There are many thunder sticks among them. They are bad. Perhaps it is they whom Tarzan seeks."

"Perhaps," admitted the slayer of Sheeta. "Where are they?"

"They were camped where the rocks sit upon the mountainside, as here." He nodded toward the cliff.

"Where?" asked Tarzan again, and this time Zugash motioned along the foothills toward the south.

9

The Great Fissure

THE MORNING SUN shone upon the bosom of Chinnereth, glancing from the breeze-born ripples that moved across its surface like vast companies of soldiers passing in review with their countless spears gleaming in the sunlight—a dazzling aspect of beauty.

But to Lady Barbara Collis it connoted something quite different—a shallow splendor concealing cruel and treacherous depths, the real Chinnereth. She shuddered as she approached its shore surrounded by the apostles, preceded by Abraham, the son of Abraham, and followed by the elders and the villagers. Among them, somewhere, she knew were the six with their great net and their fibre ropes.

How alike were they all to Chinnereth, hiding their cruelty and their treachery beneath a thin veneer of godliness! But there the parallel terminated, for Chinnereth was beautiful. She glanced at the faces of the men nearest her, and again she shuddered. " 'So God created man in his own image,' " she mused. "Who, then, created these?"

During the long weeks that fate had held her in this land of Midian she had often sought an explanation of the origin of this strange race, and the deductions of her active mind had not deviated greatly from the truth. Noting the exaggerated racial characteristics of face and form that distinguished them from other peoples she had seen, recalling their common tendency to epilepsy, she had concluded that they were the inbred descendants of a common ancestor, himself a defective and an epileptic.

This theory explained much; but it failed to explain Jezebel, who insisted that she was the child of two of these creatures and that, insofar as she knew, no new strain of blood had ever been injected into the veins of the Midian by intermating with other peoples. Yet, somehow, Lady Barbara knew that such a strain must have been introduced, though she could not guess the truth nor the antiquity of the fact that lay buried in the grave of a little slave girl.

And their religion! Again she shuddered. What a hideous travesty of the teachings of Christ! It was a confused jumble of ancient Christianity and still more ancient Judaism, handed down by word of mouth through a half imbecile people who had no written language; a people who had confused Paul the Apostle with Christ the Master and lost entirely the essence of the Master's teachings, while interpolating hideous barbarisms of their own invention. Sometimes she thought she saw in this exaggerated deviation a suggestion of parallel to other so-called Christian sects of the civilized outer world.

But now her train of thoughts was interrupted by the near approach of the procession to the shore of the lake. Here was the flat-topped lava rock of grim suggestiveness and hideous memory. How long it seemed since she had watched the six hurl their screaming victim from its well-worn surface, and yet it had been but yesterday. Now it was her turn. The Prophet and the Apostles were intoning their senseless gibberish, meant to impress the villagers with their erudition and cloak the real vacuity of their minds, a practice not unknown to more civilized sects.

She was halted now upon the smooth surface of the lava, polished by soft sandals and naked feet through the countless years that these cruel rites had been enacted beside the waters of Chinnereth. Again she heard the screams of yesterday's victim. But Lady Barbara Collis had not screamed, nor would she. She would rob them of that satisfaction at least.

Abraham, the son of Abraham, motioned the six to the fore; and they came, bearing their net and their cords. At their feet lay the lava fragment that would weight the net and its contents. The Prophet raised his hands above his head and the people knelt. In the forefront of their ranks Lady Barbara saw the golden-haired Jezebel; and her heart was touched, for there were anguish in the beautiful face and tears in the lovely eyes. Here was one, at least, who could harbor love and compassion.

"I have walked with Jehovah," cried Abraham, the son of Abraham, and Lady Barbara wondered that he did not have blisters on his feet, so often he walked with Jehovah. The levity of the conceit brought an involuntary smile to her lips, a smile that the Prophet noticed. "You smile," he said, angrily. "You smile when you should scream and beg for mercy as the others do. Why do you smile?"

"Because I am not afraid," replied Lady Barbara, though she was very much afraid.

"Why art thou not afraid, woman?" demanded the old man.

"I, too, have walked with Jehovah," she replied, "and He told me to fear not, because you are a false prophet, and—"

"Silence!" thundered Abraham, the son of Abraham. "Blaspheme no more. Jehovah shall judge you in a moment." He turned to the six. "Into the net with her!"

Quickly they did his bidding; and as they commenced to swing her body to and fro, to gain momentum against the moment that they would release their holds and cast her into the deep lake, she heard The Prophet reciting her iniquities that Jehovah was about to judge in his own peculiar way. His speech was punctuated by the screams and groans of those of the company who were seized in the grip of the now familiar attacks to which Lady Barbara had become so accustomed as to be almost as callous to as the Midians themselves.

From her pocket the girl extracted the little penknife that was her only weapon and held it firmly in one hand, the blade open and ready for the work she intended it to do. And what work was that? Surely, she could not hope to inflict instant death upon herself with that inadequate weapon! Yet, in the last stages of fear induced by utter helplessness and hopelessness one may attempt anything, even the impossible.

Now they were swinging her far out over Chinnereth. The Apostles and the elders were intoning their weird chant in voices excited to frenzy by the imminence of death, those who were not writhing upon the rocky face of the altar in the throes of seizures.

Suddenly came the word from Abraham, the son of Abraham. Lady Barbara caught her breath in a last frightened gasp. The six released their holds. A loud scream arose from the huddled villagers—the scream of a woman—and as she plunged toward the dark waters Lady Barbara knew that it was the voice of Jezebel crying out in the anguish of sorrow. Then mysterious Chinnereth closed above her head.

At that very moment Lafayette Smith, A.M., Ph.D., Sc.D., was stumbling along a rocky mountainside that walled the great crater where lay the land of Midian and Chinnereth. He was no less aware of the tragedy being enacted upon the opposite side of that stupendous wall than of the fact that he was moving directly away from the camp he was seeking. Had there been anyone there to tell him, and had they told him, that he was hopelessly lost he would have been inclined to dispute the statement, so positive was he that he was taking a shortcut to camp, which he imagined was but a little distance ahead.

Although he had been without supper and breakfast, hunger had not as yet caused him any annoyance, partially because of the fact that he had had some chocolate with him, which had materially assisted in allaying its pangs, and partially through his interest in the geologic formations that held the attention of his scholarly mind to the exclusion of such material considerations as hunger, thirst, and bodily comfort. Even the question of personal safety was relegated to the oblivion that usually engulfed all practical issues when Lafayette Smith was immersed in the pleasant waters of research.

Consequently he was unaware of the proximity of a tawny body, nor did the fixed and penetrating gaze of a pair of cruel, yellow-green eyes penetrate the armor of his preoccupation to disturb that sixth sense that is popularly supposed to warn us of unseen danger. Yet even had any premonition of threat to his life or safety disturbed him he doubtless would have ignored it, safe in the consciousness that he was adequately protected by the possession of his .32 caliber, nickel plated pistol.

Moving northward along the lower slopes of a conical mountain, the mind of the geologist became more and more deeply engrossed in the rocky story that Nature had written upon the landscape, a story so thrilling that even the thoughts of camp were forgotten; and as he made his way farther and farther from camp a great lion stalked in his wake.

What hidden urge prompted Numa thus to follow the man-thing perhaps the great cat, himself, could not have guessed. He was not hungry, for he had but recently finished a kill, nor was he a maneater, though a properly balanced combination of circumstances might easily find the scales tipped in that direction by hunger, inevitable and oft recurring. It may have been only curiosity, or, again, some motive akin to that playfulness which is inherent in all cats.

For an hour Numa followed the man—an hour of intense interest for both of them—an hour that would have been replete with far greater interest for the man, if less pleasurable, had he shared with Numa the knowledge of their propinquity. Then the man halted before a narrow vertical cleft in the rocky escarpment towering above him. Here was an interesting entry in the book of Nature! What titanic force had thus rent the solid rock of this mighty mountain? It had its own peculiar significance, but what was it? Perhaps elsewhere on the face of the mountain, that here became precipitous, there would be other evidence to point the way to a solution. Lafayette Smith looked up at the face of the cliff towering above him, he looked ahead in the direction he had been going; and then he looked back in the direction from which he had come—and saw the lion.

For a long moment the two stared at one another. Surprise and interest were the most definitely registered of the emotions that the discovery engendered in the mind of the man. Suspicion and irritability were aroused in Numa.

"Most interesting," thought Lafayette Smith. "A splendid specimen"; but his interest in lions was purely academic, and his thoughts quickly reverted to the more important phenomenon of the crack in the mountain, which now, again, claimed his undivided attention. From which it may be inferred that Lafayette Smith was either an inordinately courageous man or a fool. Neither assumption, however, would be wholly correct, especially the latter. The truth of the matter is that Lafayette Smith suffered from inexperience and impracticality. While he knew that a lion was, *per se,* a threat to longevity he saw no reason why this lion should attack him. He, Lafayette Smith, had done nothing to offend this, or any other, lion; he was attending to his own affairs and, like the gentleman he was, expected others, including lions, to be equally considerate. Furthermore, he had a childlike faith in the infallibility of his nickel plated .32 should worse develop into worst. Therefore he ignored Numa and returned to contemplation of the intriguing crack.

It was several feet wide and was apparent as far up the face of the cliff as he could see. Also there was every indication that it continued far below the present surface of the ground, but had been filled by débris brought down by erosion from above. How far into the mountain it extended he could not guess; but he hoped that it ran back, and was open, for a great distance, in which event it would offer a most unique means for studying the origin of this mountain massif.

Therefore, with this thought uppermost in his mind, and the lion already crowded into the dim background of his consciousness, he entered the narrow opening of the intriguing fissure. Here he discovered that the cleft curved gradually to the left and that it extended upward to the surface, where it was considerably wider than at the bottom, thus affording both light and air for the interior.

Thrilled with excitement and glowing with pride in his discovery, Lafayette clambered inward over the fallen rocks that littered the floor of the fissure, intent now on exploring the opening to its full extent and then working back slowly to the entrance in a more leisurely manner, at which time he would make a minute examination of whatever geological record Nature had imprinted upon the walls of this majestic corridor. Hunger, thirst, camp, and the lion were forgotten.

Numa, however, was no geologist. The great cleft aroused

no palpitant enthusiasm within his broad breast. It did not cause him to forget anything, and it intrigued his interest only to the extent of causing him to speculate on why the man-thing had entered it. Having noted the indifferent attitude of the man, his lack of haste, Numa could not attribute his disappearance within the maw of the fissure to flight, of which it bore not a single earmark; and it may be recorded here that Numa was an expert on flight. All of his life things had been fleeing from him.

It had always seemed to Numa an unfair provision of Nature that things should so almost inevitably seek to escape him, especially those things he most coveted. There were, for example, Pacco, the zebra, and Wappi, the antelope, the tenderest and most delicious of his particular weaknesses, and, at the same time, the fleetest. It would have been much simpler all around had Kota the tortoise been endowed with the speed of Pacco and Pacco with the torpidity of Kota.

But in this instance there was nothing to indicate that the man-thing was fleeing him. Perhaps, then, there was treachery afoot. Numa bristled. Very cautiously he approached the fissure into which his quarry had disappeared. Numa was beginning to think of Lafayette Smith in terms of food, now, since his long stalking had commenced to arouse within his belly the first, faint suggestions of hunger. He approached the cleft and looked in. The tarmangani was not in sight. Numa was not pleased, and he evidenced his displeasure by an angry growl.

A hundred yards within the fissure Lafayette Smith heard the growl and halted abruptly. "That damn lion!" he ejaculated. "I had forgotten all about him." It now occurred to him that this might be the beast's lair—a most unhappy contretemps, if true. A realization of his predicament at last supplanted the geologic reveries that had filled his mind. But what to do? Suddenly his faith in his trusty .32 faltered. As he recalled the appearance of the great beast the weapon seemed less infallible, yet it still gave him a certain sense of assurance as his fingers caressed its grip.

He determined that it would not be wise to retrace his steps toward the entrance at this time. Of course the lion might not have entered the fissure, might not even be harboring any intention of so doing. On the other hand, he might, in which event a return toward the opening could prove embarrassing, if not disastrous. Perhaps, if he waited a while, the lion would go away; and in the meantime, he decided, it would be discreet to go still farther along the cleft, as the lion, if it entered at all, might conceivably not proceed to the uttermost depths of the corridor. Further, there was the chance that he would find some sort of sanctuary farther in—a cave, a ledge to which he could climb, a miracle. Lafayette Smith was open to anything by this time.

And so he scrambled on, tearing his clothes and his flesh as well on sharp fragments of tumbled rock, going deeper into this remarkable corridor that seemed endless. In view of what might be behind him he hoped that it was endless. He had shuddered regularly to the oft recurring expectation of running into a blank wall just beyond that portion of the gently curving fissure that lay within his view ahead. He pictured the event. With his back to the rocky end of the cul-de-sac he would face back down the corridor, his pistol ready in his hand. Presently the lion would appear and discover him.

At this point he had some difficulty in constructing the scene, because he did not know just what the lion would do. Perhaps, seeing a man, cowed by the superior gaze of the human eye, he would turn in hasty retreat. And then again, perhaps not. Lafayette Smith was inclined to the conclusion that he would not. But then, of course, he had not had sufficient experience of wild animals to permit him to pose as an authority on the subject. To be sure, upon another occasion, while engaged in fieldwork, he had been chased by a cow. Yet even this experience had not been conclusive—it had not served to definitely demonstrate the cow's ultimate intent—for the very excellent reason that Lafayette had attained a fence two jumps ahead of her.

Confused as the issue now seemed to be by his total ignorance of leonine psychology, he was convinced that he must attempt to visualize the expectant scene that he might be prepared for the eventuality.

Forging grimly ahead over the roughly tumbled fragments, casting an occasional glance backward, he again pictured his last stand with his back against the corridor's rocky end. The lion was creeping slowly toward him, but Lafayette was waiting until there should be no chance of a miss. He was very cool. His hand was steady as he took careful aim.

Here regrets interrupted the even tenor of his musing—regrets that he had not practiced more assiduously with his pistol. The fact that he had never discharged it troubled him, though only vaguely, since he harbored the popular subconscious conviction that if a firearm is pointed in the general direction of an animate object it becomes a deadly weapon.

However, in this mental picture he took careful aim—the fact that he was utilizing the front sight only giving him no concern. He pulled the trigger. The lion staggered and almost fell. It required a second shot to finish him, and as he sank to the ground Lafayette Smith breathed a genuine sigh of relief. He felt himself trembling slightly to the reaction of the nervous strain he had been undergoing. He stopped, and, withdrawing a handkerchief from his pocket, mopped the perspiration from his forehead, smiling a little as he realized the pitch of excitement to which he had aroused himself. Doubtless the lion had already forgotten him and had gone on about his business, he soliloquized.

He was facing back in the direction from which he had come as this satisfying conclusion passed through his mind; and then, a hundred feet away, where the corridor passed from view around a curve, the lion appeared.

10

In the Clutches of the Enemy

THE "GUNNER" WAS perturbed. It was morning, and Lafayette Smith was still missing. They had searched for him until late the previous night, and now they were setting forth again. Ogonyo, the head man, acting under instructions from the "Gunner" had divided the party into pairs and, with the exception of four men left to guard the camp, these were to search in different directions combing the country carefully for trace of the missing man.

Danny had selected Obambi as his companion, a fact which irked the black boy considerably as he had been the target for a great deal of angry vituperation ever since Danny had discovered, the afternoon before, that he had left Smith alone in the mountains.

"It don't make no difference what he told you, you punk," the "Gunner" assured him, "you didn't have no business leavin' him out there alone. Now I'm goin' to take you for a walk, and if we don't find Lafayette you ain't never comin' back."

"Yes, Bwana," replied Obambi, who had not even a crude idea of what the white man was talking about. One thing, however, pleased him immensely and that was that the bwana insisted on carrying his own gun, leaving nothing for Obambi to carry but a light lunch and two fifty-round drums of ammunition. Not that the nine pounds and thirteen ounces of a Thompson submachine gun would have been an exceptionally heavy burden, but that Obambi was always glad to be relieved of any burden. He would have been mildly grateful for a load reduction of even thirteen ounces.

The "Gunner," in attempting to determine the probable route that Smith would have followed in his search for the camp, reasoned in accordance with what he assumed he would have done under like circumstances; and, knowing that Smith had been last seen well above the camp and a little to the north of it, he decided to search in a northerly direction along the foothills, it being obvious that a man would come downhill rather than go farther up in such an emergency.

The day was hot and by noon the "Gunner" was tired, sweating, and disgusted. He was particularly disgusted with Africa, which, he informed Obambi, was "a hell of a burgh."

"Geeze," he grumbled; "I've walked my lousy legs off, and I ain't been no further than from The Loop to Cicero. I been six hours, and I could of done it in twenty minutes in a taxi. Of course they ain't got no cops in Africa, but they ain't got no taxis either."

"Yes, Bwana," agreed Obambi.

"Shut up!" growled the "Gunner."

They were sitting beneath the shade of a tree on a hillside, resting and eating their lunch. A short distance below them the hillside dropped sheer in a fifty-foot cliff, a fact that was not apparent from where they sat, any more than was the palisaded village at the cliff's base. Nor did they see the man squatting by a bush at the very brink of the cliff. His back was toward them, as, from the concealment of the bush, he gazed down upon the village below.

Here, the watcher believed, was the man he sought; but he wished to make sure, which might require days of watching. Time, however, meant little or nothing to Tarzan—no more than it did to any other jungle beast. He would come back often to this vantage spot and watch. Sooner or later he would discover the truth or falsity of his suspicion that one of the white men he saw in the village below was the slave raider for whom he had come north. And so, like a great lion, the ape-man crouched, watching his quarry.

Below him Dominic Capietro and Leon Stabutch lolled in the shade of a tree outside the hut of the raider, while a half dozen slave girls waited upon them as they leisurely ate their belated breakfast.

A couple of fiery liquid bracers had stimulated their jaded spirits, which had been at low ebb after their awakening following their debauch of the previous day, though, even so, neither could have been correctly described as being in fine fettle.

Capietro, who was even more surly and quarrelsome than usual, vented his spleen upon the hapless slaves, while Stabutch ate in morose silence, which he finally broke to revert to the subject of his mission.

"I ought to get started toward the south," he said. "From all I can learn there's nothing to be gained looking for the ape-man in this part of the country."

"What you in such a hurry to find him for?" demanded Capietro. "Ain't my company good enough for you?"

" 'Business before pleasure,' you know, comrade," Stabutch reminded the Italian in a conciliatory tone.

"I suppose so," grunted Capietro.

"I should like to visit you again after I have come back from the south," suggested Stabutch.

"You may not come back."

"I shall. Peter Zveri must be avenged. The obstacle in the path of communism must be removed."

"The monkey-man killed Zveri?"

"No, a woman killed him," replied the Russian, "but the monkey-man, as you call him, was directly responsible for the failure of all Zveri's plans and thus indirectly responsible for his death."

"You expect to fare better than Zveri, then? Good luck to you, but I don't envy you your mission. This Tarzan is like a lion with the brain of a man. He is savage. He is terrible. In his own country he is also very powerful."

"I shall get him, nevertheless," said Stabutch, confidently. "If possible I shall kill him the moment I first see him, before he has an opportunity to become suspicious; or, if I cannot do that, I shall win his confidence and his friendship and then destroy him when he least suspects his danger."

Voices carry upward to a great distance, and so, though Stabutch spoke only in normal tones, the watcher, squatting at the cliff top, smiled—just the faintest suggestion of a grim smile.

So that was why the man from "Russa," of whom Goloba the head man had told him, was inquiring as to his where-abouts? Perhaps Tarzan had suspected as much, but he was glad to have definite proof.

"I shall be glad if you do kill him," said Capietro. "He would drive me out of business if he ever learned about me. He is a scoundrel who would prevent a man from earning an honest dollar."

"You may put him from your mind, comrade," Stabutch assured the raider. "He is already as good as dead. Furnish me with men, and I shall soon be on my way toward the south."

"My villains are already saddling to go forth and find men for your safari," said Capietro, with a wave of his hand in the direction of the central compound, where a score of cutthroats were saddling their horses in preparation for a foray against a distant Galla village.

"May luck go with them," said Stabutch. "I hope— What was that?" he demanded, leaping to his feet as a sudden crash of falling rock and earth came from behind them.

Capietro was also upon his feet. "A landslide," he exclaimed. "A portion of the cliff has fallen. Look! What is that?" he pointed at an object halfway up the cliff—the figure of a naked white man clinging to a tree that had found lodgment for its roots in the rocky face of the cliff. The tree, a small one, was bending beneath the weight of the man. Slowly it gave way, there was the sound of rending wood, and then the figure hur-tled downward into the village where it was hidden from the sight of the two white watchers by an intervening hut.

But Stabutch had seen the giant figure of the almost naked white long enough to compare it with the description he had had of the man for whom he had come all the long way from

Moscow. There could not be two such, of that he was certain. "It is the ape-man!" he cried. "Come, Capietro, he is ours!"

Instantly the Italian ordered several *shiftas* to advance and seize the ape-man.

Fortune is never necessarily with either the brave or the virtuous. She is, unfortunately, quite as likely to perch upon the banner of the poltroon or the blackguard. Today she deserted Tarzan completely. As he squatted upon the edge of the cliff, looking down upon the village of Dominic Capietro, he suddenly felt the earth giving beneath him. Catlike, he leaped to his feet, throwing his hands above his head, as one does, mechanically, to preserve his balance or seek support, but too late. With a small avalanche of earth and rock he slid over the edge of the cliff. The tree, growing partway down the face of the escarpment, broke his fall and, for a moment, gave him hope that he might escape the greater danger of the final plunge into the village, where, if the fall did not kill him it was quite evident that his enemies would. But only for a moment were his hopes aroused. With the breaking of the bending stem hope vanished as he plunged on downward.

Danny "Gunner" Patrick, having finished his lunch, lighted a cigarette and let his gaze wander out over the landscape that unfolded in a lovely panorama before him. City bred, he saw only a part of what there was to be seen and understood but little of that. What impressed him most was the loneliness of the prospect. "Geeze," he soliloquized, "what a hideout! No one wouldn't ever find a guy here." His eyes suddenly focused upon an object in the foreground. "Hey, feller," he whispered to Obambi, "what's that?" He pointed in the direction of the thing that had aroused his curiosity.

Obambi looked and, when they found it, his keen eyes recognized it for what it was. "It is a man, Bwana," he said. "It is the man who killed Simba in our camp that night. It is Tarzan of the Apes."

"How t'ell do you know?" demanded the "Gunner."

"There is only one Tarzan," replied the black. "It could be no other, as no other white man in all the jungle country or the mountain country or the plains country goes thus naked."

The "Gunner" rose to his feet. He was going down to have a talk with the ape-man, who, perhaps, could help him in his search for Lafayette Smith; but as he arose he saw the man below him leap to his feet and throw his arms above his head. Then he disappeared as though swallowed up by the earth. The "Gunner" knitted his brows.

"Geeze," he remarked to Obambi, "he sure screwed, didn't he?"

"What, Bwana?" asked Obambi.

"Shut up," snapped the "Gunner." "That was funny," he muttered. "Wonder what became of him. Guess I'll give him a tail. Come on," he concluded aloud to Obambi.

Having learned through experience (wholly the experience of others who had failed to do so) that attention to details is essential to the continued pursuit of life, liberty, and happiness, the "Gunner" looked carefully to his Thompson as he walked rapidly but cautiously toward the spot where Tarzan had disappeared. He saw that there was a cartridge in the chamber, that the magazine drum was properly attached and that the fire control lever was set for full automatic fire.

In the village, which he could not yet see and of the presence of which he did not dream, the *shiftas* were running toward the place where they knew the body of the fallen man must lie; and in the van were Stabutch and Capietro, when suddenly there stepped from the interior of the last hut the man they sought. They did not know that he had alighted on the thatched roof of the hut from which he had just emerged, nor that, though he had broken through it to the floor below, it had so broken his fall that he had suffered no disabling injury.

To them it seemed a miracle; and to see him thus, apparently uninjured, took the two white men so by surprise that they halted in their tracks while their followers, imitating their example, clustered about them.

Stabutch was the first to regain his presence of mind. Whipping a revolver from its holster he was about to fire point-blank at the ape-man, when Capietro struck his hand up. "Wait," growled the Italian. "Do not be too fast. I am in command here."

"But it is the ape-man," cried Stabutch.

"I know that," replied Capietro, "and for that very reason I wish to take him alive. He is rich. He will bring a great ransom."

"Damn the ransom," ejaculated Stabutch. "It is his life I want."

"Wait until I have the ransom," said Capietro, "and then you can go after him."

In the meantime Tarzan stood watching the two. He saw that his situation was fraught with exceptional danger. It was to the interest of either one of these men to kill him; and while the ransom of which one spoke might deter him temporarily he knew that but little provocation would be required to induce this one to kill him rather than to take the chance that he might escape, while it was evident that the Russian already considered that he had sufficient provocation, and Tarzan did not doubt but that he would find the means to accomplish his design even in the face of the Italian's objections.

If he could but get among them, where they could not use firearms against him, because of the danger that they might kill members of their own party, he felt that, by virtue of his superior strength, speed, and agility, he might fight his way to one of the palisaded walls of the village where he would have a fair chance to escape. Once there he could scale the palisade with the speed of Manu, the monkey, and with little danger other than from the revolvers of the two whites, since he held the marksmanship of the *shiftas* in contempt.

He heard Capietro call to his men to take him alive; and then, waiting not upon them, he charged straight for the two whites, while from his throat burst the savage growl of a wild beast that had, upon more than a single occasion in the past, wrought havoc with the nerves of human antagonists.

Nor did it fail in its purpose now. Shocked and unnerved for the instant, Stabutch fell back while Capietro, who had no desire to kill the ape-man unless it became necessary, leaped to one side and urged his followers to seize him.

For a moment bedlam reigned in the village of the white raider. Yelling, cursing men milled about a white giant who fought with his bare hands, seizing an antagonist and hurling him in the faces of others, or, using the body of another like a flail, sought to mow down those who opposed him.

Among the close-massed fighters, excited curs ran yelping and barking, while children and women upon the outskirts of the melee shrieked encouragement to the men.

Slowly Tarzan was gaining ground toward one of the coveted walls of the village where, as he stepped quickly backward to avoid a blow, he stumbled over a yapping cur and went down beneath a dozen men.

From the top of the cliff "Gunner" Patrick looked down upon this scene. "That mob has sure got him on the spot," he said aloud. "He's a regular guy, too. I guess here's where I step in for him."

"Yes, Bwana," agreed the willing Obambi.

"Shut up," said the "Gunner," and then he raised the butt of the Thompson to his shoulder and squeezed the trigger.

Mingled with the rapid reports of the machine gun were the screams and curses of wounded and frightened men and the shrieks of terrified women and children. Like snow before a spring shower, the pack that had surrounded Tarzan melted away as men ran for the shelter of their huts or for their saddled ponies.

Capietro and Stabutch were among the latter, and even before Tarzan could realize what had happened he saw the two racing through the open gates of the village.

The "Gunner," noting the satisfactory effect of his fire, had ceased, though he stood ready again to rain a hail of death down upon the village should necessity require. He had aimed only at the outskirts of the crowd surrounding the ape-man, for fear that a bullet might strike the man he was endeavoring to succor; but he was ready to risk finer shooting should any press the naked giant too closely.

He saw Tarzan standing alone in the village street like a lion at bay, and then he saw his eyes ranging about for an explanation of the burst of fire that had liberated him.

"Up here, feller!" shouted the "Gunner."

The ape-man raised his eyes and located Danny instantly. "Wait," he called; "I'll be up there in a moment."

11

The Crucifixion

As THE WATERS of Chinnereth closed over the head of Lady Barbara, the golden-haired Jezebel sprang to her feet and ran swiftly forward among the men congregated upon the great flat lava rock from which the victim of their cruel fanaticism had been hurled to her doom. She pushed apostles roughly aside as she made her way toward the brink, tears streaming from her eyes and sobs choking her throat.

Abraham, the son of Abraham, standing directly in her path, was the first to guess her purpose to throw herself into the lake and share the fate of her loved mistress. Impelled by no humanitarian urge, but rather by a selfish determination to save the girl for another fate which he already had chosen for her, the Prophet seized her as she was about to leap into the water.

Turning upon the old man like a tigress, Jezebel scratched, bit, and kicked in an effort to free herself, which she would have succeeded in doing had not the Prophet called the six executioners to his aid. Two of them seized her; and, seeing that her efforts were futile, the girl desisted; but now she turned the flood gates of her wrath upon Abraham, the son of Abraham.

"Murderer!" she cried. "Son of Satan! May Jehovah strike thee dead for this. Curses be upon thy head and upon those of all thy kin. Damned be they and thee for the foul crime thou hast committed here this day."

"Silence, blasphemer!" screamed Abraham, the son of Abraham. "Make thy peace with Jehovah, for tonight thou shalt be judged by fire. Take her back to the village," he directed the two who held her, "and make her secure in a cave. Seest thou, too, that she escapeth not."

"Fire or water, it be all the same to me," cried the girl as they dragged her away, "just so it takes me away forever from this accursed land of Midian and the mad beast who poseth as the prophet of Jehovah."

As Jezebel moved off toward the village between her two guards the villagers fell in behind them, the women calling her foul names and otherwise reviling her, and in the rear of all came the Prophet and the Apostles, leaving a score of their fellows still lying upon the ground, where they writhed, unnoticed, in the throes of epilepsy.

The impact with the surface of the water had almost stunned Lady Barbara, but she had managed to retain her senses and control of her mental and physical powers, so that, although dazed, she was able to put into effect the plan that she had nursed from the moment that she was aware of the fate to which the Prophet had condemned her.

Being an excellent swimmer and diver the thought of being immersed below the surface of Chinnereth for a few minutes had not, in itself, caused her any great mental perturbation. Her one fear had lain in the very considerable possibility that she might be so badly injured by the impact with the water, or stunned, as to be helpless to effect her own release from the net. Her relief was great, therefore, when she discovered that she was far from helpless, nor did she delay an instant in bringing her small pocketknife to play upon the fibre strands of the net that enmeshed her.

Slashing rapidly, but yet, at the same time, in accordance with a practical plan, she severed strand after strand in a straight line, as the rock dragged her downward toward the bottom. Constantly through her mind ran a single admonition—"Keep cool! Keep cool!" Should she permit herself to give away to hysteria, even for an instant, she knew that she must be lost. The lake seemed bottomless, the strands innumerable, while the knife grew constantly duller, and her strength appeared to be rapidly ebbing.

"Keep cool! Keep cool!" Her lungs were bursting. "Just a moment more! Keep cool!" She felt unconsciousness creeping upon her. She struggled to drag herself through the opening she had made in the net—her senses reeled dizzily—she was almost unconscious as she shot rapidly toward the surface.

As her head rose above the surface those standing upon the rock above her had their attention riveted upon Jezebel who was engaged at that moment in kicking the prophet of Paul, the son of Jehovah, on the shins. Lady Barbara was ignorant of all this; but it was fortunate for her, perhaps, because it prevented any of the Midians from noticing her resurrection from the deep and permitted her to swim, unseen, beneath the shelter of the overhanging rock from which she had been precipitated into the lake.

She was very weak, and it was with a prayer of thanksgiving that she discovered a narrow ledge of beach at the water's edge beneath the great lava block that loomed above her. As she dragged herself wearily out upon it she heard the voices of those upon the rock overhead—the voice of Jezebel cursing the Prophet and the old man's threat against the girl.

A thrill of pride in the courage of Jezebel warmed the heart of Lady Barbara, as did the knowledge that she had won a friend so loyal and devoted that she would put her own life in jeopardy merely for the sake of openly accusing the murderer of her friend. How magnificent she was in the primitive savagery of her denunciation! Lady Barbara could almost see her standing there defying the greatest power that her world knew, her golden hair framing her oval face, her eyes flashing, her lips curling in scorn, her lithe young body tense with emotion.

And what she had heard, and the thought of the helplessness of the young girl against the power of the vile old man, changed Lady Barbara's plans completely. She had thought to remain in hiding until night and then seek to escape this hideous valley and its mad denizens. There would be no pursuit, for they would think her dead at the bottom of Chinnereth; and thus she might seek to find her way to the outer world with no danger of interference by the people of the land of Midian.

She and Jezebel had often speculated upon the likelihood of

the existence of a possible avenue of ascent of the crater wall; and from the entrance of their cave they had chosen a spot about midway of the western face of the crater, where the rim had fallen inward, as offering the best chance of escape. Tumbled masses of rock rose here from the bottom of the valley almost to the summit of the crater, and here Lady Barbara had decided to make her first bid for freedom.

But now all was changed. She could not desert Jezebel, whose life was now definitely jeopardized because of her friendship and loyalty. But what was she to do? How could she be of assistance to the girl? She did not know. Of only one thing was she certain—she must try.

She had witnessed enough horrors in the village of the South Midians to know that whatever Abraham, the son of Abraham, planned for Jezebel would doubtless be consummated after dark, the time he chose, by preference, for all the more horrible of his so-called religious rites. Only those which took them to a distance from the village, such as immersions in the waters of Chinnereth, were performed by daylight.

With these facts in mind, Lady Barbara decided that she might, with safety, wait until after dark before approaching the village. To do so earlier might only result in her own recapture, an event that would render her helpless in effecting the succor of Jezebel, while giving the Prophet two victims instead of one.

The sound of voices above her had ceased. She had heard the vituperations of the women diminishing in the distance, and by this she had known that the party had returned to the village. It was cold beneath the shadow of the rock, with her wet clothing clinging to her tired body; and so she slipped back into the water and swam along the shore a few yards until she found a spot where she could crawl out and lie in the pleasant warmth of the sun.

Here she rested again for a few minutes, and then she cautiously ascended the bank until her eyes were on a level with the ground. At a little distance she saw a woman, lying prone, who was trying to raise herself to a sitting position. She was evidently weak and dazed, and Lady Barbara realized that she was recovering from one of those horrid seizures to which nearly all the inhabitants of the village were subject. Near her were others, some lying quietly, some struggling; and in the direction of the village she saw several who had recovered sufficiently to attempt the homeward journey.

Lying very still, her forehead concealed behind a low shrub, Lady Barbara watched and waited for half an hour, until the last of the unfortunate band had regained consciousness and self-control sufficiently to permit them to depart in the direction of their squalid habitations.

She was alone now with little or no likelihood of discovery. Her clothes were still wet and exceedingly uncomfortable; so she quickly removed them and spread in the hot sun to dry, while she luxuriated in the soothing comfort of a sun bath, alternated with an occasional dip in the waters of the lake.

Before the sun dropped to the western rim of the crater her clothing had dried; and now she sat, fully dressed again, waiting for darkness to fall. Below her lay the waters of the lake and beyond its farther shore she could dimly see the outlines of the village of the North Midians, where dwelt the mysterious "beautiful men" of Jezebel's daydreams.

Doubtless, thought Lady Barbara, the prince charming of the golden one's imagination would prove to be a whiskered Adonis with a knotted club; but, even so, it were difficult to imagine more degraded or repulsive males than those of her own village. Almost anything—even a gorilla—might seem preferable to them.

As night approached, the girl saw little lights commence to twinkle in the northern village—the cooking fires, doubtless—and then she rose and turned her face toward the village of Abraham, the son of Abraham, of Jobab and Timothy and Jezebel, toward certain danger and possible death.

As she walked along the now familiar path toward the village, the mind of Lady Barbara Collis was vexed by the seemingly hopeless problem that confronted her, while hovering upon the verge of her consciousness was that fear of the loneliness and the darkness of an unfamiliar and inhospitable country that is inherent in most of us. Jezebel had told her that dangerous beasts were almost unknown in the land of Midian, yet her imagination conjured slinking forms in the darkness and the sound of padded feet upon the trail behind her and the breathing of savage lungs. Yet ahead of her lay a real menace more terrible, perhaps, than swiftly striking talons and powerful jaws.

She recalled that she had heard that men who had been mauled by lions, and lived to narrate their experiences, had all testified uniformly to the fact that there had been no pain and little terror during the swift moments of the experience; and she knew that there was a theory propounded by certain students of animal life that the killing of the carnivores was always swift, painless, and merciful. Why was it, she wondered, that of all created things only man was wantonly cruel and only man, and the beasts that were trained by man, killed for pleasure?

But now she was nearing the village and passing from the possibility of attack by merciful beasts to the assurance of attack by merciless men, should she be apprehended by them. To reduce this risk she skirted the village at a little distance and came to the foot of the cliff where the caves were located and where she hoped to find Jezebel and, perhaps, discover a means of liberating her.

She glanced up the face of the cliff, which seemed to be deserted, most of the villagers being congregated about a group of small cooking fires near the few huts at the foot of the cliff. They often cooked thus together gossiping and praying and narrating experiences and revelations—they all received revelations from Jehovah when they "walked" with Him, which was their explanation of their epileptic seizures.

The more imaginative members of the community were the recipients of the most remarkable revelations; but, as all of them were stupid, Jehovah had not, at least during Lady Barbara's sojourn among them, revealed anything of a particularly remarkable or inspiring nature. Their gossip, like their "experiences," was mean and narrow and sordid. Each sought constantly to discover or invent some scandal or heresy in the lives of his fellows, and if the finger pointed at one not in the good graces of the Prophet or the Apostles the victim was quite likely to make a Roman holiday.

Seeing the villagers congregated about their fires, Lady Barbara commenced the ascent of the steep path that zigzagged up the face of the cliff. She moved slowly and cautiously, stopping often to look about her, both above and below; but, notwithstanding her fears and doubts she finally reached the mouth of the cave that she and Jezebel had occupied. If she hoped to find the golden one there she was disappointed; but at least, if Jezebel were not there, it was a relief to find that no one else was; and with a sense of greater security than she had felt since the dawn of this eventful day she crawled into the interior and threw herself down upon the straw pallet that the girls had shared.

Home! This rough lair, no better than that which housed the beasts of the wilds, was home now to Lady Barbara Collis whose life had been spent within the marble halls of the Earl of Whimsey. Permeating it were memories of the strange friendship and affection that had gradually united these two girls whose origins and backgrounds could scarcely have been more dissimilar. Here each had learned the language of the other, here they had laughed and sung together, here they had exchanged confidences, and here they had planned together a future in which they would not be separated. The cold walls seemed warmer because of the love and loyalty to which they had been silent witnesses.

But now Lady Barbara was here alone. Where was Jezebel? It was the answer to that question that the English girl must find. She recalled the Prophet's threat—"for tonight thou shalt be judged by fire." She must hasten, then, if she were to save Jezebel. But how was she to accomplish it in the face of all the seemingly insurmountable obstacles which confronted her?— her ignorance of where Jezebel was being held, the numbers of her enemies, her lack of knowledge of the country through which they would be forced to flee should she be so fortunate as to effect the girl's escape from the village.

She roused herself. Lying here upon her pallet would accomplish nothing. She rose and looked down toward the village; and instantly she was all alertness again, for there was Jezebel. She was standing between two guards, surrounded by many villagers who maintained an open space about her. Presently the spectators separated and men appeared carrying a burden. What was it? They laid it in the center of the open space, in front of Jezebel; and then Lady Barbara saw what it was—a large wooden cross.

A man was digging a hole at the center of the circular space that had been left around the prisoner; others were bringing brush and fagots. Now the men who guarded Jezebel seized her and bore her to the ground. They laid her upon the cross and stretched her arms out upon the wooden cross arm.

Lady Barbara was horror stricken. Were they going to perpetrate the horrible atrocity of nailing her to the cross? Abraham, the son of Abraham, stood at the head of the cross, his hands in the attitude of prayer, a personification of pious hypocrisy. The girl knew that no cruelty, however atrocious, was beyond him. She knew, too, that she was powerless to prevent the consummation of this foul deed, yet she cast discretion and self-interest to the winds, as, with a warning cry that shattered the silence of the night, she sped swiftly down the steep pathway toward the village—a self-sacrifice offered willingly upon the altar of friendship.

Startled by her scream, every eye was turned upward toward her. In the darkness they did not recognize her, but their stupid minds were filled with questioning and with terror as they saw something speeding down the cliff face toward them. Even before she reached the circle of firelight where they stood many had collapsed in paroxysms of epilepsy induced by the nervous shock of this unexpected visitation.

When she came closer, and was recognized, others succumbed, for now indeed it appeared that a miracle had been worked and that the dead had been raised again, even as they had seen the dead girl resurrected the previous day.

Pushing aside those who did not quickly enough make way for her, Lady Barbara hastened to the center of the circle. As his eyes fell upon her, Abraham, the son of Abraham, paled and stepped back. For a moment he seemed upon the verge of a stroke.

"Who are you?" he cried. "What are you doing here?"

"You know who I am," replied Lady Barbara. "Why do you tremble if you do not know that I am the messenger of Jehovah whom you reviled and sought to destroy? I am here to save the girl Jezebel from death. Later Jehovah will send His wrath upon Abraham, the son of Abraham, and upon all the people of the land of Midian for their cruelties and their sins."

"I did not know," cried the Prophet. "Tell Jehovah that I did not know. Intercede for me, that Jehovah may forgive me; and anything within my power to grant shall be yours."

So great was her surprise at the turn events had taken that Lady Barbara, who had expected only opposition and attack, was stunned for the moment. Here was an outcome so foreign to any that she had imagined that she had no response ready. She almost laughed aloud as she recalled the fears that had constantly harassed her since she had determined to attempt Jezebel's escape. And now it was all so easy.

"Liberate the girl, Jezebel," she commanded, "and then make food ready for her and for me."

"Quick!" cried the Prophet. "Raise the girl and set her free."

"Wait!" exclaimed a thin, querulous voice behind him. "I have walked with Jehovah." All turned in the direction of the speaker. He was Jobab the apostle.

"Quick! Release her!" demanded Lady Barbara, who, in this interruption and in the manner and voice of the speaker, whom she knew was one of the most fanatically intolerant of the religious bigots of Midian, saw the first spark that might grow into a flame of resistance to the will of the Prophet; for she knew these people well enough to be sure that they would grasp at any excuse to thwart the abandonment of their cruel pleasure.

"Wait!" shrieked Jobab. "I have walked with Jehovah, and He hath spoken unto me, saying: 'Behold, Jobab the Apostle, a seeming miracle shall be wrought out of Chinnereth; but be not deceived, for I say unto ye that it shall be the work of Satan; and whosoever believeth in it shall perish.'"

"Hallelujah!" shrieked a woman, and the cry was taken up

by the others. To right and left the excited villagers were being stricken by their Nemesis. A score of writhing bodies jerked and struggled upon the ground in the throes of convulsions, the horrible choking, the frothing at the mouth, adding to the horror of the scene.

For a moment, Abraham, the son of Abraham, stood silent in thought. A cunning light flickered suddenly in his crafty eyes, and then he spoke. "Amen!" he said. "Let the will of Jehovah be done as revealed to the Apostle Jobab. Let Jobab speak the word of Jehovah, and upon Jobab's head be the reward."

"Another cross," screamed Jobab; "bring another cross. Let two beacon fires light the path of Jehovah in the heavens, and if either of these be His children He will not let them be consumed," and so, as Abraham, the son of Abraham, had passed the buck to Jobab, Jobab passed it along to Jehovah, who has been the recipient of more than His share through the ages.

Futile were the threats and arguments of Lady Barbara against the bloodlust of the Midians. A second cross was brought, a second hole dug, and presently both she and Jezebel were lashed to the symbols of love and raised to an upright position. The bottoms of the crosses were sunk in the holes prepared for them and earth tamped around them to hold them upright. Then willing hands brought fagots and brushwood and piled them about the bases of the two pyres.

Lady Barbara watched these preparations in silence. She looked upon the weak, degenerate faces of this degraded people; and she could not, even in the extremity of her danger, find it in her heart to condemn them too severely for doing what supposedly far more enlightened people had done, within the memory of man, in the name of religion.

She glanced at Jezebel and found the girl's eyes upon her. "You should not have come back," said the girl. "You might have escaped." Lady Barbara shook her head. "You did it for me," continued Jezebel. "May Jehovah reward you, for I may only thank you."

"You would have done the same for me at Chinnereth," replied Lady Barbara. "I heard you defy the Prophet there."

Jezebel smiled. "You are the only creature I have ever

loved," she said; "the only one who I ever thought loved me. Of course I would die for you."

Abraham, the son of Abraham, was praying. Young men stood ready with flaming torches, the flickering light from which danced grotesquely upon the hideous features of the audience, upon the two great crosses, and upon the beautiful faces of the victims.

"Good-bye, Jezebel," whispered Lady Barbara.

"Good-bye," replied the golden one.

12

Out of the Grave

NOTWITHSTANDING THE FACT that Lafayette Smith had so recently visualized this very emergency and had, as it were, rehearsed his part in it, now that he stood face-to-face with the lion he did none of the things exactly as he had pictured. He was not at all cool when he saw the carnivore appear at the turn in the fissure; he did not face him calmly, draw a deadly bead, and fire. Nothing was in the least as he had imagined it would be. In the first place the distance between them seemed entirely inadequate and the lion much larger than he had supposed any lion could be, while his revolver seemed to shrink to proportions that represented utter futility.

All this, however, was encompassed in a single, instantaneous and overwhelming conception. No appreciable time elapsed, therefore, between the instant that he perceived the lion and that at which he commenced to jerk the trigger of his pistol, which he accomplished, without aiming, while in the act of turning to flee.

Running headlong over the jumbled rocks Lafayette Smith fled precipitately into the unknown depths of the ancient rift, at his elbow the ghastly fear that beyond each successive turn would loom the rocky terminus of his flight, while just behind him he pictured the ravenous carnivore thirsting for his blood. The fall of swiftly moving padded feet close behind him urged him to greater speed, the hot breath of the lion surged from the savage lungs to pound upon his ears like surf upon an ocean beach.

Such is the power of imagination. It is true that Numa was bounding along the bottom of the rift, but in the opposite direction to that in which Lafayette Smith bounded. Fortunately, for Lafayette, none of his wild shots had struck the lion; but the booming reverberation of the explosions in the narrow fissure had so surprised and unnerved him that he had wheeled and fled even as the man had.

Had the pursuit been as real as Lafayette imagined it, it could have urged him to no greater speed, nor could the consequent terror have nerved him to greater endurance; but physical powers have their limits, and presently the realization that his had about reached theirs forced itself upon Lafayette's consciousness and with it realization of the futility of further flight.

It was then that he turned to make his stand. He was trembling, but with fatigue rather than fear; and inwardly he was cool as he reloaded his revolver. He was surprised to discover that the lion was not on top of him, but he expected momentarily to see him appear where the fissure turned from his sight. Seating himself on a flat rock he waited the coming of the carnivore while he rested, and as the minutes passed and no lion came his wonderment increased.

Presently his scientific eye commenced to note the structure of the fissure's walls about him, and as his interest grew in the geologic facts revealed or suggested his interest in the lion waned, until, once again, the carnivore was relegated to the background of his consciousness, while in its place returned the momentarily forgotten plan to explore the rift to it farthest extent.

Recovered from the excessive fatigue of his strenuous exertion he undertook once more the exploration so rudely interrupted. Regained was the keen pleasure of discovery; forgotten, hunger, fatigue, and personal safety as he advanced along this mysterious path of adventure.

Presently the floor of the rift dropped rapidly until it was inclined at an angle that made progress difficult; and at the same time it narrowed, giving evidence that it might be rapidly pinching out. There was now barely width for him to squeeze forward between the walls when the fissure ahead of him became suddenly shrouded in gloom. Glancing up in search of an explanation of this new phenomenon Lafayette discovered that the walls far above were converging, until directly above him there was only a small streak of sky visible while ahead the rift was evidently closed entirely at the top.

As he pushed on, the going, while still difficult because of the steepness of the floor of the fissure, was improved to some extent by the absence of jumbled rocks underfoot, the closed ceiling of the corridor having offered no crumbling rim to the raging elements of the ages; but presently another handicap made itself evident—darkness, increasing steadily with each few yards until the man was groping his way blindly, though none the less determinedly, toward the unknown that lay ahead.

That an abyss might yawn beyond his next step may have occurred to him, but so impractical was he in all worldly matters while his scientific entity was in the ascendancy that he ignored the simplest considerations of safety. However, no abyss yawned; and presently, at a turning, daylight showed ahead. It was only a small patch of daylight; and when he reached the opening through which it shone it appeared, at first, that he had achieved the end of his quest—that he could proceed no farther.

Dropping to his hands and knees he essayed the feat of worming his way through the aperture, which he then discovered was amply large to accommodate his body; and a moment later he stood erect in astonished contemplation of the scene before him.

He found himself standing near the base of a lofty escarpment overlooking a valley that his practised eye recognized immediately as the crater of a long-extinct volcano. Below him spread a panorama of rolling, tree-dotted landscape, broken by occasional huge outcroppings of weathered lava rock; and in the center a blue lake danced in the rays of an afternoon sun.

Thrilling to an identical reaction such as doubtless dominated

Balboa as he stood upon the heights of Darien overlooking the broad Pacific, Lafayette Smith experienced that spiritual elation that is, perhaps, the greatest reward of the explorer. Forgotten, for the moment, was the scientific interest of the geologist, submerged by intriguing speculation upon the history of this lost valley, upon which, perhaps, the eyes of no other white man had ever gazed.

Unfortunately for the permanency of this beatific state of mind two other thoughts rudely obtruded themselves, as thoughts will. One appertained to the camp, for which he was supposed to be searching, while the other involved the lion, which was supposedly searching for him. The latter reminded him that he was standing directly in front of the mouth of the fissure, at the very spot where the lion would emerge were he following; and this suggested the impracticability of the fissure as an avenue of return to the opposite side of the crater wall.

A hundred yards away Smith espied a tree, and toward this he walked as offering the nearest sanctuary in the event the lion should reappear. Here, too, he might rest while considering plans for the future; and, that he might enjoy uninterrupted peace of mind while so engaged, he climbed up into the tree, where, straddling a limb, he leaned his back against the bole.

It was a tree of meager foliage, thus affording him an almost unobstructed view of the scene before him, and as his eyes wandered across the landscape they were arrested by something at the foot of the southern wall of the crater—something that did not perfectly harmonize with its natural surroundings. Here his gaze remained fixed as he sought to identify the thing that had attracted his attention. What it looked like he was positive that it could not be, so definitely had his preconception of the inaccessibility of the valley to man impressed itself upon his mind; yet the longer he looked the more convinced he became that what he saw was a small village of thatched huts.

And what thoughts did this recognition inspire? What noble and aesthetic emotions were aroused within his breast by the sight of this lonely village in the depths of the great crater which should, by all the proofs that he had seen, have been inaccessible to man?

No, you are wrong again. What it suggested was food. For the first time since he had become lost Lafayette Smith was acutely conscious of hunger, and when he recalled that it had been more than twenty-four hours since he had eaten anything more substantial than a few chocolates his appetite waxed ravenous. Furthermore, he suddenly realized that he was actually suffering from thirst.

At a little distance lay the lake. Glancing back toward the entrance to the fissure he discovered no lion; and so he dropped to the ground and set off in the direction of the water, laying his course so that at no time was he at any great distance from a tree.

The water was cool and refreshing; and when he had drunk his fill he became acutely conscious, for the first time during the day, of an overpowering weariness. The water had temporarily relieved the pangs of hunger, and he determined to rest a few minutes before continuing on toward the distant village. Once again he assured himself that there was no pursuing lion in evidence; and then he stretched himself at full length in the deep grass that grew near the edge of the lake, and with a low tree as protection from the hot sun relaxed his tired muscles in much needed rest.

He had not intended to sleep; but his fatigue was greater than he had supposed, so that, with relaxation, unconsciousness crept upon him unawares. Insects buzzed lazily about him, a bird alighted in the tree beneath which he lay and surveyed him critically, the sun dropped lower toward the western rim, and Lafayette Smith slept on.

He dreamed that a lion was creeping toward him through high grass. He tried to rise, but he was powerless. The horror of the situation was intolerable. He tried to cry out and frighten the lion away, but no sound issued from his throat. Then he made a final supreme effort, and the shriek that resulted awakened him. He sat up, dripping with perspiration, and looked quickly and fearfully about him. There was no lion. "Whew!" he exclaimed. "What a relief."

Then he glanced at the sun and realized that he had slept away the greater part of the afternoon. Now his hunger returned and with it recollection of the distant village. Rising, he drank again at the lake, and then started on his journey toward the base of the southern rim, where he hoped he would find friendly natives and food.

The way led for the greater part around the edge of the lake; and as dusk settled and then darkness it became more and more difficult to move except at a slow and cautious pace, since the ground was often strewn with fragments of lava that were not visible in the darkness.

Night brought the cheering sight of fires in the village; and these, seeming nearer than they really were, buoyed his spirits by the assurance that his journey was nearing completion. Yet, as he stumbled onward, the conviction arose that he was pursuing a will-o'-the-wisp, as the firelight appeared to retreat as rapidly as he advanced.

At last, however, the outlines of mean huts, illumined by the fires, became distinguishable and then the figures of people clustered about them. It was not until he was almost within the village that he saw with astonishment that the people were white, and then he saw something else that brought him to a sudden halt. Upon two crosses, raised above the heads of the villagers, were two girls. The firelight played upon their faces, and he saw that both were beautiful.

What weird, unholy rite was this? What strange race inhabited this lost valley? Who were the girls? That they were not of the same race as the villagers was apparent at the first casual glance at the degraded features of the latter.

Lafayette Smith hesitated. It was evident that he was witnessing some sort of religious rite or pageant; and he assumed that to interrupt it would prove far from a satisfactory introduction to these people, whose faces, which had already repelled him, impressed him so unfavorably that he questioned the friendliness of his reception even under the most favorable auspices.

And then a movement of the crowd opened for a moment an avenue to the center of the circle where the crosses stood; and the man was horrified by what was revealed for an instant to his amazed eyes, for he saw the dry brush and the fagots piled about the bottoms of the crosses and the young men with the flaming torches ready to ignite the inflammable piles.

An old man was intoning a prayer. Here and there villagers writhed upon the ground in what Smith thought were evidences of religious ecstasy. And then the old man gave a signal, and the torchbearers applied the flames to the dry brush.

Lafayette Smith waited to see no more. Leaping forward he thrust surprised villagers from his path and sprang into the circle before the crosses. With a booted foot he kicked the already burning brush aside; and then, with his little .32 shining in his hand, he turned and faced the astonished and angry crowd.

For a moment Abraham, the son of Abraham, was paralyzed by surprise. Here was a creature beyond his experience or his ken. It might be a celestial messenger; but the old man had gone so far now, and his crazed mind was so thoroughly imbued with the lust for torture, that he might even have defied Jehovah Himself rather than forego the pleasures of the spectacle he had arranged.

At last he found his voice. "What blasphemy is this?" he screamed. "Set upon this infidel, and tear him limb from limb."

"You will have to shoot, now," said an English voice at Smith's back, "for if you don't they will kill you."

He realized that it was one of the girls upon the crosses—another astonishing mystery in this village of mysteries, that cool English voice. Then one of the torchbearers rushed him with a maniacal shriek, and Smith fired. With a scream the fellow clutched his chest and sprawled at the American's feet; and at the report of the pistol and the sudden collapse of their fellow the others, who had been moving forward upon the intruder, fell back, while upon all sides the over-excited creatures succumbed to the curse that had descended to them from Angustus the Ephesian, until the ground was strewn with contorted forms.

Realizing that the villagers were, for the moment at least, too disconcerted and overawed by the death of their fellow to press their attack, Smith turned his attention at once to the two girls. Replacing his pistol in its holster, he cut their bonds with his pocketknife before Abraham, the son of Abraham, could collect his scattered wits and attempt to urge his followers to a renewed attack.

It was more than the work of a moment to liberate the two captives as, after he had cut the bonds that held their feet Smith had been compelled to partially support each with one arm as he severed the fibres that secured their wrists to the cross arms, lest a bone be broken or a muscle wrenched as the full weight of the victim was thrown suddenly upon one wrist.

He had cut Lady Barbara down first; and she was assisting him with Jezebel, who, having been crucified for a longer time, was unable to stand alone, when Abraham, the son of Abraham, regained sufficient composure to permit him to think and act.

Both Lady Barbara and Smith were supporting Jezebel into whose numbed feet the blood was again beginning to circulate. Their backs were toward the Prophet; and, taking advantage of their preoccupation, the old man was creeping stealthily upon them from the rear. In his hand was a crude knife, but nonetheless formidable for its crudeness. It was the blood-stained sacrificial knife of this terrible old high priest of the Midians, more terrible now because of the rage and hatred that animated the cruel, defective mind that directed the clawlike hand that wielded it.

All of his rage, all of his hatred were directed against the person of Lady Barbara, in whom he saw the author of his humiliation and his thwarted desires. Stealthily he crept upon her from behind while his followers, frozen to silence by his terrible glances, watched in breathless anticipation.

Occupied with the half-fainting Jezebel none of the three at the crosses saw the repulsive figure of the avenger as he towered suddenly behind the English girl, his right hand raised high to drive the blade deeply into her back; but they heard his sudden, choking, gasping scream and turned in time to see the knife fall from his nerveless fingers as they clutched at his throat, and to witness his collapse.

Angustus the Ephesian had reached out of a grave dug two

thousand years before, to save the life of Lady Barbara Collis—
though doubtless he would have turned over in that same grave
had he realized the fact.

13

The "Gunner" Walks

LIKE A GREAT cat, Tarzan of the Apes scaled the palisade of the raiders' village, dropped lightly to the ground upon the opposite side and ascended the cliffs a little to the south of the village where they were less precipitous. He might have taken advantage of the open gate; but the direction he chose was the shorter way; and a palisade constituted no obstacle to the foster son of Kala, the she-ape.

The "Gunner" was waiting for him upon the summit of the cliff directly behind the village, and for the second time these strangely dissimilar men met—dissimilar, and yet, in some respects, alike. Each was ordinarily quiet to taciturnity, each was self-reliant, each was a law unto himself in his own environment; but there the similarity ceased for the extremes of environment had produced psychological extremes as remotely separated as the poles.

The ape-man had been reared amidst scenes of eternal beauty and grandeur, his associates the beasts of the jungle, savage perhaps, but devoid of avarice, petty jealousy, treachery, meanness, and intentional cruelty; while the "Gunner" had known naught but the squalid aspects of scenery defiled by man, of horizons grotesque with screaming atrocities of architecture, of an earth hidden by concrete and asphaltum and littered with tin cans and garbage, his associates, in all walks of life, activated by grand and petty meannesses unknown to any but mankind.

"A machine gun has its possibilities," said the ape-man, with the flicker of a smile.

"They had you in a bad spot, mister," remarked the "Gunner."

"I think I should have gotten out all right," replied Tarzan, "but I thank you nonetheless. How did you happen to be here?"

"I been looking for my sidekick, and I happened to see you go over the edge here. Obambi here, tipped me off that you was the guy saved me from the lion,—so I was glad to step in for you."

"You are looking for whom?"

"My sidekick, Smith."

"Where is he?"

"I wouldn't be lookin' for him if I knew. He's went and lost himself. Been gone since yesterday afternoon."

"Tell me the circumstances," said Tarzan, "perhaps I can help you."

"That's what I was goin' to ask you," said the "Gunner." "I know my way around south of Madison Street, but out here I'm just a punk. I ain't got no idea where to look for him. Geeze, take a slant at them mountains. You might as well try to meet a guy at the corner of Oak and Polk as hunt for him there. I'll tell you how it happened," and then he briefly narrated all that was known of the disappearance of Lafayette Smith.

"Was he armed?" asked the ape-man.

"He thought he was."

"What do you mean?"

"He packed a shiny toy pistol, what if anybody ever shot me with it, and I found it out, I'd turn him over my knee and spank him."

"It might serve him in getting food," said Tarzan, "and that will be of more importance to him than anything else. He's not in much danger, except from men and starvation. Where's your camp?"

Danny nodded toward the south. "Back there about a thousand miles," he said.

"You'd better go to it and remain there where he can find

you if he can make his way back to it, and where I can find you if I locate him."

"I want to help you hunt for him. He's a good guy, even if he is legitimate."

"I can move faster alone," replied the ape-man. "If you start out looking for him I'll probably have to find you, too."

The "Gunner" grinned. "I guess you ain't so far off, at that," he replied. "All right, I'll beat it for camp and wait there for you. You know where our camp is at?"

"I'll find out," replied Tarzan and turned to Obambi to whom he put a few questions in the native Bantu dialect of the black. Then he turned again to the "Gunner." "I know where your camp is now. Watch out for these fellows from that village, and don't let your men wander very far from the protection of your machine gun."

"Why," demanded Danny, "what are them guys?"

"They are robbers, murderers, and slave raiders," replied Tarzan.

"Geeze," exclaimed the "Gunner," "they's rackets even in Africa, ain't they?"

"I do not know what a racket is," replied the ape-man, "but there is crime wherever there are men, and nowhere else." He turned then, without word of parting, and started upward toward the mountains.

"Geeze!" muttered the "Gunner." "That guy ain't so crazy about men."

"What, Bwana?" asked Obambi.

"Shut up," admonished Danny.

The afternoon was almost spent when the "Gunner" and Obambi approached camp. Tired and footsore as he was the white man had, nonetheless, pushed rapidly along the backtrail lest night descend upon them before they reached their destination, for Danny, in common with most city-bred humans, had discovered something peculiarly depressing and awe-inspiring in the mysterious sounds and silences of the nocturnal wilds. He wished the fires and companionship of men after the sun had set. And so the two covered the distance on the return in much less time than had been consumed in traversing it originally.

As he came in sight of the camp the brief twilight of the tropics had already fallen, the cooking fires were burning, and to a trained eye a change would have been apparent from the appearance of the camp when he had left it early that morning; but Danny's eyes were trained in matters of broads, bulls, and beer trucks and not in the concerns of camps and safaris; so, in the falling light of dusk, he did not notice that there were more men in camp than when he had left, nor that toward the rear of it there were horses tethered where no horses had been before.

The first intimation he had of anything unusual came from Obambi. "White men are in the camp, Bwana," said the black—"and many horses. Perhaps they found the mad bwana and brought him back."

"Where do you see any white men?" demanded the "Gunner."

"By the big fire in the center of camp, Bwana," replied Obambi.

"Geeze, yes, I see 'em now," admitted Danny. "They must have found old Smithy all right; but I don't see him, do you?"

"No, Bwana, but perhaps he is in his tent."

The appearance of Patrick and Obambi caused a commotion in the camp that was wholly out of proportion to its true significance. The white men leaped to their feet and drew their revolvers while strange blacks, in response to the commands of one of these, seized rifles and stood nervously alert.

"You don't have to throw no fit," called Danny, "it's only me and Obambi."

The white men were advancing to meet him now, and the two parties halted face-to-face near one of the fires. It was then that the eyes of one of the two strange white men alighted on the Thompson submachine gun. Raising his revolver he covered Danny.

"Put up your hands!" he commanded sharply.

"Wotell?" demanded the "Gunner," but he put them up as every sensible man does when thus invited at the business end of a pistol.

"Where is the ape-man?" asked the stranger.

"What ape-man? What you talkin' about? What's your racket?"

"You know who I mean—Tarzan," snapped the other.

The "Gunner" glanced quickly about the camp. He saw his own men herded under guard of villainous looking blacks in long robes that had once been white; he saw the horses tethered just beyond them; he saw nothing of Lafayette Smith. The training and the ethics of gangland controlled him on the instant. "Don't know the guy," he replied sullenly.

"You were with him today," snarled the bearded white. "You fired on my village."

"Who, me?" inquired the "Gunner" innocently. "You got me wrong, mister. I been hunting all day. I ain't seen no one. I ain't fired at nothing. Now it's my turn. What are you guys doin' here with this bunch of Ku Klux Klanners? If it's a stick up, hop to it; and get on your way. You got the drop on us, and they ain't no one to stop you. Get it over with. I'm hungry and want to feed."

"Take the gun away from him," said Capietro, in Galla, to one of his men, "also his pistol," and there was nothing for Danny "Gunner" Patrick, with his hands above his head, to do but submit. Then they sent Obambi, under escort, to be herded with the other black prisoners and ordered the "Gunner" to accompany them to the large fire that blazed in front of Smith's tent and his own.

"Where is your companion?" demanded Capietro.

"What companion?" inquired Danny.

"The man you have been travelling with," snapped the Italian. "Who else would I mean?"

"Search me," replied the "Gunner."

"What you mean by that? You got something concealed upon your person?"

"If you mean money, I ain't got none."

"You did not answer my question," continued Capietro.

"What question?"

"Where is your companion?"

"I ain't got none."

"Your head man told us there were two of you. What is your name?"

"Bloom," replied Danny.

Capietro looked puzzled. "The head man said one of you was Smith and the other Patrick."

"Never heard of 'em," insisted Danny. "The guy must of been stringin' you. I'm here alone, hunting, and my name's Bloom."

"And you didn't see Tarzan of the Apes today?"

"Never even heard of a guy with that monicker."

"Either he's lying to us," said Stabutch, "or it was the other one who fired on the village."

"Sure, it must of been two other fellows," Danny assured them. "Say, when do I eat?"

"When you tell us where Tarzan is," replied Stabutch.

"Then I guess I don't eat," remarked Danny. "Geeze, didn't I tell you I never heard of the guy? Do you think I know every monkey in Africa by his first name? Come on now, what's your racket? If we got anything you want, take it and screw. I'm sick lookin' at your mugs."

"I do not understand English so well," whispered Capietro to Stabutch. "I do not always know what he says."

"Neither do I," replied the Russian; "but I think he is lying to us. Perhaps he is trying to gain time until his companion and Tarzan arrive."

"That is possible," replied Capietro in his normal voice.

"Let's kill him and get out of here," suggested Stabutch. "We can take the prisoners and as much of the equipment as you want and be a long way from here in the morning."

"Geeze," exclaimed Danny, "this reminds me of Chi. It makes me homesick."

"How much money you pay if we don't kill you?" asked Capietro. "How much your friends pay?"

The "Gunner" laughed. "Say, mister, you're giving yourself a bum steer." He was thinking how much more one might collect for killing him, if one could make connections with certain parties on the North Side of Chicago, than for sparing his life. But here was an opportunity, perhaps, to gain time. The

"Gunner" did not wish to be killed, and so he altered his technique. "My friends ain't rich," he said, "but they might come across with a few grand. How much do you want?"

Capietro considered. This must be a rich American, for only rich men could afford these African big game expeditions. "One hundred thousand should not be excessive for a rich man like you," he said.

"Quit your kidding," said the "Gunner." "I ain't rich."

"What could you raise?" asked Capietro, who saw by the prisoner's expression of astonishment that the original bid was evidently out of the question.

"I might scrape up twenty grand," suggested Danny.

"What are grand?" demanded the Italian.

"Thousand—twenty thousand," explained the "Gunner."

"Poof!" cried Capietro. "That would not pay me for the trouble of keeping you until the money could be forwarded from America. Make it fifty thousand lire and it's a bargain."

"Fifty thousand lire? What's them?"

"A lire is an Italian coin worth about twenty cents in American money," explained Stabutch.

Danny achieved some rapid mental calculations before he replied; and when he had digested the result he had difficulty in repressing a smile, for he discovered that his offer of twenty thousand grand was actually twice what the Italian was now demanding. Yet he hesitated to agree too willingly. "That's ten thousand iron men," he said. "That's a lot of jack."

"Iron men? Jack? I do not understand," said Capietro.

"Smackers," explained Danny lucidly.

"Smackers? Is there such a coin in America?" asked Capietro, turning to Stabutch.

"Doubtless a vernacularism," said the Russian.

"Geeze, you guys is dumb," growled the "Gunner." "A smacker's a buck. Every one knows that."

"Perhaps if you would tell him in dollars it would be easier," suggested Stabutch. "We all understand the value of an American dollar."

"That's a lot more than some Americans understand,"

Danny assured him; "but it's just what I been saying right along—ten thousand dollars—and it's too damn much."

"That is for you to decide," said Capietro. "I am tired of bargaining—nobody but an American would bargain over a human life."

"What you been doing?" demanded the "Gunner." "You're the guy that started it."

Capietro shrugged. "It is not my life," he said. "You will pay me ten thousand American dollars, or you will die. Take your choice."

"Oke," said Danny. "I'll pay. Now do I eat? If you don't feed me I won't be worth nothing."

"Tie his hands," Capietro ordered one of the *shiftas*, then he fell to discussing plans with Stabutch. The Russian finally agreed with Capietro that the palisaded village of the raider would be the best place to defend themselves in the event that Tarzan enlisted aid and attacked them in force. One of their men had seen Lord Passmore's safari; and, even if their prisoner was lying to them, there was at least another white, probably well armed, who might be considered a definite menace. Ogonyo had told them that this man was alone and probably lost, but they did not know whether or not to believe the head man. If Tarzan commandeered these forces, which Capietro knew he had the influence to do, they might expect an attack upon their village.

By the light of several fires the blacks of the captured safari were compelled to break camp and, when the loads were packed, to carry them on the difficult night march toward Capietro's village. With mounted *shiftas* in advance, upon the flanks, and bringing up the rear there was no lagging and no chance to escape.

The "Gunner," plodding along at the head of his own porters, viewed the prospect of that night march with unmitigated disgust. He had traversed the route twice already since sunrise; and the thought of doing it again, in the dark, with his hands tied behind him was far from cheering. To add to his discomfort he was weak from hunger and fatigue, and now the pangs of thirst were assailing him.

"Geeze," he soliloquized, "this ain't no way to treat a regular guy. When I took 'em for a ride I never made no guy walk, not even a rat. I'll get these lousy bums yet—a thinkin' they can put Danny Patrick on the spot, an' make him walk all the way!"

14

Flight

As the choking cry broke from the lips of Abraham, the son of Abraham, Lady Barbara and Smith wheeled to see him fall, the knife clattering to the ground from his nerveless fingers. Smith was horrified, and the girl blenched, as they realized how close death had been. She saw Jobab and the others standing there, their evil faces contorted with rage.

"We must get away from here," she said. "They will be upon us in a moment."

"I'm afraid you'll have to help me support your friend," said Smith. "She cannot walk alone."

"Put your left arm around her," directed Lady Barbara. "That will leave your right hand free for your pistol. I will support her on the other side."

"Leave me," begged Jezebel. "I will only keep you from escaping."

"Nonsense," said Smith. "Put your arm across my shoulders."

"You will soon be able to walk," Lady Barbara told her, "when the blood gets back into your feet. Come! Let's get away from here while we can."

Half carrying Jezebel, the two started to move toward the circle of menacing figures surrounding them. Jobab was the first to regain his wits since the Prophet had collapsed at the critical moment. "Stop them!" he cried, as he prepared to block their way, at the same time drawing a knife from the folds of his filthy garment.

"One side, fellow!" commanded Smith, menacing Jobab with his pistol.

"The wrath of Jehovah will be upon you," cried Lady Barbara in the Midian tongue, "as it has been upon the others who would have harmed us, if you fail to let us pass in peace."

"It is the work of Satan," shrilled Timothy. "Do not let them weaken your heart with lies, Jobab. Do not let them pass!" The elder was evidently under great mental and nervous strain. His voice shook as he spoke, and his muscles were trembling. Suddenly he, too, collapsed as had Abraham, the son of Abraham. But still Jobab stood his ground, his knife raised in a definite menace against them. All around them the circle was growing smaller and its circumference more solidly knit by the forward pressing bodies of the Midians.

"I hate to do it," said Smith, half aloud, as he raised his pistol and aimed it at Jobab. The Apostle was directly in front of Lafayette Smith and little more than a yard distant when the American, aiming point-blank at his chest, jerked the trigger and fired.

An expression of surprise mingled with that of rage which had convulsed the unbecoming features of Jobab the Apostle. Lafayette Smith was also surprised and for the same reason—he had missed Jobab. It was incredible—there must be something wrong with the pistol!

But Jobab's surprise, while based upon the same miracle, was of a loftier and nobler aspect. It was clothed in the sanctity of divine revelation. It emanated from a suddenly acquired conviction that he was immune to the fire and thunder of this strange weapon that he had seen lay Lamech low but a few minutes earlier. Verily, Jehovah was his shield and his buckler!

For a moment, as the shot rang out, Jobab paused and then, clothed in the fancied immunity of this sudden revelation, he leaped upon Lafayette Smith. The sudden and unexpected impact of his body knocked the pistol from Smith's hand and simultaneously the villagers closed in upon him. A real menace now that they had witnessed the futility of the strange weapon.

Lafayette Smith was no weakling, and though his antagonist

was inspired by a combination of maniacal fury and religious fanaticism the outcome of their struggle must have been a fore-gone conclusion had there been no outside influences to affect it. But there were. Beside the villagers, there was Lady Barbara Collis.

With consternation she had witnessed the futility of Smith's marksmanship; and when she saw him disarmed and in the grip of Jobab, with others of the villagers rushing to his undoing, she realized that now, indeed, the lives of all three of them were in direct jeopardy.

The pistol lay at her feet, but only for a second. Stooping, she seized it; and then, with the blind desperation of self-preservation, she shoved the muzzle against Jobab's side and pulled the trigger; and as he fell, a hideous shriek upon his lips, she turned the weapon upon the advancing villagers and fired again. It was enough. Screaming in terror, the Midians turned and fled. A wave of nausea swept over the girl; she swayed and might have fallen had not Smith supported her.

"I'll be all right in a moment," she said. "It was so horrible!"

"You were very brave," said Lafayette Smith.

"Not as brave as you," she replied with a weak little smile; "but a better shot."

"Oh," cried Jezebel, "I thought they would have us again. Now that they are frightened, let us go away. It will require only a word from one of the apostles to send them upon us again."

"You are right," agreed Smith. "Have you any belongings you wish to take with you?"

"Only what we wear," replied Lady Barbara.

"What is the easiest way out of the valley?" asked the man, on the chance that there might be another and nearer avenue of escape than the fissure through which he had come.

"We know of no way out," replied Jezebel.

"Then follow me," directed Smith. "I'll take you out the way I came in."

They made their way from the village and out onto the dark plain toward Chinnereth, nor did they speak again until they had gone some distance from the fires of the Midians and felt that they were safe from pursuit. It was then that Lafayette Smith asked a question prompted by natural curiosity.

"How can it be possible that you young ladies know of no way out of this valley?" he asked. "Why can't you go out the way you came in?"

"I could scarcely do that," replied Jezebel; "I was born here."

"Born here?" exclaimed Smith. "Then your parents must live in the alley. We can go to their home. Where is it?"

"We just came from it," explained Lady Barbara. "Jezebel was born in the village from which we have just escaped."

"And those beasts killed her parents?" demanded Lafayette.

"You do not understand," said Lady Barbara. "Those people are her people."

Smith was dumbfounded. He almost ejaculated: "How horrible!" but stayed the impulse. "And you?" he asked presently. "Are they your people, too?" There was a note of horror in his voice.

"No," replied Lady Barbara. "I am English."

"And you don't know how you got into this valley?"

"Yes, I know—I came by parachute."

Smith halted and faced her. "You're Lady Barbara Collis!" he exclaimed.

"How did you know?" she asked. "Have you been searching for me?"

"No, but when I passed through London the papers were full of the story of your flight and your disappearance—pictures and things, you know."

"And you just stumbled onto me? What a coincidence! And how fortunate for me."

"To tell you the truth, I am lost myself," admitted Smith. "So possibly you are about as badly off as you were before."

"Scarcely," she said. "You have at least prevented my premature cremation."

"They were really going to burn you? It doesn't seem possible in this day and age of enlightenment and civilization."

"The Midians are two thousand years behind the times," she

told him, "and in addition to that they are religious, as well as congenital, maniacs."

Smith glanced in the direction of Jezebel whom he could see plainly in the light of a full moon that had but just topped the eastern rim of the crater. Perhaps Lady Barbara sensed the unspoken question that disturbed him.

"Jezebel is different," she said. "I cannot explain why, but she is not at all like her people. She tells me that occasionally one such as she is born among them."

"But she speaks English," said Smith. "She cannot be of the same blood as the people I saw in the village, whose language is certainly not the same as hers, to say nothing of the dissimilarity of their physical appearance."

"I taught her English," explained Lady Barbara.

"She wants to go away and leave her parents and her people?" asked Smith.

"Of course I do," said Jezebel. "Why should I want to stay here and be murdered? My father, my mother, my brothers, and sisters were in that crowd you saw about the crosses tonight. They hate me. They have hated me from the day I was born, because I am not like them. But then there is no love in the land of Midian—only religion, which preaches love and practices hate."

Smith fell silent as the three plodded on over the rough ground down toward the shore of Chinnereth. He was considering the responsibility that Fate had loaded upon his shoulders so unexpectedly and wondering if he were equal to the emergency, who, as he was becoming to realize, could scarcely be sure of his ability to insure his own existence in this savage and unfamiliar world.

Keenly the realization smote him that in almost thirty hours that he had been thrown exclusively upon his own resources he had discovered not a single opportunity to provide food for himself, the result of which was becoming increasingly apparent in a noticeable loss of strength and endurance. What then might he hope to accomplish with two additional mouths to feed?

And what if they encountered either savage beasts or unfriendly natives? Lafayette Smith shuddered. "I hope they can run fast," he murmured.

"Who?" asked Lady Barbara. "What do you mean?"

"Oh," stammered Lafayette. "I—I did not know that I spoke aloud." How could he tell her that he had lost confidence even in his .32? He could not. Never before in his life had he felt so utterly incompetent. His futility seemed to him to border on criminality. At any rate it was dishonorable, since it was deceiving these young women who had a right to expect guidance and protection from him.

He was very bitter toward himself; but that, perhaps, was due partly to the nervous reaction following the rather horrible experience at the village and physical weakness that was bordering on exhaustion. He was excoriating himself for having dismissed Obambi, which act, he realized, was at the bottom of all his troubles; and then he recalled that had it not been for that there would have been no one to save these two girls from the horrible fate from which he had preserved them. This thought somewhat restored his self-esteem, for he could not escape the fact that he had, after all, saved them.

Jezebel, the circulation restored to her feet, had been walking without assistance for some time. The three had lapsed into a long silence, each occupied with his own thoughts, as Smith led the way in search of the opening into the fissure.

A full African moon lighted their way, its friendly beams lessening the difficulties of the night march. Chinnereth lay upon their right, a vision of loveliness in the moonlight, while all about them the grim mass of the crater walls seemed to have closed in upon them and to hang menacingly above their heads, for night and moonlight play strange tricks with perspective.

It was shortly after midnight that Smith first stumbled and fell. He arose quickly, berating his awkwardness; but as he proceeded, Jezebel, who was directly behind him, noticed that he walked unsteadily, stumbling more and more often. Presently he fell again, and this time it was apparent to both girls that it was only with considerable effort that he arose. The third time he fell they both helped him to his feet.

"I'm terribly clumsy," he said. He was swaying slightly as she stood between them.

Lady Barbara observed him closely. "You are exhausted," she said.

"Oh, no," insisted Smith. "I'm all right."

"When did you eat last?" demanded the girl.

"I had some chocolate with me," replied Smith. "I ate the last of it this afternoon sometime."

"When did you eat a meal, I mean?" persisted Lady Barbara.

"Well," he admitted, "I had a light lunch yesterday noon, or rather day before yesterday. It must be after midnight now."

"And you have been walking all the time since?"

"Oh, I ran part of the time," he replied, with a weak laugh. "That was when the lion chased me. And I slept in the afternoon before I came to the village."

"We are going to stop right here until you are rested," announced the English girl.

"Oh, no," he demurred, "we mustn't do that. I want to get you out of this valley before daylight, as they will probably pursue us as soon as the sun comes up."

"I don't think so," said Jezebel. "They are too much afraid of the North Midians to come this far from the village; and, anyway, we have such a start that we can reach the cliffs, where you say the fissure is, before they could overtake us."

"You must rest," insisted Lady Barbara.

Reluctantly Lafayette sat down. "I'm afraid I'm not going to be much help to you," he said. "You see I am not really familiar with Africa, and I fear that I am not adequately armed for your protection. I wish Danny were here."

"Who is Danny?" asked Lady Barbara.

"He's a friend who accompanied me on this trip."

"He's had African experience?"

"No," admitted Lafayette, "but one always feels safe with Danny about. He seems so familiar with firearms. You see he is a protection guy."

"What is a protection guy?" asked Lady Barbara.

"To be quite candid," replied Lafayette, "I am not at all sure that I know myself what it is. Danny is not exactly garrulous about his past; and I have hesitated to pry into his private affairs, but he did volunteer the information one day that he had been a protection guy for a big shot. It sounded reassuring."

"What is a big shot?" inquired Jezebel.

"Perhaps a big game hunter," suggested Lady Barbara.

"No," said Lafayette. "I gather from Danny's remarks that a big shot is a rich brewer or distiller who also assists in directing the affairs of a large city. It may be just another name for political boss."

"Of course," said Lady Barbara, "it would be nice if your friend were here; but he is not, so suppose you tell us something about yourself. Do you realize that we do not even know your name?"

Smith laughed. "That's about all there is to know about me," he said. "It's Lafayette Smith, and now will you introduce me to this other young lady? I already know who you are."

"Oh, this is Jezebel," said Lady Barbara.

There was a moment's silence. "Is that all?" asked Smith.

Lady Barbara laughed. "Just Jezebel," she said. "If we ever get out of here we'll have to find a surname for her. They don't use 'em in the land of Midian."

Smith lay on his back looking up at the moon. Already he was commencing to feel the beneficial effects of relaxation and rest. His thoughts were toying with the events of the past thirty hours. What an adventure for a prosaic professor of geology, he thought. He had never been particularly interested in girls, although he was far from being a misogynist, and to find himself thus thrown into the intimate relationship of protector to two beautiful young women was somewhat disconcerting. And the moon had revealed that they were beautiful. Perhaps the sun might have a different story to tell. He had heard of such things and he wondered. But sunlight could not alter the cool, crisp, well-bred voice of Lady Barbara Collis. He liked to hear her talk. He had always enjoyed the accent and diction of cultured English folk.

He tried to think of something to ask her that he might listen to her voice again. That raised the question of just how he should address her. His contacts with nobility had been few—in fact almost restricted to a single Russian prince who had been a doorman at a restaurant he sometimes patronized, and he had never heard him addressed otherwise than as Mike. He thought Lady Barbara would be the correct formula, though that smacked a little of familiarity. Lady Collis seemed, somehow, even less appropriate. He wished he were sure. Mike would never do. Jezebel. What an archaic name! And then he fell asleep.

Lady Barbara looked down at him and raised a warning finger to her lips lest Jezebel awaken him. Then she rose and walked away a short distance, beckoning the golden one to follow.

"He is about done up," she whispered, as they seated themselves again. "Poor chap, he has had a rough time of it. Imagine being chased by a lion with only that little popgun with which to defend oneself."

"Is he from your country?" asked Jezebel.

"No, he's an American. I can tell by his accent."

"He is very beautiful," said Jezebel, with a sigh.

"After looking at Abraham, the son of Abraham, and Jobab, for all these weeks I could agree with you if you insisted that St. Ghandi is an Adonis," replied Lady Barbara.

"I do not know what you mean," said Jezebel; "but do you not think him beautiful?"

"I am less interested in his pulchritude than in his marksmanship, and that is positively beastly. He's got sand though, my word! no end. He walked right into that village and took us out from under the noses of hundreds of people with nothing but his little peashooter for protection. That, Jezebel, was top hole."

The golden Jezebel sighed. "He is much more beautiful than the men of the land of North Midian," she said.

Lady Barbara looked at her companion for a long minute; then she sighed. "If I ever get you to civilization," she said,

"I'm afraid you are going to prove something of a problem."
Wherewith she stretched herself upon the ground and was soon
asleep, for she, too, had had a strenuous day.

15

Eshbaal, the Shepherd

THE SUN SHINING on his upturned face awakened Lafayette Smith. At first he had difficulty in collecting his thoughts. The events of the previous night appeared as a dream, but when he sat up and discovered the figures of the sleeping girls a short distance from him his mind was jerked rudely back into the world of realities. His heart sank. How was he to acquit himself creditably of such a responsibility? Frankly, he did not know.

He had no doubt but that he could find the fissure and lead his charges to the outer world, but how much better off would they be then? He had no idea now, and he realized that he never had, where his camp lay. Then there was the possibility of meeting the lion again in the fissure, and if they did not there was still the question of sustenance. What were they going to use for food, and how were they going to get it?

The thought of food awoke a gnawing hunger within him. He arose and walked to the shore of the lake where he lay on his belly and filled himself with water. When he stood up the girls were sitting up looking at him.

"Good morning," he greeted them. "I was just having breakfast. Will you join me?"

They returned his salutation as they arose and came toward him. Lady Barbara was smiling. "Thank the Lord, you have a sense of humor," she said. "I think we are going to need a lot of it before we get out of this."

"I would much prefer ham and eggs," he replied ruefully.

"Now I know you're an American," she said.

"I suppose you are thinking of tea and marmalade," he rejoined.

"I am trying not to think of food at all," she replied.

"Have some lake," he suggested. "You have no idea how satisfying it is if you take enough of it."

After the girls had drunk the three set off again, led by Smith, in search of the opening to the fissure. "I know just where it is," he had assured them the night before, and even now he thought that he would have little difficulty in finding it, but when they approached the base of the cliff at the point where he had expected to find it it was not there.

Along the foot of the beetling escarpment he searched, almost frantically now, but there was no sign of the opening through which he had crawled into the valley of the land of Midian. Finally, crushed, he faced Lady Barbara. "I cannot find it," he admitted, and there was a quality of hopelessness in his voice that touched her.

"Never mind," she said. "It must be somewhere. We shall just have to keep searching until we find it."

"But it's so hard on you young ladies," he said. "It must be a bitter disappointment to you. You don't know how it makes me feel to realize that, with no one to depend on but me, I have failed you so miserably."

"Don't take it that way, please," she begged. "Anyone might have lost his bearings in this hole. These cliffs scarcely change their appearance in miles."

"It's kind of you to say that, but I cannot help but feel guilty. Yet I know the opening cannot be far from here. I came in on the west side of the valley, and that is where we are now. Yes, I am sure I must find it eventually; but there is no need for all of us to search. You and Jezebel sit down here and wait while I look for it."

"I think we should remain together," suggested Jezebel.

"By all means," agreed Lady Barbara.

"As you wish," said Smith. "We will search toward the north as far as it is possible that the opening can lie. If we don't find it we can come back here and search toward the south."

As they moved along the base of the cliff in a northerly direction Smith became more and more convinced that he was about to discover the entrance to the fissure. He thought that he discerned something familiar in the outlook across the valley from this location, but still no opening revealed itself after they had gone a considerable distance.

Presently, as they climbed the rise and gained the summit of one of the numerous low ridges that ran, buttresslike, from the face of the cliff down into the valley, he halted in discouragement.

"What is it?" asked Jezebel.

"That forest," he replied. "There was no forest in sight of the opening."

Before them spread an open forest of small trees that grew almost to the foot of the cliffs and stretched downward to the shore of the lake, forming a landscape of exceptional beauty in its parklike aspect. But Lafayette Smith saw no beauty there—he saw only another proof of his inefficiency and ignorance.

"You came through no forest on your way from the cliffs to the village?" demanded Lady Barbara.

He shook his head. "We've got to walk all the way back now," he said, "and search in the other direction. It is most disheartening. I wonder if you can forgive me."

"Don't be silly," said Lady Barbara. "One might think that you were a Cook's Tour courier who had got lost during a personally conducted tour of the art galleries of Paris and expected to lose his job in consequence."

"I feel worse than that," Smith admitted with a laugh, "and I imagine that's saying a lot."

"Look!" exclaimed Lady Barbara. "There are animals of some sort down there in the forest. Don't you see them?"

"Oh, yes," cried Jezebel, "I see them."

"What are they?" asked Smith. "They look like deer."

"They are goats," said Jezebel. "The North Midians have goats. They roam over this end of the valley."

"They look like something to eat, to me," said Lady Barbara. "Let's go down and get one of them."

"They will probably not let us catch them," suggested Lafayette.

"You've a pistol," the English girl reminded him.

"That's a fact," he agreed. "I can shoot one."

"Maybe," qualified Lady Barbara.

"I'd better go down alone," said Smith. "Three of us together might frighten them."

"You'll have to be mighty careful or you'll frighten them yourself," warned Lady Barbara. "Have you ever stalked game?"

"No," admitted the American, "I never have."

Lady Barbara moistened a finger and held it up. "The wind is right," she announced. "So all you have to do is keep out of sight and make no noise."

"How am I going to keep out of sight?" demanded Smith.

"You'll have to crawl down to them, taking advantage of trees, rocks, and bushes—anything that will conceal you. Crawl forward a few feet and then stop, if they show any sign of nervousness, until they appear unconcerned again."

"That will take a long time," said Smith.

"It may be a long time before we find anything else to eat," she reminded him, "and nothing we do find is going to walk up to us and lie down and die at our feet."

"I suppose you are right," assented Smith. "Here goes! Pray for me." He dropped to his hands and knees and crawled slowly forward over the rough ground in the direction of the forest and the goats. After a few yards he turned and whispered: "This is going to be tough on the knees."

"Not half as hard as it's going to be on our stomachs if you don't succeed," replied Lady Barbara.

Smith made a wry face and resumed his crawling while the two girls, lying flat now to conceal themselves from the quarry, watched his progress.

"He's not doing half badly," commented Lady Barbara after several minutes of silent watching.

"How beautiful he is," sighed Jezebel.

"Just at present the most beautiful things in the landscape

are those goats," said Lady Barbara. "If he gets close enough for a shot and misses I shall die—and I know he will miss."

"He didn't miss Lamech last night," Jezebel reminded her.

"He must have been aiming at someone else," commented Lady Barbara shortly.

Lafayette Smith crawled on apace. With numerous halts, as advised by Lady Barbara, he drew slowly nearer his unsuspecting quarry. The minutes seemed hours. Pounding constantly upon his brain was the consciousness that he must not fail, though not for the reason that one might naturally assume. The failure to procure food seemed a less dreadful consequence than the contempt of Lady Barbara Collis.

Now, at last, he was quite close to the nearest of the herd. Just a few more yards and he was positive that he could not miss. A low bush, growing just ahead of him, concealed his approach from the eyes of his victim. Lafayette Smith reached the bush and paused behind it. A little farther ahead he discovered another shrub still closer to the goat, a thin nanny with a large udder. She did not look very appetizing, but beneath that unprepossessing exterior Lafayette Smith knew there must be hidden juicy steaks and cutlets. He crawled on. His knees were raw and his neck ached from the unnatural position his unfamiliar method of locomotion had compelled it to assume.

He passed the bush behind which he had paused, failing to see the kid lying hidden upon its opposite side—hidden by a solicitous mamma while she fed. The kid saw Lafayette but it did not move. It would not move until its mother called it, unless actually touched by something, or terrified beyond the limit of its self-control.

It watched Lafayette crawling toward the next bush upon his itinerary—the next and last. What it thought is unrecorded, but it is doubtful that it was impressed by Lafayette's beauty.

Now the man had reached the concealment of the last bush, unseen by any other eyes than those of the kid. He drew his pistol cautiously, lest the slightest noise alarm his potential dinner. Raising himself slightly until his eyes were above the level of the bush he took careful aim. The goat was so close that a miss appeared such a remote contingency as to be of negligible consideration.

Lafayette already felt the stirring warmth of pride with which he would toss the carcass of his kill at the feet of Lady Barbara and Jezebel. Then he jerked the trigger.

Nanny leaped straight up into the air, and when she hit the ground again she was already streaking north in company with the balance of the herd. Lafayette Smith had missed again.

He had scarcely time to realize the astounding and humiliating fact as he rose to his feet when something struck him suddenly and heavily from behind—a blow that bent his knees beneath him and brought him heavily to earth in a sitting posture. No, not to earth. He was sitting on something soft that wriggled and squirmed. His startled eyes, glancing down, saw the head of a kid protruding from between his legs—little Capra hircus had been terrified beyond the limit of his self-control.

"Missed!" cried Lady Barbara Collis. "How could he!" Tears of disappointment welled to her eyes.

Eshbaal, hunting his goats at the northern fringe of the forest cocked his ears and listened. That unfamiliar sound! And so near. From far across the valley, toward the village of the South Midians, Eshbaal had heard a similar sound, though faintly from afar, the night before. Four times it had broken the silence of the valley and no more. Eshbaal had heard it and so had his fellows in the village of Elija, the son of Noah.

Lafayette Smith seized the kid before it could wriggle free, and despite its struggles he slung it across his shoulder and started back toward the waiting girls.

"He didn't miss it!" exclaimed Jezebel. "I knew he wouldn't," and she went down to meet him, with Lady Barbara, perplexed, following in her wake.

"Splendid!" cried the English girl as they came closer. "You really did shoot one, didn't you? I was sure you missed."

"I did miss," admitted Lafayette ruefully.

"But how did you get it?"

"If I must admit it," explained the man, "I sat on it. As a matter of fact it got me."

"Well, anyway, you have it," she said.

"And it will be a whole lot better eating than the one I missed," he assured them. "That one was terribly thin and very old."

"How cute it is," said Jezebel.

"Don't," cried Lady Barbara. "We mustn't think of that. Just remember that we are starving."

"Where shall we eat it?" asked Smith.

"Right here," replied the English girl. "There is plenty of deadwood around these trees. Have you matches?"

"Yes. Now you two look the other way while I do my duty. I wish I'd hit the old one now. This is like murdering a baby."

Upon the opposite side of the forest Eshbaal was once again experiencing surprise, for suddenly the goats for which he had been searching came stampeding toward him.

"The strange noise frightened them," soliloquized Eshbaal. "Perhaps it is a miracle. The goats for which I have searched all day have been made to return unto me."

As they dashed past, the trained eye of the shepherd took note of them. There were not many goats in the bunch that had strayed, so he had no difficulty in counting them. A kid was missing. Being a shepherd there was nothing for Eshbaal to do but set forth in search of the missing one. He advanced cautiously, alert because of the noise he had heard.

Eshbaal was a short, stocky man with blue eyes and a wealth of blond hair and beard. His features were regular and handsome in a primitive, savage way. His single garment, fashioned from a goatskin, left his right arm entirely free, nor did it impede his legs, since it fell not to his knees. He carried a club and a rude knife.

Lady Barbara took charge of the culinary activities after Lafayette had butchered the kid and admitted that, beyond hard-boiling eggs, his knowledge of cooking was too sketchy to warrant serious mention. "And anyway," he said, "we haven't any eggs."

Following the directions of the English girl, Smith cut a number of chops from the carcass; and these the three grilled on pointed sticks that Lady Barbara had had him cut from a nearby tree.

"How long will it take to cook them?" demanded Smith. "I could eat mine raw. I could eat the whole kid raw, for that matter, in one sitting and have room left for the old nanny I missed."

"We'll eat only enough to keep us going," said Lady Barbara; "then we'll wrap the rest in the skin and take it with us. If we're careful, this should keep us alive for three or four days."

"Of course you're right," admitted Lafayette. "You always are."

"You can have a big meal this time," she told him, "because you've been longer without food than we."

"You have had nothing for a long time, Barbara," said Jezebel. "I am the one who needs the least."

"We all need it now," said Lafayette. "Let's have a good meal this time, get back our strength, and then ration the balance so that it will last several days. Maybe I will sit on something else before this is gone."

They all laughed; and presently the chops were done, and the three fell to upon them. "Like starving Armenians," was the simile Smith suggested.

Occupied with the delightful business of appeasing wolfish hunger, none of them saw Eshbaal halt behind a tree and observe them. Jezebel he recognized for what she was, and a sudden fire lighted his blue eyes. The others were enigmas to him—especially their strange apparel.

Of one thing Eshbaal was convinced. He had found his lost kid and there was wrath in his heart. For just a moment he watched the three; then he glided back into the forest until he was out of their sight, when he broke into a run.

The meal finished, Smith wrapped the remainder of the carcass in the skin of the kid; and the three again took up their search for the fissure.

An hour passed and then another. Still their efforts were not crowned with success. They saw no opening in the stern, forbidding face of the escarpment, nor did they see the slinking figures creeping steadily nearer and nearer—a score of stocky, yellow-haired men led by Eshbaal, the Shepherd.

"We must have passed it," said Smith at last. "It just cannot be this far south," yet only a hundred yards farther on lay the elusive opening into the great fissure.

"We shall have to hunt for some other way out of the valley then," said Lady Barbara. "There is a place farther south that Jezebel and I used to see from the mouth of our cave where the cliff looked as though it might be scaled."

"Let's have a try at it then," said Smith. "Say, look there!" he pointed toward the north.

"What is it? Where?" demanded Jezebel.

"I thought I saw a man's head behind that rock," said Smith. "Yes, there he is again. Lord, look at 'em. They're all around."

Eshbaal and his fellows, realizing that they were discovered, came into the open, advancing slowly toward the three.

"The men of North Midian!" exclaimed Jezebel. "Are they not beautiful!"

"What shall we do?" demanded Lady Barbara. "We must not let them take us."

"We'll see what they want," said Smith. "They may not be unfriendly. Anyway, we couldn't escape them by running. They would overtake us in no time. Get behind me, and if they show any signs of attacking I'll shoot a few of them."

"Perhaps you had better go out and sit on them," suggested Lady Barbara, wearily.

"I am sorry," said Smith, "that my marksmanship is so poor; but, unfortunately perhaps, it never occurred to my parents to train me in the gentle art of murder. I realize now that they erred and that my education has been sadly neglected. I am only a schoolteacher, and in teaching the young intellect to shoot I have failed to learn to do so myself."

"I didn't intend to be nasty," said Lady Barbara, who detected in the irony of the man's reply a suggestion of wounded pride. "Please forgive me."

The North Midians were advancing cautiously, halting occasionally for brief, whispered conferences. Presently one of them spoke, addressing the three. "Who are you?" he demanded. "What do you in the land of Midian?"

"Can you understand him?" asked Smith, over his shoulder.

"Yes," replied both girls simultaneously.

"He speaks the same language as Jezebel's people," explained Lady Barbara. "He wants to know who we are and what we are doing here."

"You talk to him, Lady Barbara," said Smith.

The English girl stepped forward. "We are strangers in Midian," she said. "We are lost. All we wish is to get out of your country."

"There is no way out of Midian," replied the man. "You have killed a kid belonging to Eshbaal. For that you must be punished. You must come with us."

"We were starving," explained Lady Barbara. "If we could pay for the kid we would gladly do so. Let us go in peace."

The Midians held another whispered conference, after which their spokesman addressed the three again. "You must come with us," he said, "the women at least. If the man will go away we will not harm you, we do not want him; we want the women."

"What did he say?" demanded Smith, and when Lady Barbara had interpreted he shook his head. "Tell them no," he directed. "Also tell them that if they molest us I shall have to kill them."

When the girl delivered this ultimatum to the Midians they laughed. "What can one man do against twenty?" demanded their leader, then he advanced followed by his retainers. They were brandishing their clubs now, and some of them raised their voices in a savage war cry.

"You will have to shoot," said Lady Barbara. "There are at least twenty. You cannot miss them all."

"You flatter me," said Smith, as he raised his .32 and leveled it at the advancing Midians.

"Go back!" shouted Jezebel, "or you will be killed," but the attackers only came forward the faster.

Then Smith fired. At the sharp crack of the pistol the Midians halted, surprised; but no one fell. Instead, the leader hurled his club, quickly and accurately, just as Smith was about to fire again. He dodged; but the missile struck his pistol hand a glancing blow, sending the weapon flying—then the North Midians were upon them.

16

Trailing

TARZAN OF THE Apes had made a kill. It was only a small rodent, but it would satisfy his hunger until the morrow. Darkness had fallen shortly after he had discovered the spoor of the missing American, and he was forced to abandon the search until daylight came again. The first sign of the spoor had been very faint—just the slightest imprint of one corner of a boot heel, but that had been enough for the ape-man. Clinging to a bush nearby was the scarcely perceptible scent spoor of a white man, which Tarzan might have followed even after dark; but it would have been a slow and arduous method of tracking which the ape-man did not consider the circumstances warranted. Therefore he made his kill, ate, and curled up in a patch of tall grass to sleep.

Wild beasts may not sleep with one eye open, but often it seems that they sleep with both ears cocked. The ordinary night sounds go unnoticed, while a lesser sound, portending danger or suggesting the unfamiliar, may awaken them on the instant. It was a sound falling into the latter category that awoke Tarzan shortly after midnight.

He raised his head and listened, then he lowered it and placed an ear against the ground. "Horses and men," he soliloquized as he rose to his feet. Standing erect, his great chest rising and falling to his breathing, he listened intently. His sensitive nostrils, seeking to confirm the testimony of his ears, dilated to receive and classify the messages that Usha, the wind, bore to them. They caught the scent of Tongani, the baboon, so strong as almost to negate the others. Tenuous, from a great distance came the scent spoor of Sabor, the lioness, and the sweet, heavy stench of Tantor, the elephant. One by one the ape-man read these invisible messages brought by Usha, the wind; but only those interested him that spoke of horses and men.

Why did horses and men move through the night? Who and what were the men? He scarcely needed to ask himself that latter question, and only the first one interested him.

It is the business of beasts and of men to know what their enemies do. Tarzan stretched his great muscles lazily and moved down the slope of the foothills in the direction from which had come the evidence that his enemies were afoot.

The "Gunner" stumbled along in the darkness. Never in his twenty-odd years of life had he even approximated such utter physical exhaustion. Each step he was sure must be his last. He had long since become too tired even to curse his captors as he plodded on, now almost numb to any sensation, his mind a chaos of dull misery.

But even endless journeys must ultimately end; and at last the cavalcade turned into the gateway of the village of Dominic Capietro, the raider; and the "Gunner" was escorted to a hut where he slumped to the hard earth floor after his bonds had been removed, positive that he would never rise again.

He was asleep when they brought him food; but aroused himself long enough to eat, for his hunger was fully as great as his fatigue. Then he stretched out again and slept, while a tired and disgusted *shifta* nodded drowsily on guard outside the entrance to the hut.

Tarzan had come down to the cliff above the village as the raiders were filing through the gateway. A full moon cast her revealing beams upon the scene, lighting the figures of horses and men. The ape-man recognized Capietro and Stabutch, he saw Ogonyo, the head man of the safari of the young American geologist; and he saw the "Gunner" stumbling painfully along in bonds.

The ape-man was an interested spectator of all that transpired in the village below. He noted particularly the location of the hut into which the white prisoner had been thrust. He watched the preparation of food, and he noted the great quantities of liquor that Capietro and Stabutch consumed while waiting for the midnight supper being prepared by slaves. The more they drank the better pleased was Tarzan.

As he watched them, he wondered how supposedly rational creatures could consider the appellation *beast* a term of reproach and *man* one of glorification. The beasts, as he knew, held an opposite conception of the relative virtues of these two orders, although they were ignorant of most of man's asininities and degradations, their minds being far too pure to understand them.

Waiting with the patience of the unspoiled primitive nervous system, Tarzan watched from the cliff top until the village below seemed to have settled down for the night. He saw the sentries in the banquette inside the palisade, but he did not see the guard squatting in the shadow of the hut where the "Gunner" lay in heavy slumber.

Satisfied, the ape-man rose and moved along the cliff until he was beyond the village; and there, where the escarpment was less precipitous, he made his way to its base. Noiselessly and cautiously he crept to the palisade at a point that was hidden from the view of the sentries. The moon shone full upon him, but the opposite side of the palisade he knew must be in dense shadow. There he listened for a moment to assure himself that his approach had aroused no suspicion. He wished that he might see the sentries at the gate, for when he topped the palisade he would be in full view for an instant. When last he had seen them they had been squatting upon the banquette, their backs to the palisade, and apparently upon the verge of sleep. Would they remain thus?

Here, however, was a chance he must take, and so he gave the matter little thought and few regrets. What was, was; and if he could not change it he must ignore it; and so, leaping lightly upward, he seized the top of the palisade and drew himself up and over. Only a glance he threw in the direction of the sentries as he topped the barrier, a glance that told him they had not moved since he had last looked.

In the shadow of the palisade he paused to look about. There was nothing to cause him apprehension; and so he moved quickly, keeping ever in the shadows where he could, toward the hut where he expected to find the young white man. It was hidden from his view by another hut which he approached and had circled when he saw the figure of the guard sitting by the doorway, his rifle across his knees.

This was a contingency the ape-man had not anticipated, and it caused a change in his immediate plans. He drew back out of sight behind the hut he had been circling, lay down flat upon the ground, and then crawled forward again until his head protruded beyond the hut far enough to permit one eye to watch the unconscious guard. Here he lay waiting—a human beast watching its quarry.

For a long time he lay thus trusting to his knowledge of men that the moment for which he waited would arrive. Presently the chin of the *shifta* dropped to his chest; but immediately it snapped back again, erect. Then the fellow changed his position. He sat upon the ground, his legs stretched before him, and leaned his back against the hut. His rifle was still across his knees. It was a dangerous position for a man who would remain awake.

After a while his head rolled to one side. Tarzan watched him closely, as a cat watches a mouse. The head remained in the position to which it had rolled, the chin dropped, and the mouth gaped; the tempo of the breathing changed, denoting sleep.

Tarzan rose silently to his feet and as silently crept across the intervening space to the side of the unconscious man. There must be no outcry, no scuffle.

As strikes Histah, the snake, so struck Tarzan of the Apes. There was only the sound of parting vertebrae as the neck broke in the grip of those thews of steel.

The rifle Tarzan laid upon the ground; then he raised the corpse in his arms and bore it into the darkness of the hut's interior. Here he groped for a moment until he had located the body of the sleeping white, and knelt beside him. Cautiously he shook him, one hand ready to muffle any outcry the man might make, but the "Gunner" did not awaken. Tarzan shook him again more roughly and yet without results, then he slapped him heavily across the face.

The "Gunner" stirred. "Geeze," he muttered "can't you let a guy sleep? Didn't I tell you you'd get your ransom?"

Tarzan permitted a faint smile to touch his lips. "Wake up," he whispered. "Make no noise. I have come to take you away."

"Who are you?"

"Tarzan of the Apes."

"Geeze!" The "Gunner" sat up.

"Make no noise," cautioned the ape-man once more.

"Sure," whispered Danny as he raised himself stiffly to his feet.

"Follow me," said Tarzan, "and no matter what happens stay very close to me. I am going to toss you to the top of the palisade. Try not to make any noise as you climb over, and be careful when you drop to the ground on the other side to alight with your knees flexed—it is a long drop."

"You say you're going to toss me to the top of the palisade, guy?"

"Yes."

"Do you know what I weigh?"

"No, and I don't care. Keep still and follow me. Don't stumble over this body." Tarzan paused in the entrance and looked about; then he passed out, with the "Gunner" at his heels, and crossed quickly to the palisade. Even if they discovered him now he still had time to accomplish what he had set out to do, before they could interfere, unless the sentries, firing on them, chanced to make a hit; but on that score he felt little apprehension.

As they came to the palisade the "Gunner" glanced up, and his skepticism increased—a fat chance any guy would have to toss his one hundred and eighty pounds to the top of that!

The ape-man seized him by the collar and the seat of his breeches. "Catch the top!" he whispered. Then he swung the

"Gunner" backward as though he had been a fifty-pound sack of meal, surged forward and upward; and in the same second Danny Patrick's outstretched fingers clutched the top of the palisade.

"Geeze," he muttered, "if I'd missed I'd of gone clean over."

Catlike, the ape-man ran up the barrier and dropped to the ground on the outside almost at the instant that the "Gunner" alighted, and without a word started toward the cliff, where once again he had to assist the other to reach the summit.

Danny "Gunner" Patrick was speechless, partly from shortness of breath following his exertions, but more, by far, from astonishment. Here was a guy! In all his experience of brawny men, and it had been considerable, he had never met, nor expected to meet, such a one as this.

"I have located the spoor of your friend," said Tarzan.

"The what?" asked the "Gunner." "Is he dead?"

"His tracks," explained the ape-man, who was still leading the way up the slope toward the higher mountains.

"I gotcha," said the "Gunner." "But you ain't seen him?"

"No, it was too dark to follow him when I found them. We will do so in the morning."

"If I can walk," said the "Gunner."

"What's the matter with you?" demanded Tarzan. "Injured?"

"I ain't got no legs from the knees down," replied Danny. "I walked my lousy dogs off yesterday."

"I'll carry you," suggested Tarzan.

"Nix!" exclaimed Danny. "I can crawl, but I'll be damned if I'll let any guy carry me."

"It will be a hard trip if you're exhausted now," the ape-man told him. "I could leave you somewhere near here and pick you up after I find your friend."

"Nothing doing. I'm going to look for old Smithy if I wear 'em off to the hips."

"I could probably travel faster alone," suggested Tarzan.

"Go ahead," agreed the "Gunner" cheerfully. "I'll tail along behind you."

"And get lost."

"Let me come along, mister. I'm worried about that crazy nut."

"All right. It won't make much difference anyway. He may be a little hungrier when we find him, but he can't starve to death in a couple of days."

"Say," exclaimed Danny, "how come you knew them guys had taken me for a ride?"

"I thought you walked."

"Well, what's the difference? How did you know I was in that lousy burgh of theirs?"

"I was on the cliff when they brought you in. I waited until they were asleep. I am not ready to deal with them yet."

"What you goin' to do to them?"

Tarzan shrugged but made no reply; and for a long time they walked on in silence through the night, the ape-man timing his speed to the physical condition of his companion, whose nerve he was constrained to admire, though his endurance and knowledge he viewed with contempt.

Far up in the hills, where he had bedded down earlier in the night, Tarzan halted and told the "Gunner" to get what rest he could before dawn.

"Geeze, them's the pleasantest words I've heard for years," sighed Danny, as he lay down in the high grass. "You may think you've seen a guy pound his ear, but you ain't seen nothin'. Watch me," and he was asleep almost before the words had left his mouth.

Tarzan lay down at a little distance; and he, too, was soon asleep, but at the first suggestion of dawn he was up. He saw that his companion still slept, and then he slipped silently away toward a water hole he had discovered the previous day in a rocky ravine near the cliff where he had met the tribe of Zugash, the tongani.

He kept well down the slope of the foothills, for with the coming of dawn the wind had changed, and he wished to come upwind toward the water hole. He moved as silently as the disappearing shadows of the retreating night, his nostrils quivering to catch each vagrant scent borne upon the bosom of the early morning breeze.

There was deep mud at one edge of the water hole, where the earth had been trampled by the feet of drinking beasts; and near here he found that which he sought, the sticky sweetness of whose scent had been carried to his nostrils by Usha.

Low trees grew in the bottom of the ravine and much underbrush, for here the earth held its moisture longer than on the ridges that were more exposed to Kudu's merciless rays. It was a lovely sylvan glade, nor did its beauties escape the appreciative eyes of the ape-man, though the lure of the glade lay not this morning in its aesthetic charms, but rather in the fact that it harbored Horta, the boar.

Silently to the edge of the underbrush came the ape-man as Horta came down to the pool to drink. Upon the opposite side stood Tarzan, his bow and arrows ready in his hands; but the high brush precluded a fair shot, and so the hunter stepped out in full view of the boar. So quickly he moved that his arrow sped as Horta wheeled to run, catching the boar in the side behind the left shoulder—a vital spot.

With a snort of rage Horta turned back and charged. Straight through the pool he came for Tarzan; and as he came three more arrows shot with unbelievable accuracy and celerity, buried themselves deep in the breast of the great beast. Bloody foam flecked his jowls and his flashing tusks, fires of hate shot from his wicked little eyes as he sought to reach the author of his hurts and wreak his vengeance before he died.

Discarding his bow the ape-man met the mad charge of Horta with his spear, for there was no chance to elude the swift rush of that great body, hemmed, as he was, by the thick growth of underbrush. His feet braced, he dropped the point of his weapon the instant Horta was within its range, that he might have no opportunity to dodge it or strike it aside with his tusks. Straight through the chest it drove, deep into the savage heart, yet the beast still strove to reach the man-thing that held it off with a strength almost equal to its own.

But already as good as dead on his feet was Horta, the boar. His brief, savage struggles ended; and he dropped in the shallow water at the edge of the pool. Then the ape-man placed a foot upon his vanquished foe and screamed forth the hideous challenge of his tribe.

The "Gunner" sat suddenly erect, awakened out of a sound sleep. "Geeze!" he exclaimed. "What was that?" Receiving no answer he looked about. "Wouldn't that eat you?" he murmured. "He's went. I wonder has he run out on me? He didn't seem like that kind of a guy. But you can't never tell—I've had pals to double-cross me before this."

In the village of Capietro a dozing sentry snapped suddenly alert, while his companion half rose to his feet. "What was that?" demanded one.

"A hairy one has made a kill," said the other.

Sheeta, the panther, downwind, stalking both the man and the boar, stopped in his tracks; then he turned aside and loped away in easy, graceful bounds; but he had not gone far before he stopped again and raised his nose upwind. Again the scent of man; but this time a different man, nor was there any sign of the feared thunder stick that usually accompanied the scent spoor of the tarmangani. Belly low, Sheeta moved slowly up the slope toward Danny "Gunner" Patrick.

"What to do?" mused the "Gunner." "Geeze, I'm hungry! Should I wait for him or should I go on? On, where? I sure got myself in a jam all right. Where do I go? How do I eat? Hell!"

He arose and moved about, feeling out his muscles. They were lame and sore, but he realized that he was much rested. Then he scanned the distances for a sight of Tarzan and, instead, saw Sheeta, the panther, a few hundred yards away.

Danny Patrick, hoodlum, racketeer, gangster, gunman, killer, trembled in terror. Cold sweat burst from every pore, and he could feel the hair rise on his scalp. He felt a mad impulse to run; but, fortunately for Danny, his legs refused to move. He was literally, in the vernacular to which he was accustomed, scared stiff. The "Gunner," without a gun, was a very different man.

The panther had stopped and was surveying him. Caution and an hereditary fear of man gave the great cat pause, but he was angry because he had been frightened from his prey after hunting futilely all night, and he was very, very hungry. He growled, his face wrinkled in a hideous snarl; and Danny felt his knees giving beneath him.

Then, beyond the panther, he saw the high grass moving to the approach of another animal, which the "Gunner" promptly assumed was the beast's mate. There was just a single, narrow strip of this high grass; and when the animal had crossed it he, too, would see Danny, who was confident that this would spell the end. One of them might hesitate to attack a man—he didn't know—but he was sure that two would not.

He dropped to his knees and did something that he had not done for many years—he prayed. And then the grasses parted; and Tarzan of the Apes stepped into view, the carcass of a boar upon one broad shoulder. Instantly the ape-man took in the scene that his nostrils had already prepared him for.

Dropping the carcass of Horta he voiced a sudden, ferocious growl that startled Sheeta no more than it did Danny Patrick. The cat wheeled, instantly on the defensive. Tarzan charged, growls rumbling from his throat; and Sheeta did exactly what he had assumed he would do—turned and fled. Then Tarzan picked up the carcass of Horta and came up the slope to Danny, who knelt open-mouthed and petrified.

"What are you kneeling for?" asked the ape-man.

"I was just tying my boot lace," explained the "Gunner."

"Here is breakfast," said Tarzan, dropping the boar to the ground. "Help yourself."

"That sure looks good to me," said Danny. "I could eat it raw."

"That is fine," said Tarzan; and, squatting, he cut two strips from one of the hams. "Here," he said, offering one to the "Gunner."

"Quit your kidding," remonstrated the latter.

Tarzan eyed him questioningly, at the same time tearing off a mouthful of the meat with his strong teeth. "Horta is a little bit tough," he remarked, "but he is the best I could do without losing a great deal of time. Why don't you eat? I thought you were hungry."

"I got to cook mine," said the "Gunner."

"'But you said you could eat it raw," the ape-man reminded him.

"That's just a saying," explained the "Gunner." "I might at that, but I ain't never tried it."

"Make a fire, then; and cook yours," said Tarzan.

"Say," remarked Danny a few minutes later as he squatted before his fire grilling his meat, "did you hear that noise a little while ago?"

"What was it like?"

"I never heard nothing like it but once before—say I just took a tumble to myself! That was you killin' the pig. I heard you yell like that the night you killed the lion in our camp."

"We will be going as soon as you finish your meat," said Tarzan. He was hacking off several pieces, half of which he handed to the "Gunner" while he dropped the balance into his quiver. "Take these," he said. "You may get hungry before we can make another kill." Then he scraped a hole in the loose earth and buried the remainder of the carcass.

"What you doin' that for?" asked the "Gunner." "Afraid it will smell?"

"We may come back this way," explained Tarzan. "If we do Horta will be less tough."

The "Gunner" made no comment; but he assured himself, mentally, that he "wasn't no dog," to bury his meat and then dig it up again after it had rotted. The idea almost made him sick.

Tarzan quickly picked up the trail of Lafayette Smith and followed it easily, though the "Gunner" saw nothing to indicate that human foot had ever trod these hills.

"I don't see nothing," he said.

"I have noticed that," returned Tarzan.

"That," thought Danny Patrick, "sounds like a dirty crack"; but he said nothing.

"A lion picked up his trail here," said the ape-man.

"You ain't spoofin' me are you?" demanded Danny. "There ain't no sign of nothin' on this ground."

"Nothing that you can see perhaps," replied Tarzan; "but then, though you may not know it, you so-called civilized men are almost blind and quite stone deaf."

Soon they came to the fissure, and here Tarzan saw that the man and the lion had both gone in, the lion following the man, and that only the lion had come out.

"That looks tough for old Smithy, doesn't it?" said the "Gunner" when Tarzan had explained the story of the spoor.

"It may," replied the ape-man. "I'll go on in and look for him. You can wait here or follow. You can't get lost if you stay inside this crack."

"Go ahead," said Danny. "I'll follow."

The fissure was much longer than Tarzan had imagined; but some distance from the entrance he discovered that the lion had not attacked Smith, for he could see where Numa had turned about and that the man had continued on. Some recent scars on the sides of the fissure told him the rest of the story quite accurately.

"It's fortunate he didn't hit Numa," soliloquized the ape-man.

At the end of the fissure Tarzan had some difficulty in wriggling through the aperture that opened into the valley of the Land of Midian; but once through he picked up the trail of Smith again and followed it down toward the lake, while Danny, far behind him, stumbled wearily along the rough floor of the fissure.

Tarzan walked rapidly for the spoor was plain. When he came to the shore of Chinnereth he discovered Smith's tracks intermingled with those of a woman wearing well-worn European boots and another shod with sandals.

When he had first entered the valley he had seen the village of the South Midians in the distance and now he drew the false conclusion that Smith had discovered a friendly people and other whites and that he was in no danger.

His curiosity piqued by the mystery of this hidden valley, the ape-man determined to visit the village before continuing on Smith's trail. Time had never entered greatly into his calculations, trained, as he had been, by savage apes to whom, time meant less than nothing; but to investigate and to know every detail of his wilderness world was as much a part of the man as is his religion to a priest.

And so he continued rapidly on toward the distant village while Danny Patrick still crawled and stumbled slowly along the rocky floor of the fissure.

Danny was tired. Momentarily he expected to meet Tarzan returning either with Smith or with word of his death; so he stopped often to rest, with the result that when he had reached the end of the fissure and crawled through to behold the mystifying sight of a strange valley spread before him, Tarzan was already out of sight.

"Geeze!" exclaimed the "Gunner." "Who would have thought that hole led into a place like this? I wonder which way that Tarzan guy went?"

This thought occupied the "Gunner" for a few minutes. He examined the ground as he had seen Tarzan do, mistook a few spots where some little rodent had scratched up the earth, or taken a dust bath, for the footprints of a man, and set forth in the wrong direction.

17

She Is Mine!

THE STOCKY, BLOND warriors of Elija, the son of Noah, quickly surrounded and seized Lafayette Smith and his two companions. Elija picked up Smith's pistol and examined it with interest; then he dropped it into a goatskin pouch that was suspended from the girdle that held his single garment about him.

"This one," said Eshbaal, pointing to Jezebel, "is mine."

"Why?" asked Elija, the son of Noah.

"I saw her first," replied Eshbaal.

"Did you hear what he said?" demanded Jezebel of Lady Barbara.

The English girl nodded apathetically. Her brain was numb with disappointment and the horror of the situation, for in some respects their fate might be worse with these men than with those of South Midian. These were lusty, primitive warriors, not half-witted creatures whose natural passions had been weakened by generations of hereditary disease of nerve and brain.

"He wants me," said Jezebel. "Is he not beautiful?"

Lady Barbara turned upon the girl almost angrily, and then suddenly she remembered that Jezebel was little more than a child in experience and that she had no conception of the fate that might await her at the hands of the North Midians.

In their narrow religious fanaticism the South Midians denied even the most obvious phases of procreation. The subject was absolutely taboo and so hideous had ages of training and custom made it appear to them that mothers often killed their firstborn rather than exhibit these badges of sin.

"Poor little Jezebel," said Lady Barbara.

"What do you mean, Barbara?" asked the girl. "Are you not happy that the beautiful man wants me?"

"Listen, Jezebel," said Lady Barbara. "You know I am your friend, do you not?"

"My only friend," replied the girl. "The only person I ever loved."

"Then believe me when I say that you must kill yourself, as I shall kill myself, if we are unable to escape from these creatures."

"Why?" demanded Jezebel. "Are they not more beautiful than the South Midians?"

"Forget their fatal beauty," replied Lady Barbara, "but never forget what I have told you."

"Now I am afraid," said Jezebel.

"Thank God for that," exclaimed the English girl.

The North Midians marched loosely and without discipline. They seemed a garrulous race, and their arguments and speeches were numerous and lengthy. Sometimes so intent did they become on some point at argument, or in listening to a long-winded oration by one of their fellows, that they quite forgot their prisoners, who were sometimes amongst them, sometimes in advance and once behind them.

It was what Lady Barbara had been awaiting and what she had to some extent engineered.

"Now!" she whispered. "They are not looking." She halted and turned back. They were among the trees of the forest where some concealment might be found.

Smith and Jezebel had stopped at Lady Barbara's direction; and for an instant the three paused, breathless, watching the retreating figures of their captors.

"Now run!" whispered Lady Barbara. "We'll scatter and meet again at the foot of the cliff."

Just what prompted Lady Barbara to suggest that they separate Lafayette Smith did not understand. To him it seemed a foolish and unnecessary decision; but as he had a great deal more confidence in Lady Barbara's judgment in practical matters than in his own he did not voice his doubts, though he accepted her plan with certain mental reservations, which guided his subsequent acts.

The English girl ran in a southeasterly direction, while Jezebel, obeying the commands of her friend, scurried off toward the southwest. Smith, glancing to the rear, discovered no indication that their captors had, as yet, missed them. For a moment he was hesitant as to what course to pursue. The conviction still gripped him that he was the natural protector of both girls, notwithstanding the unfortunate circumstances that had nullified his efforts to function successfully in that rôle; but he saw that it was going to be still more difficult to protect them both now that they had elected to run in different directions.

However, his decision was soon made, difficult though it was. Jezebel was in her own world; contemplation of her capture by the North Midains had, so far from alarming her, appeared rather to have met with enthusiastic anticipation on her part; she could not be worse off with them than the only other people she knew.

Lady Barbara, on the other hand, was of another world—his own world—and he had heard her say that death would be preferable to captivity among these semisavages. His duty, therefore, was to follow and protect Lady Barbara; and so he let Jezebel take her way unprotected back toward the cliff, while he pursued the English girl in the direction of Chinnereth.

Lady Barbara Collis ran until she was out of breath. For several minutes she had distinctly heard the sounds of pursuit behind her—the heavy footfalls of a man. Frantic from hopelessness, she drew her pocketknife from a pocket of her jacket and opened the blade as she ran.

She wondered if she could destroy herself with this inadequate weapon. She was positive that she could not inflict either fatal or disabling injuries upon her pursuer with it. Yet the thought of self-destruction revolted her. The realization was upon her that she had about reached the limit of her endurance, and that the fatal decision could not be long averted, when her heritage of English fighting blood decided the question for her. There was but one thing it would permit—she must stand and defend herself. She stopped then, suddenly, and wheeled about, the little knife clutched in her right hand—a tigress at bay.

When she saw Lafayette Smith running toward her she collapsed suddenly and sank to the ground, where she sat with her back against the bole of a tree. Lafayette Smith, breathing hard, came and sat down beside her. Neither had any breath for words.

Lady Barbara was the first to regain her power of speech. "I thought I said we would scatter," she reminded him.

"I couldn't leave you alone," he replied.

"But how about Jezebel? You left her alone."

"I couldn't go with both of you," he reminded her, "and you know Jezebel is really at home here. It means much more to you to escape than it means to her."

She shook her head. "Capture means the same thing to either of us," she said, "But of the two I am better able to take care of myself than Jezebel—she does not understand the nature of her danger."

"Nevertheless," he insisted, "you are the more important. You have relatives and friends who care for you. Poor little Jezebel has only one friend, and that is you, unless I may consider myself a friend, as I should like to do."

"I imagine we three have the unique distinction of being the closest corporation of friends in the world," she replied, with a wan smile, "and there doesn't seem to be anyone who wants to buy in."

"The Friendless Friends Corporation, Limited," he suggested.

"Perhaps we'd best hold a directors' meeting and decide what we should do next to conserve the interests of the stockholders."

"I move we move," he said.

"Seconded." The girl rose to her feet.

"You're terribly tired, aren't you?" he asked. "But I suppose the only thing we can do is to get as far away from the territory of the North Midians as possible. It's almost certain they will try to capture us again as soon as they discover we are missing."

"If we can only find a place to hide until night," she said.

"Then we can go back to the cliffs under the cover of darkness and search for Jezebel and the place that she and I thought might be scaled."

"This forest is so open that it doesn't afford any good hiding places, but at least we can look."

"Perhaps we shall find a place near the lake," said Lady Barbara. "We ought to come to it soon."

They walked on for a considerable distance without talking, each occupied with his own thoughts; and as no sign of pursuit developed their spirits rose.

"Do you know," he said presently, "that I can't help but feel that we're going to get out of this all right in the end?"

"But what a terrible experience! It doesn't seem possible that such things could have happened to me. I can't forget Jobab." It was the first time mention had been made of the tragedy at the southern village.

"You must not give that a thought," he said. "You did the only thing possible under the circumstances. If you had not done what you did both you and Jezebel would have been recaptured, and you know what that would have meant."

"But I've killed a human being," she said. There was an awed tone in her voice.

"I killed one, too," he reminded her, "but I don't regret it in the least, notwithstanding the fact that I never killed anyone before. If I were not such a terrible marksman I should have killed another today, perhaps several. My regret is that I didn't."

"It's a strange world," he continued after a moment's reflective silence. "Now, I always considered myself rather well educated and fitted to meet the emergencies of life; and I suppose I should be, in the quiet environment of a college town; but what an awful failure I have proved to be when jolted out of my narrow little rut. I used to feel sorry for the boys who wasted their time in shooting galleries and in rabbit hunting. Men who boasted of their marksmanship merited only my contempt, yet within the last twenty-four hours I would have traded all my education along other lines for the ability to shoot straight."

"One should know something of many things to be truly educated," said the girl, "but I'm afraid you exaggerate the value of marksmanship in determining one's cultural status."

"Well, there's cooking," he admitted. "A person who cannot cook is not well educated. I had hoped one day to be an authority on geology; but with all I know of the subject, which of course isn't so much at that, I would probably starve to death in a land overrunning with game, because I can neither shoot nor cook."

Lady Barbara laughed. "Don't develop an inferiority complex at this stage," she cried. "We need every ounce of self-assurance that we can muster. I think you are top hole. You may not be much of a marksman—that I'll have to admit, and perhaps you cannot cook; but you've one thing that covers a multitude of shortcomings in a man—you are brave."

It was Lafayette Smith's turn to laugh. "That's mighty nice of you," he said. "I'd rather you thought that of me than anything else in the world; and I'd rather you thought it than anyone else, because it would mean so much to you now; but it isn't true. I was scared stiff in that village last night and when those fellows came at us today, and that's the truth."

"Which only the more definitely justifies my statement," she replied.

"I don't understand."

"Cultured and intelligent people are more ready to realize and appreciate the dangers of a critical situation than are ignorant, unimaginative types. So, when such a person stands his ground determinedly in the face of danger, or voluntarily walks into a dangerous situation from a sense of duty, as you did last night, it evidences a much higher quality of courage than that possessed by the ignorant, physical lout who hasn't brains enough to visualize the contingencies that may result from his action."

"Be careful," he warned her, "or you'll make me believe all that—then I'll be unbearably egotistical. But please don't try to convince me that my inability to cook is a hallmark of virtue."

"I—listen! What was that?" she halted and turned her eyes toward the rear.

"They have found us," said Lafayette Smith. "Go on—go as fast as you can! I'll try to delay them."

"No," she replied, "there is no use. I'll remain with you, whatever happens."

"Please!" he begged. "Why should I face them if you won't take advantage of it."

"It wouldn't do any good," she said. "They'd only get me later, and your sacrifice would be useless. We might as well give ourselves up in the hope that we can persuade them to free us later, or, perhaps, find the opportunity to escape after dark."

"You had better run," he said, "because I am going to fight. I am not going to let them take you without raising a hand in your defense. If you get away now, perhaps I can get away later. We can meet at the foot of the cliffs—but don't wait for me if you can find a way out. Now, do as I tell you!" His tone was peremptory—commanding.

Obediently she continued on toward Chinnereth, but presently she stopped and turned. Three men were approaching Smith. Suddenly one of the three swung his club and hurled it at the American, at the same instant dashing forward with his fellows.

The club fell short of its mark, dropping at Smith's feet. She saw him stoop and seize it, and then she saw another detachment of the Midians coming through the woods in the wake of the first three.

Smith's antagonists were upon him as he straightened up with the club in his hand, and he swung it heavily upon the skull of the man who had hurled it at him and who had rushed forward in advance of his fellows with hands outstretched to seize the stranger.

Like a felled ox the man dropped; and then Lady Barbara saw Smith carry the unequal battle to the enemy as, swinging the club above his head, he rushed forward to meet them.

So unexpected was his attack that the men halted and turned

to elude him, but one was too slow and the girl heard the fellow's skull crush beneath the heavy blow of the bludgeon.

Then the reinforcements, advancing at a run, surrounded and overwhelmed their lone antagonist, and Smith went down beneath them.

Lady Barbara could not bring herself to desert the man who had thus bravely, however hopelessly, sought to defend her; and when the North Midians had disarmed and secured Smith they saw her standing where she had stood during the brief engagement.

"I couldn't run away and leave you," she explained to Smith, as the two were being escorted toward the village of the North Midians. "I thought they were going to kill you, and I couldn't help you—Oh, it was awful. I couldn't leave you then, could I?"

He looked at her for a moment. "No," he answered. "*You* couldn't."

18

A Guy and a Skirt

DANNY "GUNNER" PATRICK was tired and disgusted. He had walked for several hours imagining that he was following a spoor, but he had seen nothing of his erstwhile companion. He was thirsty, and so cast frequent glances in the direction of the lake.

"T'ell!" he muttered. "I ain't goin' to tail that guy no longer till I get me a drink. My mouth feels like I'd been eating cotton for a week."

He turned away from the cliffs and started down in the direction of the lake, the inviting waters of which sparkled alluringly in the afternoon sun; but the beauties of the scene were wasted upon the "Gunner," who saw only a means of quenching his thirst.

The way led through a field of scattered boulders fallen from the towering rim above. He had to pick his way carefully among the smaller ones, and his eyes were almost constantly upon the ground. Occasionally he was compelled to skirt some of the larger masses, many of which towered above his head obstructing his view ahead.

He was damning Africa in general and this section of it in particular as he rounded the corner of an unusually large fragment of rock, when suddenly he stopped and his eyes went wide.

"Geeze!" he exclaimed aloud. "A broad!"

Before him, and coming in his direction, was a golden-haired girl attired in a single, scant piece of rough material. She saw him simultaneously and halted.

"Oh," exclaimed Jezebel with a happy smile. "Who art thou?" but as she spoke in the language of the land of Midian the "Gunner" failed to understand her.

"Geeze," he said. "I knew I must of come to Africa for something, and I guess you're it. Say kid, you're about all right. I'll tell the world you *are* all right."

"Thank you," said Jezebel in English. "I am so glad that you like me."

"Geeze," said Danny. "You talk United States, don't you? Where you from?"

"Midian," replied Jezebel.

"Ain't never heard of it. What you doin' here? Where're your people?"

"I am waiting for Lady Barbara," replied the girl, "and Smith," she added.

"Smith! What Smith?" he demanded.

"Oh, he is beautiful," confided Jezebel.

"Then he ain't the Smith I'm lookin' for," said the "Gunner." "What's he doin' here, and who's this Lady Barbara dame?"

"Abraham, the son of Abraham, would have killed Lady Barbara and Jezebel if Smith had not come and saved us. He is very brave."

"Now I know it ain't my Smith," said Danny, "though I ain't sayin' he ain't got guts. What I mean is he wouldn't know how to save no one—he's a geologist."

"Who are you?" demanded Jezebel.

"Call me Danny, kid."

"My name is not kid," she explained sweetly. "It is Jezebel."

"Jezebel! Geeze, what a monicker! You look like it ought to be Gwendolyn."

"It is Jezebel," she assured him. "Do you know who I hoped you'd be?"

"No. Now just tell me, kid, who you supposed I was, Probably President Hoover or Big Bill Thompson, eh?"

"I do not know them," said Jezebel. "I hoped that you were the 'Gunner.' "

"The 'Gunner'? What do you know about the 'Gunner,' kid?"

"My name is not kid, it is Jezebel," she corrected him, sweetly.

"Oke, Jez," conceded Danny, "but tell me who wised you up to the 'Gunner' bozo."

"My name is not Jez, it is——"

"Oh, sure kid, it's Jezebel—that's oke by me; but how about the 'Gunner'?"

"What about him?"

"I just been a-askin' you."

"But I don't understand your language," explained Jezebel. "It sounds like English, but it is not the English Lady Barbara taught me."

"It ain't English," Danny assured her, seriously; "it's United States."

"It's quite like English though, isn't it?"

"Sure," said the "Gunner." "The only difference is we can understand English but the English don't never seem to understand all of ours. I guess they're dumb."

"Oh, no, they're not dumb," Jezebel assured him. "Lady Barbara is English, and she can talk quite as well as you."

Danny scratched his head. "I didn't say they was dummies. I said they was dumb. Dummies can't talk only with their mitts. If a guy's dumb, he don't know nothing."

"Oh," said Jezebel.

"But what I asked you is, who wised you up to this 'Gunner' bozo?"

"Can you say it in English, please," asked Jezebel.

"Geeze, what could be plainer? I asked who told you about the 'Gunner' and what did they tell you?" Danny was waxing impatient.

"Smith told us. He said the 'Gunner' was a friend of his; and when I saw you I thought you must be Smith's friend, hunting for him."

"Now, what do you know about that!" exclaimed Danny.

"I have just told you what I know about it," explained the

girl; "but perhaps you did not understand me. Perhaps you are what you call dumb."

"Are you trying to kid me, kid?" demanded the "Gunner."

"My name is not——"

"Oh, all right, all right. I know what your name is."

"Then why do you not call me by my name? Do you not like it?"

"Sure, kid—I mean Jezebel—sure I like it. It's a swell handle when you get used to it. But tell me, where is old Smithy?"

"I do not know such a person."

"But you just told me you did."

"Oh, I see," cried Jezebel. "Smithy is the United States for Smith. But Smith is not old. He's quite young."

"Well, where is he?" demanded Danny, resignedly.

"We were captured by the beautiful men from North Midian," explained Jezebel; "but we escaped and ran away. We ran in different directions, but we are going to meet tonight farther south along the cliffs."

"Beautiful men?" demanded the "Gunner." "Did old Smithy let a bunch of fairies hoist him?"

"I do not understand," said Jezebel.

"*You* wouldn't," he assured her; "but say, kid—"

"My name—"

"Aw, forget it—you know who I mean. As I was saying, let's me and you stick together till we find old Smithy. What say?"

"That would be nice, the 'Gunner,' " she assured him.

"Say, call me Danny, k—Jezebel."

"Yes, Danny."

"Geeze, I never knew Danny was such a swell monicker till I heard you say it. What say we beat it for the big drink down there? I got me such a thirst my tongue's hanging out. Then we can come back to this here rock pile and look for old Smithy."

"That will be nice," agreed Jezebel. "I, too, am thirsty." She sighed. "You cannot know how happy I am, Danny."

"Why?" he asked.

"Because you are with me."

"Geeze, k—Jezebel, but you're sure a fast worker."

"I do not know what you mean," she replied, innocently.

"Well just tell me why you're happy because I'm with you."

"It is because I feel safe with you after what Smith told us. He said he always felt safe when you were around."

"So that's it? All you want is a protection guy, eh? You don't like me for myself at all, eh?"

"Oh, of course I like you, Danny," cried the girl. "I think you are beautiful."

"Yeah? Well, listen, sister. You may be a swell kidder—I dunno—or you may be just a dumb egg—but don't call me no names. I know what my pan looks like; and it ain't beautiful, and I ain't never wore a beret."

Jezebel, who only caught the occasional highspots of Danny's conversation, made no reply, and they walked on in the direction of the lake, in silence, for some time. The forest was some little distance away, on their left, and they had no knowledge of what was transpiring there, nor did any sound reach their ears to acquaint them with the misfortune that was befalling Lady Barbara and Lafayette Smith.

At the lake they quenched their thirst, after which the "Gunner" announced that he was going to rest for a while before he started back toward the cliffs. "I wonder," he said, "just how far a guy can walk, because in the last two days I've walked that far and back again."

"How far is that?" inquired Jezebel.

He looked at her a moment and then shook his head. "It's twice as far," he said, as he stretched himself at full length and closed his eyes. "Geeze, but I'm about all in," he murmured.

"In what?"

He deigned no reply, and presently the girl noted from his altered breathing that he was asleep. She sat with her eyes glued upon him, and occasionally a deep sigh broke from her lips. She was comparing Danny with Abraham, the son of Abraham, with Lafayette Smith and with the beautiful men of North Midian; and the comparison was not uncomplimentary to Danny.

The hot sun was beating down upon them, for there was no

shade here; and presently its effects, combined with her fatigue, made her drowsy. She lay down near the "Gunner" and stretched luxuriously. Then she, too, fell asleep.

The "Gunner" did not sleep very long; the sun was too hot. When he awoke he raised himself on an elbow and looked around. His eyes fell on the girl and there they rested for some time, noting the graceful contours of the lithe young body, the wealth of golden hair, and the exquisite face.

"The kid's sure some looker," soliloquized Danny. "I seen a lotta broads in my day, but I ain't never seen nothin' could touch her. She'd sure be a swell number dolled up in them Boul Mich rags. Geeze, wouldn't she knock their lamps out! I wonder where this Midian burgh is she says she comes from. If they's all as swell lookin' as her, that's the burgh for me."

Jezebel stirred and he reached over and shook her on the shoulder. "We'd better be beatin' it," he said. "We don't want to miss old Smithy and that dame."

Jezebel sat up and looked about her. "Oh," she exclaimed, "you frightened me. I thought something was coming."

"Why? Been dreaming?"

"No. You said we'd have to beat something."

"Aw, cheese it! I meant we'd have to be hittin' the trail for the big rocks."

Jezebel looked puzzled.

"Hike back to them cliffs where you said old Smithy and that Lady Barbara dame were going to meet you."

"Now I understand," said Jezebel. "All right, come on."

But when they reached the cliffs there was no sign of Smith or Lady Barbara, and at Jezebel's suggestion they walked slowly southward in the direction of the place where she and the English girl had hoped to make a crossing to the outer world.

"How did you get into the valley, Danny?" asked the girl.

"I come through a big crack in the mountain," he replied.

"That must be the same place Smith came through," she said. "Could you find it again?"

"Sure. That's where I'm headed for now."

It was only midafternoon when Danny located the opening

into the fissure. They had seen nothing of Lady Barbara and Smith, and they were in a quandary as to what was best to do.

"Maybe they come along and made their getaway while we was hittin' the hay," suggested Danny.

"I don't know what you are talking about," said Jezebel, "but what I think is that they may have located the opening while we were asleep and gone out of the valley."

"Well ain't that what I said?" demanded Danny.

"It didn't sound like it."

"Say, you trying to high-hat me?"

"High-hat?"

"Aw, what's the use?" growled the "Gunner," disgustedly. "Let's you and me beat it out of this here dump and look for old Smithy and the skirt on the other side. What say?"

"But suppose they haven't gone out?"

"Well, then we'll have to come back again; but I'm sure they must have. See this footprint?" he indicated one of his own, made earlier in the day, which pointed toward the valley. "I guess I'm getting good," he said. "Pretty soon that Tarzan guy won't have no edge on me at all."

"I'd like to see what's on the other side of the cliffs," said Jezebel. "I have always wanted to do that."

"Well, you won't see nothin' much," he assured her. "Just some more scenery. They ain't even a hot dog stand or a single speakeasy."

"What are those?"

"Well, you might call 'em filling stations."

"What are filling stations?"

"Geeze, kid, what do you think I am, a college perfessor? I never saw anyone who could ask so many questions in my whole life."

"My name——"

"Yes, I know what your name is. Now come on and we'll crawl through this hole-in-the-wall. I'll go first. You follow right behind me."

The rough going along the rocky floor of the fissure taxed the "Gunner's" endurance and his patience, but Jezebel was all excitement and anticipation. All her life she had dreamed of what might lie in the wonderful world beyond the cliffs.

Her people had told her that it was a flat expanse filled with sin, heresy, and iniquity, where, if one went too far he would surely fall over the edge and alight in the roaring flames of an eternal hades; but Jezebel had been a doubter. She had preferred to picture it as a land of flowers and trees and running water, where beautiful people laughed and sang through long, sunny days. Soon she was to see for herself, and she was much excited by the prospect.

And now at last they came to the end of the great fissure and looked out across the rolling foothills toward a great forest in the distance.

Jezebel clasped her hands together in ecstacy. "Oh, Danny," she cried, "how beautiful it is!"

"What?" asked the "Gunner."

"Oh, everything. Don't you think it is beautiful, Danny?"

"The only beautiful thing around here, k—Jezebel, is you," said Danny.

The girl turned and looked up at him with her great gray eyes. "Do you think I am beautiful, Danny?"

"Sure I do."

"Do you think I am *too* beautiful?"

"There ain't no such thing," he replied, "but if they was you're it. What made you ask?"

"Lady Barbara said I was."

The "Gunner" considered this for some moments. "I guess she's right at that, kid."

"You like to call me kid, don't you?" asked Jezebel.

"Well, it seems more friendly-like," he explained, "and it's easier to remember."

"All right, you may call me kid if you want to, but my name is Jezebel."

"That's a bet," said Danny. "When I don't think to call you Jezebel, I'll call you kid, Sister."

The girl laughed. "You're a funny man, Danny. You like to say everything wrong. I'm not your sister, of course."

"And I'm damn glad you ain't, kid."

"Why? Don't you like me?"

Danny laughed. "I never seen a kid like you before," he said. "You sure got me guessin'. But at that," he added, a little seriously for him, "they's one thing I ain't guessin' about and that's that you're a good little kid."

"I don't know what you are talking about," said Jezebel.

"And at that I'll bet you don't," he replied; "and now kid, let's sit down and rest. I'm tired."

"I'm hungry," said Jezebel.

"I ain't never see a skirt that wasn't, but why did you have to bring that up? I'm so hungry I could eat hay."

"Smith killed a kid and we ate some of that," said Jezebel. "He wrapped the rest up in the skin and I suppose he lost it when the North Midians attacked us. I wish—"

"Say," exclaimed Danny, "what a dumbbell I am!" He reached down into one of his pockets and brought out several strips of raw meat. "Here I been packin' this around all day and forgets all about it—and me starvin' to death."

"What is it?" asked Jezebel, leaning closer to inspect the unsavory morsels.

"It's pig," said Danny as he started searching for twigs and dry grass to build a fire, "and I know where they is a lot more that I thought I couldn't never eat but I know now I could— even if I had to fight with the maggots for it."

Jezebel helped him gather wood, which was extremely scarce, being limited to dead branches of a small variety of artemisia that grew on the mountainside; but at length they had collected quite a supply, and presently they were grilling pieces of the boar meat over the flames. So preoccupied were they that neither saw three horsemen draw rein at the top of a ridge a mile away and survey them.

"This is like housekeeping, ain't it?" remarked the "Gunner."

"What is that?" asked Jezebel.

"That's where a guy and his girlfriend get hitched and go to doin' their own cooking. Only in a way this is better—they ain't goin' to be no dishes to wash."

"What is hitched, Danny?" asked Jezebel.

"Why—er," Danny flushed. He had said many things to many girls in his life, many of them things that might have brought a blush to the cheek of a wooden Indian; but this was the first time, perhaps, that Danny had felt any embarrassment.

"Why—er," he repeated, "hitched means married."

"Oh," said Jezebel. She was silent for a while, watching the pork sizzling over the little flames. Then she looked up at Danny. "I think housekeeping is fun," she said.

"So do I," agreed Danny, "with you," he added and his voice was just a trifle husky. His eyes were on her; and there was a strange light in them, that no other girl had ever seen there. "You're a funny little kid," he said presently. "I never seen one like you before," and then the neglected pork fell off the end of the sharpened twig, with which he had been holding it, and tumbled into the fire.

"Geeze!" exclaimed Danny, "Look at that!" He fished the unsavory looking morsel from the ashes and flames and surveyed it. "It don't look so good, but I'm goin' to fool it. I'm goin' to eat it anyway. I wouldn't care if a elephant had sat on it for a week—I'd eat it, and the elephant, too."

"Oh, look!" cried Jezebel. "Here come some men and they are all black. What strange beasts are they sitting on? Oh, Danny, I am afraid."

At her first exclamation the "Gunner" had turned and leaped to his feet. A single look told him who the strangers were—no strangers to him.

"Beat it, kid!" he cried. "Duck back into the crack, and hit the trail for the valley. They can't follow you on gee-gees."

The three *shiftas* were already close; and when they saw that they had been discovered they spurred forward at a gallop, and yet Jezebel stood beside the little fire, wide-eyed and frightened. She had not understood the strange argot that the "Gunner" employed in lieu of English. "Beat it" and "duck" and "hit the trail" had not been included in the English idiom she had gleaned from Lady Barbara Collis. But even had she understood him it would have made no difference, for Jezebel was not of the clay that is soft in the face of danger, her little feet not of the kind that run away, leaving a companion in distress.

The "Gunner" glanced behind him and saw her. "For God's sake run, kid," he cried. "These are tough guys. I know 'em," then the *shiftas* were upon him.

To conserve ammunition, which was always scarce and difficult to obtain, they tried to ride him down, striking at him with their rifles. He dodged the leading horseman; and as the fellow reined in to wheel his mount back to the attack, the "Gunner" leaped to his side and dragged him from the saddle. The mount of a second *shifta* stumbled over the two men and fell, unhorsing its rider.

The "Gunner" seized the long rifle that had fallen from the hands of the man he had dragged down and scrambled to his feet. Jezebel watched him in wide-eyed wonder and admiration. She saw him swing the rifle like a club and strike at the third horseman, and then she saw the one he had first grappled lunge forward and, seizing him around the legs, drag him down, while the second to be unhorsed ran in now and leaped upon him just as the remaining *shifta* struck him a heavy blow on the head.

As she saw him fall, the blood gushing from an ugly wound in his head, Jezebel ran forward to him; but the *shiftas* seized her. She was thrown to the back of a horse in front of one of them, the others mounted, and the three galloped away with their prisoner, leaving Danny "Gunner" Patrick lying motionless in a welter of his own blood.

19

In the Village of Elija

As Tarzan approached the village of Abraham, the son of Abraham, he was seen by a watcher who immediately warned his fellows, with the result that when the ape-man arrived the huts were deserted, the villagers having taken refuge in the caves in the face of the towering cliff.

Abraham, the son of Abraham, from the safety of the highest cave, exhorted his people to repel the advance of this strange creature, whose partial nakedness and strange armament filled him with alarm, with the result that when Tarzan came near the base of the cliff the villagers, with much shouting, rolled rocks down the steep declivity in an effort to destroy him.

The Lord of the Jungle looked up at the howling creatures above him. Whatever his emotions his face did not reveal them. Doubtless contempt was predominant, for he read in their reception of him only fear and cowardice.

As naught but curiosity had prompted his visit to this strange village, since he knew that Smith already had quitted it, he remained only long enough for a brief survey of the people and their culture, neither of which was sufficiently attractive to detain him; and then he turned and retraced his steps toward the place on the shore of Chinnereth where he had picked up the northbound spoor of Smith and Lady Barbara and Jezebel.

He made his way in a leisurely manner, stopping beside the lake to quench his thirst and eat from his small store of boar meat; and then he lay down to rest, after the manner of beasts who have fed and are not hurried.

In the village he had quitted Abraham, the son of Abraham, gave thanks to Jehovah for their deliverance from the barbarian, though reserving proper credit to himself for his masterly defense of his flock.

And how fared it with Lady Barbara and Lafayette Smith? Following their recapture they were permitted no second opportunity to escape, as, heavily guarded, they were conducted northward toward the village of Elija, the son of Noah.

The girl was much depressed; and Smith sought to reassure her, though upon what grounds he himself could scarcely explain.

"I cannot believe that they intend to harm us," he said. "We have done nothing worse than kill one of their goats and that only because we were starving. I can pay them whatever price they name for the animal, and thus they will be recompensed and have no further cause for complaint against us."

"With what will you pay them?" asked Lady Barbara.

"I have money," replied Smith.

"Of what good would it be to them?"

"Of what good would it be to them! Why they could buy another goat if they wanted to," he replied.

"These people know nothing of money," she said. "It would be worthless to them."

"I suppose you are right," he admitted. "I hadn't thought of that. Well, I could give them my pistol, then."

"They already have it."

"But it's mine," he exclaimed. "They'll have to give it back to me."

She shook her head. "You are not dealing with civilized people guided by the codes and customs of civilization or responsible to the law-enforcing agencies with which we are familiar and which, perhaps, are all that keep us civilized."

"We escaped once," he ventured; "perhaps we can escape again."

"That, I think, is our only hope."

The village of the North Midians, where they presently

arrived, was more pretentious than that of the people at the southern end of the valley. While there were many crude huts there were also several of stone, while the entire appearance of the village was more cleanly and prosperous.

Several hundred villagers came to meet the party as soon as it was sighted, and the prisoners noted that there was no evidence of the degeneracy and disease which were such marked characteristics of the South Midians. On the contrary, these people appeared endowed with abundant health, they looked intelligent and, physically, they were a splendid race, many of them being handsome. All were golden haired and blue-eyed. That they were descended from the same stock that had produced Abraham, the son of Abraham, and his degraded flock would have appeared impossible, yet such was the fact.

The women and children pushed and jostled one another and the men in their efforts to get close to the prisoners. They jabbered and laughed incessantly, the clothing of the prisoners seeming to arouse the greatest wonder and mirth.

Their language being practically the same as that of the South Midians Lady Barbara had no difficulty in understanding what they were saying, and from scraps of their conversation which she overheard she realized that her worst fears might be realized. However, the crowd offered them no personal injury; and it was apparent that in themselves they were not inherently a cruel people, though their religion and their customs evidently prescribed harsh treatment for enemies who fell into their hands.

Upon arrival in the village Lady Barbara and Smith were separated. She was taken to a hut and put in charge of a young woman, while Smith was confined, under guard of several men, in another.

Lady Barbara's jailer, far from being ill-favored, was quite beautiful, bearing a strong resemblance to Jezebel; and she proved to be quite as loquacious as the men who had captured them.

"You are the strangest looking South Midian I ever saw," she remarked, "and the man does not look at all like one. Your hair is neither the color of those they keep nor of those they destroy—it is just between, and your garments are such as no one ever saw before."

"We are not Midians," said Lady Barbara.

"But that is impossible," cried the woman. "There are none but Midians in the land of Midian and no way to get in or out. Some say there are people beyond the great cliffs, and some say there are only devils. If you are not a Midian perhaps you are a devil; but then, of course, you are a Midian."

"We come from a country beyond the cliffs," Lady Barbara told her, "and all we want is to go back to our own country."

"I do not think Elija will let you. He will treat you as we always treat South Midians."

"And how is that?"

"The men are put to death because of their heresy; and the women, if they are good-looking, are kept as slaves. But being a slave is not bad. I am a slave. My mother was a slave. She was a South Midian who was captured by my father who owned her. She was very beautiful. After a while the South Midians would have killed her, as you do to all your beautiful women just before their first child is born.

"But we are different. We kill the bad-looking ones, both boys and girls, and also any who become subject to the strange demons which afflict the South Midians. Do you have these demons?"

"I am not a Midian, I told you," said Lady Barbara.

The woman shook her head. "It is true that you do not look like them, but if Elija ever believes you are not you are lost."

"Why?" asked Lady Barbara.

"Elija is one of those who believe that the world beyond the cliffs is inhabited by demons; so, if you are not a South Midian, you must be a demon; and he would certainly destroy you as he will destroy the man; but for my part I am one of those who say they do not know. Some say that perhaps this world around Midian is inhabited by angels. Are you an angel?"

"I am not a demon," replied Lady Barbara.

"Then you must be a South Midian or an angel."

"I am no South Midian," insisted the English girl.

"Then you are an angel," reasoned the woman. "And if you are you will have no difficulty in proving it."

"How?"

"Just perform a miracle."

"Oh," said Lady Barbara.

"Is the man an angel?" demanded the woman.

"He is an American."

"I never heard of that—is it a kind of angel?"

"Europeans do not call them that."

"But really I think Elija will say he is a South Midian, and he will be destroyed."

"Why do your people hate the South Midians so?" asked Lady Barbara.

"They are heretics."

"They are very religious," said Lady Barbara; "they pray all the time to Jehovah and they never smile. Why do you think them heretics?"

"They insist that Paul's hair was black, while we know that it was yellow. They are very wicked, blasphemous people. Once, long before the memory of man, we were all one people; but there were many wicked heretics among us who had black hair and wished to kill all those with yellow hair; so those with yellow hair ran away and came to the north end of the valley. Ever since, the North Midians have killed all those with black hair and the South Midians all those with yellow hair. Do you think Paul had yellow hair?"

"Certainly I do," said Lady Barbara.

"That will be a point in your favor," said the woman.

Just then a man came to the door of the hut and summoned Lady Barbara. "Come with me," he commanded.

The English girl followed the messenger, and the woman who had been guarding her accompanied them. Before a large stone hut they found Elija surrounded by a number of the older men of the village, while the remainder of the population was grouped in a semicircle facing them. Lafayette Smith stood before Elija, and Lady Barbara was conducted to the side of the American.

Elija, the Prophet, was a middle-aged man of not unprepossessing appearance. He was short and stocky, extremely muscular in build, and his face was adorned with a wealth of blond whiskers. Like the other North Midians he was garbed in a single garment of goatskin, his only ornament being the pistol he had taken from Smith, which he wore on a leather thong that encircled his neck.

"This man," said Elija, addressing Lady Barbara, "will not talk. He makes noises, but they mean nothing. Why will he not talk?"

"He does not understand the language of the land of Midian," replied the English girl.

"He must understand it," insisted Elija; "everyone understands it."

"He is not from Midian," said Lady Barbara.

"Then he must be a demon," said Elija.

"Perhaps he is an angel," suggested Lady Barbara; "he believes that Paul's hair was yellow."

This statement precipitated a wordy argument and so impressed Elija and his apostles that they withdrew into the interior of the hut for a secret conference.

"What's it all about, Lady Barbara?" asked Smith, who, of course, had understood nothing of what had been said.

"You believe Paul's hair was yellow, don't you?" she asked.

"I don't know what you are talking about."

"Well, I told them you were a firm believer in the yellowness of Paul's hair."

"Why did you tell them that?" demanded Smith.

"Because the North Midians prefer blonds," she replied.

"But who is Paul?"

"Was, you mean. He is dead."

"Of course I'm sorry to hear that, but who *was* he?" insisted the American.

"I am afraid you have neglected the scriptures," she told him.

"Oh, the apostle; but what difference does it make what color his hair was?"

"It doesn't make any difference," she explained. "What does make a difference is that you have stated, through me, that you believe he had yellow hair; and that may be the means of saving your life."

"What nonsense!"

"Of course—the other fellow's religion is always nonsense; but not to him. You are also suspected of being an angel. Can you imagine!"

"No! Who suspects me?"

"It was I; or at least I suggested it, and I am hoping Elija will now suspect it. If he does we are both safe, provided that, in your celestial capacity, you will intercede for me."

"You are as good as saved then," he said, "for inasmuch as I cannot speak their language you can put any words you wish into my mouth without fear of being called to account."

"That's a fact, isn't it?" she said, laughing. "If our emergency were not so critical I could have a lot of fun, couldn't I?"

"You seem to find fun in everything," he replied, admiringly, "even in the face of disaster."

"Perhaps I am whistling in the dark," she said.

They talked a great deal while they waited for Elija and the apostles to return, for it helped them to tide over the anxious minutes of nervous strain that slowly dragged into hours. They could hear the chatter and buzz of conversation within the hut, as Elija and his fellows debated, while, outside, the villagers kept up a constant babel of conversation.

"They like to talk," commented Smith.

"And perhaps you have noticed an idiosyncrasy of the North Midians in this respect?" she asked.

"Lots of people like to talk."

"I mean that the men gabble more than the women."

"Perhaps in self-defense."

"Here they come!" she exclaimed as Elija appeared in the doorway of the hut, fingering the pistol he wore as an ornament.

Darkness was already falling as the Prophet and the twelve apostles filed out to their places in the open. Elija raised his hands in a signal for silence and when quiet had been restored he spoke.

"With the aid of Jehovah," he said, "we have wrestled with a mighty question. There were some among us who contended that this man is a South Midian, and others that he is an angel. Mighty was the weight of the statement that he believes that Paul had yellow hair, for if such is the truth then indeed he is not a heretic; and if he is no heretic he is not a South Midian, for they, as all the world knows, are heretics. Yet again, it was brought forth that if he is a demon he might still claim that he believed in the yellowness of Paul, in order that he might deceive us.

"How were we to know? We must know lest we, through our ignorance, do sin against one of His angels and bring down the wrath of Jehovah upon our heads.

"But at last I, Elija, the son of Noah, True Prophet of Paul, the son of Jehovah, discovered the truth. The man is no angel! The revelation descended upon me in a burst of glory from Jehovah Himself—the man cannot be an angel because he has no wings!"

There was an immediate burst of "Amens" and "Hallelujahs" from the assembled villagers, while Lady Barbara went cold with dread.

"Therefore," continued Elija, "he must be either a South Midian or a demon, and in either case he must be destroyed."

Lady Barbara turned a pale face toward Lafayette Smith—pale even through its coating of tan. Her lip trembled, just a little. It was the first indication of a weaker, feminine emotion that Smith had seen this remarkable girl display.

"What is it?" he asked. "Are they going to harm you?"

"It is you, my dear friend," she replied. "You must escape."

"But how?" he asked.

"Oh, I don't know; I don't know," she cried. "There is only one way. You will have to make a break for it—now. It is dark. They will not expect it. I will do something to engage their attention, and then you make a dash for the forest."

He shook his head. "No," he said. "We shall go together, or I do not go."

"Please," she begged, "or it will be too late."

Elija had been talking to one of his apostles, and now he raised his voice again so that all might hear. "Lest we have mistaken the divine instructions of Jehovah," he said, "we shall place this man in the mercy of Jehovah and as Jehovah wills so shall it be. Make ready the grave. If he is indeed an angel he will arise unharmed."

"Oh, go; please go!" cried Lady Barbara.

"What did he say?" demanded Smith.

"They are going to bury you alive," she cried.

"And you," he asked; "what are they going to do to you?"

"I am to be held in slavery."

With sharpened sticks and instruments of bone and stone a number of men were already engaged in excavating a grave in the center of the village street before the hut of Elija, who stood waiting its completion surrounded by his apostles. The Prophet was still toying with his newfound ornament, concerning the purpose and mechanism of which he was wholly ignorant.

Lady Barbara was urging Smith to attempt escape while there was yet an opportunity, and the American was considering the best plan to adopt.

"You will have to come with me," he said. "I think if we make a sudden break right back through the village toward the cliffs we shall find our best chance for success. There are fewer people congregated on that side."

From the darkness beyond the village on the forest side a pair of eyes watched the proceedings taking place before the hut of Elija. Slowly, silently the owner of the eyes crept closer until he stood in the shadow of a hut at the edge of the village.

Suddenly Smith, seizing Lady Barbara's hand, started at a run toward the north side of the village; and so unexpected was his break for liberty that, for a moment, no hand was raised to stay him; but an instant later, at a cry from Elija, the entire band leaped in pursuit, while from the shadow of the hut where he had stood concealed the watcher slipped forward into the village where he stood near the hut of Elija watching the pursuit of the escaped prisoners. He was alone, for the little central compound of the village had emptied as by magic, even the women and children having joined in the chase.

Smith ran swiftly, holding tightly to the girl's hand; and close on their heels came the leaders of the pursuit. No longer did the village fires light their way; and only darkness loomed ahead, as the moon had not yet risen.

Gradually the American bore to the left, intending to swing in a half circle toward the south. There was yet a chance that they might make good their escape if they could outdistance the nearer of their pursuers until they reached the forest, for their strait gave them both speed and endurance far above normal.

But just as success seemed near they entered a patch of broken lava rock, invisible in the darkness; and Smith stumbled and fell dragging Lady Barbara down with him. Before they could scramble to their feet the leading Midian was upon them.

The American freed himself for a moment and struggled to his feet; and again the fellow sought to seize him, but Smith swung a heavy blow to his chin and felled him.

Brief, however, was this respite, for almost immediately both the American and the English girl were overwhelmed by superior numbers and once again found themselves captives, though Smith fought until he was overpowered, knocking his antagonists to right and left.

Miserably dejected, they were dragged back to the village compound, their last hope gone; and again the Midians gathered around the open grave to witness the torture of their victim.

Smith was conducted to the edge of the excavation, where he was held by two stalwart men, while Elija raised his voice in prayer, and the remainder of the assemblage knelt, bursting forth occasionally with hallelujahs and amens.

When he had concluded his long prayer the Prophet paused. Evidently there was something on his mind which vexed him. In fact it was the pistol which dangled from the thong about his neck. He was not quite sure of its purpose, and he was about to destroy the only person who might tell him.

To Elija the pistol was quite the most remarkable possession that had ever fallen into his hands, and he was filled with a great curiosity concerning it. It might be, he argued, some magic talisman for averting evil, or, upon the other hand, it might be the charm of a demon or a sorcerer, that would work evil upon him. At that thought he quickly removed the thong from about his neck, but he still held the weapon in his hand.

"What is this?" he demanded, turning to Lady Barbara and exhibiting the pistol.

"It is a weapon," she said. "Be careful or it will kill someone."

"How does it kill?" asked Elija.

"What is he saying?" demanded Smith.

"He is asking how the pistol kills," replied the girl.

A brilliant idea occurred to the American. "Tell him to give it to me, and I will show him," he said.

But when she translated the offer to Elija he demurred. "He could then kill me with it," he said, shrewdly.

"He won't give it to you," the girl told Smith. "He is afraid you want to kill him."

"I do," replied the man.

"Tell him," said Elija, "to explain to me how I may kill someone with it."

"Repeat my instructions to him very carefully," said Smith, after Lady Barbara had translated the demand of the prophet. "Tell him how to grasp the pistol," and when Lady Barbara had done so and Elija held the weapon by the grip in his right hand, "now tell him to place his index finger through the guard, but warn him not to pull the trigger."

Elija did as he was bid. "Now," continued Smith, "explain to him that in order to see how the weapon operates he should place one eye to the muzzle and look down the barrel."

"But I can see nothing," expostulated Elija when he had done as Lady Barbara directed. "It is quite dark down the little hole."

"He says it is too dark in the barrel for him to see anything," repeated Lady Barbara to the American.

"Explain to him that if he pulls the trigger there will be a light in the barrel," said Smith.

"But that will be murder," exclaimed the girl.

"It is war," said Smith, "and in the subsequent confusion we may escape."

Lady Barbara steeled herself. "You could see nothing

because you did not press the little piece of metal beneath your index finger," she explained to Elija.

"What will that do?" demanded the prophet.

"It will make a light in the little hole," said Lady Barbara.

Elija again placed his eye against the muzzle; and this time he pulled the trigger; and as the report cracked the tense silence of the watching villagers Elija, the son of Noah, pitched forward upon his face.

Instantly Lady Barbara sprang toward Smith, who simultaneously sought to break away from the grip of the men who held him; but they, although astonished at what had occurred, were not to be caught off their guard, and though he struggled desperately they held him.

For an instant there was a hushed silence; and then pandemonium broke loose as the villagers realized that their prophet was dead, slain by the wicked charm of a demon; but at the very outset of their demands for vengeance their attention was distracted by a strange and remarkable figure that sprang from the hut of Elija, stooped and picked up the pistol that had fallen from the hands of the dead man, and leaped to the side of the prisoner struggling with his guards.

This was such a man as none of them had ever seen—a giant white man with a tousled shock of black hair and with gray eyes that sent a shiver through them, so fierce and implacable were they. Naked he was but for a loincloth of skin, and the muscles that rolled beneath his brown hide were muscles such as they never had seen before.

As the newcomer sprang toward the American one of the men guarding Smith, sensing that an attempt was being made to rescue the prisoner, swung his club in readiness to deal a blow against the strange creature advancing upon him. At the same time the other guard sought to drag Smith from the compound.

The American did not at first recognize Tarzan of the Apes, yet, though he was not aware that the stranger was bent upon his rescue, he sensed that he was an enemy of the Midians, and so struggled to prevent his guard from forcing him away.

Another Midian seized Lady Barbara with the intention of

carrying her from the scene, for all the villagers believed that the strange giant was a friend of the prisoners and had come to effect their release.

Smith was successful in tearing himself free from the man who held him, and immediately sprang to the girl's assistance, felling her captor with a single blow, just as Tarzan leveled the American's pistol at the guard who was preparing to cudgel him.

The sound of this second shot and the sight of their fellow dropping to the ground, as had Elija, filled the Midians with consternation; and for a moment they fell back from the three, leaving them alone in the center of the compound.

"Quick!" called Tarzan to Smith. "You and the girl get out of here before they recover from their surprise. I will follow you. That way," he added, pointing toward the south.

As Lafayette Smith and Lady Barbara hurried from the village Tarzan backed slowly after them, keeping the little pistol in full view of the frightened villagers, who, having seen two of their number die beneath its terrifying magic, were loath to approach it too closely.

Until out of range of a thrown club Tarzan continued his slow retreat; then he wheeled and bounded off into the night in pursuit of Lafayette Smith and Lady Barbara Collis.

20

The Best Three out of Five

THOUGH JEZEBEL WAS terrified by the black faces of her captors and by the strange beasts they bestrode, the like of which she had never even imagined, her fear for herself was outweighed by her sorrow. Her one thought was to escape and return to the side of the "Gunner," even though she believed him dead from the terrific blow that his assailant had struck him.

She struggled violently to free herself from the grasp of the man in front of whom she rode; but the fellow was far too powerful; and, though she was difficult to hold, at no time was there the slightest likelihood that she might escape. Her efforts, however, angered him and at last he struck her, bringing to the girl a realization of the futility of pitting her puny strength against his. She must wait, then, until she could accomplish by stealth what she could not effect by force.

The village of the raiders lay but a short distance from the point at which she had been captured, and but a few minutes had elapsed since that event when they rode up to its gates and into the central compound.

The shouts that greeted the arrival of a new and beautiful prisoner brought Capietro and Stabutch to the doorway of their hut.

"Now what have the black devils brought in?" exclaimed Capietro.

"It looks like a young woman," said Stabutch.

"It is," cried Capietro, as the *shiftas* approached the hut with their prisoner. "We shall have company, eh, Stabutch? Who have you there, my children?" he demanded of the three who were accompanying Jezebel.

"The price of a chief's ransom, perhaps," replied one of the blacks.

"Where did you find her?"

"Above the village a short distance, when we were returning from scouting. A man was with her. The man who escaped with the help of the ape-man."

"Where is he! Why did you not bring him, also?" demanded Capietro.

"He fought us, and we were forced to kill him."

"You have done well," said Capietro. "She is worth two of him—in many ways. Come girl, hold up your head, let us have a look at that pretty face. Come, you need not fear anything— if you are a good girl you will find Dominic Capietro a good fellow."

"Perhaps she does not understand Italian," suggested Stabutch.

"You are right, my friend; I shall speak to her in English."

Jezebel had looked up at Stabutch when she heard him speak a language she understood. Perhaps this man would be a friend, she thought; but when she saw his face her heart sank.

"What a beauty!" ejaculated the Russian.

"You have fallen in love with her quickly, my friend," commented Capietro. "Do you want to buy her?"

"How much do you want for her?"

"Friends should not bargain," said the Italian. "Wait, I have it! Come, girl," and he took Jezebel by the arm and led her into the hut, where Stabutch followed them.

"Why was I brought here?" asked Jezebel. "I have not harmed you. Let me go back to Danny; he is hurt."

"He is dead," said Capietro; "but don't you grieve, little one. You now have two friends in place of the one you have lost. Soon you will forget him; it is easy for a woman to forget."

"I shall never forget him," cried Jezebel. "I want to go back to him—perhaps he is not dead." Then she broke down and cried.

Stabutch stood eyeing the girl hungrily. Her youth and her beauty aroused a devil within him, and he made a mental vow that he would possess her. "Do not cry," he said, kindly. "I am your friend. Everything will be all right."

The new tone in his voice gave hope to Jezebel, and she looked up at him gratefully. "If you are my friend," she said, "take me away from here and back to Danny."

"After a while," replied Stabutch, and then to Capietro, "How much?"

"I shall not sell her to my good friend," replied the Italian. "Let us have a drink, and then I shall explain my plan."

The two drank from a bottle standing on the earth floor of the hut. "Sit down," said Capietro, waving Jezebel to a seat on the dirty rug. Then he searched for a moment in his duffle bag and brought out a deck of soiled and grimy cards. "Be seated, my friend," he said to Stabutch. "Let us have another drink, and then you shall hear my plan."

Stabutch drank from the bottle and wiped his lips with the back of his hand. "Well," he said, "what is it?"

"We shall play for her," exclaimed the Italian, shuffling the deck, "and whoever wins, keeps her."

"Let us drink to that," said Stabutch. "Five games, eh, and the first to win three takes her?"

"Another drink to seal the bargain!" exclaimed the Italian. "The best three out of five!"

Stabutch won the first game, while Jezebel sat looking on in ignorance of the purpose of the bits of pasteboard, and only knowing that in some way they were to decide her fate. She hoped the younger man would win, but only because he had said that he was her friend. Perhaps she could persuade him to take her back to Danny. She wondered what kind of water was in the bottle from which they drank, for she noticed that it wrought a change in them. They talked much louder now and shouted strange words when the little cards were thrown upon the rug, and then one would appear very angry while the other always laughed immoderately. Also they swayed and lurched in a peculiar manner that she had not noticed before they had drunk so much of the water from the bottle.

Capietro won the second game and the third. Stabutch was furious, but now he became very quiet. He exerted all his powers of concentration upon the game, and he seemed almost sober as the cards were dealt for the fourth game.

"She is as good as mine!" cried Capietro, as he looked at his hand.

"She will never be yours," growled the Russian.

"What do you mean?"

"I shall win the next two games."

The Italian laughed loudly. "That is good!" he cried. "We should drink to that." He raised the bottle to his lips and then passed it to Stabutch.

"I do not want a drink," said the Russian, in a surly tone, pushing the bottle aside.

"Ah, ha! My friend is getting nervous. He is afraid he is going to lose and so he will not drink. Sapristi! It is all the same to me. I get the brandy and the girl, too."

"Play!" snapped Stabutch.

"You are in a hurry to lose," taunted Capietro.

"To win," corrected Stabutch, and he did.

Now it was the Italian's turn to curse and rage at luck, and once again the cards were dealt and the players picked up their hands.

"It is the last game," said Stabutch.

"We have each won two," replied Capietro. "Let us drink to the winner—although I dislike proposing a toast to myself," and he laughed again, but this time there was an ugly note in his laughter.

In silence, now, they resumed their play. One by one the little pasteboards fell upon the rug. The girl looked on in wondering silence. There was a tenseness in the situation that she felt, without understanding. Poor little Jezebel, she understood so little!

Suddenly, with a triumphant oath, Capietro sprang to his feet. "I win!" he cried. "Come, friend, drink with me to my good fortune."

Sullenly the Russian drank, a very long draught this time.

There was a sinister gleam in his eye as he handed the bottle back to Capietro. Leon Stabutch was a poor loser.

The Italian emptied the bottle and flung it to the ground. Then he turned toward Jezebel and stooping lifted her to her feet. "Come, my dear," he said, his coarse voice thick from drink, "Give me a kiss."

Jezebel drew back, but the Italian jerked her roughly to him and tried to draw her lips to his.

"Leave the girl alone," growled Stabutch. "Can't you see she is afraid of you?"

"What did I win her for?" demanded Capietro. "To leave her alone? Mind your own business."

"I'll make it my business," said Stabutch. "Take your hands off her." He stepped forward and laid a hand on Jezebel's arm. "She is mine by rights anyway."

"What do you mean?"

"You cheated. I caught you at it in the last game."

"You lie!" shouted Capietro and simultaneously he struck at Stabutch. The Russian dodged the blow and closed with the other.

Both were drunk and none too steady. It required much of their attention to keep from falling down. But as they wrestled about the interior of the hut a few blows were struck—enough to arouse their rage to fury and partially to sober them. Then the duel became deadly, as each sought the throat of the other.

Jezebel, wide-eyed and terrified, had difficulty in keeping out of their way as they fought to and fro across the floor of the hut; and so centered was the attention of the two men upon one another that the girl might have escaped had she not been more afraid of the black men without than of the whites within.

Several times Stabutch released his hold with his right hand and sought for something beneath his coat and at last he found it—a slim dagger. Capietro did not see it.

They were standing in the center of the hut now, their arms locked about one another, and resting thus as though by mutual consent. They were panting heavily from their exertions, and neither seemed to have gained any material advantage.

Slowly the Russian's right hand crept up the back of his

adversary. Jezebel saw, but only her eyes reflected her horror. Though she had seen many people killed she yet had a horror of killing. She saw the Russian feel for a spot on the other's back with the point of his thumb. Then she saw him turn his hand and place the dagger point where his thumb had been.

There was a smile upon Stabutch's face as he drove the blade home. Capietro stiffened, screamed, and died. As the body slumped to the ground and rolled over on its back the murderer stood over the corpse of his victim, a smile upon his lips, and his eyes upon the girl.

But suddenly the smile died as a new thought came to the cunning mind of the slayer and his eyes snapped from the face of Jezebel to the doorway of the hut where a filthy blanket answered the purpose of a door.

He had forgotten the horde of cutthroats who had called this thing upon the floor their chief! But now he recalled them and his soul was filled with terror. He did not need to ask himself what his fate would be when they discovered his crime.

"You have murdered him!" cried the girl suddenly, a note of horror in her voice.

"Be quiet!" snapped Stabutch. "Do you want to die? They will kill us when they discover this."

"I did not do it," protested Jezebel.

"They will kill you just the same—afterwards. They are beasts."

Suddenly he stooped, seized the corpse by the ankles and, dragging it to the far end of the hut, he covered it with rugs and clothing.

"Now keep quiet until I come back," he said to Jezebel. "If you give an alarm I'll kill you myself before they have a chance to."

He rummaged in a dark corner of the hut and brought forth a revolver with its holster and belt, which he buckled about his hips, and a rifle which he leaned beside the doorway.

"When I return be ready to come with me," he snapped, and raising the rug that covered the doorway, he stepped out into the village.

Quickly he made his way to where the ponies of the band

were tethered. Here were several of the blacks loitering near the animals.

"Where is the head man?" he asked, but none of them understood English. He tried to tell them by means of signs, to saddle two horses, but they only shook their heads. If they understood him, as they doubtless did, they refused to take orders from him.

At this juncture the head man, attracted from a nearby hut, approached. He understood a little pidgin English, and Stabutch had no difficulty in making him understand that he wanted two horses saddled; but the head man wanted to know more. Did the chief want them?

"Yes, he wants them," replied Stabutch. "He sent me to get them. The chief is sick. Drink too much." Stabutch laughed and the head man seemed to understand.

"Who go with you?" asked the head man.

Stabutch hesitated. Well, he might as well tell him—everyone would see the girl ride out with him anyway. "The girl," he said.

The head man's eyes narrowed. "The Chief say?" he asked.

"Yes. The girl thinks the white man not dead. The Chief send me to look for him."

"You take men?"

"No. Man come back with us if girl say so. Be afraid of black men. No come."

The other nodded understandingly and ordered two horses saddled and bridled. "Him dead," he offered.

Stabutch shrugged. "We see," he replied, as he led the two animals toward the hut where Jezebel awaited him.

The head man accompanied him, and Stabutch was in terror. What if the man insisted on entering the hut to see his chief? Stabutch loosened the revolver in its holster. Now his greatest fear was that the shot might attract others to the hut. That would never do. He must find some other way. He stopped and the head man halted with him.

"Do not come to the hut yet," said Stabutch.

"Why?" asked the head man.

"The girl is afraid. If she sees you she will think we are

deceiving her, and she may refuse to show me where the man is. We promised her that no black man would come."

The head man hesitated. Then he shrugged and turned back. "All right," he said.

"And tell them to leave the gates open till we have gone," called Stabutch.

At the hut door he called to the girl. "All ready," he said, "and hand me my rifle when you come out"; but she did not know what a rifle was and he had to step in and get it himself.

Jezebel looked at the horses with dismay.

At the thought of riding one of these strange beasts alone she was terrified. "I cannot do it," she told Stabutch.

"You will have to—or die," he whispered. "I'll lead the one you ride. Here, hurry."

He lifted her into the saddle and showed her how to use the stirrups and hold the reins. Then he put a rope about the neck of her horse; and, mounting his own, he led hers out through the village gateway while half a hundred murderers watched them depart.

As they turned upward toward the higher hills the setting sun projected their shadows far ahead, and presently night descended upon them and hid their sudden change of direction from any watchers there may have been at the village gates.

21

An Awakening

D ANNY "GUNNER" PATRICK opened his eyes and stared up at the blue African sky. Slowly consciousness returned and with it the realization that his head pained severely. He raised a hand and felt of it. What was that? He looked at his hand and saw that it was bloody.

"Geeze!" he muttered. "They got me!" He tried to recall how it had happened. "I know the finger was on me, but how the hell did they get me? Where was I?" His thoughts were all back in Chicago, and he was puzzled. Vaguely he felt that he had made his getaway, and yet they had "got" him. He could not figure it out.

Then he turned his head slightly and saw lofty mountains looming near. Slowly and painfully he sat up and looked around, Memory, partial and fragmentary, returned. "I must have fell off them mountains," he mused, "while I was lookin' for camp."

Gingerly he rose to his feet and was relieved to find that he was not seriously injured—at least his arms and legs were intact. "My head never was much good. Geeze, it hurts, though."

A single urge dominated him—he must find camp. Old Smithy would be worrying about him if he did not return. Where was Obambi? "I wonder if he fell off too," he muttered, looking about him. But Obambi, neither dead nor alive, was not in sight; and so the "Gunner" started upon his fruitless search for camp.

At first he wandered toward the northwest, directly away from Smith's last camp. Tongani, the baboon, sitting upon his sentinel rock, saw him coming and sounded the alarm. At first Danny saw only a couple of "monkeys" coming toward him, barking and growling. He saw them stop occasionally and place the backs of their heads against the ground and he mentally classified them as "nutty monks"; but when their numbers were swollen to a hundred and he finally realized the potential danger lying in those powerful jaws and sharp fangs, he altered his course and turned toward the southwest.

For a short distance the tongani followed him, but when they saw that he intended them no harm they let him proceed and returned to their interrupted feeding, while the man, with a sigh of relief, continued on his way.

In a ravine Danny found water, and with the discovery came a realization of his thirst and his hunger. He drank at the same pool at which Tarzan had slain Horta, the boar; and he also washed the blood from his head and face as well as he could. Then he continued on his aimless wandering. This time he climbed higher up the slope toward the mountains, in a southeasterly direction, and was headed at last toward the location of the now abandoned camp. Chance and the tongani had set him upon the right trail.

In a short time he reached a spot that seemed familiar; and here he stopped and looked around in an effort to recall his wandering mental faculties, which he fully realized were not functioning properly.

"That bat on the bean sure knocked me cuckoo," he remarked, half aloud. "Geeze, what's that?" Something was moving in the tall grass through which he had just come. He watched intently and a moment later saw the head of Sheeta, the panther, parting the grasses a short distance from him. The scene was suddenly familiar.

"I gotcha Steve!" exclaimed the "Gunner." "Me and that Tarzan guy flopped here last night—now I remember."

He also remembered how Tarzan had chased the panther

away by "running a bluff on him," and he wondered if he could do the same thing.

"Geeze, what a ornery lookin' pan! I'll bet you got a rotten disposition—and that Tarzan guy just growled and ran at you, and you beat it. Say, I don't believe it, if I did see it myself. Whyinell don't you go on about your business, you big stiff? You give me the heeby-jeebies." He stooped and picked up a fragment of rock. "Beat it!" he yelled, as he hurled the missile at Sheeta.

The great cat wheeled and bounded away, disappearing in the tall grass that the "Gunner" could now see waving along the path of the panther's retreat. "Well, what do you know about that?" ejaculated Danny. "I done it! Geeze, these lions ain't so much."

His hunger now claimed his attention as his returning memory suggested a means of appeasing it. "I wonder could I do it?" he mused, as he hunted around on the ground until he had found a thin fragment of rock, with which he commenced to scrape away the dirt from a loose heap that rose a few inches above the contour of the surrounding ground. "I wonder could I!"

His digging soon revealed the remains of the boar Tarzan had cached against their possible return. With his pocketknife the "Gunner" hacked off several pieces, after which he scraped the dirt back over the body and busied himself in the preparation of a fire, where he grilled the meat in a sketchy fashion that produced culinary results which ordinarily would have caused him to turn up his nose in disgust. But today he was far from particular and bolted the partially cooked and partially charred morsels like a ravenous wolf.

His memory had returned now up to the point of the meal he had eaten at this same spot with Tarzan—from there on until he had regained consciousness a short time before, it was a blank. He knew now that he could find his way back to camp from the point above the raiders' village where he and Obambi had lunched, and so he turned his footsteps in that direction.

When he had found the place, he crept on down to the edge

of the cliff where it overlooked the village; and here he lay down to rest and to spy upon the raiders, for he was very tired.

"The lousy bums!" he ejaculated beneath his breath, as he saw the *shiftas* moving about the village. "I wish I had my typewriter, I'd clean up that dump."

He saw Stabutch emerge from a hut and walk down to the horses. He watched him while he talked to the blacks there and to the head man. Then he saw the Russian leading two saddled horses back to the hut.

"That guy don't know it," he muttered, "but the finger is sure on him. I'll get him on the spot some day if it takes the rest of my natural life. Geeze, glom the broad!" Stabutch had summoned Jezebel from the hut. Suddenly a strange thing happened inside the head of Danny "Gunner" Patrick. It was as though someone had suddenly raised a window shade and let in a flood of light. He saw everything perfectly now in retrospection. With the sight of Jezebel his memory had returned!

It was with difficulty that he restrained an urge to call out and tell her that he was there; but caution stilled his tongue, and he lay watching while the two mounted and rode out of the gateway.

He rose to his feet and ran along the ridge toward the north, parallel to the course they were taking. It was already dusk. In a few minutes it would be dark. If he could only keep them in sight until he knew in what direction they finally went!

Exhaustion was forgotten as he ran through the approaching night. Dimly now he could see them. They rode for a short distance upward toward the cliffs; and then, just before the darkness swallowed them, he saw them turn and gallop away toward the northwest and the great forest that lay in that direction.

Reckless of life and limb, the "Gunner" half stumbled, half fell down the cliffs that here had crumbled away and spilled their fragments out upon the slope below.

"I gotta catch 'em, I gotta catch 'em," he kept repeating to himself. "The poor kid! The poor little kid! So help me God, if I catch 'em, what I won't do to that ———— if he's hurt her!"

On through the night he stumbled, falling time and again only to pick himself up and continue his frantic and hopeless search for the little golden-haired Jezebel who had come into his life for a few brief hours to leave a mark upon his heart that might never be erased.

Gradually the realization of it crept upon him as he groped blindly into the unknown, and it gave him strength to go on in the face of such physical exhaustion as he had never known before.

"Geeze," he muttered, "I sure must of fell hard for that kid."

22

By a Lonely Pool

NIGHT HAD FALLEN; and Tarzan of the Apes, leading Lady. Barbara Collis and Lafayette Smith from the valley of the land of Midian, did not see the spoor of Jezebel and the "Gunner."

His two charges were upon the verge of exhaustion, but the ape-man led them on through the night in accordance with a plan he had decided upon. He knew that there were two more whites missing—Jezebel and Danny Patrick—and he wanted to get Lady Barbara and Smith to a place of safety that he might be free to pursue his search for these others.

To Lady Barbara and Smith the journey seemed interminable, yet they made no complaint, for the ape-man had explained the purpose of this forced march to them; and they were even more anxious than he concerning the fate of their friends.

Smith supported the girl as best he could; but his own strength was almost spent, and sometimes his desire to assist her tended more to impede than to aid her. Finally she stumbled and fell; and when Tarzan, striding in advance, heard and returned to them he found Smith vainly endeavoring to lift Lady Barbara.

This was the first intimation the ape-man had received that his charges were upon the verge of exhaustion, for neither had voiced a single complaint; and when he realized it he lifted Lady Barbara in his arms and carried her, while Smith, relieved at least of further anxiety concerning her, was able to keep going, though he moved like an automaton, apparently without conscious volition. Nor may his state be wondered at, when one considers what he had passed through during the preceding three days.

With Lady Barbara, he marveled at the strength and endurance of the ape-man, which, because of his own weakened state, seemed unbelievable even as he witnessed it.

"It is not much farther," said Tarzan, guessing that the man needed encouragement.

"You are sure the hunter you told us of has not moved his camp?" asked Lady Barbara.

"He was there day before yesterday," replied the ape-man. "I think we shall find him there tonight."

"He will take us in?" asked Smith.

"Certainly, just as you would, under similar circumstances, take in anyone who needed assistance," replied the Lord of the Jungle. "He is an Englishman," he added, as though that fact in itself were a sufficient answer to their doubts.

They were in a dense forest now, following an ancient game trail; and presently they saw lights flickering ahead.

"That must be the camp," exclaimed Lady Barbara.

"Yes," replied Tarzan, and a moment later he called out in a native dialect.

Instantly came an answering voice; and a moment later Tarzan halted upon the edge of the camp, just outside the circle of beast fires.

Several askaris were on guard, and with them Tarzan conversed for a few moments; then he advanced and lowered Lady Barbara to her feet.

"I have told them not to disturb their bwana," the ape-man explained. "There is another tent that Lady Barbara may occupy, and the head man will arrange to have a shelter thrown up for Smith. You will be perfectly safe here. The men tell me their bwana is Lord Passmore. He will doubtless arrange to get you out to railhead. In the meantime I shall try to locate your friends."

That was all—the ape-man turned and melted into the black night before they could voice any thanks.

"Why he's gone!" exclaimed the girl. "I didn't even thank him."

"I thought he would remain here until morning," said Smith. "He must be tired."

"He seems tireless," replied Lady Barbara. "He is a superman, if ever there was one."

"Come," said the head man, "your tent is over here. The boys are arranging a shelter for the bwana."

"Good night, Mr. Smith," said the girl. "I hope you sleep well."

"Good night, Lady Barbara," replied Smith. "I hope we wake up sometime."

And as they prepared for this welcome rest Stabutch and Jezebel were riding through the night, the man completely confused and lost.

Toward morning they drew rein at the edge of a great forest, after riding in wide circles during the greater part of the night. Stabutch was almost exhausted; and Jezebel was but little better off, but she had youth and health to give her the reserve strength that the man had undermined and wasted in dissipation.

"I've got to get some sleep," he said, dismounting.

Jezebel needed no invitation to slip from her saddle for she was stiff and sore from this unusual experience. Stabutch led the animals inside the forest and tied them to a tree. Then he threw himself upon the ground and was almost immediately asleep.

Jezebel sat in silence listening to the regular breathing of the man. "Now would be the time to escape," she thought. She rose quietly to her feet. How dark it was! Perhaps it would be better to wait until it became light enough to see. She was sure the man would sleep a long time, for it was evident that he was very tired.

She sat down again, listening to the noises of the jungle. They frightened her. Yes, she would wait until it was light;

then she would untie the horses, ride one and lead the other away so that the man could not pursue her.

Slowly the minutes crept by. The sky became lighter in the east, over the distant mountains. The horses became restless. She noticed that they stood with ears pricked up and that they looked deeper into the jungle and trembled.

Suddenly there was the sound of crashing in the underbrush. The horses snorted and surged back upon their ropes, both of which broke. The noise awakened Stabutch, who sat up just as the two terrified animals wheeled and bolted. An instant later a lion leaped past the girl and the man, in pursuit of the two fleeing horses.

Stabutch sprang to his feet, his rifle in his hands. "God!" he exclaimed. "This is no place to sleep," and Jezebel's opportunity had passed.

The sun was topping the eastern mountains. The day had come. Soon the searchers would be ahorse. Now that he was afoot, Stabutch knew that he must not loiter. However, they must eat, or they would have no strength to proceed; and only by his rifle could they eat.

"Climb into that tree, little one," he said to Jezebel. "You will be safe there while I go and shoot something for our breakfast. Watch for the lion, and if you see him returning this way shout a warning. I am going farther into the forest to look for game."

Jezebel climbed into the tree, and Stabutch departed upon the hunt for breakfast. The girl watched for the lion, hoping it would return, for she had determined that she would give no warning to the man if it did.

She was afraid of the Russian because of things he had said to her during that long night ride. Much that he had said she had not understood at all, but she understood enough to know that he was a bad man. But the lion did not return, and presently Jezebel dozed and nearly fell out of the tree.

Stabutch, hunting in the forest, found a water hole not far from where he had left Jezebel; and here he hid behind bushes waiting for some animal to come down to drink. Nor had he long to wait before he saw a creature appear suddenly upon the opposite side of the pool. So quietly had it come that the Russian had not dreamed that a creature stirred within a mile of his post. The most surprising feature of the occurrence, however, was that the animal thus suddenly to step into view was a man.

Stabutch's evil eyes narrowed. It was *the* man—the man he had traveled all the way from Moscow to kill. What an opportunity! Fate was indeed kind to him. He would fulfill his mission without danger to himself, and then he would escape with the girl—that wondrous girl! Stabutch had never seen so beautiful a woman in his life, and now he was to possess her—she was to be his.

But first he must attend to the business of the moment. What a pleasant business it was, too. He raised his rifle very cautiously and aimed. Tarzan had halted and turned his head to one side. He could not see the rifle barrel of his enemy because of the bush behind which Stabutch hid and the fact that his eyes were centered on something in another direction.

The Russian realized that he was trembling, and he cursed himself under his breath. The nervous strain was too great. He tensed his muscles in an effort to hold his hands firm and the rifle steady and immovable upon the target. The front sight of the rifle was describing a tiny circle instead of remaining fixed upon that great chest which offered such a splendid target.

But he must fire! The man would not stand there thus forever. The thought hurried Stabutch, and as the sight passed again across the body of the ape-man the Russian squeezed the trigger.

At the sound of the shot Jezebel's eyes snapped open. "Perhaps the lion returned," she soliloquized, "or maybe the man has found food. If it were the lion, I hope he missed it."

Also, as the rifle spoke, the target leaped into the air, seized a low-hung branch and disappeared amidst the foliage of the trees above. Stabutch had missed—he should have relaxed his muscles rather than tensed them.

The Russian was terrified. He felt as must one who stands upon the drop with the noose already about his neck. He turned and fled. His cunning mind suggested that he had better not return where the girl was. She was already lost to him, for he could not be burdened with her now in this flight, upon the success of which hung his very life. Accordingly he ran toward the south.

As he rushed headlong through the forest he was already out of breath when he felt a sudden sickening pain in his arm and at the same instant saw the feathered tip of an arrow waving beside him as he ran.

The shaft had pierced his forearm, its tip projecting from the opposite side. Sick with terror Stabutch increased his speed. Somewhere above him was his Nemesis, whom he could neither see nor hear. It was as though a ghostly assassin pursued him on silent wings.

Again an arrow struck him, sinking deep into the triceps of his other arm. With a scream of pain and horror Stabutch halted and, dropping upon his knees, raised his hands in supplication. "Spare me!" he cried. "Spare me! I have never wronged you. If you will spare——"

An arrow, speeding straight, drove through the Russian's throat. He screamed and clutched at the missile and fell forward on his face.

Jezebel, listening in the tree, heard the agonized shriek of the stricken man; and she shuddered. "The lion got him," she whispered. "He was wicked. It is the will of Jehovah!"

Tarzan of the Apes dropped lightly from a tree and warily approached the dying man. Stabutch, writhing in agony and terror, rolled over on his side. He saw the ape-man approaching, his bow and arrow ready in his hand, and, dying, reached for the revolver at his hip to complete the work that he had come so far to achieve and for which he was to give his life.

No more had his hand reached the grip of his weapon than the Lord of the Jungle loosed another shaft that drove deep through the chest of the Russian, deep through his heart. Without a sound Leon Stabutch collapsed; and a moment later there rang through the jungle the fierce, uncanny victory cry of the bull ape.

As the savage notes reverberated through the forest Jezebel

slid to the ground and fled in terror. She knew not where nor to what fate her flying feet led her. She was obsessed by but a single idea—to escape from the terrors of that lonely spot.

23

Captured

WITH THE COMING of day the "Gunner" found himself near a forest. He had heard no sound of horses all during the night; and now that day had come, and he could see to a distance, he scanned the landscape for some sign of Stabutch and Jezebel but without success.

"Geeze," he muttered, "there ain't no use, I gotta rest. The poor little kid! If I only knew where the rat took her; but I don't, and I gotta rest." He surveyed the forest. "That looks like a swell hideout. I'll lay up there and grab off a little sleep. Geeze, I'm all in."

As he walked toward the forest his attention was attracted to something moving a couple of miles to the north of him. He stopped short, and looked more closely as two horses, racing from the forest, dashed madly toward the foothills, pursued by a lion.

"Geeze!" exclaimed the "Gunner," "those must be their horses. What if the lion got her!"

Instantly his fatigue was forgotten; and he started at a run toward the north; but he could not keep the pace up for long; and soon he was walking again, his brain a turmoil of conjecture and apprehension.

He saw the lion give up the chase and turn away almost immediately, cutting up the slope in a northeasterly direction. The "Gunner" was glad to see him go, not for his own sake so much as for Jezebel, whom, he reasoned, the lion might not have killed after all. There was a possibility, he thought, that she might have had time to climb a tree. Otherwise, he was positive, the lion must have killed her.

His knowledge of lions was slight. In common with most people, he believed that lions wandered about killing everything so unfortunate as to fall into their pathways—unless they were bluffed out as he had bluffed the panther the day before. But of course, he reasoned, Jezebel wouldn't have been able to bluff a lion.

He was walking close to the edge of the forest, making the best time that he could, when he heard a shot in the distance. It was the report of Stabutch's rifle as he fired at Tarzan. The "Gunner" tried to increase his speed. There was too much doing there, where he thought Jezebel might be, to permit of loafing; but he was too exhausted to move rapidly.

Then, a few minutes later, the Russian's scream of agony was wafted to his ears and again he was goaded on. This was followed by the uncanny cry of the ape-man, which, for some reason, Danny did not recognize, though he had heard it twice before. Perhaps the distance and the intervening trees muffled and changed it.

On he plodded, trying occasionally to run; but his overtaxed muscles had reached their limit; and he had to give up the attempt, for already he was staggering and stumbling even at a walk.

"I ain't no good," he muttered, "nothing but a lousy punk. Here's a guy beatin' it with my girl, and I ain't even got the guts to work my dogs. Geeze, I'm a flop."

A little farther on he entered the forest so that he could approach the spot, where he had seen the horses emerge, without being seen, if Stabutch were still there.

Suddenly he stopped. Something was crashing through the brush toward him. He recalled the lion and drew his pocket-knife. Then he hid behind a bush and waited, nor did he have long to wait before the author of the disturbance broke into view.

"Jezebel!" he cried, stepping into her path. His voice trembled with emotion.

With a startled scream the girl halted, and then she recognized him. "Danny!" It was the last straw—her overwrought nerves went to pieces; and she sank to the ground, sobbing hysterically.

The "Gunner" took a step or two toward her. He staggered, his knees gave beneath him, and he sat down heavily a few yards from her; and then a strange thing happened. Tears welled to the eyes of Danny "Gunner" Patrick; he threw himself facedown on the ground; and he, too, sobbed.

For several minutes they lay there, and then Jezebel gained control of herself and sat up. "Oh, Danny," she cried. "Are you hurt? Oh, your head! Don't die, Danny."

He had quelled his emotion and was roughly wiping his eyes on his shirtsleeve. "I ain't dyin'," he said; "but I oughta. Some one oughta bump me off—a great big stiff like me, cryin'!"

"It's because you've been hurt, Danny," said Jezebel.

"Naw, it ain't that. I been hurt before, but I ain't bawled since I was a little kid—when my mother died. It was something else. I just blew up when I seen you, and knew that you was O. K. My nerves went blooey—just like that!" He snapped his fingers. "You see," he added, hesitantly, "I guess I like you an awful lot, kid."

"I like you, Danny," she told him. "You're top hole."

"I'm what? What does that mean?"

"I don't know," Jezebel admitted. "It's English, and you don't understand English, do you?"

He crawled over closer to her and took her hand in his. "Geeze," he said, "I thought I wasn't never goin' to see you again. Say," he burst out violently, "did that bum hurt you any, kid?"

"The man who took me away from the black men in the village, you mean?"

"Yes."

"No, Danny. After he killed his friend we rode all night. He was afraid the black men would catch him."

"What became of the rat? How did you make your getaway?"

She told him all that she knew, but they were unable to

account for the sounds both had heard or to guess whether or not they had portended the death of Stabutch.

"I wouldn't be much good, if he showed up again," said Danny. "I gotta get my strength back some way."

"You must rest," she told him.

"I'll tell you what we'll do," he said. "We'll lay around here until we are rested up a bit; then we'll beat it back up toward the hills where I know where they's water and something to eat. It ain't very good food," he added, "but it's better than none. Say, I got some of it in my pocket. We'll just have a feed now." He extracted some dirty scraps of half-burned pork from one of his pockets and surveyed them ruefully.

"What is it?" asked Jezebel.

"It's pig, kid," he explained. "It don't look so hot, does it? Well, it don't taste no better than it looks; but it's food, and that's what we are needin' bad right now. Here, hop to it." He extended a handful of the scraps toward her. "Shut your eyes and hold your nose, and it ain't so bad," he assured her. "Just imagine you're in the old College Inn."

Jezebel smiled and took a piece of the meat. "United States is a funny language, isn't it, Danny?"

"Why, I don't know—is it?"

"Yes, I think so. Sometimes it sounds just like English and yet I can't understand it at all."

"That's because you ain't used to it," he told her; "but I'll learn you if you want me to. Do you?"

"Oke, kid," replied Jezebel.

"You're learnin' all right," said Danny, admiringly.

They lay in the growing heat of the new day and talked together of many things, as they rested. Jezebel told him the story of the land of Midian, of her childhood, of the eventful coming of Lady Barbara and its strange effect upon her life; and Danny told her of Chicago, but there were many things in his own life that he did not tell her—things that, for the first time, he was ashamed of. And he wondered why he was ashamed.

As they talked, Tarzan of the Apes quitted the forest and set out upon his search for them, going upward toward the hills, intending to start his search for their spoor at the mouth of the fissure. If he did not find it there he would know that they were still in the valley; if he did find it, he would follow it until he located them.

At break of day a hundred *shiftas* rode out of their village. They had discovered the body of Capietro, and now they knew that the Russian had tricked them and fled, after killing their chief. They wanted the girl for ransom, and they wanted the life of Stabutch.

They had not ridden far when they met two riderless horses galloping back toward the village. The *shiftas* recognized them at once, and knowing that Stabutch and the girl were now afoot they anticipated little difficulty in overhauling them.

The rolling foothills were cut by swales and canyons; so that at times the vision of the riders was limited. They had been following downward along the bottom of a shallow canyon for some time, where they could neither see to a great distance nor be seen; and then their leader turned his mount toward higher ground, and as he topped the summit of a low ridge he saw a man approaching from the direction of the forest.

Tarzan saw the *shifta* simultaneously and changed his direction obliquely to the left, breaking into a trot. He knew that if that lone rider signified a force of mounted *shiftas* he would be no match for them; and, guided by the instinct of the wild beast, he sought ground where the advantage would be with him—the rough, rocky ground leading to the cliffs, where no horse could follow him.

With a yell to his followers, the *shifta* chieftain put spurs to his horse and rode at top speed to intercept the ape-man; and close behind him came his yelling, savage horde.

Tarzan quickly saw that he could not reach the cliffs ahead of them; but he maintained his steady, tireless trot that he might be that much nearer the goal when the attack came. Perhaps he could hold them off until he reached the sanctuary of the cliffs, but certainly he had no intention of giving up without exerting every effort to escape the unequal battle that must follow if they overtook him.

With savage yells the *shiftas* approached, their loose cotton garments fluttering in the wind, their rifles waving above their heads. The chief rode in the lead; and when he was near enough, the ape-man, who had been casting occasional glances rearward across a brown shoulder, stopped, wheeled and let an arrow drive at his foe; then he was away again as the shaft sank into the breast of the *shifta* chieftain.

With a scream, the fellow rolled from his saddle; and for a moment the others drew rein, but only for a moment. Here was but a single enemy, poorly armed with primitive weapons—he was no real menace to mounted riflemen.

Shouting their anger and their threats of vengeance, they spurred forward again in pursuit; but Tarzan had gained and the rocky ground was not far away.

Spreading in a great half circle, the *shiftas* sought to surround and head off their quarry, whose strategy they had guessed the moment that they had seen the course of his flight. Now another rider ventured too near, and for a brief instant Tarzan paused to loose another arrow. As this second enemy fell, mortally wounded, the ape-man continued his flight to the accompaniment of a rattle of musketry fire; but soon he was forced to halt again as several of the horsemen passed him and cut off his line of retreat.

The hail of slugs screaming past him or kicking up the dirt around him gave him slight concern, so traditionally poor was the marksmanship of these roving bands of robbers, illy equipped with ancient firearms with which, because of habitual shortage of ammunition, they had little opportunity to practice.

Now they pressed closer, in a rough circle of which he was the center; and, firing across him from all sides, it seemed impossible that they should miss him; but miss him they did, though their bullets found targets among their own men and horses, until one, who had supplanted the slain chief, took command and ordered them to cease firing.

Turning again in the direction of his flight, Tarzan tried to shoot his way through the cordon of horsemen shutting off his retreat; but, though each arrow sped true to its mark, the yelling horde closed in upon him until, his last shaft spent, he was the center of a closely milling mass of shrieking enemies.

Shrilly above the pandemonium of battle rose the cries of the new leader. "Do not kill! Do not kill!" he screamed, "It is Tarzan of the Apes, and he is worth the ransom of a ras!"

Suddenly a giant black threw himself from his horse full upon the Lord of the Jungle, but Tarzan seized the fellow and hurled him back among the horsemen. Yet closer and closer they pressed; and now several fell upon him from their saddles, bearing him down beneath the feet of the now frantic horses.

Battling for life and liberty, the ape-man struggled against the overpowering odds that were being constantly augmented by new recruits who hurled themselves from their mounts upon the growing pile that overwhelmed him. Once he managed to struggle to his feet, shaking most of his opponents from him; but they seized him about the legs and dragged him down again; and presently succeeded in slipping nooses about his wrists and ankles, thus effectually subduing him.

Now that he was harmless many of them reviled and struck him; but there were many others who lay upon the ground, some never to rise again. The *shiftas* had captured the great Tarzan, but it had cost them dear.

Now some of them rounded up the riderless horses, while others stripped the dead of their weapons, ammunition, and any other valuables the living coveted. Tarzan was raised to an empty saddle, where he was securely bound; and four men were detailed to conduct him and the horses of the dead to the village, the wounded accompanying them, while the main body of the blacks continued the search for Stabutch and Jezebel.

24

The Long Night

THE SUN WAS high in the heavens when Lady Barbara, refreshed by her long, undisturbed sleep, stepped from her tent in the camp of Lord Passmore. A smiling, handsome black boy came running toward her. "Breakfast soon be ready," he told her. "Lord Passmore very sorry. He have to go hunt."

She asked after Lafayette Smith and was told that he had just awakened, nor was it long before he joined her; and soon they were breakfasting together.

"If Jezebel and your friend were here," she said, "I should be very happy. I am praying that Tarzan finds them."

"I am sure he will," Smith assured her, "though I am only worried about Jezebel. Danny can take care of himself."

"Doesn't it seem heavenly to eat a meal again?" the girl remarked. "Do you know it has been months since I have eaten anything that even vaguely approximated a civilized meal. Lord Passmore was fortunate to get such a cook for his safari. I had no such luck."

"Have you noticed what splendid-looking fellows all his men are?" asked Smith. "They would make that aggregation of mine resemble fourth-rate roustabouts with hookworm and sleeping sickness."

"There is another very noticeable thing about them," said Lady Barbara.

"What is that?"

"There is not a single piece of cast-off European finery among them—their garb is native, pure and simple; and, while I'll have to admit there isn't much to it, it lends a dignity to them that European clothing would change to the absurd."

"I quite agree with you," said Smith. "I wonder why I didn't get a safari like this."

"Lord Passmore is evidently an African traveler and hunter of long experience. No amateur could hope to attract such men as these."

"I shall hate to go back to my own camp, if I stay here very long," said Smith; "but I suppose I'll have to; and that suggests another unpleasant feature of the change."

"And what is that?" she asked.

"I shan't see you any more," he said with a simple directness that vouched for the sincerity of his regret.

The girl was silent for a moment, as though the suggestion had aroused a train of thought she had not before considered. "That is true, isn't it?" she remarked, presently. "We shan't see each other any more—but not for always. I'm sure you'll stop and visit me in London. Isn't it odd what old friends we seem? And yet we only met two days ago. Or, maybe, it doesn't seem that way to you. You see I was so long without seeing a human being of my own world that you were quite like a long-lost brother, when you came along so unexpectedly."

"I have the same feeling," he said, "as though I had known you forever—and—," he hesitated, "—as though I could never get along without you in the future." He flushed a little as he spoke those last words.

The girl looked up at him with a quick smile—a sympathetic, understanding smile. "It was nice of you to say that," she said. "Why it sounded almost like a declaration," she added, with a gay, friendly laugh.

He reached across the little camp table and laid a hand upon hers. "Accept it as such," he said, "I'm not very good at saying things—like that."

"Let's not be serious," she begged. "Really, we scarcely know each other, after all."

"I have known you always," he replied. "I think we were amoebas together before the first Cambrian dawn."

"Now you've compromised me," she cried, laughingly, "for I'm sure there were no chaperons way back there. I hope that you were a proper amoeba. You didn't kiss me, did you?"

"Unfortunately for me amoebas have no mouths," he said, "but I've been profiting by several millions of years of evolution just to remedy that defect."

"Let's be amoebas again," she suggested.

"No," he said, "for then I couldn't tell you that I—I—" He choked and flushed.

"Please! Please, don't tell me," she cried. "We're such ripping friends—don't spoil it."

"Would it spoil it?" he asked.

"I don't know. It might. I am afraid."

"Can't I ever tell you?" he asked.

"Perhaps, someday," she said.

A sudden burst of distant rifle fire interrupted them. The blacks in the camp were instantly alert. Many of them sprang to their feet, and all were listening intently to the sounds of this mysterious engagement between armed men.

The man and the girl heard the head man speaking to his fellows in some African dialect. His manner showed no excitement, his tones were low but clear. It was evident that he was issuing instructions. The men went quickly to their shelters, and a moment later Lady Barbara saw the peaceful camp transformed. Every man was armed now. As by magic a modern rifle and a bandoleer of cartridges were in the possession of each black. White feathered headdresses were being adjusted and war paint applied to glossy hides.

Smith approached the head man. "What is the matter?" he asked. "Is something wrong?"

"I do not know, Bwana," replied the black; "but we prepare."

"Is there any danger?" continued the white.

The head man straightened to his full, impressive height. "Are we not here?" he asked.

Jezebel and the "Gunner" were walking slowly in the direction of the distant water hole and the cached boar meat, following the bottom of a dip that was the mouth of a small canyon that led up into the hills.

They were stiff and lame and very tired; and the wound on the "Gunner's" head pained; but, notwithstanding, they were happy as, hand in hand, they dragged their weary feet toward water and food.

"Geeze, kid," said Danny, "it sure is a funny world. Just think, if I hadn't met old Smithy on board that ship me and you wouldn't never have met up. It all started from that," but then Danny knew nothing of Angustus the Ephesian.

"I got a few grand salted away, kid, and when we get out of this mess we'll go somewhere where nobody doesn't know me and I'll start over again. Get myself a garage or a filling station, and we'll have a little flat. Geeze, it's goin' to be great showin' you things. You don't know what you ain't seen—movies and railroads and boats! Geeze! You ain't seen nothin' and nobody ain't going to show you nothin', only me."

"Yes, Danny," said Jezebel, "it's going to be ripping," and she squeezed his hand.

Just then they were startled by the sound of rifle fire ahead. "What was that?" asked Jezebel.

"It sounded like the Valentine Massacre," said Danny, "but I guess it's them toughs from the village. We better hide, kid." He drew her toward some low bushes; and there they lay down, listening to the shouts and shots that came down to them from where Tarzan fought for his life and liberty with the odds a hundred to one against him.

After a while the din ceased, and a little later the two heard the thudding of many galloping hoofs. The sound increased in volume as it drew nearer, and Danny and Jezebel tried to make themselves as small as possible beneath the little bush in the inadequate concealment of which they were hiding.

At a thundering gallop the *shiftas* crossed the swale just above them, and all but a few had passed when one of the stragglers discovered them. His shout, which attracted the attention of others, was carried forward until it reached the new chief, and presently the entire band had circled back to learn what their fellow had discovered.

Poor "Gunner"! Poor Jezebel! Their happiness had been short lived. Their recapture was effected with humiliating ease. Broken and dejected, they were soon on their way to the village under escort of two black ruffians.

Bound, hands and feet, they were thrown into the hut formerly occupied by Capietro and left without food or water upon the pile of dirty rugs and clothing that littered the floor.

Beside them lay the corpse of the Italian which his followers, in their haste to overtake his slayer, had not taken the time to remove. It lay upon its back, the dead eyes staring upward.

Never before in his life had the spirits of Danny Patrick sunk so low, for the very reason, perhaps, that never in his life had they risen so high as during the brief interlude of happiness he had enjoyed following his reunion with Jezebel. Now he saw no hope ahead, for, with the two white men eliminated, he feared that he might not even be able to dicker with these ignorant black men for the ransom that he would gladly pay to free Jezebel and himself.

"There goes the garage, the filling station, and the flat," he said, lugubriously.

"Where?" asked Jezebel.

"Flooie," explained Danny.

"But you are here with me," said the golden one; "so I do not care what else there is."

"That's nice, kid; but I ain't much help, all tied up like a Christmas present. They sure picked out a swell bed for me— feels like I was lyin' on a piece of the kitchen stove." He rolled himself to one side and nearer Jezebel. "That's better," he said, "but I wonder what was that thing I was parked on."

"Maybe your friend will come and take us away," suggested Jezebel.

"Who, Smithy? What would he take us with—that dinky toy pistol of his?"

"I was thinking of the other that you told me about."

"Oh, that Tarzan guy! Say, kid, if he knew we was here he'd walk in and push all these nutty dumps over with one mitt and kick the whole gang over the back fence. Geeze, you bet I wish he was here. There is one big shot, and I don't mean maybe."

In a hut on the edge of the village was the answer to the "Gunner's" wish, bound hand and foot, as was the "Gunner," and, apparently, equally helpless. Constantly the ape-man was working on the thongs that confined his wrists—twisting, tugging, pulling.

The long day wore on and never did the giant captive cease his efforts to escape; the thongs were heavy and securely tied, yet little by little he felt that they were loosening.

Toward evening the new chief returned with the party that had been searching for Stabutch. They had not found him; but scouts had located the camp of Lord Passmore, and now the *shiftas* were discussing plans for attacking it on the morrow.

They had not come sufficiently close to it to note the number of armed natives it contained; but they had glimpsed Smith and Lady Barbara; and, being sure that there were not more than two white men, they felt little hesitation in attempting the raid, since they were planning to start back for Abyssinia on the morrow.

"We will kill the white man we now have," said the chief, "and carry the two girls and Tarzan with us. Tarzan should bring a good ransom and the girls a good price."

"Why not keep the girls for ourselves," suggested another.

"We shall sell them," said the chief.

"Who are you, to say what we shall do?" demanded the other. "You are no chief."

"No," growled a villanous looking black squatting beside the first objector.

He who would be chief leaped, catlike, upon the first speaker, before any was aware of his purpose. A sword gleamed for an instant in the light of the new-made cook fires and fell with terrific force upon the skull of the victim.

"Who am I?" repeated the killer, as he wiped the bloody blade upon the garment of the slain man. "I am chief!" He looked around upon the scowling faces about him. "Is there any who says I am not chief?" There was no demur. Ntale was chief of the *shifta* band.

Inside the dark interior of the hut where he had lain bound all day without food or water the ape-man tugged and pulled until the sweat stood in beads upon his body, but not in vain. Gradually a hand slipped through the stretched thong, and he was free. Or at least his hands were, and it took them but a moment to loosen the bonds that secured his ankles.

With a low, inaudible growl he rose to his feet and stepped to the doorway. Before him lay the village compound. He saw the *shiftas* squatting about while slaves prepared the evening meal. Nearby was the palisade. They must see him as he crossed to it, but what matter?

He would be gone before they could gather their wits. Perhaps a few stray shots would be fired; but then, had they not fired many shots at him this morning, not one of which had touched him?

He stepped out into the open, and at the same instant a burly black stepped from the next hut and saw him. With a shout of warning to his fellows the man leaped upon the escaping prisoner. Those at the fires sprang to their feet and came running toward the two.

Within their prison hut Jezebel and Danny heard the commotion and wondered.

The ape-man seized the black who would have stopped him and wheeling him about to form a shield for himself, backed quickly toward the palisade.

"Stay where you are," he called to the advancing *shiftas*, in their own dialect. "Stay where you are, or I will kill this man."

"Let him kill him then," growled Ntale. "He is not worth the ransom we are losing," and with a shout of encouragement to his followers he leaped quickly forward to intercept the ape-man.

Tarzan was already near the palisade as Ntale charged. He raised the struggling black above his head and hurled him upon the advancing chief, and as the two went down he wheeled and ran for the palisade.

Like Manu the monkey he scaled the high barrier. A few

scattered shots followed him, but he dropped to the ground out-side unscathed and disappeared in the growing gloom of the advancing night.

The long night of their captivity dragged on and still the "Gunner" and Jezebel lay as they had been left, without food or drink, while the silent corpse of Capietro stared at the ceiling.

"I wouldn't treat nobody like this," said the "Gunner," "not even a rat."

Jezebel raised herself to one elbow. "Why not try it?" she whispered.

"What?" demanded Danny. "I'd try anything once."

"What you said about a rat made me think of it," said Jezebel. "We have lots of rats in the land of Midian. Some-times we catch them—they are very good to eat. We make traps, but if we do not kill the rats soon after they are caught they gnaw their way to freedom—they gnaw the cords which bind the traps together."

"Well, what of it?" demanded Danny. "We ain't got no rats, and if we had—well, I won't say I wouldn't eat 'em, kid; but I don't see what it's got to do with the mess we're in."

"We're like the rats, Danny," she said. "Don't you see? We're like the rats and—we can gnaw our way to freedom!"

"Well, kid," said Danny, "if you want to gnaw your way through the side of this hut, hop to it; but if I gets a chance to duck I'm goin' through the door."

"You do not understand, Danny," insisted Jezebel. "You are an egg that cannot talk. I mean that I can gnaw the cords that fasten your wrists together."

"Geeze, kid!" exclaimed Danny. "Dumb ain't no name for it, and I always thought I was the bright little boy. You sure got a bean, and I don't mean maybe."

"I wish I knew what you are talking about, Danny," said Jezebel, "and I wish you would let me try to gnaw the cords from your wrist. Can't you understand what I'm talking about?"

"Sure, kid, but I'll do the gnawing—my jaws are tougher. Roll over, and I'll get busy. When you're free you can untie me."

Jezebel rolled over on her stomach and Danny wriggled into

position where he could reach the thongs at her wrists with his teeth. He fell to work with a will, but it was soon evident to him that the job was going to be much more difficult than he had anticipated.

He found, too, that he was very weak and soon tired; but though often he was forced to stop through exhaustion, he never gave up. Once, when he paused to rest, he kissed the little hands that he was trying to liberate. It was a gentle, reverent kiss, quite unlike the "Gunner"; but then love is a strange force, and when it is aroused in the breast of a man by a clean and virtuous woman it makes him always a little tenderer and a little better.

Dawn was lifting the darkness within the hut, and still the "Gunner" gnawed upon the thongs that it seemed would never part. Capietro lay staring at the ceiling, his dead eyes rolled upward, just as he had lain there staring through all the long hours of the night, unseeing.

The *shiftas* were stirring in the village, for this was to be a busy day. Slaves were preparing the loads of camp equipment and plunder that they were to carry toward the north. The fighting men were hastening their breakfasts that they might look to their weapons and their horse gear before riding out on their last raid from this village, against the camp of the English hunter.

Ntale the chief was eating beside the fire of his favorite wife. "Make haste, woman," he said. "I have work to do before we ride."

"You are chief now," she reminded him. "Let others work."

"This thing I do myself," replied the black man.

"What do you do that is so important that I must hasten the preparation of the morning meal?" she demanded.

"I go to kill the white man and get the girl ready for the journey," he replied. "Have food prepared for her. She must eat or she will die."

"Let her die," replied the woman. "I do not want her around. Kill them both."

"Shut thy mouth!" snapped the man. "I am chief."

"If you do not kill her, I shall," said the woman. "I shall not cook for any white bitch."

The man rose. "I go to kill the man," he said. "Have breakfast for the girl when I return with her."

25

The Waziri

"THERE!" GASPED THE "Gunner."

"I am free!" exclaimed Jezebel.

"And my jaws is wore out," said Danny.

Quickly Jezebel turned and worked upon the thongs that confined the "Gunner's" wrists before taking the time to loose her ankles. Her fingers were quite numb, for the cords had partially cut off the circulation from her hands; and she was slow and bungling at the work. It seemed to them both that she would never be done. Had they known that Ntale had already arisen from his breakfast fire with the announcement that he was going to kill the "Gunner," they would have been frantic; but they did not know it, and perhaps that were better, since to Jezebel's other handicaps was not added the nervous tension that surely would have accompanied a knowledge of the truth.

But at last the "Gunner's" hands were free; and then both fell to work upon the cords that secured their ankles, which were less tightly fastened.

At last the "Gunner" arose. "The first thing I do," he said, "is to find out what I was lyin' on yesterday. It had a familiar feel to it; and, if I'm right—boy!"

He rummaged among the filthy rags at the end of the hut, and a moment later straightened up with a Thompson sub-machine gun in one hand and his revolver, belt, and holster in the other—a grin on his face.

"This is the first break I've had in a long time," he said. "Everything's jake now, sister."

"What are those things?" asked Jezebel.

"Them's the other half of 'Gunner' Patrick," replied Danny. "Now, bring on the dirty rats!"

As he spoke, Ntale the chief drew aside the rug at the doorway and looked in. The interior of the hut was rather dark, and at first glance he could not make out the figures of the girl and the man standing at the far side; but, silhouetted as he was against the growing morning light beyond the doorway, he was plainly visible to his intended victim; and Danny saw that the man carried a pistol ready in his hand.

The "Gunner" had already buckled his belt about him. Now he transferred the machine gun to his left hand and drew his revolver from its holster. He did these things quickly and silently. So quickly that, as he fired, Ntale had not realized that his prisoners were free of their bonds—a thing he never knew, as, doubtless, he never heard the report of the shot that killed him.

At the same instant that the "Gunner" fired, the report of his revolver was drowned by yells and a shot from a sentry at the gate, to whom the coming day had revealed a hostile force creeping upon the village.

As Danny Patrick stepped over the dead body of the chief and looked out into the village he realized something of what had occurred. He saw men running hastily toward the village gates and scrambling to the banquette. He heard a fusilade of shots that spattered the palisade, splintering the wood and tearing through to fill the village with a screaming, terror-stricken mob.

His knowledge of such things told him that only high-powered rifles could send their projectiles through the heavy wood of the palisade. He saw the *shiftas* on the banquette returning the fire with their antiquated muskets. He saw the slaves and prisoners cowering in a corner of the village that was freer from the fire of the attackers than other portions.

He wondered who the enemies of the *shiftas* might be, and

past experience suggested only two possibilities—either a rival "gang" or the police.

"I never thought I'd come to it, kid," he said.

"Come to what, Danny?"

"I hate to tell you what I been hopin'," he admitted.

"Tell me, Danny," she said. "I won't be angry."

"I been hopin' them guys out there was cops. Just think o' that, kid! Me, 'Gunner' Patrick, a-hopin' the cops would come!"

"What are cops, Danny?"

"Laws, harness bulls—Geeze, kid, why do you ask so many questions? Cops is cops. And I'll tell you why I hope it's them. If it ain't cops it's a rival mob, and we'd get just as tough a break with them as with these guys."

He stepped out into the village street. "Well," he said, "here goes Danny Patrick smearin' up with the police. You stay here, kid, and lie down on your bread basket, so none of them slugs'll find you, while I go out and push the smokes around."

Before the gate was a great crowd of *shiftas* firing through openings at the enemy beyond. The "Gunner" knelt and raised the machine gun to his shoulder. There was the vicious b-r-r-r as of some titanic rattle snake; and a dozen of the massed *shiftas* collapsed, dead or screaming, to the ground.

The others turned and, seeing the "Gunner," realized that they were caught between two fires, for they remembered the recent occasion upon which they had witnessed the deadly effects of this terrifying weapon.

The "Gunner" spied Ogonyo among the prisoners and slaves huddled not far from where he stood, and the sight of him suggested an idea to the white man.

"Hey! Big feller, you!" He waved his hand to Ogonyo. "Come here! Bring all them guys with you. Tell 'em to grab anything they can fight with if they want to make their getaway."

Whether or not Ogonyo understood even a small part of what the "Gunner" said, he seemed at least to grasp the main idea; and presently the whole mob of prisoners and slaves, except the women, had placed themselves behind Danny.

The firing from the attacking force had subsided somewhat since Danny's typewriter had spoken, as though the leader of that other party had recognized its voice and guessed that white prisoners within the village might be menaced by his rifle fire. Only an occasional shot, aimed at some specific target, was coming into the village.

The *shiftas* had regained their composure to some extent and were preparing their horses and mounting, with the evident intention of executing a sortie. They were leaderless and confused, half a dozen shouting advice and instructions at the same time.

It was at this moment that Danny advanced upon them with his motley horde armed with sticks and stones, an occasional knife and a few swords hastily stolen from the huts of their captors.

As the *shiftas* realized that they were menaced thus seriously from the rear, the "Gunner" opened fire upon them for the second time, and the confusion that followed in the village compound gave the attackers both within and without a new advantage.

The *shiftas* fought among themselves for the loose horses that were now stampeding in terror about the village; and as a number of them succeeded in mounting they rode for the village gates, overthrowing those who had remained to defend them. Some among them forced the portals open; and as the horsemen dashed out they were met by a band of black warriors, above whose heads waved white plumes, and in whose hands were modern high-powered rifles.

The attacking force had been lying partially concealed behind a low ridge, and as it rose to meet the escaping *shiftas* the savage war cry of the Waziri rang above the tumult of the battle.

First to the gates was Tarzan, war chief of the Waziri, and while Muviro and a small detachment accounted for all but a few of the horsemen who had succeeded in leaving the village, the ape-man, with the remaining Waziri, charged the demoralized remnants of Capietro's band that remained within the palisade.

Surrounded by enemies, the *shiftas* threw down their rifles and begged for mercy, and soon they were herded into a corner of the village under guard of a detachment of the Waziri.

As Tarzan greeted the "Gunner" and Jezebel he expressed his relief at finding them unharmed.

"You sure come at the right time," Danny told him. "This old typewriter certainly chews up the ammunition, and that last burst just about emptied the drum; but say, who are your friends? Where did you raise this mob?"

"They are my people," replied Tarzan.

"Some gang!" ejaculated the "Gunner," admiringly; "but say, have you seen anything of old Smithy?"

"He is safe at my camp."

"And Barbara," asked Jezebel; "where is she?"

"She is with Smith," replied Tarzan. "You will see them both in a few hours. We start back as soon as I arrange for the disposal of these people." He turned away and commenced to make enquiries among the prisoners of the *shiftas*.

"Is he not beautiful!" exclaimed Jezebel.

"Hey, sister, can that 'beautiful' stuff," warned the "Gunner," "and from now on remember that I'm the only 'beautiful' guy you know, no matter what my pan looks like."

Quickly Tarzan separated the prisoners according to their tribes and villages, appointed head men to lead them back to their homes and issued instructions to them as he explained his plans.

The weapons, ammunition, loot and belongings of the *shiftas* were divided among the prisoners, after the Waziri had been allowed to select such trifles as they desired. The captured *shiftas* were placed in charge of a large band of Gallas with orders to return them to Abyssinia and turn them over to the nearest ras.

"Why not hang them here?" asked the Galla head man. "We shall then save all the food they would eat on the long march back to our country, besides saving us much trouble and worry in guarding them—for the ras will certainly hang them."

"Take them back, as I tell you," replied Tarzan. "But if they give you trouble do with them as you see fit."

It took little more than an hour to evacuate the village. All of

Smith's loads were recovered, including Danny's precious ammunition and extra drums for his beloved Thompson; and these were assigned to Smith's porters, who were once again assembled under Ogonyo.

When the village was emptied it was fired in a dozen places; and, as the black smoke curled up toward the blue heavens, the various parties took their respective ways from the scene of their captivity, but not before the several head men had come and knelt before the Lord of the Jungle and thanked him for the deliverance of their people.

26

The Last Knot Is Tied

LAFAYETTE SMITH AND Lady Barbara had been mystified witnesses to the sudden transformation of the peaceful scene in the camp of Lord Passmore. All day the warriors had remained in readiness, as though expecting a summons; and when night fell they still waited.

Evidences of restlessness were apparent; and there was no singing and little laughter in the camp, as there had been before. The last that the two whites saw, as they retired for the night, were the little groups of plumed warriors squatting about their fires, their rifles ready to their hands; and they were asleep when the summons came and the sleek, black fighting men melted silently into the dark shadows of the forest, leaving only four of their number to guard the camp and the two guests.

When Lady Barbara emerged from her tent in the morning she was astonished to find the camp all but deserted. The boy who acted in the capacity of personal servant and cook for her and Smith was there and three other blacks. All were constantly armed; but their attitude toward her had not changed, and she felt only curiosity relative to the other altered conditions, so obvious at first glance, rather than apprehension.

When Smith joined her a few minutes later he was equally at a loss to understand the strange metamorphosis that had transformed the laughing, joking porters and askaris into painted warriors and sent them out into the night so surreptitiously, nor could they glean the slightest information from their boy, who, though still courteous and smiling, seemed by some strange trick of fate suddenly to have forgotten the very fair command of English that he had exhibited with evident pride on the previous day.

The long day dragged on until midafternoon without sign of any change. Neither Lord Passmore nor the missing blacks returned, and the enigma was as baffling as before. The two whites, however, seemed to find much pleasure in one another's company; and so, perhaps, the day passed more rapidly for them than it did for the four blacks, waiting and listening through the hot, drowsy hours.

But suddenly there was a change. Lady Barbara saw her boy rise and stand in an attitude of eager listening. "They come!" he said, in his own tongue, to his companions. Now they all stood and, though they may have expected only friends, their rifles were in readiness for enemies.

Gradually the sound of voices and of marching men became distinctly audible to the untrained ears of the two whites, and a little later they saw the head of a column filing through the forest toward them.

"Why there's the 'Gunner'!" exclaimed Lafayette Smith. "And Jezebel, too. How odd that they should be together."

"With Tarzan of the Apes!" cried Lady Barbara. "He has saved them both."

A slow smile touched the lips of the ape-man as he witnessed the reunion of Lady Barbara and Jezebel and that between Smith and the "Gunner"; and it broadened a little, when, after the first burst of greetings and explanations, Lady Barbara said, "It is unfortunate that our host, Lord Passmore, isn't here."

"He is," said the ape-man.

"Where?" demanded Lafayette Smith, looking about the camp.

"I am 'Lord Passmore,' " said Tarzan.

"You?" exclaimed Lady Barbara.

"Yes. I assumed this rôle when I came north to investigate the rumors I had heard concerning Capietro and his band, believing that they not only would suspect no danger, but hoping, also, that they would seek to attack and plunder my safari as they have those of others."

"Geeze," said the "Gunner." "What a jolt they would of got!"

"That is why we never saw 'Lord Passmore,' " said Lady Barbara, laughing. "I thought him a most elusive host."

"The first night I left you here," explained Tarzan, "I walked into the jungle until I was out of sight, and then I came back from another direction and entered my tent from the rear. I slept there all night. The next morning, early, I left in search of your friends—and was captured myself. But everything has worked out well, and if you have no other immediate plans I hope that you will accompany me back to my home and remain a while as my guests while you recover from the rather rough experiences Africa has afforded you. Or, perhaps," he added, "Professor Smith and his friend wish to continue their geological investigations."

"I, ah, well, you see," stammered Lafayette Smith; "I have about decided to abandon my work in Africa and devote my life to the geology of England. We, or, er—you see, Lady Barbara—"

"I am going to take him back to England and teach him to shoot before I let him return to Africa. Possibly we shall come back later, though."

"And you, Patrick," asked Tarzan, "are you remaining to hunt, perhaps?"

"Nix, mister," said Danny, emphatically, "We're goin' to California and buy a garage and filling station."

"We?" queried Lady Barbara.

"Sure," said the "Gunner", "me and Jez."

"Really?" exclaimed Lady Barbara. "Is he in earnest, Jezebel?"

"Oke, kid—isn't it ripping?" replied the golden one.

TARZAN
AND THE
CITY OF GOLD

Contents

1

Savage Quarry

Down out of Tigre and Amhara upon Gojam and Shoa and Kaffa come the rains from June to September, carrying silt and prosperity from Abyssinia to the eastern Sudan and to Egypt, bringing muddy trails and swollen rivers and death and prosperity to Abyssinia.

Of these gifts of the rains, only the muddy trails and the swollen rivers and death interested a little band of *shiftas* that held out in the remote fastnesses of the mountains of Kaffa. Hard men were these mounted bandits, cruel criminals without even a vestige of culture such as occasionally leavens the activities of rogues, lessening their ruthlessness. Kaficho and Galla they were, the offscourings of their tribes, outlaws, men with prices upon their heads.

It was not raining now; and the rainy season was drawing to a close, for it was the middle of September; but there was still much water in the rivers, and the ground was soft after a recent rain.

The *shiftas* rode, seeking loot from wayfarer, caravan, or village; and as they rode, the unshod hoofs of their horses left a plain spoor that one might read upon the run; not that that caused the *shiftas* any concern, because no one was looking for them. All that anyone in the district wished of the *shiftas* was to keep out of their way.

A short distance ahead of them, in the direction toward

which they were riding, a hunting beast stalked its prey. The wind was blowing from it toward the approaching horsemen; and for this reason their scent spoor was not borne to its sensitive nostrils, nor did the soft ground give forth any sound beneath the feet of their walking mounts that the keen ears of the hunter might detect during the period of concentration and mild excitement attendant upon the stalk.

Though the stalker did not resemble a beast of prey, such as the term connotes to the mind of man, he was one nevertheless; for in his natural haunts he filled his belly by the chase and by the chase alone; neither did he resemble the mental picture that one might hold of a typical British lord, yet he was that too—he was Tarzan of the Apes.

All beasts of prey find hunting poor during a rain, and Tarzan was no exception to the rule. It had rained for two days, and as a result Tarzan was hungry. A small buck was drinking in a stream fringed by bushes and tall reeds, and Tarzan was worming his way upon his belly through short grass to reach a position from which he might either charge or loose an arrow or cast a spear. He was not aware that a group of horsemen had reined in upon a gentle rise a short distance behind him where they sat in silence regarding him intently.

Usha, the wind, who carries scent, also carries sound. Today, Usha carried both the scent and the sound of the *shiftas* away from the keen nostrils and the ears of the ape-man. Perhaps, endowed as he was with supersensitive perceptive faculties, Tarzan should have sensed the presence of an enemy; but "Even the worthy Homer sometimes nods."

However self-sufficient an animal may be it is endowed with caution, for there is none that has not its enemies. The weaker herbivora must be always on the alert for the lion, the leopard, and man; the elephant, the rhinoceros, and the lion may never relax their vigilance against man; and man must always be on guard against these and others. Yet one may not say that such caution connotes either fear or cowardice; for Tarzan, who was without fear, was the personification of caution, especially when he was far from his own stamping grounds as he was today and every creature a potential enemy.

The combination of ravenous hunger with the opportunity to satisfy it may have placed caution in abeyance as, oftentimes, a certain recklessness born of pride in his might did; but, be that as it may, the fact remains that Tarzan was wholly ignorant of the presence of that little knot of villainous bandits who were quite prepared to kill him, or anyone else, for a few poor weapons or for nothing at all.

The circumstances that brought Tarzan northward into Kaffa are not a part of this story. Perhaps they were not urgent, for the Lord of the Jungle loves to roam remote fastnesses still unspoiled by the devastating hand of civilization and needs but trifling incentive to do so. Still unsated with adventure, it may be that Abyssinia's three hundred fifty thousand square miles of semisavagery held an irresistible lure for him in their suggestion of mysterious back country and in the ethnological secrets they have guarded from time immemorial.

Wanderer, adventurer, outcast, Greek phalanx, and Roman legion, all have entered Abyssinia within times chronicled in history or legend never to reappear; and it is even believed by some that she holds the secret of the lost tribes of Israel. What wonders, then, what adventures, might not her remote corners reveal!

At the moment, however, Tarzan's mind was not occupied by thoughts of adventure; he did not know that it loomed threateningly behind him; his concern and his interest were centered upon the buck which he intended should satisfy the craving of his ravenous hunger. He crept cautiously forward. Than he, not even Sheeta, the leopard, stalks more silently or more stealthily.

From behind, the white-robed *shiftas* moved from the little rise where they had been watching him in silence, moved down toward him with spear and long-barreled matchlock. They were puzzled. Never before had they seen a white man like this one; but if curiosity were in their minds, there was only murder in their hearts.

The buck raised his head occasionally to glance about him, wary, suspicious; and when he did so, Tarzan froze into immobility. Suddenly the animal's gaze centered for an instant upon something in the direction of the ape-man; then it wheeled and bounded away. Instantly Tarzan glanced behind him, for he knew that it had not been he who had frightened his quarry but something beyond and behind him that the alert eyes of Wappi had discovered; and that quick glance revealed a half dozen horsemen moving slowly toward him, told him what they were, and explained their purpose; for, knowing that they were *shiftas*, he knew that they came only to rob and kill—knew that here were enemies more ruthless than Numa.

When they saw that he had discovered them, the horsemen broke into a gallop and bore down upon him, waving their weapons and shouting. They did not fire, evidently holding in contempt this primitively armed victim, but seemed to purpose riding him down and trampling him beneath the hoofs of their horses or impaling him upon their spears. Perhaps they thought that he would seek safety in flight, thereby giving them the added thrill of the chase; and what quarry could give the hunter greater thrills than man!

But Tarzan did not turn and run. He knew every possible avenue of escape within the radius of his vision for every danger that might reasonably be expected to confront him here, for it is the business of the creatures of the wild to know these things if they are to survive; and so he knew that there was no escape from mounted men by flight. But this knowledge threw him into no panic. Could the requirements of self-preservation have been best achieved by flight, he would have fled; but as they could not, he adopted the alternative quite as a matter of course—he stood to fight, ready to seize upon any fortuitous circumstance that might offer a chance of escape.

Tall, magnificently proportioned, muscled more like Apollo than like Hercules, garbed only in a narrow G-string of lion skin with a lion's tail depending before and behind, he presented a splendid figure of primitive manhood that suggested more, perhaps, the demigod of the forest than it did man. Across his back hung his quiver of arrows and a light, short spear; the loose coils of his grass rope lay across one bronzed shoulder; at his hip swung the hunting knife of his father, the knife that had given the boy-Tarzan the first suggestion of his coming supremacy over the other beasts of the jungle on that far-gone day when his youthful hand drove it into the heart of Bolgani, the gorilla; in his left hand was his bow and between the fingers four extra arrows.

As Ara, the lightning, so is Tarzan for swiftness. The instant that he had discovered and recognized the menace creeping upon him from behind and known that he had been seen by the horsemen he had leaped to his feet, and in the same instant strung his bow. Now, perhaps even before the leading *shiftas* realized the danger that confronted them, the bow was bent, the shaft sped.

Short but powerful was the bow of the ape-man; short, that it might be easily carried through the forest and the jungle; powerful, that it might send its shafts through the toughest hide to a vital organ of its prey. Such a bow was this that no ordinary man might bend it.

Straight through the heart of the leading *shifta* drove the first arrow, and as the fellow threw his arms above his head and lunged from his saddle four more arrows sped with lightning-like rapidity from the bow of the ape-man, and every arrow found a target. Another *shifta* dropped to ride no more, and three were wounded.

Only seconds had elapsed since Tarzan had discovered his danger, and already the four remaining horsemen were upon him. The three who were wounded were more interested in the feathered shafts protruding from their bodies than in the quarry they had expected so easily to overcome; but the fourth was whole, and he thundered down upon the ape-man with his spear set for the great bronzed chest.

There could be no retreat for Tarzan; there could be no side-stepping to avoid the thrust for a step to either side would have carried him in front of one of the other horsemen. He had but a single slender hope for survival, and that hope, forlorn though it appeared, he seized upon with the celerity, strength, and agility that make Tarzan Tarzan. Slipping his bowstring about his neck after his final shot, he struck up the point of the menacing weapon of his antagonist, and grasping the man's arm swung himself to the horse's back behind the rider.

As steel-thewed fingers closed upon the *shifta's* throat he voiced a single piercing scream; then a knife drove home beneath his left shoulder blade, and Tarzan hurled the body from the saddle. The terrified horse, running free with flying reins, tore through the bushes and the reeds into the river, while the remaining *shiftas*, disabled by their wounds, were glad to abandon the chase upon the bank, though one of them, retaining more vitality than his companions, did raise his matchlock and send a parting shot after the escaping quarry.

The river was a narrow, sluggish stream but deep in the channel; and as the horse plunged into it, Tarzan saw a commotion in the water a few yards downstream and then the outline of a long, sinuous body moving swiftly toward them. It was Gimla, the crocodile. The horse saw it too and, becoming frantic, turned upstream in an effort to escape. Tarzan climbed over the high cantle of the Abyssinian saddle and unslung his spear in the rather futile hope of holding the reptile at bay until his mount could reach the safety of the opposite bank toward which he was now attempting to guide him.

Gimla is as swift as he is voracious. He was already at the horse's rump, with opened jaws, when the *shifta* at the river's edge fired wildly at the ape-man. It was well for Tarzan that the wounded man had fired hurriedly; for simultaneously with the report of the firearm, the crocodile dove; and the frenzied lashing of the water about him evidenced the fact that he had been mortally wounded.

A moment later the horse that Tarzan rode reached the opposite bank and clambered to the safety of dry land. Now he was under control again; and the ape-man wheeled him about and sent a parting arrow across the river toward the angry, cursing bandits upon the opposite side, an arrow that found its mark in the thigh of the already wounded man who had unwittingly rescued Tarzan from a serious situation with the shot that had been intended to kill him.

To the accompaniment of a few wild and scattered shots, Tarzan of the Apes galloped toward a nearby forest into which he disappeared from the sight of the angry *shiftas*.

2

The White Prisoner

FAR TO THE south a lion rose from his kill and walked majestically to the edge of a nearby river. He cast not so much as a single glance at the circle of hyenas and jackals that had ringed him and his kill waiting for him to depart and which had broken and retreated as he rose. Nor, when the hyenas rushed in to tear at what he had left, did he appear even to see them.

There were the pride and bearing of royalty in the mien of this mighty beast; and to add to his impressiveness were his great size, his yellow, almost golden, coat, and his great black mane. When he had drunk his fill, he lifted his massive head and voiced a roar, as is the habit of lions when they have fed and drunk; and the earth shook to this thunderous voice, and a hush fell upon a jungle.

Now he should have sought his lair and slept, to go forth again at night and kill; but he did not do so. He did not do at all what might have been expected of a lion under similar circumstances. He raised his head and sniffed the air, and then he put his nose to the ground and moved to and fro like a hunting dog searching for a game scent. Finally he halted and voiced a low roar; then, with head raised, he moved off along a trail that led toward the north. The hyenas were glad to see him go; so were the jackals, who wished that the hyenas would go also. Ska, the vulture, circling above, wished that they would all leave.

At about the same time, many marches to the north, three angry, wounded *shiftas* viewed their dead comrades and cursed

the fate that had led them upon the trail of the strange white
giant; then they stripped the clothing and weapons from their
dead fellows and rode away, loudly vowing vengeance should
they ever again come upon the author of their discomfiture and
secretly hoping that they never would. They hoped that they
were done with him, but they were not.

Shortly after he had entered the forest, Tarzan swung to an
overhanging branch beneath which his mount was passing and
let the animal go its way. The ape-man was angry; the *shiftas*
had frightened away his dinner. That they had sought to kill
him annoyed him far less than the fact that they had spoiled his
hunting. Now he must commence his search for meat all over
again, but when he had filled his belly he would look into this
matter of *shiftas*. Of this he was certain.

Tarzan had considered the gastronomic potentialities of the
bandit's horse, but had discarded the idea. On several occasions in the past he had been forced to eat horse meat, but he
had not liked it. Although he was hungry, he was far from fam-
ished; and so he preferred to hunt again until he found flesh
more palatable, nor was it long before he had made his kill and
eaten.

Satisfied, he lay up for a while in the crotch of a tree, but not
for long. His active mind was considering the matter of the
shiftas. Here was something that should be looked into. If the
band were on the march, he need not concern himself about
them; but if they were permanently located in this district, that
was a different matter; for Tarzan expected to be here for some
time; and it was well to know the nature, the number, and the
location of all enemies. Furthermore, he felt that he could not
let them escape without some additional punishment for the
inconvenience they had caused him.

Returning to the river, Tarzan crossed it and took up the
plain trail of the *shiftas*. It led him up and down across some
low hills and then down into the narrow valley of the stream
that he had crossed farther up. Here the floor of the valley was
forested, the river winding through the wood. Into this wood
the trail led.

It was almost dark now; the brief equatorial twilight was

rapidly fading into the night; the nocturnal life of the forest and the hills was awakening; from down among the deepening shadows of the valley came the coughing grunts of a hunting lion. Tarzan sniffed the warm air rising from the valley toward the mountains; it carried with it the odors of a camp and the scent spoor of man. He raised his head, and from his deep chest rumbled a full-throated roar. Tarzan of the Apes was hunting too.

In the gathering shadows he stood then erect and silent, a lonely figure standing in solitary grandeur upon that desolate hillside. Swiftly the silent night enveloped him; his figure merged with the darkness that made hill and valley, river and forest one. Not until then did Tarzan move; then he stepped down on silent feet toward the forest. Now was every sense alert, for now the great cats would be hunting. Often his sensitive nostrils quivered as they searched the air; no slightest sound escaped his keen ears.

As he advanced, the man scent became stronger, guiding his steps. Nearer and nearer sounded the deep cough of the lion; but of Numa Tarzan had little fear at present, knowing that the great cat, being upwind, could not be aware of his presence. Doubtless Numa had heard the ape-man's roar, but he could not know that its author was approaching him.

Tarzan had estimated the lion's distance down the valley and the distance that lay between himself and the forest and had guessed that he would reach the trees before their paths crossed. He was not hunting for Numa, the lion, and with the natural caution of the wild beasts, he would avoid an encounter. It was not food either that he hunted, for his belly was full, but man, the arch-enemy of all created things.

It was difficult for Tarzan to think of himself as a man, and his psychology was more often that of the wild beast than the human, nor was he particularly proud of his species. While he appreciated the intellectual superiority of man over other creatures, he harbored contempt for him because he had wasted the greater part of his inheritance. To Tarzan, as to many other created things, contentment is the highest ultimate goal of achievement, and health and culture the principal avenues along which man may approach this goal. With scorn the ape-man viewed the overwhelming majority of mankind which was wanting in either one essential or the other, when not wanting in both. He saw the greed, the selfishness, the cowardice, and the cruelty of man; and, in view of man's vaunted mentality, he knew that these characteristics placed man upon a lower spiritual scale than the beasts, while barring him eternally from the goal of contentment.

So now, as he sought the lair of the man-things, it was not in the spirit of one who seeks his own kind but of a beast which reconnoiters the position of an enemy. The mingled odors of a camp grew stronger in his nostrils, the scents of horses and men and food and smoke. To you or to me, alone in a savage wilderness, engulfed in darkness, cognizant of the near approach of a hunting lion, these odors would have been most welcome; but Tarzan's reaction to them was that of the wild beast that knows man only as an enemy—his snarling muscles tensed as he smothered a low growl.

As Tarzan reached the edge of the forest the lion was but a short distance to his right and approaching; so the ape-man took to the trees, through which he swung silently toward the camp of the *shiftas*. Numa heard him then and roared, and the men in the camp threw more wood upon the beast fire.

To a tree overlooking the camp, Tarzan made his way. Below him he saw a band of some twenty men with their horses and equipment. A rude boma of branches and brush had been erected about the campsite as a partial protection against wild beasts, but more dependence was evidently placed upon the fire which they kept burning in the center of the camp.

In a single quick glance the ape-man took in the details of the scene below him, and then his eyes came to rest upon the only one that aroused either interest or curiosity, a white man who lay securely bound a short distance from the fire.

Ordinarily, Tarzan was no more concerned by the fate of a white man than by that of a black man or any other created thing to which he was not bound by ties of friendship; the life of a man meant less to Tarzan of the Apes than the life of an ape. But in this instance there were two factors that made the life of the captive a matter of interest to the Lord of the Jungle. First, and probably predominant, was his desire to be further avenged upon the *shiftas* for their wanton attack upon him, which had frightened away his intended kill; the second was curiosity, for the white man that lay bound below him was different from any that he had seen before, at least insofar as his apparel was concerned.

His only garment appeared to be a habergeon made up of ivory discs that partially overlay one another, unless certain ankle, wrist, neck, and head ornaments might have been considered to possess such utilitarian properties as to entitle them to a similar classification. Except for these, his arms and legs were naked. His head rested upon the ground with the face turned away from Tarzan so that the ape-man could not see his features but only that his hair was heavy and black.

As he watched the camp, seeking for some suggestion as to how he might most annoy or inconvenience the bandits, it occurred to Tarzan that a just reprisal would consist in taking from them something that they wanted, just as they had deprived him of the buck he had desired. Evidently they wished the prisoner very much or they would not have gone to the trouble of securing him so carefully; so this fact decided Tarzan to steal the white man from them. Perhaps curiosity also had a considerable part in inducing this decision, for the strange apparel of the prisoner had aroused within the ape-man a desire to know more concerning him.

To accomplish his design, he decided to wait until the camp slept; and setting himself comfortably in a crotch of the tree, he prepared to keep his vigil with the tireless patience of the hunting beast he was. As he watched, he saw several of the *shiftas* attempt to communicate with their prisoner; but it was evident that neither understood the other.

Tarzan was familiar with the language spoken by the Kafichos and Gallas, and the questions that they put to their prisoner aroused his curiosity still further. There was one question that they asked him in many different ways, in several dialects, and in signs which the captive either did not understand or pretended not to. Tarzan was inclined to believe that the latter was true, for the sign language was such that it could scarcely be misunderstood. They were asking him the way to a place where there was much ivory and gold, but they got no information from him.

"The pig understands us well enough," growled one of the *shiftas*; "he is just pretending that he does not."

"If he won't tell us, what is the use of carrying him around with us and feeding him?" demanded another. "We might as well kill him now."

"We will let him think it over tonight," replied one who was evidently the leader, "and if he still refuses to speak in the morning, we will kill him then."

This decision they attempted to transmit to the prisoner both by words and signs, and then they squatted about the fire and discussed the occurrences of the day and their plans for the future. The principal topic of their conversation was the strange white giant who had slain three of their number and escaped upon one of their horses; and after this had been debated thoroughly and in detail for some time, and the three survivors of the encounter had boasted severally of their deeds of valor, they withdrew to the rude shelters they had constructed and left the night to Tarzan, Numa, and a single sentry.

The silent watcher among the shadows of the tree waited on in patience until the camp should be sunk in deepest slumber and, waiting, planned the stroke that was to rob the *shiftas* of their prey and satisfy his own desire for revenge. As he patiently bided his time, there came strongly to his nostrils the scent spoor of Numa, the lion; and he guessed that the carnivore, attracted by the presence of the horses, was coming to investigate the camp. That he would enter it, he doubted, for the sentry was keeping the fire blazing brightly; and Numa seldom dares the fearful mystery of flames unless goaded by extreme hunger.

At last the ape-man felt that the time had come when he might translate his plan into action; all but the sentry were wrapped in slumber, and even he was dozing beside the fire. As noiselessly as the shadow of a shadow Tarzan descended from the tree, keeping well in the shadow cast by the beast fire.

For a moment he stood in silence, listening. He heard the breathing of Numa in the darkness beyond the circle of fire-light, and knew that the king of beasts was near and watching. Then he looked from behind the great bole of the tree and saw that the sentry's back was still turned toward him. Silently he moved into the open; stealthily, on soundless feet, he crept toward the unsuspecting bandit. He saw the matchlock across the fellow's knees; and for it he had respect, as have all jungle animals that have been hunted.

Closer and closer he came to his prey. At last he crouched directly behind him. There must be no noise, no outcry. Tarzan waited. Beyond the rim of fire waited Numa, expectant, for he saw that very gradually the flames were diminishing. A bronzed hand shot quickly forward, fingers of steel gripped the brown throat of the sentry almost at the instant that a knife was driven from below his left shoulder blade into his heart. The sentry was dead without knowing that death threatened him, a merciful ending.

Tarzan withdrew the knife from the limp body and wiped the blade upon the once-white robe of his victim; then he moved softly toward the prisoner who was lying in the open. For him, they had not bothered to build a shelter. As he made his way toward the man, Tarzan passed close to two of the shelters in which lay members of the band; but he made no noise that might awaken them. When he approached the captive more closely, he saw in the diminishing light of the fire that the man's eyes were open and that he was regarding Tarzan with level, though questioning, gaze. The ape-man put a finger to his lips to enjoin silence, and then he came and knelt beside the man and cut the thongs that secured his wrists and ankles; then he helped him to his feet, for the thongs had been drawn tightly, and his legs were numb.

For a moment he waited while the stranger tested his feet and moved them rapidly in an effort to restore circulation; then he beckoned him to follow, and all would have been well but for Numa, the lion. At this moment, either to voice his anger against the flames or to terrify the horses into a stampede, he elected to voice a thunderous roar.

So close was the lion that the sudden shattering of the deep silence of the night startled every sleeper to wakefulness. A dozen men seized their matchlocks and leaped from their shelters. In the waning light of the fire they saw no lion; but they saw their liberated captive, and they saw Tarzan of the Apes standing beside him.

Among those who ran from the shelters was the least seriously wounded of Tarzan's victims of the afternoon. Instantly recognizing the bronzed white giant, he shouted loudly to his companions, "It is he! It is the white demon who killed our friends today."

"Kill him!" screamed another.

"Kill them both!" cried the leader of the *shiftas*.

Completely surrounding the two white men, the *shiftas* advanced upon them; but they dared not fire because of fear that they might wound one of their own comrades. Nor could Tarzan loose an arrow nor cast a spear, for he had left all his weapons except his rope and his knife hidden in the tree above the camp that he might move with the utmost freedom and in silence while seeking to liberate the captive.

One of the bandits, more courageous, probably because less intelligent, than his fellows, rushed to close quarters with musket clubbed. It was his undoing. The man-beast crouched, growling; and, as the other was almost upon him, charged. The musket butt, hurtling through the air to strike him down, he dodged; and then he seized the weapon and wrenched it from the *shifta's* grasp as though it had been a toy in a child's hands.

Tossing the matchlock at the feet of his companion, Tarzan laid hold upon the rash Galla, spun him around, and held him as a shield against the weapons of his fellows. But despite this reverse the other *shiftas* gave no indication of giving up the battle. They saw before them two men practically defenseless, and now with redoubled shouts they pushed closer.

Two of them rushed in behind the ape-man, for it was he they feared the more; but they were to learn that their former prisoner might not be considered lightly. He had picked up the musket that Tarzan had cast aside and, grasping it close to the muzzle, was using it as a club. The heavy butt struck the foremost bandit heavily upon the side of the head, dropping him like a felled ox; and as it swung again, the second bandit leaped back barely in time to avoid a similar fate.

A quick backward glance assured Tarzan that his companion was proving himself a worthy ally, but it was evident that they could not hope to hold out long against the superior numbers pitted against them. Their only hope, he believed, lay in making a sudden, concerted rush through the thin line of foemen surrounding them, and he sought to convey his plan to the man standing back to back with him; but though he spoke to him in English and in the several continental languages with which the ape-man was familiar the only reply he received was in a language that he himself had never before heard.

What was he to do? They must go together, and both must understand the purpose animating Tarzan. But how was that possible if they could not communicate with one another? Tarzan turned and touched the other lightly on the shoulder; then he jerked his thumb in the direction he intended going and beckoned with a nod of his head.

Instantly the man nodded his understanding and wheeled about as Tarzan started to charge, still bearing the struggling *shifta* in his grasp; but the *shiftas* were determined not to let these two escape; and while they could not fire for fear of killing their comrade, they stood their ground with clubbed muskets and with spears; so that the outcome looked dark indeed for the Lord of the Jungle and his companion.

Using the man in his grasp as a flail, Tarzan sought to mow down those standing between him and liberty; but there were many of them, and presently they succeeded in dragging their comrade from the clutches of the ape-man. Now it seemed that the situation of the two whites was hopeless, for there was no longer anything to prevent the bandits using their matchlocks to advantage. The *shiftas* were in such a transport of rage that nothing less than the extermination of these two foes would satisfy them; but Tarzan and the other pressed on so closely that the muskets were useless against them for the moment; though presently some of the *shiftas* withdrew a little to one side where they might have free use of their weapons.

One fellow in particular was well placed to fire without endangering any of his fellows, and raising his matchlock to his shoulder he took careful aim at Tarzan.

3

Cats by Night

As the man raised his weapon to his shoulder to fire at Tarzan, a scream of warning burst from the lips of one of his comrades, to be drowned by the throaty roar of Numa, the lion, as the swift rush of his charge carried him over the boma into the midst of the camp.

The man who would have killed Tarzan cast a quick backward glance as the warning cry apprised him of his danger; and when he saw the lion he cast away his rifle in his excitement and terror, his terrified scream mingled with the voice of Numa, and in his anxiety to escape the fangs of the maneater he rushed into the arms of the ape-man.

The lion, momentarily confused by the firelight and the swift movement and the shouts of the men, paused, crouching, as he looked to right and left. In that brief instant Tarzan seized the fleeing *shifta*, lifted him high above his head, and hurled him into the face of Numa; then, as the lion seized its prey and its great jaws closed upon the head and shoulder of the hapless bandit, he motioned to his companion to follow him, and, running directly past the lion, leaped the boma at the very point that Numa had leaped it. Close at his heels was the white captive of the *shiftas*, and before the bandits had recovered from the first shock and surprise of the lion's unexpected charge the two had disappeared in the shadows of the night.

Just outside the camp Tarzan left his companion for a moment while he swung into the tree where he had left his weapons and recovered them; then he led the way out of the valley up into the hills. At his elbow trotted the silent white man he had rescued from certain death at the hands of the Kaficho and Galla bandits.

During the brief encounter in the camp Tarzan had noted with admiration the strength, agility, and courage of the stranger who had aroused both his interest and his curiosity. Here, seemingly, was a man moulded to the dimensions of Tarzan's own standards, a quiet, resourceful, courageous fighting man. Radiating that intangible aura which we call personality, even in his silences he impressed the ape-man with a conviction that loyalty and dependability were innate characteristics of the man; so Tarzan, who ordinarily preferred to be alone, was not displeased to have the companionship of this stranger.

The moon, almost full, had risen above the black mountain mass to the east, shedding her soft light on hill and valley and forest, transforming the scene once more into that of a new world which was different from the world of daylight and from the world of moonless night, a world of strange grays and silvery greens.

Up toward a fringe of forest that clothed the upper slopes of the foothills and dipped down into canyon and ravine the two men moved as noiselessly as the passing shadow of a cloud, yet to one hidden in the dark recesses of the wood above, their approach was not unheralded, for on the breath of Usha, the wind, it was borne ahead of them to the cunning nostrils of the prince of hunters.

Sheeta, the panther, was hungry. For several days prey had been scarce and elusive. Now, in his nostrils, the scent of the man-things grew stronger as they drew nearer. It was the pure scent of man that came to him unvitiated by the hated odor of the flame-belching thunder stick that he feared and hated. Eagerly, Sheeta, the panther, awaited the coming of the men.

Within the forest, Tarzan sought a tree where they might lie up for the night. He had eaten and was not hungry. Whether or not his companion had eaten was his own concern. This was a law of the jungle from which Tarzan might deviate for a weak or wounded companion but not for a strong man able to provide for himself. Had he killed, he would have shared his kill; but he would not go forth and hunt for another.

Tarzan found a branch that forked horizontally. With his hunting knife he cut other branches and laid them across the two arms of the Y thus formed. Over this rude platform he spread leaves; and then he lay down to sleep, while from an adjacent tree upwind Sheeta watched him. Sheeta also watched the other man-thing on the ground between the two trees. The great cat did not move; he seemed scarcely to breathe. Even Tarzan was unaware of his presence, yet the ape-man was restless. A sense so delicate that he was not objectively aware of its existence seemed to warn him that all was not well. He listened intently and sniffed the air but detected nothing amiss. Below him, his companion was making his bed upon the ground in preference to risking the high-flung branches of the trees to which he was unaccustomed. It was the man upon the ground that Sheeta watched.

At last, his bed of leaves and grasses arranged to suit him, Tarzan's companion lay down. Sheeta waited. Gradually, almost imperceptibly the sinuous muscles were drawing the hindquarters forward beneath the sleek body in preparation for the spring. Sheeta edged forward on the great limb upon which he crouched, but in doing so he caused the branch to move slightly and the leaves at its end to rustle just a little. Your ears or mine would not have been conscious of any noise, but the ears of Tarzan are not as are yours or mine.

He heard; and his eyes, turning quickly, sought and found the intruder. At the same time instant Sheeta launched himself at the man lying on his rude pallet on the ground below; and as Sheeta sprang so did Tarzan. What happened happened very quickly; it was a matter of seconds only.

As the two beasts sprang, Tarzan voiced a roar that was intended both to warn his companion and to distract the attention of Sheeta from his prey. The man upon the ground leaped quickly to one side, prompted more by an instinctive reaction than by reason. The panther's body brushed him as it struck the ground, but the beast's thoughts were now upon the thing that had voiced that menacing roar rather than upon its intended prey.

Wheeling as he leaped aside, the man turned and saw the savage carnivore just as Tarzan landed full upon the beast's back. He heard the mingled growls of the two as they closed in battle, and his scalp stiffened as he realized that the sounds coming from the lips of his companion were quite as bestial as those issuing from the throat of the carnivore.

Tarzan sought a hold about the neck of the panther, while the great cat instantly attempted to roll over on its back that it might rip the body of its antagonist to shreds with the terrible talons that armed its hind feet. But this strategy the ape-man had anticipated; and rolling beneath Sheeta as Sheeta rolled, he locked his powerful legs beneath the belly of the panther; then the great cat leaped to its feet again and sought to shake the man-thing from its back; and all the while a mighty arm was tightening about its neck, closing off its wind.

With frantic leaps and bounds the panther hurled itself about in the moonlight while Tarzan's companion stood unarmed and helpless. Twice he had tried to run in and assist the ape-man, but both times the two bodies had struck him and sent him spinning across the ground. Now he saw a new factor being injected into the battle; Tarzan had succeeded in drawing his knife. Momentarily the blade flashed before his eyes; then it was buried in the body of Sheeta. The cat, screaming from pain and rage, redoubled its efforts to dislodge the creature clinging to it in the embrace of death; but again the knife fell.

Now Sheeta stood trembling upon uncertain feet as once again the knife was plunged deeply into his side; then, his great voice forever stilled, he sank lifeless to the ground as the ape-man rolled from beneath him and sprang to his feet.

The man whose life Tarzan had saved came forward and laid a hand upon the shoulder of the ape-man, speaking a few words in a low voice but in a tongue that Tarzan did not understand though he guessed that it expressed the gratitude that the manner of the man betokened.

What thoughts were in the mind of Tarzan's companion? Twice within an hour this strange white man had saved him from death. For what reasons, the man could not guess. That sentiments of friendship and loyalty were aroused in his breast would seem only natural if he possessed either honor or gratitude, but of this we can have no knowledge until we know him better. As yet he is not even a name to us; and, following the policy of Tarzan, we shall not judge him until we know him better; then we may learn to like him, or we may have reason to despise him.

Influenced by the attack of the panther and knowing that Numa was abroad, Tarzan, by signs, persuaded the man to come up into the tree; and here the ape-man helped him construct a nest similar to his own. For the balance of the night they slept in peace, and the sun was an hour old before either stirred the following morning; then the ape-man rose and stretched himself.

Nearby, the other man sat up and looked about him. His eyes met Tarzan's, and he smiled and nodded. For the first time the ape-man had an opportunity to examine his new acquaintance by daylight. The man had removed his single garment for the night, covering himself with leaves and branches. Now as he rose, his only garment was a G-string, and Tarzan saw six feet of well-muscled, well-proportioned body topped by a head that seemed to bespeak breeding and intelligence. The man's features were strong, clear-cut, and harmoniously placed; the face was more noticeable for strength and rugged masculinity than for beauty.

The wild beast in Tarzan looked into the brown eyes of the stranger and was satisfied that here was one who might be trusted; the man in him noted the headband that confined the black hair, saw the strangely wrought ivory ornament in the center of the forehead, the habergeon that he was now donning, the ivory ornaments on wrists and ankles, and found his curiosity piqued.

The ivory ornament in the center of the headband was shaped like a concave, curved trowel, the point of which projected above the top of the man's head and curved forward. His wristlets and anklets were of long flat strips of ivory laid close together and fastened around the limbs by leather thongs that were laced through holes piercing the strips near their tops and bottoms. His sandals were of heavy leather, apparently elephant hide, and were supported by leather thongs fastened to the bottoms of his anklets.

On each arm below the shoulder he wore an ivory disc upon which was carved a design; about his neck was a band of smaller ivory discs elaborately carved, and from the lowest of these a strap ran down to his habergeon, which was also supported by shoulder straps. Depending from each side of his headband was another ivory disc of large size, above which was a smaller disc. The larger discs covered his ears. Heavy, curved, wedge-shaped pieces of ivory were held, one upon each shoulder, by the same straps that supported his habergeon.

That all these trappings were solely for purposes of ornamentation Tarzan did not believe. He saw that almost without exception they would serve as a protection against a cutting weapon such as a sword or battle-ax; and he could not but wonder where the stalwart warrior who wore them had had his genesis, for nowhere in the world, so far as Tarzan knew, was there a race of men wearing armor and ornaments such as these.

But speculation concerning this matter was relegated to the background of his thoughts by hunger and recollection of the remains of yesterday's kill that he had hung high in a tree of the forest farther up the river; so he dropped lightly to the ground, motioning the young warrior to follow him; and set off in the direction of his cache, keeping his keen senses always on the alert for enemies.

Cleverly hidden by leafy branches, the meat was intact when Tarzan reached it. He cut several strips and tossed them down to the warrior waiting on the ground below; then he cut some for himself and crouching in a crotch proceeded to eat it raw. His companion watched him for a moment in surprise; then he made fire with a bit of steel and flint and cooked his own portion.

As he ate, Tarzan's active mind was considering plans for the future. He had come to Abyssinia for a specific purpose, though the matter was not of such immediate importance that it demanded instant attention. In fact, in the philosophy that a lifetime of primitive environment had inspired, time was not an important consideration. The phenomenon of this ivory-armored warrior aroused questions that intrigued his interest to a far greater extent than did the problems that had brought him thus far from his own stamping grounds, and he decided that the latter should wait the solving of the riddle of this seeming anachronism that his new-made acquaintance presented.

Having no other means of communication than signs rendered an exchange of ideas between the two difficult, but when they had finished their meal and Tarzan had descended to the ground he succeeded in asking his companion in what direction he wished to go. The warrior pointed in a northeasterly direction toward the high mountains; and, as plainly as he could through the medium of signs, invited Tarzan to accompany him to his country. This invitation Tarzan accepted and motioned the other to lead the way.

For days that stretched to weeks the two men struck deeper and deeper into the heart of a stupendous mountain system. Always mentally alert and eager to learn, Tarzan took advantage of the opportunity provided by time and propinquity to learn the language of his companion, and he proved such an apt pupil that they were soon able to make themselves understood to one another.

Among the first things that Tarzan learned was that his companion's name was Valthor, while Valthor took the earliest opportunity to evince an interest in the ape-man's weapons; and as he was unarmed, Tarzan spent a day in making a spear and bow and arrows for him. Thereafter, as Valthor taught the Lord of the Jungle to speak his language, Tarzan instructed the former in the use of the bow, the spear being already a familiar weapon to the young warrior.

Thus the days and the weeks passed and the two seemed no nearer the country of Valthor than when they had started from the vicinity of the camp of the *shiftas*. Tarzan found game of certain varieties plentiful in the mountains, and it was he who kept their larder supplied. The impressive scenery that was marked by rugged grandeur held the interest of the ape-man undiminished. He hunted, and he enjoyed the beauties of unspoiled nature, practically oblivious of the passage of time.

But Valthor was less patient; and at last, late one day when they found themselves at the head of a blind canyon where stupendous cliffs barred further progress, he admitted defeat. "I am lost," he said simply.

"That," remarked Tarzan, "I could have told you many days ago."

Valthor looked at him in surprise. "How could you know that," he demanded, "when you yourself do not know in what direction my country lies?"

"I know," replied the ape-man, "because during the past week you have led the way toward the four points of the compass, and today we are within five miles of where we were a week ago. Across this ridge at our right, not more than five miles away, is the little stream where I killed the ibex and the gnarled old tree in which we slept that night just seven suns ago."

Valthor scratched his head in perplexity, and then he smiled. "I cannot dispute you," he admitted. "Perhaps you are right, but what are we going to do?"

"Do you know in what direction your country lies from the camp in which I found you?" asked Tarzan.

"Thenar is due east of that point," replied Valthor; "of that I am positive."

"Then we are directly southwest of it now, for we have traveled a considerable distance toward the south since we entered the higher mountains. If your country lies in these mountains then it should not be difficult to find it if we can keep moving always in a northeasterly direction."

"This jumble of mountains with their twisting canyons and gorges confuses me," Valthor admitted. "You see, in all my life before I have never been farther from Thenar than the valley of Onthar, and both these valleys are surrounded by landmarks with which I am so familiar that I need no other guides. It has never been necessary for me to consult the positions of the sun, the moon, nor the stars before; and so they have been of no help to me since we set out in search of

Thenar. Do you believe that you could hold a course toward the northeast in this maze of mountains? If you can, then you had better lead the way rather than I."

"I can go toward the northeast," Tarzan assured him, "but I cannot find your country unless it lies in my path."

"If we reach a point within fifty or a hundred miles of it, from some high eminence we shall see Xarator," explained Valthor; "and then I shall know my way to Thenar, for Xarator is almost due west of Athne."

"What are Xarator and Athne?" demanded Tarzan.

"Xarator is a great peak the center of which is filled with fire and molten rock. It lies at the north end of the valley of Onthar and belongs to the men of Cathne, the City of Gold. Athne, the City of Ivory, is the city from which I come. The men of Cathne, in the valley of Onthar, are the enemies of my people."

"Tomorrow, then," said Tarzan, "we shall set out for the city of Athne in the valley of Thenar."

As Tarzan and Valthor ate meat that they had cut from yesterday's kill and carried with them, many weary miles to the south a black-maned lion lashed his tail angrily and voiced a savage growl as he stood over the body of a buffalo calf he had killed and faced an angry bull pawing the earth and bellowing a few yards away.

Rare is the beast that will face Gorgo, the buffalo, when rage inflames his red-rimmed eyes; but the great lion showed no intention of leaving its prey even in the face of the bull's threatened charge. He stood his ground. The roars of the lion and the bull mingled in a savage, thunderous dissonance that shook the ground, stilling the voices of the lesser people of the jungle.

Gorgo gored the earth, working himself into a frenzy of rage. Behind him, bellowing, stood the mother of the slain calf. Perhaps she was urging her lord and master to avenge the murder. The other members of the herd had bolted into the thickest of the jungle leaving these two to contest with Numa his right to his kill, leaving vengeance to those powerful horns backed by that massive neck.

With a celerity and agility that belied his great weight, the bull charged. That two such huge beasts could move so quickly and so lightly seemed incredible, as it seemed incredible that any creature could either withstand or avoid the menace of those mighty horns; but the lion was ready, and as the bull was almost upon him, he leaped to one side, reared upon his hind feet and with one massive, taloned paw struck the bull a terrific blow on the side of its head that wheeled it half around and sent it stumbling to its knees, half stunned and bleeding, its great jawbone crushed and splintered. And before Gorgo could regain his feet, Numa leaped full upon his back, buried his teeth in the bulging muscles of the great neck, and with one paw reached for the nose of the bellowing bull, jerking the head back with a mighty surge that snapped the vertebrae.

Instantly the lion was on his feet again facing the cow, but she did not charge. Instead, bellowing, she crashed away into the jungle leaving the king of beasts standing with his forefeet upon his latest kill.

That night Numa fed well; yet when he had gorged himself he did not lie up as a lion should, but continued toward the north along the mysterious trail he had been following for many days.

4

Down the Flood

THE NEW DAY dawned cloudy and threatening. The season of rains was over, but it appeared that a belated storm was gathering above the lofty peaks through which Tarzan and Valthor were searching for the elusive valley of Thenar. The chill of night was dissipated by no kindly warmth of sunlight. The two men shivered as they rose from their rude beds among the branches of a tree.

"We shall eat later," announced Tarzan, "after a little climbing has put warmth into our blood."

"If we are lucky enough to find anything to eat," rejoined Valthor.

"Tarzan seldom goes hungry," replied the ape-man. "He will not go hungry today. When Tarzan is ready to hunt, we shall eat."

Down the box canyon they went until Tarzan found a place where they might ascend the precipitous sidewall; then they toiled upward, the warrior from Athne confident that each step would be his last as he clung to the steep face of the canyon wall but too proud to reveal his fear to the agile ape-man climbing so easily above him. But he did not fall, and at last the two stood upon the summit of a mighty ridge that led upward toward lofty peaks.

Valthor's heart was pounding and he was breathing heavily, but Tarzan showed no sign of exertion. He was about to continue on up the ridge, when he glanced at his companion and saw his condition; then he squatted on the ground with a laconic "Rest now"; and Valthor was glad to rest.

All day they moved toward the northeast. Sometimes it rained a little, and always it threatened to rain more. A great storm seemed always to be gathering, yet it never broke during the long day. Tarzan made a kill before noon, and they ate; but immediately afterward they started on again. The cold, damp, sunless air offered them no incentive for tarrying on the way.

It was late in the afternoon when they ascended out of a deep gorge and stood upon a lofty plateau. In the near foreground were no mountains, but at a distance lofty peaks were visible dimly through a light drizzle of rain. Suddenly Valthor voiced an exclamation of elation. "We have found it!" he cried. "There is Xarator!"

Tarzan looked in the direction that the other pointed and saw a mighty, flat-topped peak in the distance, directly above which low clouds were reflecting a dull red light. "So that is Xarator!" he remarked. "And Thenar is directly east of it?"

"Yes," replied Valthor; "which means that Onthar must be just below the edge of this plateau, almost directly in front of us. Come!"

The two walked quickly over the level, grassy ground for a mile or two to come at length to the edge of the plateau beyond which, and below them, stretched a wide valley.

"We are almost at the southern end of Onthar," said Valthor. "There is Cathne, the City of Gold. See it—in the bend of the river at this end of that forest? It is a rich city, but its people are the enemies of my people."

Through the rain, Tarzan saw a walled city between a forest and a river. The houses were nearly all white, and there were many domes of dull yellow. The river, which ran between them and the city, was spanned by a bridge that was also a dull yellow color in the twilight of the late afternoon storm. Tarzan saw that the river extended the full length of the valley, a distance of fourteen or fifteen miles, being fed by smaller streams coming down out of the mountains. Also extending the length of the valley was what appeared to be a well-marked road. Near the center of the valley it branched, one fork following an affluent of the main stream with which it disappeared into the mouth of a canyon on the eastern side of the valley. Directly below them and extending to the northern extremity of Onthar was a level plain dotted with trees; across the river, a forest stretched from the farther bank to the steep hills that bounded Onthar on the east and southeast.

Tarzan's eyes wandered back to the city of Cathne. "Why do you call it the City of Gold?" he asked.

"Do you not see the golden domes and the Bridge of Gold?" demanded Valthor.

"Are they covered with gold paint?" inquired Tarzan.

"They are covered with solid gold," replied Valthor. "The gold on some of the domes is an inch thick, and the bridge is built of solid blocks of gold."

Tarzan lifted his eyebrows. As he looked down upon this seemingly deserted and peaceful valley he could not but conjure another picture—a picture of what it would be if word of these vast riches were carried to the outside world, bringing the kindly beneficences of modern civilization and civilized men to Onthar. How the valley would hum and roar then with the sweet music of mill and factory! What a gorgeous spectacle would be painted against the African sky by tall chimneys spouting black smoke to hang like a sable curtain above the golden domes of Cathne!

"Where do they find their gold?" he asked.

"Their mines lie in the hills directly south of the city," replied Valthor.

"And where is your country, Thenar?" asked the ape-man.

"Just beyond the hills east of Onthar. Do you see where the river and the road cut through the forest about five miles above the city? You can see them entering the hills just beyond the forest."

"Yes," replied Tarzan; "I see."

"The road and the river run through the Pass of the Warriors into the valley of Thenar; a little northeast of the center of the valley lies Athne, the City of Ivory; there, beyond the pass, is my country."

"How far are we from Athne?" enquired Tarzan.

"About twenty-five miles, possibly a little less," replied Valthor.

"We might as well start now, then," suggested the ape-man, "for in this rain it will be more comfortable to be on the march than to lie up until morning; and in your city we can find a dry place to sleep I presume."

"Certainly," replied Valthor, "but it will not be safe to attempt to cross Onthar by daylight. We should certainly be seen by the sentries on the gates of Cathne, and as these people are our enemies the chances are that we should never cross the valley without being either killed or taken prisoners. It will be bad enough at night on account of the lions, but by day it will be infinitely worse as we shall have both men and lions to contend with."

"What lions?" demanded Tarzan.

"The men of Cathne breed lions, and there are many at large in the valley," explained Valthor. "That great plain that you see below us, stretching the full length of the valley on this side of the river, is called the Field of the Lions. We shall be safer if we cross it after dark."

"Whatever you wish," agreed Tarzan with a shrug; "it is all the same to me if we start now or wait until dark."

"It is not very comfortable here," remarked the Athnean. "The rain is cold."

"I have been uncomfortable before," replied Tarzan; "rains do not last forever."

"If we were in Athne we should be very comfortable," sighed Valthor. "In my father's house there are fireplaces; even now the flames are roaring about great logs, and all is warmth and comfort."

"Above the clouds the sun is shining," replied Tarzan, "but we are not above the clouds; we are here where the sun is not shining and there is no fire, and we are cold." A faint smile touched his lips. "It does not warm me to speak of fires or the sun."

"Nevertheless, I wish I were in Athne," insisted Valthor. "It is a splendid city, and Thenar is a lovely valley. In Thenar we raise goats and sheep and elephants. In Thenar there are no lions except those that stray in from Onthar; those we kill. Our farmers raise vegetables and fruits and hay; our artisans manufacture leather goods; they make cloth from the hair of goats and the wool of sheep; our carvers work in ivory and wood.

"We trade a little with the outside world, paying for what we buy with ivory and gold. Were it not for the Cathneans we should lead a happy, peaceful life without a care."

"What do you buy from the outside world, and of whom do you buy it?" asked Tarzan.

"We buy salt, of which we have none of our own," explained Valthor. "We also buy steel for our weapons and black slaves and occasionally a white woman, if she be young and pretty. These things we buy from a band of *shiftas*. With this same band we have traded since before the memory of man. *Shifta* chiefs and kings of Athne have come and gone, but our relations with this band have never altered. I was searching for them when I became lost and was captured by another band."

"Do you never trade with the people of Cathne?" asked the ape-man.

"Once each year there is a week's truce during which we trade with them in peace. They give us gold and foodstuffs and hay in exchange for the women, the salt, and the steel we buy from the *shiftas*, and the cloth, leather, and ivory that we produce.

"Besides mining gold, the Cathneans breed lions for war and sport, raise fruits, vegetables, cereals, and hay and work in gold and, to a lesser extent, in ivory. Their gold and their hay are the products most valuable to us; and of these we value the hay more, for without it we should have to decrease our elephant herds."

"Why should two peoples so dependent upon one another fight?" asked Tarzan.

Valthor shrugged. "I do not know; perhaps it is just a custom. Yet, though we talk much of wanting peace, we should miss the thrills and excitement that peace does not hold." His eyes brightened. "The raids!" he exclaimed. "There is a sport for men! The Cathneans come with their lions to hunt our goats, our sheep, our elephants, and us. They take heads for trophies, and above all they value the head of man. They try to take our women, and when they succeed then there is war, if the family of the woman seized be of sufficient importance.

"When we wish sport we go into Onthar after gold and women or just for the sport of killing men or capturing slaves. The greatest game of all is to sell a woman to a Cathnean for much gold and then take her away from him in a raid. No, I do not think that either we or the Cathneans would care for peace."

As Valthor talked, the invisible sun sank lower into the west; heavy clouds, dark and ominous, hid the peaks to the north, settling low over the upper end of the valley. "I think we may start now," he said; "it will soon be dark."

Downward through a gully, the sides of which hid them from the city of Cathne, the two men made their way toward the floor of the valley. From the heavy storm clouds burst a flash of lightning followed by the roar of thunder; upon the upper end of the valley the storm god loosed his wrath; water fell in a deluge of masses wiping from their sight the hills beyond the storm.

By the time they reached level ground the storm was upon them and the gully they had descended a raging mountain torrent. The swift night had fallen; utter darkness surrounded them, darkness frequently broken by vivid flashes of lightning. The pealing of the constant thunder was deafening. The rain engulfed them in solid sheets like the waves of the ocean. It was, perhaps, the most terrific storm that either of these men had ever seen.

They could not converse; only the lightning prevented their becoming separated, as it alone permitted Valthor to keep his course across the grassy floor of the valley in the direction of the City of Gold where they would find the road that led to the Pass of the Warriors and on into the valley of Thenar.

Presently they came within sight of the lights of the city, a few dim lights framed by the casements of windows; and a moment later they were on the road and were moving northward against the full fury of the storm. And such a storm! As they moved toward its center it grew in intensity; against the wind that accompanied it they waged a grim battle that was sometimes to them and sometimes to the wind, for often it stopped them in their tracks and forced them back.

For miles they pitted their muscles against the Herculean strength of the storm god; and the rage of the storm god seemed to rise against them, knowing no bounds, as though he was furious that these two puny mortals should pit their strength against his. Suddenly, as though in a last titanic effort to overcome them, the lightning burst into a mighty blaze that illuminated the entire valley for seconds, the thunder crashed as it had never crashed before, and a mass of water fell that crushed the two men to earth.

As they staggered to their feet again foot-deep water swirled about their legs; they stood in a broad, racing torrent that rushed past them toward the river; but in that last effort the storm god had spent his force. The rain ceased; through a rift in the dark clouds the moon looked down, perhaps in wonder, upon a drowned world; and Valthor led the way again toward the Pass of the Warriors. The last storm of the rainy season was over.

It is seven miles from the Bridge of Gold, that is the gateway to the city of Cathne, to the ford where the road to Thenar crosses the river; and it required three hours for Valthor and Tarzan to cover the distance, two hours for the first third and one hour for the remainder; but at last they stood at the river's brink.

A boiling flood confronted them, tearing down a widened river toward the city of Cathne. Valthor hesitated. "Ordinarily," he said to Tarzan, "the water is little more than a foot deep. It must be three feet deep now."

"And it will soon be deeper," commented the ape-man. "Only a small portion of the storm waters have had time to reach this point from the hills and the upper valley. If we are going to cross tonight, we shall have to do it now."

"Very well," replied Valthor, "but follow me; I know the ford."

As the Athnean stepped into the water the clouds closed again beneath the moon and plunged the world once more into darkness. As Tarzan followed he could scarcely see his guide ahead of him; and as Valthor knew the ford he moved more rapidly than the ape-man with the result that presently Tarzan could not see him at all, but he felt his way toward the opposite bank without thought of disaster.

The force of the stream was mighty; but mighty, too, are the thews of Tarzan of the Apes. The water, which Valthor had thought to be three feet in depth, was soon surging to the ape-man's waist, and then he missed the ford and stepped into a hole. Instantly the current seized him and swept him away; not even the giant muscles of Tarzan could cope with the might of the flood.

The Lord of the Jungle fought the swirling waters in an effort to reach the opposite shore, but in their embrace he was powerless. Was the storm god proud or resentful to see one of his children succeed where he had failed? That is a difficult question to answer, for gods are strange creatures; they give to those who have and take from those who have not; they punish whom they love and are jealous and resentful; in which they resemble the creatures who conceived them.

Finding even his great strength powerless and weakening, Tarzan gave up the struggle to reach the opposite bank and devoted his efforts to keeping his nose above the surface of the angry flood. Even this was none too easy of accomplishment, as the rushing waters had a trick of twisting him about or turning him over. Often his head was submerged, and sometimes he floated feetfirst and sometimes headfirst; but he tried to rest his muscles as best he could against the time when some vagary of the torrent might carry him within reach of the bank upon one side or the other.

He knew that several miles below the city of Cathne the river entered a narrow gorge, for that he had seen from the edge of the plateau from which he had first viewed the valley of Onthar; and Valthor had told him that beyond the gorge it tumbled in a mighty falls a hundred feet to the bottom of a rocky canyon. Should he not succeed in escaping the clutches of the torrent before it carried him into the gorge his doom was sealed, but Tarzan felt neither fear nor panic. His life had been in jeopardy often during his savage existence, yet he still lived.

He wondered what had become of Valthor. Perhaps he, too, was being hurtled along either above or below him. But such was not the fact. Valthor had reached the opposite bank in safety and waited there for Tarzan. When the ape-man did not appear within a reasonable time, the Athnean shouted his name aloud; but though he received no answer he was still not sure that Tarzan was not upon the opposite side of the river, the loud roaring of which might have drowned the sound of the voice of either.

Then Valthor decided to wait until daylight, rather than abandon his friend in a country with which he was entirely unfamiliar. That the Athnean remained bespoke his loyalty as well as the high esteem in which he held the ape-man, for the dangers that might beset Tarzan in Onthar would prove even a greater menace to Valthor, an hereditary enemy of the Cathneans.

Through the long night he waited and, with the coming of dawn, eagerly scanned the opposite bank of the river, his slender hope for the safety of his friend dying when daylight failed to reveal any sign of him. Then, at last, he was convinced that Tarzan had been swept away to his death by the raging flood; and, with a heavy heart, he turned away from the river and resumed his interrupted journey toward the Pass of the Warriors and the Valley of Thenar.

5

The City of Gold

As Tarzan battled for his life in the swirling waters of the swollen river he lost all sense of time; the seemingly interminable struggle against death might have been enduring without beginning, might endure without end, insofar as his numbed senses were concerned. His efforts to delay the apparently inevitable end were now purely mechanical, instinctive reactions to the threat against self-preservation. The cold water had sapped the vitality of his mind as well as of his body, yet, while his heart beat, neither would admit defeat; subconsciously, without active volition, they sought to preserve him. It was well that they did.

Turnings in the river cast him occasionally against one shore and then the other. Always, then, his hands reached up in an attempt to grasp something that might stay his mad rush toward the falls and death; and at last success crowned their efforts—his fingers closed upon the stem of a heavy vine that trailed down the bank into the swirling waters, closed and held.

Instantly, almost miraculously, new life seemed to be instilled into the veins of the ape-man by the feel of that stout support in his grasp. Quickly he seized it with both hands; the river clutched at his body and tried to drag it onward toward its doom; but the vine held, and so did Tarzan.

Hand over hand the man dragged himself out of the water and onto the bank, where he lay for several minutes; then he rose slowly to his feet, shook himself like some great lion, and looked about him in the darkness, trying to penetrate the impenetrable night. Faintly, as through shrubbery, he thought that he saw a light shining dimly in the distance. Where there was a light, there should be men. Tarzan moved cautiously forward to investigate.

He knew that he had crossed the river but that he was a long distance from the point at which he had entered it. He wondered what had become of Valthor; and determined, after he had investigated the light, to start up the river in search of him; even though he feared that his companion had been swept away by the flood, as he had.

But a few steps from the river Tarzan encountered a wall, and when he was close to the wall he could no longer see the light. Reaching upward, he discovered that the top of the wall was still above the tips of his outstretched fingers; but walls which were made to keep one out also invited one to climb them. The ape-man, filled with the curiosity of the beast, desired now more than ever to investigate the light he had seen.

Stepping back a few paces, he ran toward the wall and sprang upward. His extended fingers gripped the top of the wall and clung there. Slowly he drew himself up, threw a leg across the capstones, and looked to see what might be seen upon the opposite side of the wall.

He did not see much; a square of dim light forty or fifty feet away; that was all, and it did not satisfy curiosity. Silently he lowered himself to the ground upon the same side as the light and moved cautiously forward. Beneath his bare feet he felt stone flagging, and guessed that he was in a paved courtyard.

He had crossed about half the distance to the light when the retreating storm flashed a farewell bolt from the distance. This distant lightning but barely sufficed to momentarily relieve the darkness surrounding the ape-man, revealing a low building, a lighted window, a deeply recessed doorway in the shelter of which stood a man. It also revealed Tarzan to the man in the doorway.

Instantly the silence was shattered by the brazen clatter of a gong. The door swung open, and men bearing torches rushed out. Tarzan, impelled by the natural caution of the beast, turned to run; but as he did so, he saw other open doors upon his flanks; and armed men with torches were rushing from these as well.

Realizing that flight was useless. Tarzan stood still with folded arms as the men converged upon him from three directions. Perhaps his insatiate curiosity prompted him to await quietly the coming of the men as much as a realization of the futility of flight. Tarzan wanted to see what the men were like and what they would do. He knew that he must be in the City of Gold, and his imagination was inflamed. If they threatened him, he could still fight; if they imprisoned him, he could escape; so, at least, thought Tarzan, whose self-confidence was in proportion to his great size and his giant strength.

The torches carried by some of the men showed Tarzan that he was in a paved, quadrangular courtyard enclosed by buildings upon three sides and the wall he had scaled upon the fourth. Their light also revealed the fact that he was being surrounded by some fifty men armed with spears, the points of which were directed toward him in a menacing circle.

"Who are you?" demanded one of the men as the cordon drew tightly about him. The language in which the man spoke was the same as that which Tarzan had learned from Valthor, the common language of the enemy cities of Athne and Cathne.

"I am a stranger from a country far to the south," replied the ape-man.

"What are you doing inside the walls of the palace of Nemone?" The speaker's voice was threatening, his tone accusatory. Tarzan sensed that the presence of a stranger here was a crime in itself; but this made the situation all the more interesting; while the name, Nemone, possessed a quality that fired his interest.

"I was crossing the river far above here when the flood caught me and swept me down; it was only by chance that I finally made a landing here."

The man who had been questioning him shrugged. "Well," he admitted, "it is not for me to question you anyway. Come!

You will have a chance to tell your story to an officer; but he will not believe it either."

As the men conducted Tarzan toward one of the buildings, he thought that they seemed more curious than hostile. It was evident, however, that they were only common warriors without responsibility and that he might find the attitude of the officer class entirely different.

They conducted him into a large, low-ceilinged room which was furnished with rough benches and tables; upon the walls hung weapons, spears and swords; and there were shields of elephant hide studded with gold bosses. But there were other things in this strange room that compelled the interest of the ape-man far more than did the weapons and the shields; upon the walls were mounted the heads of animals; there were the heads of sheep and goats and lions and elephants. Among these, sinister and forbidding, were the scowling heads of men. The sight of them reminded Tarzan of the stories Valthor had told him of these men of Cathne.

Two men guarded Tarzan in one corner of the room, while another was dispatched to notify a superior of the capture; the remainder loafed about the room, talking, playing games, cleaning their weapons. The prisoner took the opportunity to examine his captors.

They were well set up men, many of them not ill-favored, though for the most part of ignorant and brutal appearance. Their helmets, habergeons, wristlets, and anklets were of elephant hide heavily embossed with gold studs. Long hair from the manes of lions fringed the tops of their anklets and wristlets and was also used for ornamental purposes along the crests of their helmets and upon some of their shields and weapons. The elephant hide that composed their habergeons was cut into discs, and the habergeon fabricated in a manner similar to that one of ivory which Valthor had worn. In the center of each shield was a heavy boss of solid gold. Upon the harnesses and weapons of these common soldiers was a fortune in the precious metal.

While Tarzan, immobile, silent, surveyed the scene with eyes that seemed scarcely to move yet missed no detail, two warriors entered the room; and the instant that they crossed the threshold silence fell upon the men congregated in the chamber; and Tarzan knew by that these were officers, though their trappings would have been sufficient evidence of their superior stations in life.

Habergeons and helmets, wristlets and anklets were all of gold and ivory, as were the hilts and scabbards of their short, daggerlike swords. The two presented a gorgeous picture against the background of the grim room and the relatively somber trappings of the common soldiers.

At a word of command from one of the two, the common warriors fell back, clearing one end of the room; then the two seated themselves at a table and ordered Tarzan's guards to bring him forward. As the Lord of the Jungle halted before them both men surveyed him critically.

"Why are you in Onthar?" demanded one who was evidently the superior, since he propounded all the questions during the interview.

Tarzan answered this and other questions as he had answered similar ones at the time of his capture, but he sensed from the attitudes of the two officers that neither was impressed with the truth of his statements. They seemed to have preconceived a conviction concerning him that nothing which he might say could alter.

"He does not look much like an Athnean," remarked the younger man.

"That proves nothing," snapped the other. "Naked men look like naked men. He might pass for your own cousin were he garbed as you are garbed."

"Perhaps you are right, but why is he here? A man does not come alone from Thenar to raid in Onthar. Unless—" he hesitated; "unless he was sent to assassinate the Queen!"

"I had thought of that," said the older man. "Because of what happened to the last Athnean prisoner we took, the Athneans are very angry with the Queen. Yes, they might easily attempt to assassinate her."

"For what other reason would a stranger enter the palace grounds? He would know that he must die if he were caught."

"Of course, and this man expected to die; but he intended killing the Queen first. He was willing to martyr himself for Athne."

Tarzan was almost amused as he contemplated the ease with which these two convinced themselves that what they wanted to believe true, was true; but he realized that this form of one-sided trial might prove disastrous to him if his fate were to be decided by such a tribunal and so he was prompted to speak.

"I have never been in Athne," he said quietly. "I am from a country far to the south. An accident brought me here. I am not an enemy. I have not come to kill your Queen or any other. Until today I did not know that your city existed." This was a long speech for Tarzan of the Apes. He was almost positive that it would not influence his captors, yet there was a chance that they might believe him. He wished to remain among these people until his curiosity concerning them had been satisfied, and he felt that he might only do this by winning their confidence; if they imprisoned him, he would see nothing while he was in prison; and when he got out of prison, he would see but little more; as he would then be concerned only with the business of escape.

Men are peculiar, and none knew this better than Tarzan, who, because he had seen rather less of men than of beasts, had been inclined to study those whom he had seen. Now he was studying the two men who were questioning him. The elder he judged to be a man accustomed to the exercise of great power; cunning, ruthless, cruel. Tarzan did not like him. His was the instinctive appraisal of the wild beast.

The younger man was of an entirely different mold. He was intelligent rather than cunning; his countenance bespoke a frank and open nature. The ape-man judged that he was both honest and courageous. It was true that he had agreed with all that the elder man had said, almost in contradiction of his own original statement that Tarzan did not resemble an Athnean; but in that the ape-man saw confirmation of his belief in the younger man's intelligence. Only a fool contradicts his superior for no good purpose.

While he was certain that the younger man had little

authority, compared with that exercised by his superior, yet Tarzan thought best to address him rather than the other because he thought that he might win an ally in the younger man and was sure that he could never influence the elder unless it was very much to the latter's interests to be influenced. And so, when he spoke again, he spoke to the younger of the two officers.

"Are these men of Athne like me?" he asked.

For an instant the officer hesitated; then he said, quite frankly, "No; they are not like you. You are unlike any man that I have seen."

"Are their weapons like my weapons?" continued the ape-man. "There are mine over in the corner of the room; your men took them away from me. Look at them."

Even the elder officer seemed interested. "Bring them here," he ordered one of the warriors.

The man brought them and laid them on the table before the two officers: the spear, the bow, the quiver of arrows, the grass rope, and the knife. The two men picked them up one by one and examined them carefully. Both seemed interested.

"Are they like the weapon of the Athneans?" demanded Tarzan. Of course he knew that they were not, but he thought it best not to acquaint these men with the fact that he had been consorting with one of their enemies.

"They are nothing like them," admitted the younger man. "What do you suppose this thing is for, Tomos?" he asked his companion as he examined Tarzan's bow.

"It may be a snare of some sort," replied Tomos; "probably for small animals—it would be useless against anything large."

"Let me take it," suggested Tarzan, "and I will show you how it is used."

The younger man handed the bow to the ape-man.

"Be careful, Gemnon," cautioned Tomos; "this may be a trick, a subterfuge by which he hopes to get possession of a weapon with which to kill us."

"He cannot kill us with that thing," replied Gemnon. "Let's see how he uses it. Go ahead— Let's see, what did you say your name is?"

"Tarzan," replied the Lord of the Jungle, "Tarzan of the Apes."

"Well, go ahead, Tarzan; but see that you don't attempt to attack any of us."

Tarzan stepped to the table and took an arrow from his quiver; then he glanced about the room. On the wall at the far end a lion's head with open mouth hung near the ceiling. With what appeared but a single swift motion he fitted the arrow to the bow, drew the feathered shaft to his shoulder, and released it.

Every eye in the room had been upon him, for the common warriors had been interested spectators of what had been transpiring; every eye saw the shaft quivering now where it protruded from the center of the lion's mouth; and an involuntary exclamation broke from every throat, an exclamation in which were mingled surprise and applause.

"Take the thing away from him, Gemnon," snapped Tomos. "It is not a safe weapon in the hands of an enemy."

Tarzan tossed the bow to the table. "Do the Athneans use this weapon?" he asked.

Gemnon shook his head. "We know no men who use such a weapon," he replied.

"Then you must know that I am no Athnean," stated Tarzan, looking squarely at Tomos.

"It makes no difference where you are from," snapped Tomos; "you are an enemy."

The ape-man shrugged but remained silent. He had accomplished all that he had hoped for. He was sure that he had convinced them both that he was not an Athnean and had aroused the interest of the younger man, Gemnon. Something might come of this; though just what, he did not know himself.

Gemnon had leaned close to Tomos and was whispering in the latter's ear, evidently urging some action upon him. Tarzan could not hear what he was saying. The elder man listened impatiently; it was clear that he was not in accord with the suggestion of his junior.

"No," he said when the other had finished. "I will not permit anything of the sort. The life of the Queen is too sacred to risk by permitting this fellow any freedom. We shall lock him up for the night, and tomorrow decide what shall be done with him." He turned to a warrior who seemed to be an under-officer. "Take this fellow to the strong house," he said, "and see that he does not escape." Then he rose and strode from the room, followed by his younger companion.

When they had gone, the man in whose charge Tarzan had been left picked up the bow and examined it. "What do you call this thing?" he demanded.

"A bow," replied the ape-man.

"And these?"

"Arrows."

"Will they kill a man?"

"With them I have killed men and lions and buffaloes and elephants," replied Tarzan. "Would you like to learn how to use them?" Perhaps, he thought, a little kindly feeling in the guardroom might be helpful to him later on. Just at present he was not thinking of escape; these people and the City of Gold were far too interesting to leave until he had seen more of them.

The man fingering the bow hesitated. Tarzan guessed that he wished to try his hand with the weapon but feared to delay carrying out the order of his officer.

"It will take but a moment," suggested Tarzan. "See, let me show you."

Half reluctantly the man handed him the bow and Tarzan selected another arrow.

"Hold them like this," he directed and placed the bow and arrow correctly in the other's hands. "Tell your men to stand aside; you may not shoot accurately at first. Aim at the lion's head, as I did. Now draw the bowstring back as far as you can."

The man, of stocky, powerful build, tugged at the bowstring; but the bow that Tarzan bent so easily he could scarcely bend at all. When he released the arrow it flew but a few feet and dropped to the floor. "What's wrong?" he demanded.

"It requires practice," the ape-man told him.

"There is a trick to it," insisted the under-officer. "Let me see you do it again."

The other warriors, watching with manifest interest, whispered among themselves or commented openly. "It takes a strong man to bend that stick," said one.

"Althides is a strong man," retorted another.

"But he is not strong enough."

Althides, the under-officer, watched intently while Tarzan strung the bow again and bent it; he saw how easily the stranger flexed the heavy wood, and he marveled. The other men looked on in open admiration, and this time a shout of approval arose as Tarzan's second arrow crowded the first in the mouth of the lion. When the symbols of high authority are absent men can be human.

Althides scratched his head. "I shall have to lock you up now," he said, "or old Tomos will have my head on the wall of his palace; but I shall practice with this strange weapon until I learn to use it. Are you sure that there is no trick in bending that thing you call a bow?"

"There is no trick to it," Tarzan assured him. "Make yourself a lighter bow and you will find it easier, or bring me the material and I will make one for you."

"That I will do," exclaimed Althides. "Come now and be locked up."

A guard accompanied Tarzan across the courtyard to another building where he was placed in a room which, in the light of the torches borne by his escort, he saw had another occupant; then they left him, locking the heavy door behind them; and Tarzan heard their footsteps dying away across the courtyard as they took themselves and their torches off, leaving him in darkness.

He could not see his companion, but he could hear his breathing. He wondered with whom fate had cast him in this remote dungeon of the City of Gold.

6

The Man Who Stepped on a God

Now that the torches were gone the room was very dark, but Tarzan lost no time in starting to investigate his prison. First he groped his way to the door, which he found to be constructed of solid planking with a small, square hole cut in it about the height of his eyes. There was no sign of lock or latch upon the inside and no way of ascertaining how it was secured from the outside.

Leaving the door, Tarzan moved slowly along the walls, feeling carefully over the stone surface. He knew that the other occupant of the cell was sitting on a bench in one corner at the far end. He could still hear him breathing. As he examined the room Tarzan approached closer and closer to his fellow prisoner.

In the rear wall the ape-man discovered a window. It was small and high set. The night was so dark that he could not tell whether it opened onto the outdoors or into another apartment of the building. As an avenue of escape the window appeared quite useless, as it was much too small to accommodate the body of a man.

As Tarzan was examining the window he was close to the corner where the other man sat, and now he heard a movement there. He also noticed that the fellow's breathing had increased in rapidity, as though he were nervous or excited. At last a voice sounded through the darkness.

"What are you doing?" it demanded.

"Examining the cell," replied Tarzan.

"It will do you no good, if you are looking for a way to escape," said the voice. "You won't get out of here until they take you out, no more than I shall."

Tarzan made no reply. There seemed nothing to say; and Tarzan seldom speaks, even when others might find much to say. He went on with his examination of the room. Passing the other occupant, he felt along the fourth and last wall; but his search revealed nothing to repay the effort. He was in a small, rectangular cell of stone that was furnished with a long bench at one end and had a door and a window letting into it.

Tarzan walked to the far end of the room and sat down upon the bench. He was cold, wet, and hungry; but he was unafraid. He was thinking of all that had transpired since night had fallen and left him to the mercy of the storm; he wondered what the morrow held for him. It occurred to him that perhaps he had made a mistake in not attempting a break for liberty before his captors had succeeded in locking him in a cell from which there seemed little likelihood that he could escape at all, for in common with all animals he loathed captivity. However, here he was, locked up securely; and there seemed nothing to do but make the best of it. Someday they would take him out or unlock his cell door; then, unless he had learned that their intentions toward him were prompted by friendliness, he would take advantage of any opportunity that might be offered to escape.

Presently the man in the corner of the cell addressed him. "Who are you?" he asked. "When they brought you in I saw by the light of the torches that you are neither a Cathnean nor an Athnean." The man's voice was coarse, his tones gruff; he demanded rather than requested. This did not please Tarzan, so he did not reply. "What's the matter?" growled his fellow prisoner. "Are you dumb?" His voice was raised angrily.

"Nor deaf," replied the ape-man. "You do not have to shout at me."

The other was silent for a short time; then he spoke in an altered tone. "We may be locked in this hole together for a long time," he said. "We might as well be friends."

"As you will," replied Tarzan, his involuntary shrug passing unnoticed in the darkness of the cell.

"My name is Phobeg," said the man; "what is yours?"

"Tarzan," replied the ape-man.

"Are you either Cathnean or Athnean?"

"Neither; I am from a country far to the south."

"You would be better off had you stayed there," offered Phobeg. "How do you happen to be here in Cathne?"

"I was lost," explained the ape-man, who had no intention of telling the entire truth and thus identifying himself as a friend of one of the Cathneans' enemies. "I was caught in the flood and carried down the river to your city. Here they captured me and accused me of coming to assassinate your Queen."

"So they think you came to assassinate Nemone! Well, whether you did come for that purpose or not will make no difference."

"What do you mean?" demanded Tarzan.

"I mean that in any event you will be killed in one way or another," explained Phobeg, "whatever way will best amuse Nemone."

"Nemone is your Queen?" inquired the ape-man indifferently.

"By the mane of god, she is all that and more!" exclaimed Phobeg fervently. "Such a Queen there never has been in Onthar or Thenar before nor ever will be again. By the teeth of the great one! She makes them all stand around, the priests, the captains, and the councillors."

"But why should she have me destroyed who am only a stranger that became lost?"

"We keep no white men prisoners, only blacks as slaves. Now, were you a woman you would not be killed; and were you a very good-looking woman (not too good-looking, however) you would be assured a life of ease and luxury. But you are only a man; so you will be killed to furnish a pleasurable break in the monotony of Nemone's life."

"And what would happen to a *too* good-looking woman?" asked Tarzan.

"Enough, if Nemone saw her," replied Phobeg meaningly. "To be more beautiful than the Queen is equivalent to high treason in the estimation of Nemone. Why, men hide their wives and daughters if they think that they are too beautiful; but there are few who would risk hiding an alien prisoner.

"I know a man who has a very ugly wife," continued Phobeg, "who never comes out of her house in the daytime. She tells her neighbors that her husband keeps her hidden for fear Nemone will see her. Then there was another who *was* too beautiful. Her husband tried to keep her hidden from Nemone, but one day the Queen saw her and ordered her nose and ears cut off. Yes, I am glad that I am an ugly man rather than a beautiful woman."

"Is the Queen beautiful?" asked Tarzan.

"Yes, by the claws of the all-high, she is the most beautiful woman in the world."

"Knowing her policy, as you have explained it," remarked the ape-man, "I can readily believe that she may be the most beautiful woman in Cathne and quite sure of remaining so as long as she lives and is Queen."

"Do not mistake me," said Phobeg; "Nemone *is* beautiful; but," and he lowered his voice to a whisper, "she is a she-Satan. Even I who have served her faithfully may not look to her for mercy."

"What did you do to get here?" inquired the ape-man.

"I accidentally stepped on god's tail," replied Phobeg gloomily.

The man's strange oaths had not gone unnoticed by Tarzan, and now this latest remarkable reference to deity astounded him; but contact with strange peoples had taught him to learn certain things concerning them by observation and experience rather than by direct questioning, matters of religion being chief among these; so now he only commented, "And therefore you are being punished."

"Not yet," replied Phobeg. "The form of my punishment has not yet been decided. If Nemone has other amusements I may escape punishment, or I may come through my trial successfully and be freed; but the chances are all against me, for Nemone seldom has sufficient bloody amusement to sate her.

"Of course, if she leaves the decision of my guilt or innocence to the chances of an encounter with a single man I shall doubtless be successful in proving the latter, for I am very strong; and there is no better sword- or spearman in Cathne; but I should have less chance against a lion, while, faced by the eternal fires of frowning Xarator, all men are guilty."

Although the man spoke the language Valthor had taught the ape-man and he understood the words, the meaning of what he said was as Greek to Tarzan. He could not quite grasp what the amusements of the Queen had to do with the administration of justice even though the inferences to be derived from Phobeg's remarks seemed apparent; the conclusion was too sinister to be entertained by the noble mind of the Lord of the Jungle.

He was still considering the subject and wondering about the eternal fires of frowning Xarator when sleep overcame his physical discomforts and merged his speculations with his dreams; and to the south another jungle beast crouched in the shelter of a rocky ledge while the storm that had betrayed Tarzan to new enemies wasted its waning wrath and passed on into the nothingness that is the sepulcher of storms; then as the new day dawned bright and clear he arose and stepped out into the sunlight, the great lion that we have seen before, the great lion with the golden coat and the black mane.

He sniffed the morning air and stretched, yawning. His sinuous tail twitched nervously as he looked about over the vast domain that was his because he was there, as every wilderness is the domain of the king of beasts while his majesty is in residence.

From the slight elevation upon which he stood, his yellow-green eyes surveyed a broad plain, tree dotted. There was game there in plenty: wildebeest, zebra, giraffe, koodoo, and hartebeest; and the king was hungry, for the rain had prevented his making a kill the previous night. He blinked his yellow-green eyes in the new sunlight and strode majestically down toward the plain and his breakfast, as, many miles to the north, a black slave accompanied by two warriors brought breakfast to another lord of the jungle in a prison cell at Cathne.

At the sound of footsteps approaching his prison Tarzan awoke and arose from the cold stone floor where he had been sleeping. Phobeg sat upon the edge of the wooden bench and watched the door.

"They bring us food or death," he said; "one never knows."

The ape-man made no reply. He stood there waiting until the door swung open and the slave entered with the food in a rough earthen bowl and water in a glazed jug; he looked at the two warriors standing in the open doorway and at the sunlit court-yard beyond them. What was passing in that savage mind? Perhaps the warriors would have been less at ease could they have known, but the ape-man made no move. Curiosity kept him prisoner there quite as much as armed men or sturdy door, and now he only *looked* beyond the two warriors who were eyeing him intently. They had not been on duty the night before and had not seen him, but they had heard of him. His feat with his strange weapon been told them by their fellows.

"So this is the wild-man!" exclaimed one.

"You had better be careful, Phobeg," said the other. "I should hate to be locked up in a cell with a wild-man"; then, laughing at his joke, he slammed the door after the slave had come out; and the three went away.

Phobeg was appraising Tarzan with a new eye; his naked-ness took on a new meaning in the light of that descriptive term, wild-man. Phobeg noted the great height of his cellmate, the expanse of his chest, and his narrow hips; but he greatly underestimated the strength of the symmetrical muscles that flowed so smoothly beneath the bronzed hide; then he glanced at his own gnarled and knotted muscles and was satisfied.

"So you are a wild-man!" he demanded. "How wild are you?"

Tarzan turned slowly toward the speaker. He thought that he recognized thinly veiled sarcasm in the tone of Phobeg's voice. For the first time he saw his companion in the light of day. He saw a man a few inches shorter than himself but of mighty build, a man of great girth and bulging muscles, a man who might outweigh the Lord of the Jungle by fifty pounds. He noted his prominent jaw, his receding forehead, and his small eyes. In silence Tarzan regarded Phobeg.

"Why don't you answer?" demanded the Cathnean.

"Do not be a fool," admonished Tarzan. "I recall that last night you said that as we might be confined here for a long time we might as well be friends. We cannot be friends by insulting one another. Food is here. Let us eat."

Phobeg grunted and inserted one of his big paws into the pot the slave had brought. As there was no knife or fork or spoon, Tarzan had no alternative but to do likewise if he wished to eat; and so he too took food from the pot with his fingers. The food was meat; it was tough and stringy and undercooked; had it been raw Tarzan had been better suited.

Phobeg chewed assiduously upon a mouthful of the meat until he had reduced the fibers to a pulp that would pass down his throat. "An old lion must have died yesterday," he remarked, "a very old lion."

"If we acquire the characteristics of the creatures we eat, as many men believe," Tarzan replied, "we should soon die of old age on this diet."

"Yesterday I had a piece of goat's meat from Thenar," said Phobeg. "It was strong and none too tender, but it was better than this. I am accustomed to good food. In the temple the priests live as well as the nobles do in the palace, and so the temple guard lives well on the leavings of the priests. I was a member of the temple guard. I was the strongest man on the guard. I am the strongest man in Cathne. When raiders come from Thenar, or when I am taken there on raids the nobles marvel at my strength and bravery. I am afraid of nothing. With my bare hands I have killed men. Did you ever see a man like me?"

"No," admitted the ape-man.

"Yes, it is well that we should be friends," continued Phobeg, "well for you. Everyone wants to be friends with me, for they have learned that my enemies get their necks twisted. I take them like this, by the head and the neck," and with his great paws he went through a pantomine of seizing and twisting; "then, crack! their spines break. What do you think of that?"

"I should think that your enemies would find that very uncomfortable," replied Tarzan.

"Uncomfortable!" ejaculated Phobeg. "Why, man, it kills them!"

"At least they can no longer hear," commented the Lord of the Jungle.

"Of course they cannot hear; they are dead. I do not see what that has to do with it."

"That does not surprise me," Tarzan assured him.

"What does not surprise you?" demanded Phobeg. "That they are dead? or that they cannot hear?"

"I am not easily surprised by anything," explained the ape-man.

Beneath his low forehead Phobeg's brows were knitted in thought. He scratched his head. "What were we talking about?" he demanded.

"We were trying to decide which would be more terrible," explained Tarzan patiently, "to have you for a friend or an enemy."

Phobeg looked at his companion for a long time. One could almost see the laborious effort of cerebration going on beneath that thick skull. Then he shook his head. "That is not what we were talking about at all," he grumbled. "Now I have forgotten. I never saw anyone as stupid as you. When they called you a wild-man they must have meant a crazy man. And I have got to remain locked in here with you for no one knows how long."

"You can always get rid of me," said Tarzan quite seriously.

"How can I get rid of you?" demanded the Cathnean.

"You can twist my neck, like this." Tarzan mimicked the pantomime in which Phobeg had explained how he rid himself of his enemies.

"I *could* do it," boasted Phobeg, "but then they *would* kill me. No, I shall let you live."

"Thanks," said Tarzan.

"Or at least while we are locked up here together," added Phobeg.

Experience had taught Tarzan that the more stupid or ignorant the man the more egotistical he was likely to be, but he had never before encountered such an example of crass stupidity and stupendous egotism as Phobeg presented. To be locked up at all with this brainless mass of flesh was bad enough in itself; but to be on bad terms with it at the same time would make matters infinitely less bearable, and so Tarzan determined to brook everything other than actual physical abuse that he might lighten the galling burden of incarceration.

Loss of liberty represented for Tarzan, as it does for all creatures endowed with brains, the acme of misery, more to be avoided than physical pain, yet, with stoic fortitude he accepted his fate without a murmur of protest; and while his body was confined between the narrow confines of four walls of stone his memories roved the jungle and the veldt and lived again the freedom and the experiences of the past.

He recalled the days of his childhood when fierce Kala, the she-ape that had suckled him at her hairy breast in his infancy, had protected him from the dangers of their savage life; and he recalled her gentleness and her patience with this backward child who must still be carried in her arms long after the balus of her companion shes were able to scurry through the trees seeking their own food and even able to protect themselves against their enemies by flight if nothing more.

These were his first impressions of life, dating back perhaps to his second year while he was still unable to swing through the trees or even make much progress upon the ground. After that he had developed rapidly, far more rapidly than a pampered child of civilization, for upon the quick development of his cunning and his strength depended his life.

With a faint smile he recalled the rage of old Tublat, his foster father, when Tarzan had deliberately undertaken to annoy him. Old "Broken-nose" had always hated Tarzan because the helplessness of his long-drawn infancy had prevented Kala from bearing other apes. Tublat had argued in the meager language of the apes that Tarzan was a weakling that would never become strong enough or clever enough to be of value to the tribe. He wanted Tarzan killed; and he tried to get old Kerchak, the king, to decree his death; so when Tarzan grew old enough to understand, he hated Tublat and sought to annoy him in every way that he could.

His memories of those days brought only smiles now, save only the great tragedy of his life, the death of Kala; but that had occurred later, when he was almost a grown man. She had been saved to him while he needed her most and not taken away until after he was amply able to fend for himself and meet the other denizens of the jungle upon an equal footing. But it was not the protection of those great arms and mighty fangs that he had missed, that he still missed even today; he had missed the maternal love of that savage heart, the only mother-love that he had ever known.

And now his thoughts turned naturally to other friends of the jungle of whom Kala had been first and greatest. There were his many friends among the great apes; there was Tantor, the elephant; there was Jad-bal-ja, the Golden Lion; there was little Nkima. Poor little Nkima! Much to his disgust and amid loud howls, Nkima had been left behind this time when Tarzan set out upon his journey into the north country; but the little monkey had contracted a cold and the ape-man did not wish to expose him to the closing rains of the rainy season.

Tarzan regretted a little that he had not brought Jad-bal-ja with him, for though he could do very well for considerable periods without the companionship of man, he often missed that of the wild beasts that were his friends. Of course the Golden Lion was sometimes an embarrassing companion when one was in contact with human beings; but he was a loyal friend and good company, for only occasionally did he break the silence.

Tarzan recalled the day that he had captured the tiny cub and how he had taught the bitch, Za, to suckle it. What a cub he had been! All lion from the very first. Tarzan sighed as he thought of the days that he and the Golden Lion had hunted and fought together.

7

Nemone

TARZAN HAD THOUGHT, when he went without objection into the prison cell at Cathne, that the next morning he would be questioned and released, or at least be taken from the cell; and once out of the cell again, Tarzan had no intention of returning to it, the Lord of the Jungle being very certain of his own prowess.

But they had not let him out the next morning nor the next nor the next. Perhaps he might have made a break for liberty when food was brought; but each time he thought that the next day would bring his release, and waited.

Imprisonment of any nature galled him, but this experience was rendered infinitely more irksome by the presence of Phobeg. The man annoyed Tarzan; he was ignorant, a braggart, and inclined to be quarrelsome. In the interests of peace the ape-man had tolerated more from his cell-mate than he would have under ordinary circumstances; and Phobeg, being what he was, had assumed that the other's toleration was prompted by fear. Believing this, he became more arrogant and overbearing, ignorant of the fact that he was playing with death.

Phobeg had been imprisoned longer than had Tarzan, and the confinement was making him moody. Sometimes he sat for hours staring at the floor, or, at others, he would mumble to himself, carrying on long conversations which were always acrimonious and that usually resulted in working him up into a rage; then he might seek to vent his spleen upon Tarzan. The fact that Tarzan remained silent under such provocation increased Phobeg's ire; but it also prevented an actual break between them, for it is still a fact, however trite the saying, that it takes two to make a quarrel; and Tarzan would not quarrel; at least, not yet.

"Nemone won't get much entertainment out of you," growled Phobeg this morning after one of his tirades had elicited no response from the ape-man.

"Well, even so," replied Tarzan, "you should more than make up to her any amusement value that I may lack."

"That I will," exclaimed Phobeg. "If it is fighting she wants, she shall see such fighting as she has never seen before when she matches Phobeg with either man or beast; but you! Bah! She will have to pit you against some half-grown child if she wishes to see any fight at all. You have no courage; your veins are filled with water. If she is wise she will dump you into Xarator. By god's tail! I should like to see you there. I'll bet my best habergeon they could hear you scream in Athne."

The ape-man was standing gazing at the little rectangle of sky that he could see through the small, barred opening in the door. He remained silent after Phobeg had ceased speaking, totally ignoring him as though he had not spoken, as though he did not exist. Phobeg became furious. He rose from the bench upon which he had been sitting.

"Coward!" he cried. "Why don't you answer me? By the yellow fangs of Thoos! I've a mind to beat some manners into you, so that you will know enough to answer when your betters speak." He took a step in the direction of the ape-man.

Slowly Tarzan turned toward the angry man, his level gaze fixed upon the other's eyes, and waited. He said nothing, but his attitude was an open book that even the stupid Phobeg could read. And Phobeg hesitated.

Just what might have happened no man may know, for at that instant four warriors came and swung the door of the cell open. "Come with us," said one of them, "both of you."

Phobeg sullenly, Tarzan with the savage dignity of Numa, accompanied the four warriors across the open courtyard and through a doorway that led into a long corridor at the end of which they were ushered into a large room. Here, behind a table, sat seven warriors trapped in ivory and gold. Among them Tarzan recognized the two who had questioned him the night of his capture, old Tomos and the younger Gemnon.

"These are nobles," whispered Phobeg to Tarzan. "That one at the center of the table is old Tomos, the Queen's councillor. He would like to marry the Queen, but I guess he is too old to suit her. The one on his right is Erot. He used to be a common warrior like me; but Nemone took a fancy to him, and now he is the Queen's favorite. She won't marry him though, for he is not of noble blood. The young fellow on Tomos's left is Gemnon. He is from an old and noble family. Warriors who have served him say he is a very decent sort."

As Phobeg gossiped, the two prisoners and their guard had been standing just inside the doorway waiting to be summoned to advance, and Tarzan had had an opportunity to note the architecture and furnishings of the room. The ceiling was low and was supported by a series of engaged columns at regular intervals about the four walls. Between the columns along one side of the room behind the table at which the nobles were seated were unglazed windows, and there were three doorways: that through which Tarzan and Phobeg had been brought, which was directly opposite the windows, and one at either end of the room. The doors themselves were beautifully carved and highly polished, some of the panels containing mosaics of gold and ivory and bits of colored substances.

The floor was of stone, composed of many pieces of different shapes and sizes; but all so nicely fitted that joints were barely discernible. On the floor were a few small rugs either of the skins of lions or of a stiff and heavy wool weave. These latter contained simple designs in several colors and resembled the work of primitive people such as the Navajos of southwestern America.

Upon the walls were paintings depicting battle scenes in which lions and elephants took part with warriors, and always the warriors with the elephants appeared to be suffering defeat, while the warriors with the lions were collecting many heads from fallen foemen. Above these mural paintings was a row of mounted heads encircling the room. These were similar to those Tarzan had seen in the guardroom the night of his coming to Cathne and differed from them only in that they were better specimens and better mounted. Perhaps, too, the heads of men predominated here, scowling down upon their enemies.

But now Tarzan's examination of the room was interrupted by the voice of Tomos. "Bring the prisoners forward," he directed the under-officer who was one of the four warriors escorting them.

When the two men had been halted upon the opposite side of the table from the nobles, Tomos pointed at Tarzan's companion. "Which is this one?" he demanded.

"He is called Phobeg," replied the under-officer.

"What is the charge against him?"

"He profaned Thoos."

"Who brought the charge?"

"The high priest."

"It was an accident," Phobeg hastened to explain. "I meant no disrespect."

"Silence!" snapped Tomos. Then he pointed at Tarzan. "And this one?" he demanded. "Who is he?"

"This is the one who calls himself Tarzan," explained Gemnon. "You will recall that you and I examined him the night he was captured."

"Yes, yes," said Tomos; "I recall. He carried some sort of strange weapon."

"Is he the man of whom you told me," asked Erot, "the one who came from Athne to assassinate the Queen?"

"This is the one," replied Tomos; "he came at night during the last storm and succeeded in making his way into the palace grounds after dark before he was discovered and arrested."

"He does not greatly resemble an Athnean," commented Erot.

"I am not," said Tarzan.

"Silence!" commanded Tomos.

"Why should I be silent?" demanded Tarzan. "There is none other to speak for me than myself; therefore I shall speak for myself. I am no enemy of your people, nor are my people at war with yours. I demand my liberty!"

"He demands his liberty," mimicked Erot and laughed aloud as though it was a good joke; "the slave *demands* his liberty!"

Tomos half rose from his seat, his face purple with rage. He banged the table with his fist. He pointed a finger at Tarzan. "Speak when you are spoken to, slave, and not otherwise; and when Tomos, the councillor, tells you to be silent, be silent."

"I have spoken," said Tarzan; "when I choose to speak again, I shall speak."

"We have a way of silencing impudent slaves, forever," sneered Erot.

"It is evident that he is a man from a far country," interjected Gemnon. "It is not strange that he neither understands our customs nor recognizes the great among us. Perhaps we should listen to him. If he is not an Athnean and no enemy, why should we imprison him or punish him?"

"He came over the palace walls at night," retorted Tomos. "He could have come for but one purpose, to kill our Queen; therefore he must die. The manner of his death shall be at the pleasure of Nemone, our sweet and gracious Queen."

"He told us that the river washed him down to Cathne," persisted Gemnon. "It was a very dark night and he did not know where he was when he finally succeeded in crawling ashore; it was only chance that brought him to the palace."

"A pretty story but not plausible," countered Erot.

"Why not plausible?" demanded Gemnon. "I think it quite plausible. We know that no man could have swum the river in the flood that was raging that night, and that this man could not have reached the spot at which he climbed the wall except by swimming the river or crossing the Bridge of Gold. We know that he did not cross the bridge, because the bridge was well guarded and no one crossed that night. Knowing therefore that he did not cross the bridge and could not have swum the river, we know that the only way he could have reached that particular spot upon the river's bank was by being swept downstream from above. I believe his story, and I believe that we should treat him as an honorable warrior from some distant kingdom until we have better reasons than we now have for believing otherwise."

"I should not care to be the one to defend a man who came here to kill the Queen," sneered Erot meaningly.

"Enough of this!" said Tomos curtly. "The man shall be judged fairly and destroyed as Nemone thinks best."

As he ceased speaking, a door at one end of the room opened and a noble resplendent in ivory and gold stepped into the chamber. Halting just within the threshold, he faced the nobles at the table.

"The Queen!" he announced in a loud voice and then stepped aside.

All eyes turned in the direction of the doorway and at the same time the nobles rose to their feet and then kneeled upon the floor, facing the doorway through which the Queen would enter. The warriors on guard, including those with Tarzan and Phobeg, did likewise, Phobeg following their example. Everyone in the room kneeled except the noble who had announced the Queen, or rather every Cathnean. Tarzan of the Apes did not kneel.

"Down, jackal!" growled one of the guards in a whisper, and then amidst deathly silence a woman stepped into view and paused, framed in the carved casing of the doorway. Regal, she stood there glancing indolently about the apartment; then her eyes met those of the ape-man and, for a moment, held there on his. A slight frown of puzzlement contracted her straight brows as she continued on into the room, approaching the table and the kneeling men.

Behind her followed a half dozen richly arrayed nobles, resplendent in burnished gold and gleaming ivory, but as they crossed the chamber Tarzan saw only the gorgeous figure of the Queen. She was clothed more simply than her escort; but that form, which her apparel revealed rather than hid, required no embellishments other than those with which nature had endowed it. She was far more beautiful than the crude Phobeg had painted her.

A narrow diadem set with red stones encircled her brow, confining her glossy black hair; upon either side of her head, covering her ears, a large golden disc depended from the diadem; while from its rear rose a slender filament of gold that curved forward, supporting a large red stone above the center of her head. About her throat was a simple golden band that held a brooch and pendant of ivory in the soft hollow of her neck. Upon her upper arms were similar golden bands supporting triangular, curved ornaments of ivory. A broad band of gold mesh supported her breasts, the band being embellished with horizontal bands of red stones, while from its upper edge depended five narrow triangles of ivory, a large one in the center and two smaller ones on either side.

A girdle about her hips was of gold mesh. It supported another ivory triangle the slender apex of which curved slightly inward between her legs and also her scant skirt of black monkey hair that fell barely to her knees, conforming perfectly to the contours of her body.

About her wrists were numerous bracelets of ivory and gold and around her ankles were vertical strips of ivory held together by leather thongs, identical in form to those worn by Valthor and by the Cathnean men. Her feet were shod with dainty sandals; and as she moved upon them silently across the stone floor, her movements seemed to Tarzan a combination of the seductive languor of the sensualist and the sinuous grace and savage alertness of the tigress.

That she was marvelously beautiful by the standards of any land or any time grew more apparent to the Lord of the Jungle as she came nearer to him, yet her presence exhaled a subtle essence that left him wondering if her beauty were the reflection of a nature all good or all evil, for her mien and bearing suggested that there could be no compromise—Nemone, the Queen, was all one or all the other.

She kept her eyes upon him as she crossed the room slowly, and Tarzan did not drop his own from hers. There was neither boldness nor rudeness in his gaze, perhaps there was not even interest—it was the noncommittal, cautious appraisal of the wild beast that watches a creature which it neither fears nor desires.

The quizzical frown still furrowed Nemone's smooth brow

as she reached the end of the table where the nobles kneeled. It was not an angry frown, and there might have been in it much of interest and something of amusement, for unusual things interested and amused Nemone, so rare were they in the monotony of her life; and it was certainly unusual to see one who did not accord her the homage due a queen.

As she halted she turned her eyes upon the kneeling nobles. "Arise!" she commanded, and in that single word the vibrant qualities of her rich, deep voice sent a strange thrill through the ape-man. "Who is this that does not kneel to Nemone?" she demanded, her gaze now returned to the bronzed figure standing impassively before her.

As Tarzan had been standing behind the nobles as they had turned to face Nemone when they kneeled, only two of his guards had been aware of his dereliction; but now as they arose and faced about, their countenances were filled with horror and rage when they discovered that the strange captive had so affronted their Queen.

Tomos went purple again. He spluttered with rage. "He is an ignorant and impudent savage, my Queen," he said; "but as he is about to die his actions are of no consequence."

"Why is he about to die?" demanded Nemone. "And how is he to die?"

"He is to die because he came here in the dead of night to assassinate your majesty," explained Tomos; "the manner of his death rests of course in the hands of our gracious Queen."

Nemone's dark eyes, veiled behind long lashes, appraised the ape-man, lingering upon his bronzed skin and the rolling contours of his muscles; then rose to the handsome face until her eyes met his. "Why did you not kneel?" she asked.

"Why should I kneel to you who they have said will have me killed?" demanded Tarzan. "Why should I kneel to you who are not my Queen? Why should I, Tarzan of the Apes, who kneels to no one, kneel to you?"

"Silence!" cried Tomos. "Your impertinence knows no bounds. Do you not realize, ignorant slave, low savage, that you are addressing Nemone, the Queen!"

Tarzan made no reply; he did not even look at Tomos; his

eyes were fixed upon Nemone. She fascinated him; but whether as a thing of beauty or a thing of evil, he did not know. He only knew that few women, other than La, the High Priestess of the Flaming God, had ever so wholly aroused his interest and his curiosity.

Tomos turned to the under-officer in command of the escort that was guarding Tarzan and Phobeg. "Take them away!" he snapped. "Take them back to their cell until we are ready to destroy them."

"Wait," said Nemone. "I would know more of this man," and then she turned to Tarzan. "So you came to kill me!" Her voice was smooth, almost caressing. At the moment the woman reminded Tarzan of a cat that is playing with its victim. "Perhaps they chose a good man for the purpose; you look as though you might be equal to any feat of arms."

"Killing a woman is no feat of arms," replied Tarzan. "I do not kill women. I did not come here to kill you."

"Then why did you come to Onthar?" inquired the Queen in her silky voice.

"That I have already explained twice to that old man with the red face," replied Tarzan, nodding in the general direction of Tomos. "Ask him; I am tired of explaining to people who have already decided to kill me."

Tomos trembled with rage and half drew his slender, dagger-like sword. "Let me destroy him, my Queen," he cried. "Let me wipe out the affront he has put upon my beloved ruler."

Nemone had flushed angrily at Tarzan's words, but she did not lose control of herself. "Sheathe your sword, Tomos," she commanded icily; "Nemone is competent to decide when she is affronted and what steps to take. The fellow is indeed impertinent; but it seems to me that if he affronted anyone, it was Tomos he affronted and not Nemone. However, his temerity shall not go unpunished. Who is this other?"

"He is a temple guard named Phobeg," explained Erot. "He profaned Thoos."

"It would amuse us," said Nemone, "to see these two men fight upon the Field of the Lions. Let them fight without other weapons than those which Thoos has given them. To the victor, freedom," she hesitated momentarily, "freedom within limits. Take them away!"

8

Upon the Field of the Lions

TARZAN AND PHOBEG were back in their little stone cell; the ape-man had not escaped. He had had no opportunity to escape on the way back to his prison, for the warriors who guarded him had redoubled their vigilance, having been cautioned to do so by Erot, and the point of two spears had been kept constantly against his body.

Phobeg was moody and thoughtful. The attitude of his fellow prisoner during their examination by the nobles, his seeming indifference to the majesty and power of Nemone, had tended to alter Phobeg's former estimate of the ape-man's courage. He realized now that the fellow was either a very brave man or a very great fool; and he hoped that he was the latter; for Phobeg was to be pitted against him upon the Field of the Lions, possibly on the morrow.

Phobeg was stupid, but past experience had taught him something of the psychology of mortal combat. He knew that when a man went into battle fearing his antagonist he was already handicapped and partly defeated. Now Phobeg did not fear Tarzan; he was too stupid and too ignorant to anticipate fear. Facing probable defeat and death, he could be overcome by fear and even cowardice; but he was of too low an order, mentally, to visualize either in imagination, except in a rather vague and hazy way.

Tarzan, on the other hand, was of an entirely different temperament; and though he never knew fear it was for a very different reason. Being intelligent and imaginative, he could visualize all the possibilities of an impending encounter; but he could never know fear, because death held no terrors for him; and he had learned to suffer physical pain without the usually attendant horrors of mental anguish. Therefore, if he thought about the coming combat at all, he was not overconfident nor fearful nor nervous. Could he have known what was in the fellow's mind when he commenced to speak he would have been amused.

"It will doubtless be tomorrow," said Phobeg grimly.

"What will be tomorrow?" enquired the ape-man.

"The combat in which I shall kill you," explained the cheerful Phobeg.

"Oh, so you are going to kill me! Phobeg, I am surprised. I thought that you were my friend." Tarzan's tone was serious, though a brighter man than Phobeg might have discovered in it a note of banter; but Phobeg was not bright at all, and he thought that Tarzan was already commencing to throw himself upon his mercy.

"It will soon be over," Phobeg assured him. "I promise that I shall not let you suffer long."

"I suppose that you will twist my neck like this," said Tarzan, pretending to twist something with his two hands.

"M-m-m, perhaps," admitted Phobeg: "but I shall have to throw you about a bit first. We must amuse Nemone, you know."

"Surely, by all means!" assented Tarzan. "But suppose you should not be able to throw me about? Suppose that I should throw you about? Would that amuse Nemone? Or perhaps it would amuse you!"

Phobeg laughed. "It amuses me very much just to think about it," he said, "and I hope that it amuses you to think about it, for that is as near as you will ever come to throwing Phobeg about; have I not told you that I am the strongest man in Cathne?"

"Oh, of course," admitted Tarzan. "I had forgotten that for the moment."

"You would do well to try to remember it," advised Phobeg, "or otherwise our combat will not be interesting at all."

"And Nemone would not be amused! That would be sad. We should make it as interesting and exciting as possible, and you must not conclude it too soon."

"You are right about that," agreed Phobeg. "The better it is the more generous will Nemone feel toward me when it is over; she may even give me a donation in addition to my liberty if we amuse her well.

"By the belly of Thoos!" he exclaimed, slapping his thigh. "We must make a good fight of it and a long one. Now listen! How would this be? At first we shall pretend that you are defeating me; I shall let you throw me about a bit. You see? Then I shall get the better of it for a while, and then you. We shall take turns up to a certain point, and then, when I give you the cue, you must pretend to be frightened, and run away from me. I shall then chase you all over the arena, and that will give them a good laugh. When I catch you at last (and you must let me catch you right in front of Nemone) I shall then twist your neck and kill you, but I will do it as painlessly as possible."

"You are very kind," said Tarzan grimly.

"Do you like the plan?" demanded Phobeg. "Is it not a splendid one?"

"It will certainly amuse them," agreed Tarzan, "if it works."

"If it works! Why should it not work? It will, if you do your part."

"But suppose *I* kill *you*?" enquired the Lord of the Jungle.

"There you go again!" exclaimed Phobeg. "I must say that you are a good fellow after all, for you will have your little joke; and I can tell you that there is no one who enjoys a little joke more than Phobeg."

"I hope that you are in the same mood tomorrow," remarked Tarzan.

When the next day dawned the slave and the guard came with a large breakfast for the two prisoners, the best meal that had been served them since they had been imprisoned.

"Eat well," advised one of the warriors, "that you may have strength to fight a good fight for the entertainment of the

Queen. For one of you it is the last meal; so you had both better enjoy it to the full, since there is no telling for which one of you it is the last."

"It is the last for him," said Phobeg, jerking a thumb in the direction of Tarzan.

"It is thus that the betting goes," said the warrior, "but even so one cannot always be sure. The stranger is a large man, and he looks strong."

"There is none so strong as Phobeg," the former temple guard reminded them.

The warrior shrugged. "Perhaps," he admitted, "but I am not betting any money on either of you."

"Twenty drachmas to ten that he runs away from me before the fight is over," offered Phobeg.

"And if he kills you, who will pay me?" demanded the warrior. "No, that is not a good bet," and he went out and closed and locked the door behind him.

An hour later a large detachment of warriors came and took Tarzan and Phobeg from the prison. They led them through the palace grounds and out into an avenue bordered by old trees. It was a lovely avenue flanked by the white and gold homes of the nobles and the great two-storied palace surmounted by its golden domes.

Here were throngs of people waiting to see the start of the pageant and companies of warriors standing at ease, leaning upon their spears. It was an interesting sight to Tarzan who had been so long confined in the gloomy prison. He noted the dress of the civilians and the architecture of the splendid houses that could be glimpsed between the trees. He saw that the men wore short tunics or jerkins that were quite similar to the habergeons worn by the warriors, except that they were of a solid piece of cloth or light leather rather than of discs of elephant hide. The women wore short skirts of hair or cloth or leather, scant, clinging skirts that terminated just above the knees; a band to confine the breasts, sandals, and ornaments completed their simple attire.

Tarzan and Phobeg were escorted west along the avenue; and as they passed, the crowd commented upon them. There were many who knew Phobeg; some shouted encouragement to him; others taunted and insulted him. It appeared that Phobeg's popularity was not citywide. They discussed Tarzan freely but with no malice. He interested them, and there was much speculation as to his chances in a fight against the burly temple guard. The ape-man heard many wagers offered and taken; some were on him and some against; but it was evident that Phobeg was the favored of the bettors.

At the end of the avenue Tarzan saw the great Bridge of Gold that spanned the river. It was a splendid structure built entirely of the precious metal. Two golden lions of heroic size flanked the approach from the city, and as he was led across the bridge the ape-man saw two identical lions guarding the western end.

Out upon the plain that is called the Field of the Lions a crowd of spectators was filing toward a point about a mile from the city where many people were congregated, and toward this assemblage the detachment escorted the two gladiators. Here was a large, oval arena excavated to a depth of twenty or thirty feet in the floor of the plain. Upon the excavated earth piled symmetrically around the edges of the pit, and terraced from the plain level to the top, were arranged slabs of stone to serve as seats. At the east end of the arena was a wide ramp descending into it. Spanning the ramp was a low arch surmounted by the loges of the Queen and high nobility.

As Tarzan passed beneath the arch and descended the ramp toward the arena, he saw that nearly half the seats were already taken. The people were eating food that they had brought with them, and there was much laughter and talking. Evidently it was a gala day. He asked Phobeg.

"This is part of the celebration that annually follows the ending of the rainy season," explained the Cathnean. "There is entertainment of some sort here at least once a month and oftener when the weather permits. You will have an opportunity to see all the events before I kill you, as our combat will undoubtedly be the last event upon the program."

The warriors conducted the two men to the far end of the arena where a terrace had been cut partway up the sloping side of the arena, a wooden ladder leaning against the wall giving access to it. Here, upon this terrace, Tarzan and Phobeg were installed with a few warriors to serve as guards.

Presently, from the direction of the city, Tarzan heard the music of drums and trumpets.

"Here they come!" cried Phobeg.

"Who?" asked Tarzan.

"The Queen and the lion men," replied his adversary.

"What are the lion men?" enquired Tarzan.

"They are the nobles," explained Phobeg. "Really only the hereditary nobles are members of the clan of lions, but we usually speak of all nobles as lion men. Erot is a noble because Nemone has created him one; but he is not a lion man, as he was not born a noble."

"Cleave my skull! but I bet he hates that," commented one of the guard.

"He'd give a right eye to be a lion man," said Phobeg.

"It's too late now," observed the warrior; "he should have picked his parents more carefully."

"He claims that he did pick a noble father," explained Phobeg, "but his mother denies it."

Another warrior laughed. "Son of a noble!" he scoffed. "I know old Tibdos, the husband of Erot's mother; I know him well. He cleans the lions' cages at the breeding farm. Erot looks just like him. Son of a noble!"

"Son of a she-jackal!" growled Phobeg. "I wish I were to fight him today instead of this poor fellow."

"You feel sorry for him?" enquired a warrior.

"Yes, in a way," replied Phobeg. "He is not a half bad fellow, and I have nothing against him except that he is stupid. He cannot seem to understand the simplest things. He does not seem to realize that I am the strongest man in Cathne and that I am going to kill him this afternoon, unless they get through with the other events early and I kill him this morning."

"How do you know that he does not realize these things?" demanded the warrior.

"Because he has never given any sign that he is very much afraid."

"Possibly he does not believe that you can kill him," suggested the warrior.

"Then that proves that he is very stupid; but stupid or not, I am going to kill him. I am going to twist his neck until his spine breaks. I can scarcely wait to get my hands on him; of all the things that I love there is no sensation equal to that of killing a man. I love that better than I love women."

Tarzan glanced at the great hulk squatting beside him. "The French have a word for that," he remarked.

"I do not know what you are talking about," growled Phobeg.

"I am not surprised."

"There he goes again!" exclaimed Phobeg. "What sense is there to that? Did I not tell you that he is stupid?"

Now the blaring of the trumpets and the beating of the drums burst with increased volume upon their ears, and Tarzan saw that the musicians were marching down the ramp into the arena at the far end of the great oval. At the same time the tumult in the stands increased as new thousands surged over the rim of the stadium and sought seats among the thousands already there.

Behind the music marched a company of warriors, and from each spear head fluttered a colored pennon. It was a stirring and colorful picture, but nothing to what followed.

A few yards in rear of the warriors came a chariot of gold drawn by four maned lions, where, half reclining upon a couch draped with furs and gaily colored cloths, rode Nemone, the Queen. Sixteen black slaves held the lions in leash; and at either side of the chariot marched six nobles resplendent in gold and ivory, while a huge black, marching behind, held a great, red parasol over the Queen. Squatting upon little seats above the rear wheels of the chariot were two small blackamoors wielding feathered fans above her.

At sight of the chariot and its royal occupant, the people in the stands arose and then kneeled down in salute to their ruler, while wave after wave of applause rolled round the amphitheater as the pageant slowly circled the arena.

Behind Nemone's chariot marched another company of

warriors; these were followed by a number of gorgeously decorated wooden chariots, each drawn by two lions and driven by a noble; following these marched a company of nobles on foot, while a third company of warriors brought up the rear.

When the column had circled the arena Nemone quit her chariot and ascended to her loge above the ramp amid the continued cheering of the populace, the chariots driven by the nobles lined up in the center of the arena, the royal guard formed across the entrance to the stadium, and the nobles who had no part in the games went to their private loges.

There followed then in quick succession contests in dagger throwing and in the throwing of spears, feats of strength and skill, and foot races. Upon every event wagers were laid and the whole stadium was a bedlam of shouted wagers and odds, of curses, groans, hoots, laughter, and applause.

In the loges of Nemone and the nobles great sums changed hands upon every event. The Queen was an inveterate gambler, winning or losing a fortune upon the cast of a single dagger. When she won she smiled, and she smiled too when she lost; but men knew that contestants upon whom Nemone won regularly through the year were the recipients of royal favors, while those upon whom she consistently lost often disappeared.

When the minor sports were completed the chariot races began; and upon these the betting dwarfed all the other betting of the day, and men and women acted like maniacs as they encouraged a favorite driver, applauded a winner, or berated an unfortunate loser.

Two drivers raced in each event, the distance being always the same, one lap of the arena, for lions cannot maintain high speed for great distances. After each race the winner received a pennon from the Queen, while the loser drove up the ramp and out of the stadium amid the hoots of those who had lost money on him. Then two more raced, and when the last pair had finished the winners paired off for new events. Thus, by elimination, the contestants were eventually reduced to two, winners in each event in which they had contested. This, then, was the premiere racing event of the day, and the noise and the betting that it engendered surpassed all that had gone before.

The winner of this final race was acclaimed champion of the day and was presented with a golden helmet by Nemone herself, and even those who had bet upon his rival and lost their money added their voices to the ovation that the noisy throng accorded him as he drove proudly around the arena and disappeared up the ramp beneath the arch of the Queen, his golden helmet shining bravely in the sun.

"Now," said Phobeg in a loud voice, "the people are going to see something worthwhile. It is what they have been waiting for, and they will not be disappointed. If you have a god, fellow, pray to him, for you are about to die."

"Are you not going to permit me to run around the arena first while you chase me?" demanded Tarzan.

9

"Death! Death!"

A SCORE OF slaves were busily cleaning up the arena following the departure of the lion-drawn chariots, the audience was standing and stretching itself, nobles were wandering from loge to loge visiting their friends, men and women were settling up past wagers and making new ones. The sounds of many voices enveloped the stadium in one mighty discord. The period was one of intermission between events.

Tarzan was annoyed. Crowds irritated his nerves. The sound of human voices was obnoxious to him. Through narrowed lids he surveyed the scene. If ever a wild beast looked upon its enemies it was then.

Phobeg was still boasting in a loud voice that was clearly audible to at least a portion of the audience sitting just above the gladiators' ledge. The attitude of the temple guard was anything but soothing to the Lord of the Jungle, but by no sign did he intimate that he heard him after his first retort.

Already the betting was running high on this last event of the day, though only a small proportion of the audience had had a fair view of the two contestants by which they might compare them. Phobeg, however, was known by reputation and was the favorite, the odds running as high as ten to one against Tarzan.

In the royal loge Nemone lay back luxuriously in the great chair that was half a throne and half a couch. She had lost heavily during the day, but she showed no ill humor. However, the nobles surrounding her were ill at ease and hoped that she would win on this last event. Each was determined to bet heavily upon the strange wild-man with Nemone, so that she might win back all that she had lost to them upon earlier events, for all were assured that Nemone would back Phobeg, it being her custom to bet heavily upon all favorites.

Erot was particularly anxious that the Queen should win back what he had won from her. For some time he had been a trifle uncertain as to his position in the good graces of his sovereign; he had sensed, perhaps, that he was slipping a little; and he had had sufficient experience to know that winning money from Nemone constituted nothing less than a tremendous shove to one who had started to slip.

Therefore Erot, with the other nobles, having determined to let Nemone win their money on Phobeg sent slaves out into the audience secretly to place money enough on Phobeg to reimburse them what they lost to Nemone on Tarzan. The plan was accurately figured and neatly worked, and when the day was over Nemone would be winner and so would they, all of their losses having been more than made up by their winnings on Phobeg, which the common people would have paid.

This large volume of money going suddenly among the audience which was already favoring Phobeg and offering large odds against Tarzan found very little Tarzan money available at ten to one. The natural result was that to place their money at all they had to offer large odds, and to reimburse themselves of their losses to Nemone, or rather their assumed losses, for no wagers had yet been laid in the royal loge, they were compelled to put up enormous sums as the odds soared upward finally until it took one hundred Phobeg drachmas to cover one of Tarzan's.

Now a trumpet sounded, and the warriors guarding Tarzan and Phobeg ordered them down into the arena and paraded them once around it that the people might compare the gladiators and choose a favorite. As they passed before the royal loge Nemone leaned forward with half-closed eyes surveying the tall stranger and the squat Cathnean.

Erot, the Queen's favorite, watched her. "A thousand drachmas on the stranger!" he cried.

"I am betting on the stranger, too," interjected another noble eagerly.

"So am I," said Nemone.

Erot and the other nobles were amazed; this upset their plans completely. Of course they would win more money, but one always felt safer losing to Nemone than winning from her.

"You will lose your money," Erot told her.

"Then why did you offer to bet on the stranger?" demanded the Queen.

"The odds were so attractive that I was tempted into taking a chance," explained Erot quickly.

"What are the odds now?"

"One hundred to one."

"And you think the stranger may not have even one chance in a hundred of winning?" demanded Nemone, toying idly with the hilt of her dagger.

"Phobeg is the strongest man in Cathne," said Erot. "I really think that the stranger has no chance at all against him; he is as good as dead already."

"Very well then, if you feel that way about it you should bet on Phobeg," whispered Nemone softly. "I am going to wager 100,000 drachmas on the stranger. How much of this do you wish, my dear Erot?"

"I wish that my Queen would not risk her money on him at all," said Erot; "I am grieved when my beloved Queen loses."

"You bore me, Erot." Nemone gestured impatiently and then, turning to the other nobles, "Is there none here who will cover my drachmas?"

Instantly they were all eager to accomodate her. To win a hundred thousand drachmas from the Queen in addition to all that they would win from the common people was too much for their cupidity; they even forgot Nemone's possible wrath in their anxiety to accommodate her now that it was certain that her decision could not be altered, and in a few minutes the bets had been recorded.

"He has a fine physique," commented Nemone, her eyes upon the jungle lord, "and he is taller than the other."

"But look at Phobeg's muscles," Erot reminded her. "This Phobeg has killed many men; they say that he twists their necks and breaks their spines."

"We shall see," was the Queen's only comment.

Erot thought that he would not like to be in Phobeg's sandals, for if the stranger did not kill him Nemone most certainly would see that he did not long survive, who had robbed her of a hundred thousand drachmas.

Now the two men were posted in the arena a short distance from the royal loge, and the captain of the stadium was giving them their instructions which were extremely simple: they were to remain inside the arena and try to kill one another with their bare hands, though the use of elbows, knees, feet, or teeth was not barred; there were no other rules governing the combat. The winner was to receive his freedom, though even this had been qualified by Nemone.

"When the trumpet sounds you may attack," said the captain of the stadium. "And may Thoos be with you."

Tarzan and Phobeg had been placed ten paces apart. Now they stood waiting the signal. Phobeg swelled his chest and beat upon it with his fists; he flexed his arms, swelling the great muscles of his biceps until they stood out like great knotty balls; then he hopped about, warming up his leg muscles. He was attracting all the attention, and that pleased him excessively.

Tarzan stood quietly, his arms folded loosely across his chest, his muscles relaxed. He appeared totally unconscious of the presence of the noisy multitude or even of Phobeg, but he was not unconscious of anything that was transpiring about him. His eyes and his ears were alert; it would be Tarzan who would hear the first note of the trumpet's signal; Tarzan was ready!

Tarzan cared nothing for the stupid men-things making silly noises in their throats, gathered here to see two fellow creatures that had never harmed them try to kill one another for their pleasure; he did not care what they thought about him; to him they were less than the droppings of lions that the slaves had swept up in the arena.

He did not wish to kill Phobeg, nor did he wish to be killed; but Phobeg disgusted him, and he would have liked to punish the man for his ridiculous egotism. He realized that his antagonist was a mighty man and that it might not be an easy thing to punish him without taking a great deal of punishment himself, but this risk he did not mind so that he could halt his own punishment short of crippling or death. His gaze chanced to cross the royal loge; it halted there; the eyes of Nemone met his and held them. What strange eyes were hers—so beautiful, with fires burning far beneath the surface, so mysterious!

The trumpet pealed, and Tarzan's eyes swung back to Phobeg. A strange silence fell upon the amphitheater. The two men approached one another, Phobeg strutting and confident, Tarzan with the easy, graceful stride of a lion.

"Say your prayers, fellow!" shouted the temple guard. "I am going to kill you; but first I shall play with you for the amusement of Nemone."

Phobeg came closer and reached for Tarzan. The ape-man let him seize him by the shoulders; then Tarzan cupped his two hands and brought the heels of them up suddenly and with great force beneath Phobeg's chin and at the same time pushed the man from him. The great head snapped back, and the fellow's huge bulk hurtled backward a dozen paces, where Phobeg sat down heavily.

A groan of surprise arose from the audience, interspersed with cheers from those who had wagered on Tarzan. Phobeg scrambled to his feet; his face was contorted with rage; in an instant he had gone berserk. With a roar, he charged the ape-man.

"No quarter!" he screamed. "I kill you *now*!"

"Kill! Kill!" shouted the Phobeg adherents. "Death! Death! Give us a death!"

"Don't you wish to throw me about a bit first?" asked Tarzan in a low voice, as he lightly sidestepped the other's mad charge.

"No!" screamed Phobeg, turning clumsily and charging again. "I kill! I kill!"

Tarzan caught the outstretched hands and spread them wide; then a bronzed arm, lightninglike, clamped about Phobeg's short neck; the ape-man wheeled suddenly about, leaned forward, and hurled his antagonist over his head. Phobeg fell heavily to the sandy gravel of the arena.

Nemone leaned from the royal loge, her eyes flashing, her bosom heaving. Erot was but one of many nobles who experienced a constriction of the diaphragm. Nemone turned to him. "Would you like to bet a little more on the strongest man in Cathne?" she asked.

Erot smiled a sickly smile. "The battle has only commenced," he said.

"But already it is as good as over," taunted Nemone.

Phobeg arose but this time more slowly, nor did he charge again but approached his antagonist warily; his tactics now were very different from what they had been. He wanted to get close enough to Tarzan to get a hold; that was all he desired, just a hold; then, he knew, he could crush the man with his great strength.

Perhaps the ape-man sensed what was in the mind of his foe, perhaps it was just chance that caused him to taunt Phobeg by holding his left wrist out to the other; but whatever it was, Phobeg seized upon the opportunity and, grasping Tarzan's wrist, sought to drag the ape-man into his embrace; then Tarzan stepped in quickly, struck Phobeg a terrific blow in the face with his right fist, seized the wrist of the hand that held his, and, again whirling quickly beneath his victim, threw him heavily once more, using Phobeg's arm as a lever and his own shoulder as a fulcrum.

This time Phobeg had difficulty in arising at all. He came up very slowly. The ape-man was standing over him. The blood froze in the veins of the Cathnean as he heard the low, beastlike growl rumbling in the throat of the stranger.

Suddenly Tarzan stooped and seized Phobeg, and lifting him bodily, held him above his head. "Shall I run now, Phobeg?" he growled, "or are you too tired to chase me?" Then he hurled the man to the ground again a little nearer to the royal loge where Nemone sat, tense and thrilling.

Like a lion with its prey, the Lord of the Jungle followed the man who had taunted him and would have killed him; twice again he picked him up and hurled him closer to the end of the arena. Now the fickle crowd was screaming to Tarzan to kill Phobeg; Phobeg, the strongest man in Cathne; Phobeg, who twisted men's necks until their spines cracked.

Again Tarzan seized his antagonist and held him above his head. Phobeg struggled weakly, but he was quite helpless. Tarzan walked to the side of the arena near the royal loge and hurled the great body up into the audience.

"Take your strong man," he said; "Tarzan does not want *him*." Then he walked away and stood before the ramp, waiting, as though he demanded his freedom.

Amid shrieks and howls that called to Tarzan's mind only the foulest of wild beasts, the loathsome hyena, the crowd hurled the unhappy Phobeg back into the arena. "Kill him! Kill him!" they screamed.

Nemone leaned from her loge. "Kill him, Tarzan!" she cried.

Tarzan shrugged with disgust and turned away.

"Kill him, slave!" commanded a noble from his luxurious loge.

"I shall not kill him," replied the ape-man.

Nemone arose in her loge. She was flushed and excited. "Tarzan!" she cried, and when the ape-man glanced up at her, "why do you not kill him?"

"Why should I kill him?" demanded Tarzan. "He cannot harm me, and I kill only in self-defense or for food; but I do not eat human flesh, so why should I kill him?"

Phobeg, bruised, battered, and helpless, arose weakly to his feet and stood reeling drunkenly. He heard the voice of the pitiless mob screaming for his death. He saw his antagonist standing a few paces away in front of the ramp, paying no attention to him, and dimly and as though from a great distance he had heard him refuse to kill him. He had heard, but he did not comprehend. He expected to be killed, for such was the custom and the law of the arena. He had sought to kill this man; he would have shown him no mercy; so he could not understand the mercy of Tarzan's indifference that had been extended to him.

Phobeg's bloodshot eyes wandered helplessly about the arena, seeking nothing or no one in particular; sympathy was not to be found there, nor mercy, nor any friend; such were not for the vanquished. The frenzied bloodlust of the mob fascinated him. A few minutes ago it had been acclaiming him; now it condemned him to death. His gaze reached the royal loge as Erot leaned far out and shouted to Tarzan standing below.

"Kill him, fellow!" he cried. "It is the Queen's command."

Phobeg's eyes dropped to the figure of the ape-man, and he braced himself for a final effort to delay the inevitable. He knew that he had met one mightier than himself and that he must die when the other wished; but the law of self-preservation compelled him to defend himself, however hopelessly.

The ape-man glanced up at the Queen's favorite. "Tarzan kills only whom it pleases him to kill." He spoke in a low voice that yet carried to the royal loge. "I shall not kill Phobeg."

"You fool," cried Erot, "do you not understand that it is the Queen's wish, that it is the Queen's command, which no one may disobey and live, that you kill the fellow?"

"If the Queen wants him killed, why doesn't she send you down to do it? She is your Queen, not mine." There was neither awe nor respect in the voice of the ape-man.

Erot looked horrified. He glanced at the Queen. "Shall I order the guard to destroy the impudent savage?" he asked.

Nemone shook her head. Her countenance remained inscrutable, but a strange light burned in her eyes. "We give them both their lives," she said. "Set Phobeg free, and bring the other to me in the palace"; then she rose as a sign that the games were over.

Many miles to the south of the Field of the Lions in the valley of Onthar a lion moved restlessly just within the confines of a forest. He paced rapidly first in one direction and then in another; his movements were erratic; sometimes his nose was near the ground and, again, it was in the air as though he were searching for something or someone. Once he raised his head and lifted his great voice in a roar that shook the earth and sent Manu, the monkey, fleeing through the trees with his brothers and sisters. In the distance a bull elephant trumpeted, and then silence fell once more upon the jungle.

10

In the Palace of the Queen

A DETACHMENT OF common warriors commanded by an under-officer had escorted Tarzan to the stadium, but he returned to the city in the company of nobles. Several of them had clustered about him immediately following the gesture of Nemone that had suggested to them that this stranger might be the recipient of further royal favors.

Congratulating him upon his victory, praising his prowess, asking innumerable questions, they followed him from the arena, and at the top of the ramp another noble accosted him. It was Gemnon.

"The Queen has commanded me to accompany you to the city and look after you," he explained. "This evening I am to bring you to her in the palace; but in the meantime you will want to bathe and rest, and I imagine that you might welcome some decent food after the prison fare you have been eating recently."

"I shall be glad of a bath and good food," replied Tarzan, "but why should I rest? I have been doing nothing else for several days."

"But you have just come through a terrific battle for your life!" exclaimed Gemnon. "You must be tired."

Tarzan shrugged his broad shoulders. "Perhaps you had better look after Phobeg instead," he replied. "It is he who needs rest; I am not tired."

327

Gemnon laughed. "Phobeg should consider himself lucky to be alive. If anyone looks after him it will be himself."

They were walking toward the city now. The other nobles had joined their own parties or had dropped behind, and Gemnon and Tarzan were alone, if two may be said to be alone who are surrounded by a chattering mob through which bodies of armed men and lion-drawn chariots are making their slow way. Those near Tarzan were discussing him animatedly, but because of the nobles they kept their distance from him. They commented upon his giant strength and the deceptive appearance of his muscular development, the flowing symmetry of which scarce proclaimed the titanic power of the steel thews of the Lord of the Jungle.

"You are popular now," commented Gemnon.

"A few minutes ago they were screaming at Phobeg to kill me," Tarzan reminded him.

"I am really surprised that they are so friendly," remarked Gemnon. "You cheated them of a death—the one thing they are all hoping and praying to see when they go to the stadium. It is for this they pay their lepta for admission. Also, most of them lost more money betting on Phobeg; but those who won on you should love you, for they won much; the odds were as high as one hundred to one against you.

"It is the nobles, though, who have the greatest grievance against you," continued Gemnon, grinning. "Several of them lost their entire fortunes. Those closest to Nemone always have to cover her bets; and, believing that she would bet on Phobeg, they placed large bets on him among the audience to cover their losses to Nemone; then Nemone insisted upon betting on you, and they had to bet more money on Phobeg—ten million drachmas to cover Nemone's hundred thousand. I estimate that that one small group lost close to twenty million drachmas."

"And Nemone won ten million?" asked Tarzan.

"Yes," replied Gemnon; "which may account for the fact that you are alive now."

"Why should I not be alive?"

"You flouted the Queen; before thousands of her people you refused to obey her direct command. No, not even the ten million drachmas can account for it; there is some other reason why Nemone spared you. Perhaps she is contemplating for you a death that will give her greater satisfaction. Knowing Nemone as I do, I cannot believe that she will let you live; she would not be Nemone if she forgave so serious an affront to her majesty."

"Phobeg was going to kill me," Tarzan reminded him.

"But Nemone is not Phobeg. Nemone is Queen, and—"

"And what?" asked the ape-man.

Gemnon shrugged. "I was thinking aloud, which is a bad habit for one who enjoys life. Doubtless you may live long enough to know her better than you do now and then you can do your own thinking—but do not do it aloud."

"Did you lose much on Phobeg?" enquired Tarzan.

"I won; I bet on you. I met one of Erot's slaves who was going to place some of his master's money on Phobeg; I took it all. You know I had seen a little more of you than the other nobles and I believed that you had a chance, but I was backing your intelligence and agility against Phobeg's strength, stupidity, and awkwardness; even I did not dream that you were stronger than he."

"And the odds were good!"

Gemnon smiled. "Too good to be overlooked; it was more than a reasonable gamble. But I cannot understand Nemone; she is a great bettor but no gambler. She always puts her money on the favorite, and may Thoos help him if he does not win."

"A woman's intuition," suggested the ape-man.

"I think not; Nemone is too practical and calculating to act on intuition alone; she had some other reason. What it is, none knows but Nemone. The same mysterious motivation saved your life today or, perhaps I should say, prolonged it."

"I am going to see her this evening," said Tarzan, "and doubtless I shall affront her again; it seems that I have done so both times that I have seen her."

"Do not forget that she practically sentenced you to death for the first offense," Gemnon reminded him. "At that time she must have been certain that Phobeg would kill you. If I were you I should not annoy her."

When they reached the city, Gemnon took Tarzan to his own quarters in the palace. These consisted of a bedroom and bath in addition to a living room that was shared with another officer. Here Tarzan found the usual decorations of weapons, shields, and mounted heads in addition to pictures painted on leather. He saw no books, nor any other printed matter; neither was there any sign of writing materials in the rooms. He wanted to question Gemnon on this subject, but he found that he had never learned any word for writing or for a written language.

The bath interested the ape-man. The tub was a coffinlike affair made of clay and baked; the plumbing fixtures were apparently all of solid gold. While questioning Gemnon he learned that the water was brought from the mountains east of the city through clay pipes of considerable size and distributed by means of pressure tanks distributed throughout all of urban Cathne.

Gemnon summoned a slave to prepare the bath, and when Tarzan had finished, a meal was awaiting him in the living room. While he was eating, and Gemnon lounged near in conversation, another young noble entered the apartment. He had a narrow face and rather unpleasant eyes, nor was he overly cordial when Gemnon introduced him to Tarzan.

"Xerstle and I are quartered together," Gemnon explained.

"I have orders to move out," snapped Xerstle.

"Why is that?" asked Gemnon.

"To make room for your friend here," replied Xerstle sourly, and then he went into his own room mumbling something about slaves and savages.

"He does not seem pleased," remarked Tarzan.

"But I am," replied Gemnon in a low voice. "Xerstle and I have not gotten along well together. We have nothing in common. He is one of Erot's friends and was elevated from nothing after Erot became Nemone's favorite. He is the son of a foreman at the mines. If they had elevated his father he would have been an acquisition to the nobility, for he is a splendid man; but Xerstle is a rat—like his friend, Erot."

"I have heard something of your nobility," said Tarzan; "I

understand that there are two classes of nobles, and that one class rather looks upon the other with contempt even though a man of the lower class may hold a higher title than many of those in the other class."

"We do not look upon them with contempt if they are worthy men," replied Gemnon. "The old nobility, the Lion Men of Cathne, is hereditary; the other is but temporary—for the lifetime of the man who has received it as a special mark of favor from the throne. In one respect at least it reflects greater glory on its possessor than does hereditary nobility, as it is often the deserved reward of merit. I am a noble by accident of birth; had I not been born a noble I might never have become one. I am a lion man because my father was; I may own lions because, beyond the memory of man, an ancient ancestor of mine led the king's lions to battle."

"What did Erot do to win his patent of nobility?" enquired the ape-man.

Gemnon grimaced. "Whatever services he has rendered have been personal; he has never served the state with distinction. If he owns any distinction, it is that of being the prince of flatterers, the king of sycophants."

"Your Queen seems too intelligent a woman to be duped by flattery."

"No one is, always."

"There are no sycophants among the beasts," said Tarzan.

"What do you mean by that?" demanded Gemnon. "Erot is almost a beast."

"You malign the beasts. Did you ever see a lion that fawned upon another creature to curry favor?"

"But beasts are different," argued Gemnon.

"Yes; they have left all the petty meannesses to man."

"You do not think very highly of men."

"None does who thinks, who compares them with the beasts."

"We are what we are born," rejoined Gemnon; "some are beasts, some are men, and some are men who behave like beasts."

"But none, thank God, are beasts that behave like men," retorted Tarzan, smiling.

Xerstle, entering from his room, interrupted their conversation. "I have gathered my things together," he said; "I shall send a slave for them presently." His manner was short and brusque. Gemnon merely nodded in assent, and Xerstle departed.

"He does not seem pleased," commented the ape-man.

"May Xarator have him!" ejaculated Gemnon; "though he would serve a better purpose as food for my lions," he added as an afterthought, "if they would eat him."

"You own lions?" enquired Tarzan.

"Certainly," replied Gemnon. "I am a lion man and must own lions. It is a caste obligation. Each lion man must own lions of war to fight in the service of the Queen. I have five. In times of peace I use them for hunting and racing. Only royalty and the lion men may own lions."

The sun was setting behind the mountains that rimmed the western edge of the Field of the Lions as a slave entered the apartment with a lighted cresset which he hung at the end of a chain depending from the ceiling.

"It is time for the evening meal," announced Gemnon, rising.

"I have eaten," replied Tarzan.

"Come anyway; it may interest you to meet the other nobles of the palace."

Tarzan arose. "Very well," he said and followed Gemnon from the apartment.

Forty nobles were assembled in a large dining room on the main floor of the palace as Gemnon and Tarzan entered. Tomos was there and Erot and Xerstle; several of the others Tarzan also recognized as having been seen by him before either in the council room or at the stadium. A sudden silence fell upon the assemblage as he entered, as though the men had been interrupted while discussing either him or Gemnon.

"This is Tarzan," announced Gemnon by way of introduction as he led the ape-man to the table.

Tomos, who sat at the head of the table, did not appear pleased. Erot was scowling; it was he who spoke first. "This table is for nobles," he said, "not for slaves."

"By his own prowess and the grace of her majesty, the Queen, this man is here as my guest," said Gemnon quietly. "If one of my equals takes exception to his presence, I will be glad to discuss the matter with swords," and then he turned to Tarzan. "Because this man sits at table with nobles of my own rank I apologize for the inference he intended you to draw from his words. I hope you are not offended."

"Does the jackal offend the lion?" asked the ape-man.

The meal was not a complete success socially. Erot and Xerstle whispered together. Tomos did not speak but applied himself assiduously to the business of eating. Several of Gemnon's friends engaged Tarzan in conversation; and he found one or two of them agreeable, but others were inclined to be patronizing. Possibly they would have been surprised and their attitude toward him different had they known that their guest was a peer of England, but then again this might have made little impression upon them inasmuch as none of them had ever heard of England. However, Tarzan did not enlighten them. He did not care what they thought, and so the meal progressed with many silences.

When Tomos arose and the others were free to go, Gemnon conducted Tarzan to the apartments of the Queen after returning to his own apartments to don a more elaborate habergeon, helmet, and equipment.

"Do not forgot to kneel when we enter the presence of Nemone," cautioned Gemnon, "and do not speak until she addresses you."

A noble received them in a small anteroom where he left them while he went to announce their presence to the Queen, and as they waited Gemnon's eyes watched the tall stranger standing quietly near him.

"Have you no nerves?" he asked presently.

"What do you mean?" demanded the ape-man.

"I have seen the bravest warriors tremble who had been summoned before Nemone," explained his companion.

"I have never trembled," replied Tarzan. "How is it done?"

"Perhaps Nemone will teach you to tremble."

"Perhaps, but why should I tremble to go where a jackal does not tremble to go?"

"I do not understand what you mean by that," said Gemnon puzzled.

"Erot is in there."

Gemnon grinned. "But how do you know that?" he asked.

"I know," said Tarzan; he did not think it necessary to explain that when the noble had opened the door his sensitive nostrils had caught the scent spoor of the Queen's favorite.

"I hope not," said Gemnon, an expression of concern upon his countenance. "If he is there this may be a trap from which you will never come out alive."

"One might fear the Queen," replied Tarzan, "but not the jackal."

"It is the Queen of whom I was thinking."

The noble returned to the anteroom. He nodded to Tarzan. "Her majesty will receive you now," he said. "You may go, Gemnon; your attendance will not be required." Then he turned to the ape-man once more. "When I open the door and announce you, enter the room and kneel. Remain kneeling until the Queen tells you to arise, and do not speak until after her majesty addresses you. Do you hear?"

"I hear," replied Tarzan. "Open the door!"

Gemnon, just leaving the anteroom by another doorway, heard and smiled; but the noble did not smile. He frowned. The bronzed giant had spoken to him in a tone of command, but the noble did not know what to do about it; so he opened the door. But he got some revenge, or at least he thought that he did.

"The slave, Tarzan!" he announced in a loud voice.

The Lord of the Jungle stepped into the adjoining chamber, crossed to the center of it, and stood erect, silently regarding Nemone. He did not kneel. Erot was there standing at the foot of a couch upon which the Queen reclined upon fat pillows. The Queen regarded Tarzan from her deep eyes without any change of expression, but Erot scowled angrily.

"Kneel, you fool!" he commanded.

"Silence!" admonished Nemone. "It is I who give commands." Erot flushed and fingered the golden hilt of his sword.

Tarzan neither spoke nor moved nor took his eyes from the eyes of Nemone. Though he had thought her beautiful before, he realized now that she was even more gorgeous than he had believed it possible for any woman to be.

"I shall not need you again tonight, Erot," said Nemone; "you may go now."

Now Erot paled and then turned fiery red. He started to speak but thought better of it; then he backed to the doorway, executed a bow that brought him to one knee, arose, and departed.

As Tarzan had crossed the threshold his observing eyes had noted every detail of the room's interior almost in a single, sweeping glance. The chamber was not large, but it was magnificent in its conception and its appointments. Columns of solid gold supported the ceiling, the walls were tiled with ivory, the floor a mosaic of colored stones upon which were scattered rugs of colored stuff and the skins of animals, among which was one that attracted the ape-man's instant attention—the skin of a man tanned with the head on.

On the walls were paintings, for the most part very crude, and the usual array of heads of animals and men, and at one end of the room a great lion was chained between two of the golden Doric columns. He was a very large lion with a tuft of white hair in his mane directly in the center of the back of his neck. From the instant that Tarzan entered the room the lion eyed him malevolently, and Erot had scarcely passed out and closed the door behind him when the beast sprang to his feet with a terrific roar and leaped at the ape-man. The chains stopped him and he dropped down, growling.

"Belthar does not like you," said Nemone who had remained unmoved when the beast sprang. She noticed, too, that Tarzan had not started nor given any other indication that he had heard the lion or seen him; and she was pleased.

"He but reflects the attitude of all Cathne," replied Tarzan.

"That is not true," contradicted Nemone.

"No?"

"*I* like you." Nemone's voice was low and caressing. "You defied me before my people at the stadium today, but I did not have you destroyed. Do you suppose that I should have permitted you to live if I had not liked you? You do not kneel to me. No one else in the world has ever refused to do that and lived. I have never seen a man like you. I do not understand you. I am beginning to think that I do not understand myself. The leopard does not become a sheep in a few hours, yet it seems to me that I have changed as much as that since I first saw you; but that is not solely because I like you; I think that it is more because there is something mysterious about you that I cannot fathom. You have piqued my curiosity."

"And when that is satisfied you will kill me, perhaps?" asked Tarzan, a half smile curving his lip.

"Perhaps," admitted Nemone with a low laugh. "Come here and sit down beside me; I want to talk with you; I want to know more about you."

"I shall see that you do not learn too much," Tarzan assured her as he crossed to the couch and seated himself facing her, while Belthar growled and strained at his chains.

"In your own country you are no slave," said Nemone; "but I do not need to ask that; your every act has proved it. Perhaps you are a king?"

Tarzan shook his head. "I am Tarzan," he said, as though that explained everything, setting him above kings.

"Are you a lion man? You *must* be," insisted the Queen.

"It would not make me better nor worse; so what difference does it make? You might make Erot a king, but he would still be Erot."

A sudden frown darkened Nemone's countenance. "What do you mean by that?" she demanded. There was a suggestion of anger in her tone.

"I mean that a title of nobility does not make a man noble, that you may call a jackal a lion; but he will still be a jackal."

"Do you not know that I am supposed to be very fond of Erot," she demanded, "or that you may drive my patience too far?"

Tarzan shrugged. "You show execrable taste."

Nemone sat up very straight. Her eyes flashed. "I should have you killed!" she cried. Tarzan said nothing. He just kept his eyes on hers. She could not tell whether or not he was laughing at her. Finally she sank back on her pillows with a gesture of resignation. "What is the use?" she demanded. "You probably would not let me get any satisfaction from killing you anyway, and by this time I should be accustomed to being affronted."

"What you are not accustomed to is hearing the truth. Everyone is afraid of you. The reason you are interested in me is because I am not. It might do you good to hear the truth more often."

"For instance?"

"I am not going to undertake the thankless job of regenerating royalty," Tarzan assured her with a laugh.

"Let us stop quarreling. Nemone forgives you."

"I do not quarrel," said Tarzan; "only the weak and the wrong quarrel."

"Now answer my question. Are you a lion man in your own country?"

"I am a noble," replied the ape-man, "but I can tell you that that means little; a ditch digger may become a noble if he control enough votes, or a rich brewer if he subscribe a large amount of money to the political party in power."

"And which were you," demanded Nemone, "a ditchdigger or a rich brewer?"

"Neither," laughed Tarzan.

"Then why are you a noble?" insisted the Queen.

"For even less reason than either of those," admitted the ape-man. "I am a noble through no merit of my own but by an accident of birth; my family for many generations has been noble."

"Ah!" exclaimed Nemone. "It is just as I thought; you *are* a lion man!"

"And what of it?" demanded Tarzan.

"It simplifies matters," she explained, but she did not amplify the explanation nor did Tarzan either understand or enquire as to its implication. As a matter of fact he was not greatly interested in the subject.

Nemone extended a hand and laid it on his, a soft, warm

hand that trembled just a little. "I am going to give you your freedom," she said, "but on one condition."

"And what is that?" asked the ape-man.

"That you remain here, that you do not try to leave Onthar— or me." Her voice was eager and just a little husky, as though she spoke under suppressed emotion.

Tarzan remained silent. He would not promise, and so he did not speak. He realized, too, how easy it would be to remain if Nemone bid one do so. She fascinated him; she seemed to exercise a subtle influence, mysterious, hypnotic; yet he was determined to make no promise.

"I will make you a noble of Cathne," whispered Nemone. She was sitting erect now, her face close to Tarzan's. He could feel the warmth of her body close to his; the aura of some exotic scent was in his nostrils; her fingers closed upon his arm with a fierceness that hurt. "I will have made for you helmets of gold and habergeons of ivory, the most magnificent in Cathne; I will give you lions, fifty, a hundred; you shall be the richest, the most powerful noble of my court!"

The Lord of the Jungle felt weak beneath the spell of her burning eyes. "I do not want *such* things," he said.

Her soft arm crept up about his neck. A tender light, that was new to them, welled in the eyes of Nemone, the Queen of Cathne. "Tarzan!" she whispered.

And then a door at the far end of the chamber opened and a Negress entered. She had been very tall, but now she was old and bent; her scraggly wool was scant and white. Her withered lips were twisted into something that might have been either a snarl or a grin, revealing her toothless gums. She stood in the doorway leaning upon a staff and shaking her head, an ancient, palsied hag.

At the interruption Nemone straightened and looked around. The expression that had transformed and softened her countenance was swept away by a sudden wave of rage, inarticulate but no less terrible.

The old hag tapped upon the floor with her staff; her head nodded ceaselessly like that of some grotesque and horrible doll, and her lips were still contorted in what Tarzan realized now was no smile but a hideous snarl. "Come!" she cackled. "Come! Come! Come!"

Nemone sprang to her feet and faced the woman. "M'duze!" she screamed. "I could kill you! I could tear you to pieces! Get out of here!"

But the old woman only tapped with her staff and cackled, "Come! Come! Come!"

Slowly Nemone approached her. As one drawn by an invisible and irresistible power the Queen crossed the chamber, the old hag stepped aside, and the Queen passed on through the doorway into the darkness of a corridor beyond. The old woman turned her eyes upon Tarzan, and, snarling, backed through the doorway after Nemone. Noiselessly the door closed behind them.

Tarzan had arisen as Nemone arose. For an instant he hesitated and then took a step toward the doorway in pursuit of the Queen and the old hag; then he heard a door open and a step behind him, and turned to see the noble who had ushered him into Nemone's presence standing just within the threshold.

"You may return to the quarters of Gemnon," announced the noble politely.

Tarzan shook himself as might a lion; he drew a palm across his eyes as one whose vision has been clouded by a mist; then he drew a deep sigh and moved toward the doorway as the noble stepped aside to let him pass, but whether it was a sigh of relief or regret, who may say?

As the Lord of the Jungle passed out of the chamber, Belthar sprang to the ends of his chains with a thunderous roar.

11

The Lions of Cathne

WHEN GEMNON ENTERED the living room of their quarters the morning after Tarzan's audience with Nemone, he found the ape-man standing by the window looking out over the palace grounds.

"I am glad to see you here this morning," said the Cathnean.

"And surprised, perhaps," suggested the Lord of the Jungle.

"I should not have been surprised had you never returned," replied Gemnon. "How did she receive you? And Erot? I suppose he was glad to have you there!"

Tarzan smiled. "He did not appear to be, but it did not matter much as the Queen sent him away immediately."

"And you were alone with her all evening?" Gemnon appeared incredulous.

"Belthar and I," Tarzan corrected him. "Belthar does not seem to like me any better than Erot does."

"Yes, Belthar would be there," commented Gemnon. "She usually has him chained near her. But do not be offended if he does not like you; Belthar likes no one. Perhaps I should qualify that by saying that he likes no one alive, for he is very fond of dead men. Belthar is a maneater. How did Nemone treat you?"

"She was gracious," Tarzan assured him, "and that, too, notwithstanding the fact that the first thing that I did offended her royal majesty."

"And what was that?" demanded Gemnon.

"I remained standing when I should have kneeled," explained Tarzan.

"But I told you to kneel," exclaimed Gemnon.

"So did the noble at the door."

"And you forgot?"

"No."

"You refused to kneel? and she did not have you destroyed! It is incredible."

"But it is true, and she offered to make me a noble and give me a hundred lions."

Gemnon shook his head. "What enchantment have you worked to so change Nemone?"

"None; it was I who was under a spell. I have told you these things because I do not understand them. You are the only friend I have in Cathne, and I come to you for an explanation of much that was mysterious in my visit to the Queen last night; I doubt that I or another can ever understand the woman herself. She can be tender or terrible, weak or strong within the span of a dozen seconds. One moment she is the autocrat, the next the obedient vassal of a slave."

"Ah!" exclaimed Gemnon; "so you saw M'duze! I'll warrant she was none too cordial."

"No," admitted the ape-man. "As a matter of fact she did not pay any attention to me; she just ordered Nemone out of the room, and Nemone went. The remarkable feature of the occurrence lies in the fact that, though the Queen did not want to leave and was very angry about it, she obeyed the old black woman meekly."

"There are many legends surrounding M'duze," said Gemnon; "but there is one that is whispered more often than the others, though you may rest assured that it is only whispered and, at that, only among trusted friends.

"M'duze has been a slave in the royal family since the days of Nemone's grandfather; she was only a child then, a few years older than the King's son, Nemone's father. The oldsters recall that she was a fine-looking young Negress, and the legend that is only whispered is that Nemone is her daughter.

"About a year after Nemone was born, in the tenth year of

her father's reign, the Queen died under peculiar and suspicious circumstances just before she was to have been confined. The child, a son, was born just before the Queen expired. He was named Alextar, and he still lives."

"Then why is he not king?" demanded Tarzan.

"That is a long story of mystery and court intrigue and murder, perhaps, of which more is surmised than is actually known by more than two now living. Perhaps Nemone knows, but that is doubtful though she must guess close to the truth.

"Immediately following the death of the Queen the influence of M'duze increased and became more apparent. M'duze favored Tomos, a noble of little or no importance at the time; and from that day the influence and power of Tomos grew. Then, about a year after the death of the Queen, the King died. It was so obvious that he had been poisoned that a revolt of the nobles was barely averted; but Tomos, guided by M'duze, conciliated them by fixing the guilt upon a slave woman of whom M'duze was jealous and executing her.

"For ten years Tomos ruled as regent for the boy, Alextar. During this time he had, quite naturally, established his own following in important positions in the palace and in the council. Alextar was adjudged insane and imprisoned in the temple; Nemone, at the age of twelve, was crowned Queen of Cathne.

"Erot is a creature of M'duze and Tomos, a situation that has produced a contretemps that would be amusing were it not so tragic. Tomos wishes to marry Nemone, but M'duze will not permit it, and, if another theory is correct, her objection is well grounded. This theory is that Tomos, and not the old king, is the father of Nemone. M'duze wishes Nemone to marry Erot, but Erot is not a lion man, and, so far, the Queen has refused to break this ancient custom that requires the ruler to marry into this highest class of Cathneans.

"M'duze is insistent upon the marriage because she can control Erot; and she discourages any interest which Nemone may manifest in other men, which undoubtedly accounts for her having interrupted the Queen's visit with you.

"You may rest assured that M'duze is your enemy, and it

may be of value to you to recall that whoever has stood in the old hag's path has died a violent death. Beware of M'duze and Tomos and Erot; and, as a friend, I may say to you in confidence, beware of Nemone, also. And now let us forget the cruel and sordid side of Cathne and go for that walk I promised you for this morning that you may see the beauty of the city and the riches of her citizens."

Along avenues bordered by old trees Gemnon led Tarzan between the low, white and gold homes of nobles, glimpses of which were discernible only occasionally through grilled gateways in the walls that enclosed their spacious grounds. For a mile they walked along the stone-flagged street. Passing nobles greeted Gemnon, some nodding to his companion; artisans, tradesmen, and slaves stopped to stare at the strange, bronzed giant who had overthrown the strongest man in Cathne.

Then they came to a high wall that separated this section of the city from the next. Massive gates, swung wide now and guarded by warriors, opened into a portion of the city inhabited by better class artisans and tradesmen. Their grounds were less spacious, their houses smaller and plainer; but evidences of prosperity and even affluence were apparent everywhere.

Beyond this was a meaner district, yet even here all was orderly and neat, nor was there any sign of abject poverty in either the people or their homes. Here, as in the other portions of the city, they occasionally met a tame lion either wandering about or lying before the gate of its master's grounds.

Presently the ape-man's attention was attracted by a lion a short distance ahead of them; the beast was lying on the body of a man which it was devouring.

"Your streets do not seem to be entirely safe for pedestrians," commented the Lord of the Jungle, indicating the feeding lion with a nod of the head.

Gemnon laughed. "You notice that the pedestrians do not seem to be much concerned," he replied, calling attention to the people passing to and fro past the lion and its prey, merely turning aside enough to avoid them. "The lions must eat."

"Do they kill many of your citizens?"

"Very few. The man you see there died, and his corpse was

thrown into the street for the lions. The lion did not kill him. You see he is naked; that shows that he was dead before the lion got him. When a person dies, if there be no one who can or will pay for a funeral cortege, the body is disposed of in this way if not diseased; those who die of disease and those whose relatives can afford a funeral cortege find their last resting place in Xarator, though there are also many of the latter that are thrown to the lions by preference. You know we think a great deal of lions here in Cathne, and it is no disgrace but rather the contrary to be devoured by one. You see, our god is a lion."

"Do the lions eat human flesh exclusively?" inquired Tarzan.

"No. We hunt sheep, goats, and elephants in Thenar to provide them with food when there is not enough human flesh to keep them well fed, for we must keep them from hunger if we are to prevent them turning maneaters."

"Then they never kill men for food?"

"Oh, yes, occasionally; but a lion that develops that habit is destroyed; and, after all, only a few old pets are turned loose in the streets. There are about five hundred lions inside the city, and all but a few of these are kept in enclosures on their owners' property. The best racing and hunting lions are kept in private stables.

"The Queen has fully three hundred full-grown males; these are the war lions. Some of the Queen's lions are trained for racing and some for hunting; she likes to hunt, and now that the rainy season is over the hunting lions of Nemone will doubtless soon be in the field."

"Where do you get all these lions?" asked the ape-man.

"We raise them ourselves," explained Gemnon. "Outside the city is a breeding plant where the females are kept. It is maintained by Nemone, and each lion man who owns females pays a stipulated sum for their keep. We raise a great many lions, for there are many killed each year in hunting, during raids, and in war. You see, we hunt elephants with them; and in these hunts many lions are killed. The Atheneans also kill a number each year when we take our lions into Thenar to hunt or raid and quite a few escape. Most of these are still running wild in the valley or in Thenar, and there are some wild lions that have come in from the mountains. All of these are very ferocious."

As they talked they continued on toward the center of the city until they came to a large square that was bounded on all sides by shops. Here were many people. All classes from nobles to slaves mingled before the shops and in the great open square of the marketplace. There were lions held by slaves who were exhibiting them for sale for their noble masters who dickered with prospective purchasers, other nobles.

. Near the lion market was the slave block; and as slaves, unlike lions, might be owned by anyone, there was brisk bidding on the part of many wishing to buy. A huge, black Galla was on the block as Tarzan and Gemnon paused to watch the scene. The man was entirely naked that the buyers might examine him for blemishes; his expression was one of unconcern ordinarily, though occasionally he shot a venomous glance at the owner who was expatiating upon his virtues.

"For all the interest he shows," remarked Tarzan, "one might think that being sold like a piece of merchandise or a bullock was a daily occurrence in his life."

"Not quite daily," replied Gemnon, "but no novelty. He has been sold many times. I know him well; I used to own him."

"Look at him!" shouted the seller. "Look at those arms; look at those legs; look at that back! He is as strong as an elephant, and not a blemish on him. Sound as a lion's tooth he is; never ill a day in his life. And docile! a child can handle him."

"He is so refractory that no one can handle him," commented Gemnon in a whisper to the ape-man. "That is the reason I had to get rid of him; that is the reason he is up for sale so often."

"There seem to be plenty of customers interested in him," observed Tarzan.

"Do you see that slave in the red tunic?" asked Gemnon. "He belongs to Xerstle, and he is bidding on that fellow. He knows all about him, too; he knew him when the man belonged to me."

"Then why does he want to buy him?" asked the ape-man.

"I do not know, but there are other uses to which a slave may be put than labor. Xerstle may not care what sort of a disposition the fellow has or even whether he will work. If he owned lions I might think that he was buying the fellow for lion food as he will probably go cheap."

It was Xerstle's slave who bought the Galla as Tarzan and Gemnon moved on to look at the goods displayed in the shops. There were many articles of leather, wood, ivory, or gold; there were dagger-swords, spears, shields, habergeons, helmets, and sandals. One shop displayed nothing but articles of apparel for women; another, perfumes and incense; there were jewelry shops, vegetable shops, and meat shops. The last displayed dried meats and fish and carcasses of goats and sheep. The fronts of these shops were heavily barred to prevent passing lions from raiding them, Gemnon explained.

Wherever Tarzan went he attracted attention; and a small crowd always followed him, for he had been recognized the moment that he had entered the marketplace. Boys and girls clustered about him gazing at him admiringly, and men and women who had been at the stadium the previous day told those who had not how this stranger giant had lifted Phobeg above his head and hurled him up among the audience.

"Let's get out of here," suggested the Lord of the Jungle; "I do not like crowds."

"Suppose we go back to the palace and look at the Queen's lions," said Gemnon.

"I would rather look at lions than people," Tarzan assured him.

The war lions of Cathne were kept in stables within the royal grounds at a considerable distance from the palace. The building was of stone neatly laid and painted white; in it each lion had his separate cage; and outside were yards surrounded by high stone walls near the tops of which pointed sticks, set close together and inclined downward on the inside of the walls, kept the lions from escaping. In these yards the lions exercised themselves; there was another, larger arena where they were trained by a corps of keepers under the supervision of nobles;

here the racing lions were broken to harness and the hunting lions taught to obey the commands of the hunter, to trail, to charge, to retrieve.

As Tarzan entered the stable a familiar scent spoor impinged upon his nostrils. "Belthar is here," he remarked to Gemnon.

"It is possible," replied the noble, "but I don't understand how you know it."

As they were walking along in front of the cages inspecting the lions that were inside, Gemnon, who was in advance, suddenly halted. "How do you do it?" he demanded. "Last night you knew that Erot was with Nemone though you could not see him and no one could have informed you; and now you knew that Belthar was here, and, sure enough, he is!"

Tarzan approached and stood beside Gemnon, and the instant that Belthar's eyes fell upon him the beast leaped against the bars of his cage in an effort to seize the ape-man, at the same time voicing an angry roar that shook the building.

Instantly keepers came running to the spot, certain that something had gone amiss; but Gemnon assured them that it was only Belthar exhibiting his bad temper.

"He does not like me," said Tarzan.

"If he ever got you, he would make short work of you," said a head keeper.

"It is evident that he would like to," replied the ape-man.

"He is a bad one and a man-killer," said Gemnon after the keepers had departed, "but Nemone will not have him destroyed. Occasionally he is loosed in the palace arena with someone who has incurred Nemone's disfavor; thus she derives pleasure from the sufferings of the culprit.

"Formerly he was her best hunting lion, but the last time he was used he killed four men and nearly escaped. He has already eaten three keepers who ventured into the arena with him, and he will eat more before good fortune rids us of him.

"Nemone is supposed to entertain a superstition that in some peculiar way her life and the life of Belthar are linked by some mysterious, supernatural bond and that when one dies the other must die. Naturally, under the circumstances, it is neither politic nor safe to suggest that she destroy the old devil. It is odd that he has conceived such a violent dislike for you."

"I have met lions before which did not like me," said Tarzan.

"May you never meet Belthar in the open, my friend!"

12

The Man in the Lion Pit

As Tarzan and Gemnon turned away from Belthar's cage a slave approached the ape-man and addressed him. "Nemone, the Queen, commands your presence immediately," he said; "you are to come to the ivory room; the noble Gemnon will wait in the anteroom. These are the commands of Nemone, the Queen."

"What now? I wonder," remarked Tarzan as they walked through the royal grounds toward the palace.

"No one ever knows why he is summoned to an audience with Nemone until he gets there," commented Gemnon; "one may be going to receive an honor or hear his death sentence. Nemone is capricious. She is always bored and always seeking relief from her boredom. Oftentimes she finds strange avenues of escape that makes one wonder if her mind—but no! such thoughts may not even be whispered among friends."

When Tarzan presented himself he was immediately admitted to the ivory room, where he found Nemone and Erot much as he had found them the preceding night. Nemone greeted him with a smile that was almost pathetically eager; but Erot only scowled darkly, making no effort to conceal his hatred.

"We are having a diversion this morning," Nemone explained, "and we summoned you and Gemnon to enjoy it with us. A party raiding in Thenar a day or so ago captured an Athnean noble; we are going to have some sport with him this morning."

Tarzan nodded. He did not understand what she meant, and he was not particularly interested. He was thinking of M'duze and the night before; wondering what was in the mind of the strange, fascinating woman before him.

Nemone turned to Erot. "Go and tell them we are ready," she directed, "and ascertain if all is in readiness for us."

Erot flushed and backed toward the door, still scowling. "And you need not hurry," added the Queen; "we are not impatient to witness the entertainment. Let them take their time, and be sure to see that all is well ordered."

"It shall be as the Queen commands," replied Erot in a surly tone.

When the door had closed behind him, Nemone motioned Tarzan to a seat upon the couch. "I am afraid that Erot does not like you," she said, smiling. "He is furious that you do not kneel to me, and that I do not compel you to do so. I really do not know, myself, why I do not; but I guess why. Have you not, perhaps, guessed why, too?"

"There might be two reasons, either of which would be sufficient," replied the ape-man.

"And what are they? I have been curious to know how you explained it."

"Consideration of the customs of a stranger and courtesy to a guest," suggested Tarzan.

Nemone considered for a moment. "Yes," she admitted, "either is a fairly good reason, but neither is really in keeping with the customs of the court of Nemone. And then they are practically the same thing; so they constitute only one reason. Is there not another?"

"Yes," replied Tarzan; "there is an even better one; the one which probably influences you to overlook my dereliction."

"And what is it?"

"The fact that you cannot make me kneel."

A hard look flashed in the Queen's eyes; it was not the answer she had been hoping for. Tarzan's eyes did not leave hers; she saw amusement in them. "Oh, why do I endure it!" she cried, and with the query her anger melted. "You should not try to make it so hard for me to be nice to you," she said almost appealingly. "Why do you not meet me halfway? Why are you not nice to me, Tarzan?"

"I wish to be nice to you, Nemone," he replied; "but not at the price of my self-respect; but that is not the only reason why I shall never kneel to you."

"What is the other reason?" she demanded.

"That I wish you to like me; you would not like me if I cringed to you."

"Perhaps you are right," she admitted musingly. "Everyone cringes, until the sight of it disgusts me; yet I am angry when they do not cringe. Why is that?"

"You will be offended if I tell you," warned the ape-man.

"In the past two days I have been accustomed to being offended," she replied with a grimace of resignation; "so you might as well tell me."

"You are angry if they do not cringe, because you are not quite sure of yourself. You wish this outward evidence of their subservience that you may be constantly reassured that you are Queen of Cathne."

"Who says that I am not Queen of Cathne?" she demanded, instantly on the defensive. "Who says that will find that I am and that I have the power of life and death. If I chose, I could have you destroyed in an instant."

"You do not impress me," said Tarzan. "I have not said that you are not Queen of Cathne, only that your manner may often suggest your own doubts. A queen should be so sure of herself that she can always afford to be gracious and merciful."

For a while Nemone sat in silence, evidently pondering the thought that Tarzan had suggested. "They would not understand," she said at last; "if I were gracious and merciful they would think me weak; then they would take advantage of me; and eventually they would destroy me. You do not know them. But you are different; I can be gracious and merciful to you and you will never try to take advantage of my kindness; you will not misunderstand it.

"Oh, Tarzan, I wish that you would promise to remain in Cathne. If you will, there is nothing that you may not have from Nemone. I would build you a palace second only to my own. I would be very good to you; we—you could be very happy here."

The ape-man shook his head. "Tarzan can be happy in the jungle only."

Nemone leaned close to him; she seized him fiercely by the shoulders. "I will make you happy here," she whispered passionately. "You do not know Nemone. Wait! The time will come when you will want to stay—for me!"

"Erot and M'duze and Tomos may think differently," Tarzan reminded her.

"I hate them!" cried Nemone. "If they interfere this time, I shall kill them all; this time I shall have my own way; she shall not rob me of all happiness. But do not speak of her; never speak her name to me again. And as for Erot," she snapped her fingers. "I crush a worm beneath my sandal, and no one misses it. No one would miss Erot, least of all I; I have long been tired of him. He is a stupid, egotistical fool; but he is better than nothing."

The door opened and Erot entered unceremoniously; he kneeled, but the act was nearer a gesture than an accomplished fact. Nemone flashed an angry look at him.

"Before you enter our presence," she said coldly, "see to it that you are properly announced and that we have expressed a desire to receive you."

"But your majesty," objected Erot, "have I not been in the habit of—"

"You have gotten into bad habits," she interrupted; "see that you mend them. Is the diversion arranged?"

"All is in readiness, your majesty," replied the crestfallen Erot.

"Come then!" directed Nemone, motioning Tarzan to follow her.

In the anteroom they found Gemnon waiting, and the Queen bid him accompany them. Preceded and followed by armed guards, the three passed along several corridors and through a number of rooms, then up a stairway to the second floor of the palace. Here they were conducted to a balcony overlooking a small enclosed court. The windows opening onto this court from the first story of the building were heavily barred; and from just below the top of the parapet, behind which the Queen and her party sat, sharpened stakes protruded, giving the court the appearance of a miniature arena for wild animals.

As Tarzan looked down into the courtyard, wondering a little what the nature of the diversion was to be, a door at one end swung open and a young lion stepped out into the sunlight, blinking his eyes and looking about. When he saw those on the balcony looking down at him, he growled.

"He is going to make a good lion," remarked Nemone. "From a cub, he has always been vicious."

"What is he doing in here?" asked Tarzan, "or what is he going to do?"

"He is going to entertain us," replied Nemone. "Presently an enemy of Cathne will be turned into the pit with him, the Athnean who was captured in Thenar."

"And if he kills the lion you will give him his liberty?" demanded Tarzan.

Nemone laughed. "I promise that I will, but he will not kill the lion."

"He might," said Tarzan; "men have killed lions before."

"With their bare hands?" asked Nemone.

"You mean the man will not be armed?" demanded Tarzan incredulously.

"Why, of course not," exclaimed Nemone. "He is not being put in there to kill or wound a fine young lion but to be killed."

"And he has no chance then! That is not sport; it is murder!"

"Perhaps you would like to go down and defend him," sneered Erot. "The Queen would give the fellow his liberty if he had a champion who would kill the lion, for that is the custom."

"It is a custom that is without a precedent since I have been Queen," said Nemone. "It is true that it is a law of the arena, but I have yet to see a champion volunteer to take the risk."

The lion paced across the courtyard and stood directly beneath the balcony, glaring up at them. He was a splendid beast, young but full-grown.

"He is going to be a mean customer," remarked Gemnon.

"He already is," rejoined the Queen. "I was going to make a racing lion of him, but after he killed a couple of trainers I decided that he would make a better hunting lion for grand hunts. There is the Athnean." She pointed down into the courtyard. "He is a fine-looking young fellow."

Tarzan glanced at the stalwart figure in ivory standing upon the opposite side of the small arena bravely awaiting its fate; then the lion turned its head slowly in the direction of the prey it had not yet seen. At the same instant Tarzan seized the hilt of Erot's daggerlike sword, tore the weapon from its sheath, and, stepping to the top of the parapet, leaped for the lion below.

So quickly and so silently had he moved that none was aware of his intent until it had been accomplished. Gemnon voiced an ejaculation of astonishment; Erot, of relief; while Nemone cried out in genuine terror and alarm. Leaning over the parapet, the Queen saw the lion struggling to tear the body that had crushed it to the stone flagging or escape from beneath it. The horrid growls of the beast reverberated in the narrow confines of the pit, and mingled with them were the growls of the beast-man on its back. One bronzed arm was about the maned neck of the carnivore, two powerful legs were locked around its middle, and the sharp point of Erot's sword was awaiting the opportune instant to plunge into the savage heart. The Athnean was running toward the two embattled beasts.

"By Thoos!" exclaimed Nemone. "If the lion kills him, I will have it torn limb from limb. It must not kill him! Go down there, Erot, and help him; go, Gemnon!"

Gemnon did not wait, but springing to the parapet, he lowered himself by the stakes and dropped into the courtyard. Erot hung back. "Let him take care of himself," he grumbled.

Nemone turned to the guard standing behind her. She was white with apprehension because of Tarzan and with rage and disgust at Erot. "Throw him into the pit!" she commanded, pointing at the cringing favorite; but Erot did not wait to be thrown, and a moment later he had followed Gemnon to the stone flagging of the courtyard.

Neither Erot nor Gemnon nor the man from Athne were needed to save Tarzan from the lion, for already he had sunk the sword into the tawny side. Twice again the point drove into the wild heart before the roaring beast collapsed upon the white stones, and its great voice was stilled forever.

Then Tarzan rose to his feet. For a moment the men about him, the Queen leaning across the parapet above, the City of Gold, all were forgotten. Here was no English lord but a beast of the jungle that had made its kill. With one foot upon the carcass of the lion, the ape-man raised his face toward the heavens, and from the heart of the palace of Nemone rose the hideous victory cry of the bull ape that has killed.

Gemnon and Erot shuddered, and Nemone drew back in terror; but the Athnean was unmoved; he had heard that savage challenge before. He was Valthor. And now Tarzan turned; all the savagery faded from his countenance as he stretched forth a hand and laid it on Valthor's shoulder. "We meet again, my friend," he said.

"And once again you save my life!" exclaimed the Athnean noble.

The two men had spoken in low tones that had not carried to the ears of Nemone or the others in the balcony; Erot, fearful that the lion might not be dead, had run to the far end of the court, where he was cowering behind a column; that Gemnon might have heard did not concern Tarzan, who trusted the young Cathnean. But those others must not know that he had known Valthor before, or immediately the old story that Tarzan had come from Athne to assassinate Nemone would be revived and then only a miracle could save either of them.

His hand still upon Valthor's shoulder, Tarzan spoke again rapidly in a whisper. "They must not know that we are acquainted," he said. "They are looking for an excuse to kill me, some of them; but as far as you are concerned they do not have to look for any."

Nemone was now calling orders rapidly to those about her. "Go down and let Tarzan out of the arena, Tarzan and Gemnon; send them to me. Erot may go to his quarters until I give further orders; I do not wish to see him again. Take the Athnean back to his cell; later I will decide how he shall be destroyed."

She spoke in the imperious tones of one long accustomed to

absolute authority and implicit obedience, and her voice carried plainly to the ears of the men in the arena. It brought the chill of sudden fear to the heart of Erot, who saw his influence waning and recalled tales he had heard of the fate of other royal favorites who had outlived their charm. Into his cunning brain flew a score of schemes to reinstate himself, and each was based upon the elimination of the giant that had supplanted him in the affections of the Queen. He would fly to Tomos, to M'duze; neither of these could afford to see the stranger take Erot's place in the boudoir councils of Nemone and become a power behind the throne.

Tarzan heard the Queen's commands with surprise and resentment, and, wheeling, he looked up at her. "This man is free by your own word," he reminded her. "If he be returned to a cell, I shall go with him, for I have told him that he would be free."

"Do with him as you please," cried Nemone; "he is yours. Only come up to me, Tarzan. I thought that you would be killed, and I am still frightened."

Erot and Gemnon heard those words with vastly different emotions; each recognized that they signalized a change in the affairs of the court of Cathne. Gemnon anticipated the effects of a better influence injected into the councils of Nemone, and was pleased. Erot saw the flimsy structure of his temporary grandeur and reflected authority crumbling to ruin. Both were astonished by this sudden revealment of a new Nemone, whom none had ever before seen bow to the authority of another than M'duze.

Accompanied by Gemnon and Valthor, Tarzan returned to the balcony where Nemone, her composure regained, awaited them. For a moment, moved by excitement and apprehension for Tarzan's safety, she had revealed a feminine side of her character that few of her intimates might even have suspected she possessed; but now she was the Queen again. She surveyed Valthor haughtily and yet with interest.

"What is your name, Athnean?" she demanded.

"Valthor," he replied and added, "of the house of Xanthus."

"We know the house," remarked Nemone; "its head is a

king's councillor; a most noble house and close to the royal line in both blood and authority."

"My father is the head of the house of Xanthus," said Valthor.

"Your head would have made a noble trophy for our walls," sighed Nemone, "but we have given our promise that you shall be freed."

"My head would have been honored by a place among your majesty's trophies," replied Valthor, the faintest trace of a smile upon his lips; "but it shall have to be content to wait a more propitious event."

"We shall look forward with keen anticipation to that moment," rejoined Nemone graciously; "but in the meantime we will arrange an escort to return you to Athne, and hope for better fortune the next time that you fall into our hands. Be ready then early tomorrow to return to your own country."

"I thank your majesty," replied Valthor; "I shall be ready, and when I go I shall carry with me, to cherish through life, the memory of the gracious and beautiful Queen of Cathne."

"Our noble Gemnon shall be your host until tomorrow," announced Nemone. "Take him with you now to your quarters, Gemnon, and let it be known that he is Nemone's guest, whom none may harm."

Tarzan would have accompanied Gemnon and Valthor, but Nemone detained him. "You will return to my apartments with me," she directed; "I wish to talk with you."

As they walked through the palace, the Queen did not precede her companion as the etiquette of the court demanded but moved close at his side, looking up into his face as she talked. "I was frightened, Tarzan," she confided. "It is not often that Nemone is frightened by the peril of another, but when I saw you leap into the arena with the lion my heart stood still. Why did you do it, Tarzan?"

"I was disgusted with what I saw," replied the ape-man shortly.

"Disgusted! What do you mean?"

"The cowardliness of the authority that would permit an

unarmed and utterly defenseless man to be forced into an arena with a lion," explained Tarzan candidly.

Nemone flushed. "You know that that authority is I," she said coldly.

"Of course I know it," replied the ape-man, "but that only renders it the more odious."

"What do you mean?" she snapped. "Are you trying to drive me beyond my patience? If you knew me better you would know that that is not safe, not even for you, before whom I have already humbled myself."

"I am not seeking to try your patience," replied the ape-man quietly, "for I am neither interested nor concerned in your powers of self-control. I am merely shocked that one so beautiful may at the same time be so heartless. Were you a little more human, Nemone, you would be irresistible."

The flush faded from the Queen's face, the anger from her eyes; she moved on in silence, her mood suddenly introspective; and when they reached the anteroom leading to her private chambers, she halted at the threshold of the latter and laid a hand gently upon the arm of the man at her side.

"You are very brave," she said. "Only a very brave man would have leaped into the arena with the lion to save a stranger; but only the bravest of the brave could have dared to speak to Nemone as you have spoken, for the death that the lion deals may be merciful compared with that which Nemone deals when she has been affronted. Yet perhaps you knew that I would forgive you. Oh, Tarzan, what magic have you exercised to win such power over me!" She took him by the hand then and led him toward the doorway of her chambers. "In here, alone together, you shall teach Nemone how to be human!" As the door swung open there was a new light in the eyes of the Queen of Cathne, a softer light than had ever before shone in those beautiful depths; and then it faded, to be replaced by a cold, hard glitter of bitterness and hate. Facing them, in the center of the apartment, stood M'duze.

She stood there, bent and horrible, wagging her head and tapping the stone floor with her staff. She spoke no word, but fixed them with her baleful glare. As one held in the grip of a

power she is unable to resist, Nemone moved slowly toward
the ancient hag, leaving Tarzan just beyond the threshold.
Slowly and silently the door closed between them. Beyond it
the ape-man heard, faintly, the tapping of the staff upon the
colored stones of the mosaic.

13

Assassin in the Night

A GREAT LION moved silently from the south across the border of Kaffa. If he were following a trail, the heavy rain that had terminated the wet season must have obliterated it long since; yet he moved on with a certain assurance that betokened no sign of doubt.

Why was he there? What urge had drawn him thus, contrary to the habits and customs of his kind, upon this long and arduous journey? Where was he bound? What or whom did he seek? Only he, Numa, the lion, king of beasts, knew.

In his quarters in the palace, Erot paced the floor, angry and disconsolate. Sprawled on a bench, his feet wide apart, sat Xerstle deep in thought. The two men were facing a crisis, and they were terrified. Had Erot definitely fallen from the favor of the Queen, Xerstle would be dragged down with him; of that there was no doubt.

"But there must be *something* you can do," insisted Xerstle.

"I have seen both Tomos and M'duze," replied Erot wearily, "and they have promised to help. It means as much to them as it does to me. But Nemone is infatuated with this stranger. Even M'duze, who has known her all her life, has never seen her so affected by a passion as now. Even she feels that she may not be able to control the Queen in the face of her mad attachment for the naked barbarian.

"None knows Nemone better than does M'duze, and I can tell you, Xerstle, the old hag is frightened. Nemone hates her, and if the attempted thwarting of this new passion arouses her anger sufficiently it may sweep away the fear that the Queen has already held for M'duze, and she will destroy her. It is this that M'duze fears. And you can imagine how terrified old Tomos is! Without M'duze he would be lost, for Nemone tolerates him only because M'duze demands it."

"But there must be some way," again insisted Xerstle.

"There is no way so long as this fellow, Tarzan, is able to turn Nemone's heart to water," answered Erot. "Why, he does not even kneel to her; and he speaks to her as one might to a naughty slave girl. By the mane of Thoos! I believe that if he kicked her she would like it."

"But there *is* a way!" exclaimed Xerstle in a sudden whisper. "Listen!" and then he launched forth into a detailed explanation of his plan. Erot sat listening to his friend, an expression of rapt interest upon his face. A slave girl came from Xerstle's bedchamber, crossed the living room where the two men talked, and departed into the corridor beyond; but so engrossed were Erot and Xerstle that neither was aware that she had come or that she had gone.

In their quarters that evening Gemnon and Tarzan partook of the final meal of the day, for neither had enjoyed the prospect of again eating with the other nobles. Valthor slept in the bedroom, having asked not to be disturbed until morning.

"When you have definitely displaced Erot conditions will be different," explained Gemnon; "then they will fawn upon you, shower you with attentions, and wait upon your every whim."

"That will never occur," snapped the ape-man.

"Why not?" demanded his companion. "Nemone is mad about you. There is nothing that she would not do for you, absolutely nothing. Why, man, you can rule Cathne if you so choose."

"But I do not choose," replied Tarzan. "Nemone may be mad, but I am not; and even were I, I could never be mad enough to accept a position that had once been filled by Erot. The idea disgusts me; let us talk of something pleasant."

"Very well," consented Gemnon with a smile. "Perhaps I

think you are foolish, but I admit that I cannot help but admire your courage and your decency.

"And now for something more pleasant! Something very much more pleasant! I am going to take you visiting tonight. I am going to take you to see the most beautiful girl in Cathne."

"I thought that there could be no woman in Cathne more beautiful than the Queen," objected Tarzan.

"There would not be if Nemone knew of her," replied Gemnon, "but fortunately she does not know; she has never seen this girl, and may Thoos forbid that she ever does!"

"You are much interested," remarked the ape-man, smiling.

"I am in love with her," explained Gemnon simply.

"And Nemone has never seen her? I should think that a difficult condition to maintain, for Cathne is not large; and if the girl be of the same class as you many other nobles must know of her beauty. One would expect such news to come quickly to the ears of Nemone."

"She is surrounded by very loyal friends, this girl of whom I speak," replied Gemnon. "She is Doria, the daughter of Thudos. Her father is a very powerful noble and head of the faction which wishes to place Alextar on the throne. Only Nemone's knowledge of his great power preserves his life, but owing to the strained relations that exist between Nemone and his house neither he nor members of his family are often at court. Thus it has been easier to prevent knowledge of the great beauty of Doria coming to Nemone."

As the two men were leaving the palace a short time later they came unexpectedly upon Xerstle, who was most effusive in his greetings. "Congratulations, Tarzan!" he exclaimed, halting the companions. "That was a most noble feat you performed in the lion pit today. All the palace is talking about it, and let me be among the first to tell you how glad I am that you have won the confidence of our gracious and beautiful Queen by your bravery, strength, and magnanimity."

Tarzan nodded in acknowledgment of the man's avowal and started to move on, but Xerstle held him with a gesture. "We must see more of one another," he continued. "I am arranging a grand hunt, and I must have you as my guest of honor. There will be but a few of us, a most select party; and I can assure you of good sport. When all the arrangements are completed, I will let you know the day of the hunt; and now good-bye and good luck to you!"

"I care nothing about him or his grand hunt," said Tarzan as he and Gemnon continued on toward the home of Doria.

"Perhaps it would be well to accept," advised Gemnon. "That fellow and his friends will bear watching, and if you are with them occasionally you can watch them that much better."

Tarzan shrugged. "If I am still here, I shall go with him if you think best."

"If you are still here!" exclaimed Gemnon. "You certainly are not expecting to get away from Cathne, are you?"

"Why, certainly," replied Tarzan. "I may go any day, or night; there is nothing to hold me here, and I have given no promise that I would not escape when I wished."

Gemnon smiled a wry smile that Tarzan did not see in the semidarkness of the ill-lit avenue through which they were passing. "That will make it extremely interesting for me," he remarked.

"Why?" demanded the ape-man.

"Nemone turned you over into my keeping. If you escape while I am responsible for you she will have me destroyed."

A frown knit the brows of the Lord of the Jungle. "I did not know that," he said; "but you need not worry; I shall not go until you have been relieved of responsibility." A sudden smile lighted his countenance. "I think I shall ask Nemone to give me over into the keeping of Erot or Xerstle."

Gemnon chuckled. "What a story that would make!" he cried.

An occasional torch only partially dispelled the gloom beneath the overhanging trees that bordered the avenue that led toward the palace of Thudos. At the intersection of a narrow alleyway, beneath the branches of a wide-spreading oak a dark figure lurked in the shadows as Tarzan and Gemnon approached. The keen eyes of the ape-man saw and recognized it as the figure of a man before they came close enough to be in danger; and Tarzan was ready even though he had no suspicion that the man's presence there was in any way concerned with him, for it is the business of the jungle-bred to be always ready, whether danger threatens or not.

Just as the two came opposite the figure, Tarzan heard his name whispered in a hoarse voice. He stopped. "Beware of Erot!" whispered the voice. "Tonight!" Then the figure wheeled and lumbered into the denser shadows of the narrow alleyway; but in the glimpse that Tarzan got of it there was a familiar roll to the great body, just as there had been a suggestion of familiarity in the voice.

"Now who do you suppose that is?" demanded Gemnon. "Come on! We'll capture him and find out," and he started as though to pursue the stranger down the alley.

Tarzan laid a restraining hand upon his shoulder. "No," he said; "it was someone who has tried to befriend me. If he wishes to conceal his identity, it is not for me to reveal it."

"You are right," assented Gemnon.

"And I think I would have learned no more by pursuing him than I already know. I recognized him by his voice and his gait, and then, as he turned to leave, a movement in the air brought his scent spoor to my nostrils. I think I would recognize that a mile away, for it is very strong; it always is in powerful men and beasts."

"Why was he afraid of you?" asked Gemnon.

"He was not afraid of me; he was afraid of you because you are a noble."

"He need not have been, if he is a friend of yours. I would not have betrayed him."

"I know that, but he could not. You are a noble, and so you might be a friend of Erot. I do not mind telling you who it was, because I know you would not use the knowledge to harm him; but you will be surprised; I surely was. It was Phobeg."

"No! Why should he befriend the man who defeated and humiliated him, and almost killed him?"

"Because he did *not* kill him. Phobeg is a simpleminded fellow, but he is the type that would not be devoid of gratitude. He is the sort that would bestow doglike devotion upon one who was more powerful than he, for he worships physical prowess."

At the palace of Thudos the two men were ushered into a magnificent apartment by a slave after the guard at the entrance had recognized Gemnon and permitted them to pass. In the soft light of a dozen cressets they awaited the coming of the daughter of the house to whom the slave had carried Gemnon's ring to evidence the identity of her caller. The richness of the furnishings of the room were scarcely less magnificent than those Tarzan had seen in the palace of Nemone; and again, here, were the trophies of the chase prominent among the decorations upon the walls.

A human head, surmounted by a golden helmet, frowned down from sightless eyes from a place of honor above the main entrance. Though shrunken and withered in death there was still strength and majesty in its appearance; and Tarzan gazed for some moments at it, intrigued by the thought of all that had passed within that dry and ghastly skull before it found its way to grace the trophies upon the palace walls of the noble Thudos. What fierce or kindly thoughts, what hates, what loves, what rages had been born and lived and died behind that parchment forehead? What tales those dried and shriveled lips might tell could the hot blood of the fighting man give them life once more!

"A splendid trophy," commented Gemnon, attracted by his companion's evident interest in the head. "It is the most valuable trophy in Cathne; there is no other to equal it, and there may never be another. That head belonged to a king of Athne. Thudos took it himself in battle as a young man."

"I rather like the idea," said Tarzan thoughtfully. "In the world from which I come men fill their trophy rooms with the heads of creatures who are not their enemies, who would be their friends if man would let them. Your most valued trophies are the heads of your enemies who have had an equal opportunity to take your head. Yes, it is a splendid idea!"

The light fall of soft sandals upon stone announced the coming of their hostess, and both men turned toward the doorway leading into a small open garden from which she was coming. Tarzan saw a girl of exquisite beauty; but whether she were more beautiful than Nemone he could not say, there are so many things that enter into the making of a beautiful countenance; yet he acknowledged to himself that Thudos was wise in keeping her hidden from the Queen.

She greeted Gemnon with the sweet familiarity of an old friend, and when Tarzan was presented her manner was cordial and unaffected, yet always the fact that she was the daughter of Thudos seemed a part of her.

"I saw you in the stadium," she said, and then, with a laugh, "I lost many drachmas because of you."

"I am sorry," said Tarzan. "Perhaps had I known that you were betting on Phobeg I should have let him kill me."

"That is an idea," exclaimed Doria, laughing. "If you fight in the stadium again I shall tell you beforehand which man I am placing my money on, and then I shall be sure to win."

"I see that I must make you like me so well that you will not want to bet on my opponent."

"From what I have seen of him," interjected Gemnon, "I think Tarzan will always be a safe bet—in an arena."

"What do you mean?" demanded the girl. "There is the suggestion of another significance in your words."

"I am afraid my friend will not be so safe in a boudoir," laughed the young noble.

"We have already heard that he has been more than successful," said Doria with just the faintest note of something that might have been disgust.

"Do not judge him too harshly," pleaded Gemnon; "he is still doing his best to get himself destroyed."

"That should not be difficult in the palace of Nemone, though we have already heard startling tales of his refusal to kneel before the Queen. One who has survived that may not have as much to fear as we have imagined," returned Doria.

"Your Queen understands why I do not kneel," explained Tarzan. "It is through no disrespect nor boorish bravado, but because of the habits of a lifetime and the exigencies of my existence. Had I not been commanded to kneel, I might have knelt. I am afraid that I cannot explain the psychology of my position so that another may understand it; but it is plain to me that I must not bow to any authority against my will, unless I am compelled to do so by force."

The three had spent the evening in pleasant conversation, and Gemnon and Tarzan were about to leave, when a middle-aged man entered the room. It was Thudos, the father of Doria. He greeted Gemnon cordially and seemed pleased to meet Tarzan whom he immediately commenced to question relative to the world outside the valleys of Onthar and Thenar.

Thudos was a strikingly handsome man, with strong features, an athletic build, and eyes that were serious and stern that yet had wrinkles at their corners that betokened much laughter. His was a face that one might trust, for integrity, loyalty, and courage had left their imprints plainly upon it, at least for eyes as observant as those of the Lord of the Jungle.

When the two guests rose to leave again, Thudos seemed satisfied with his appraisal of the stranger. "I am glad that Gemnon brought you," he said. "The very fact that he did convinces me that he has confidence in your friendship and loyalty, for, as you may already know, the position of my house at the court of Nemone is such that we receive only assured friends within our walls."

"I understand," replied the ape-man. He made no other reply, but both Thudos and Doria felt that here was a man who might be trusted.

As the two men entered the avenue in front of the palace of their host, a figure slunk into the shadow of a tree a few paces from them; and neither saw it. Then they walked leisurely toward their apartments in the palace, discussing the noble Thudos and his matchless daughter.

"I have been curious to ask you," said Tarzan, "how Doria dared come to the stadium when her life is constantly in danger should her beauty become known to the Queen?"

"She is always disguised when she goes abroad," replied Gemnon. "A few touches by an expert hand and hollows appear in her cheeks and beneath her eyes, her brow is wrinkled; and behold! she is no longer the most beautiful woman in the world. Nemone would not give her a second thought if she saw her, but still care is taken to see that Nemone does not see her too closely even then. It is informers we fear the most. Thudos never sells a slave who has seen Doria, and once a new slave enters the palace walls he never leaves them again until long years of service have proved him, and his loyalty is unquestioned.

"It is a monotonous life for Doria, the penalty she pays for beauty; but all that we can do is hope and pray that relief will come someday in the death of Nemone or the elevation of Alextar to the throne."

Valthor was asleep on Tarzan's couch when the ape-man entered his bedroom. He had had little rest since his capture, and, in addition, he was suffering from a slight wound; so Tarzan moved softly that he might not disturb him and made no light in the room, the darkness of which was partially dispelled by the moonlight.

Spreading some skins on the floor against the wall opposite the window, the ape-man lay down and was soon asleep, while in the apartment above him two men crouched in the dark beside the window that was directly above that in Tarzan's bedroom.

For a long time they crouched there in silence. One was a large, powerful man; the other smaller and lighter. Fully an hour passed before either moved other than to change a cramped position for one more comfortable; then the smaller man arose. One end of a long rope was knotted about his body beneath his armpits; in his right hand he carried a slim dagger-sword.

Cautiously and silently he went to the window and looked out, his careful gaze searching the grounds below; then he sat on the sill and swung his legs through the window. The larger man, holding the rope firmly with both hands, braced himself. The smaller turned over on his belly and slid out of the window. Hand over hand, the other lowered him; his head disappeared below the sill.

Very carefully, so as to make no noise, the larger man lowered the smaller until the feet of the latter rested on the sill of Tarzan's bedroom window. Here the man reached in and took hold of the casing; then he jerked twice upon the rope to acquaint his fellow with the fact that he had reached his destination safely and the other let the rope slip through his fingers loosely as the movements of the man below dragged it slowly out.

The smaller man stepped gingerly to the floor inside the room. Without hesitation he moved toward the bed, his weapon raised and ready in his hand. He made no haste; his one purpose for the present appeared to be the achievement of absolute silence. It was evident that he feared to awaken the sleeper. Even when he reached the bed he stood there for a long time searching with his eyes for the right spot to strike that the blow might bring instant death. The assassin knew that Gemnon slept in another bedroom across the living room; what he did not know was that Valthor, the Athnean, lay stretched on the bed beneath his keen weapon.

As the assassin hesitated, Tarzan of the Apes opened his eyes. Though the intruder had made no sound his mere presence in the room had aroused the ape-man; perhaps the effluvium from his body, impinging upon the sensitive nostrils of the sleeping beast-man, carried the same message to the alert brain that sound would have carried.

It is said that a sleeping dog awakened by the touch of a cart-wheel reacts so quickly that he can escape harm by leaping aside before the wheel crushes him. I do not believe this; but I am convinced that the so-called lower animals awaken in full and complete possession of all their faculties; not slowly, faculty by faculty, as is the case with man. Thus awoke Tarzan, master of all his powers.

At the instant that he opened his eyes he saw the stranger in the room, saw the dagger raised above the form of the sleeping Valthor, read the whole story in a single glance, and in the same moment arose and leaped upon the unsuspecting murderer who was dragged back from his victim at the very instant that his weapon was descending.

As the two men crashed to the floor, Valthor awoke and sprang from his cot; but by the time he had discovered what was transpiring the would-be assassin lay dead upon the floor, and Tarzan of the Apes stood with one foot upon the body of his kill. For an instant the ape-man hesitated, his face upturned as the weird scream of the victorious bull ape trembled on his lips; but then he shook his head, and only a low growl rumbled upward from the deep chest.

Valthor had heard these growls before and was neither surprised nor shocked. The man in the room above had heard only beasts growl, and the sound made him hesitate and wonder. He had heard, too, the crash of the two bodies as Tarzan had hurled the other to the floor, and while he had not interpreted that correctly it had suggested resistance and put him on his guard. Cautiously he stepped closer to the window and looked out, listening.

In the room below, Tarzan of the Apes seized the corpse of the man who had come to kill him and hurled it through the window into the grounds beneath. The man above saw and, turning, slunk from the room and vanished among the dark shadows of the palace corridors.

14

The Grand Hunt

WITH THE BREAKING of dawn Tarzan and Valthor arose, for the latter was to set out upon his journey to Athne early. The previous evening a slave had been directed to serve breakfast at daybreak, and the two men now heard him arranging the table in the adjoining room.

"We have met again, and again we part," commented Valthor as he fastened his sandal straps to the ivory guards that encircled his ankles. "I wish that you were going with me to Athne, my friend."

"I would go with you were it not for the fact that Gemnon's life would be forfeited should I leave Cathne while he is responsible for me," replied the ape-man, "but you may rest assured that some day I shall pay you a visit in Athne."

"I never expected to see you alive again after we were separated by the flood," continued Valthor, "and when I recognized you in the lion pit I could not believe my own eyes. Four times at least you have saved my life, Tarzan; and you may be assured of a warm welcome in the house of my father at Athne whenever you come."

"The debt, if you feel that there was one, is wiped out," Tarzan assured him, "since you saved my life last night."

"I saved your life! What are you talking about?" demanded Valthor. "How did I save your life?"

"By sleeping in my bed," explained the Lord of the Jungle.

Valthor laughed. "A courageous, a heroic act!" he mocked.

"But nevertheless it saved my life," insisted the ape-man.

"What saved whose life?" demanded a voice at the door.

"Good morning, Gemnon!" greeted Tarzan. "My compliments and congratulations!"

"Thanks! But what about?" demanded the Cathnean.

"Upon your notable ability as a sound sleeper," explained Tarzan, smiling.

Gemnon shook his head dubiously. "Your words are beyond me. What are you talking about?"

"You slept last night through an attempted assassination, the killing of the culprit, and the disposition of the body. Phobeg's warning was no idle gossip."

"You mean that someone came here last night to kill you?"

"And almost killed Valthor instead," and then Tarzan briefly narrated the events of the attempt upon his life.

"Had you ever seen the man before?" asked Gemnon. "Did you recognize him?"

"I paid little attention to him," admitted Tarzan; "I threw him out of the window; but I do not recall having seen him before."

"Was he a noble?"

"No, he was a common warrior. Perhaps you will recognize him when you see him."

"I shall have to have a look at him and report the matter at once," said Gemnon. "Nemone is going to be furious when she hears this."

"She may have instigated it herself," suggested Tarzan; "she is half mad."

"Hush!" cautioned Gemnon. "It is death even to whisper that thought. No, I do not believe it was Nemone; but were you to accuse Erot, M'duze, or Tomos I could easily agree to that. I must go now, and if I do not return before you leave, Valthor, be assured that I have enjoyed entertaining you. It is unfortunate that we are enemies and that the next time we meet we shall have to endeavor to take one another's head."

"It is unfortunate and foolish," replied Valthor.

"But it is the custom," Gemnon reminded him.

"Then may we never meet, for I could never take pleasure in killing you."

"Here's to it, then," cried Gemnon, raising his hand as though it held a drinking horn. "May we never meet again!" and with that he turned and left them.

Tarzan and Valthor had but scarcely finished their meal when a noble arrived to tell them that Valthor's escort was ready to depart, and a moment later, with a brief farewell, the Athnean left.

Tarzan's liking for Valthor, combined with his curiosity to see the City of Ivory, determined him to visit the valley of Thenar before he returned to his own country; but that is a matter apart, having nothing to do with this story, which has seen the last of the likable young noble of Athne.

By Nemone's command the ape-man's weapons had been returned to him, and he was engaged in inspecting them, looking to the points and feathers of his arrows, his bowstring, and his grass rope, when Gemnon returned. The Cathnean was quite evidently angry and not a little excited. This was one of the few occasions upon which Tarzan had seen his warder other than smiling and affable.

"I have had a bad half hour with the Queen," explained Gemnon. "I was lucky to get away with my life. She is furious over this attempt upon your life and blames me for neglect of duty. What am I to do? Sit on your windowsill all night?"

Tarzan laughed. "I am an embarrassment," he said lightly, "and I am sorry; but how can I help it? It was an accident that brought me here; it is perversity that keeps me, the perversity of a spoiled woman."

"You had better not tell her that, nor let another than me hear you say it," Gemnon cautioned him.

"I may tell her," laughed Tarzan; "I am afraid I have never acquired that entirely human accomplishment called diplomacy."

"She has sent me to summon you; and I warn you to exercise a little judgment, even though you have no diplomacy. She is like a raging lion, and whoever arouses her further will be in for a mauling."

"What does she want of me?" demanded Tarzan. "Am I to remain in this house, caged up like a pet dog, to run at the beck of a woman?"

"She is investigating this attempt upon your life and has summoned others to be questioned," Gemnon explained.

Gemnon led the way to a large audience chamber where the nobles of the court were congregated before a massive throne on which the Queen sat, her beautiful brows contracted in a frown. As Tarzan and Gemnon entered the room, she looked up; but she did not smile. A noble advanced and led the two men to seats near the foot of the throne.

As Tarzan glanced about the faces of those near him, he saw Tomos, and Erot, and Xerstle. Erot was nervous; he fidgeted constantly upon his bench; he played with his fingers and with the hilt of his sword; occasionally he glanced appealingly up at Nemone, but if she recognized that he was there, her expression did not acknowledge it.

"We have been awaiting you," said the Queen as Tarzan took his seat. "It appears that you did not exert yourself to hasten in response to our command."

Tarzan looked up at her with an amused smile. "On the contrary, your majesty, I returned at once with the noble Gemnon," he explained respectfully.

"We have summoned you to tell the story of what happened in your apartment last night that resulted in the killing of a warrior." She then turned to a noble standing at her side and whispered a few words in his ear, whereupon the man quit the room. "You may proceed," she said, turning again to Tarzan.

"There is little to tell," replied the ape-man, rising. "A man came to my room to kill me, but I killed him instead."

"How did he enter your room?" demanded Nemone. "Where was Gemnon? Did he admit the fellow?"

"Of course not," replied Tarzan. "Gemnon was asleep in his own room; the man who would have killed me was lowered from the window of the apartment above mine and entered through my window; there was a long rope tied about his body."

"How did you know he came to kill you? Did he attack you?"

"Valthor, the Athnean, was sleeping in my bed; I was sleeping on the floor. The man did not see me, for the room was dark. He went to the bed where he thought I was sleeping. I woke as he stood over Valthor, his sword raised in his hand ready to strike. Then I killed him and threw his body out of the window."

"Did you recognize him? Had you ever seen him before?" asked the Queen.

"I did not recognize him."

There was a noise at the entrance to the audience chamber that caused Nemone to glance up. Four slaves bore a stretcher into the room and laid it at the foot of the throne; on it was the corpse of a man.

"Is this the fellow who attempted your life?" demanded Nemone.

"It is," replied Tarzan.

She turned suddenly upon Erot. "Did you ever see this man before?" she demanded.

Erot arose. He was white and trembled a little. "But your majesty, he is only a common warrior," he countered; "I may have seen him often, yet have forgotten him; that would not be strange, I see so many of them."

"And you," the Queen addressed a young noble standing near, "have you ever seen this man before?"

"Often," replied the noble; "he was a member of the palace guard and in my company."

"How long has he been attached to the palace?" demanded Nemone.

"Not a month, your majesty."

"And before that? Do you know anything about his prior service?"

"He was attached to the retinue of a noble, your majesty," replied the young officer hesitantly.

"What noble?" demanded Nemone.

"Erot," replied the witness in a low voice.

The Queen looked long and searchingly at Erot. "You have

a short memory," she said presently, an undisguised sneer in her voice, "or perhaps you have so many warriors in your retinue that you cannot recall one who has been out of your service for a month!"

Erot was pale and shaken. He looked long at the face of the dead man before he spoke again. "I do recall him now, your majesty, but he does not look the same. Death has changed him; that is why I did not recognize him immediately."

"You are lying," snapped Nemone. "There are some things about this affair that I do not understand; what part you have had in it, I do not know; but I am sure that you had some part, and I am going to find out what. In the meantime you are banished from the palace; there may be others," she looked meaningly at Tomos, "but I shall find them all out, and when I do it will be the lion pit for the lot!"

Rising, she descended from the throne, and all knelt save Tarzan. As she passed him on her way from the chamber, she paused and looked long and searchingly into his eyes. "Be careful," she whispered; "your life is in danger. I dare not see you for a while, for there is one so desperate that not even I could protect you should you visit my apartments again. Tell Gemnon to quit the palace and take you to his father's house. You will be safer there, but even then far from safe. In a few days I shall have removed the obstacles that stand between us; until then, Tarzan, good-bye!"

The ape-man bowed, and the Queen of Cathne passed on out of the audience chamber. The nobles rose. They drew away from Erot and clustered about Tarzan. In disgust the ape-man drew away. "Come, Gemnon," he said; "there is nothing to keep us here longer."

Xerstle blocked their way as they were leaving the chamber. "Everything is ready for the grand hunt," he exclaimed, rubbing his palms together genially. "I thought this tiresome audience would prevent our starting today, but it is still early. The lions and the quarry are awaiting us at the edge of the forest. Get your weapons and join me in the avenue."

Gemnon hesitated. "Who are hunting with you?" he asked.

"Just you and Tarzan and Pindes," explained Xerstle; "a small and select company that ensures a good hunt."

"We will come," said the ape-man.

As the two returned to their quarters to get their weapons Gemnon appeared worried. "I am not sure that it is wise to go," he said.

"And why not?" enquired Tarzan.

"This may be another trap for you."

The ape-man shrugged. "It is quite possible, but I cannot remain cooped up in hiding. I should like to see what a grand hunt is; I have heard the term so often since I came to Cathne. Who is Pindes? I do not recall him."

"He was an officer of the guard when Erot became the Queen's favorite, but through Erot he was dismissed. He is not a bad fellow but weak and easily influenced; however, he must hate Erot, and so I think you have nothing to fear from him."

"I have nothing to fear from anyone," Tarzan assured him.

"Perhaps you think not, but be on guard."

"I am always on guard; had I not been I should have been dead long ago."

"Your self-complacency may be your undoing," growled Gemnon testily.

Tarzan laughed. "I appreciate both danger and my own limitations, but I cannot let fear rob me of my liberty and the pleasures of life; fear is to be more dreaded than death. You are afraid, Erot is afraid, Nemone is afraid; and you are all unhappy. Were I afraid, I should be unhappy but no safer. I prefer to be simply cautious. And by the way, speaking of caution, Nemone instructed me to tell you to take me from the palace and keep me in your father's house. She says the palace is no safe place for me. I really think that it is M'duze who is after me."

"M'duze and Erot and Tomos," said Gemnon; "there is a triumvirate of greed and malice and duplicity that I should hate to have upon my trail."

At his quarters, Gemnon gave orders that his and Tarzan's belongings be moved to the house of his father while the two men were hunting; then they went to the avenue where they found Xerstle and Pindes awaiting them. The latter was a man of about thirty, rather good-looking but with a weak face and eyes that invariably dropped from a direct gaze. He met Tarzan with great cordiality, and as the four men walked along the main avenue of the city toward the eastern gate he was most affable.

"You have never been on a grand hunt?" he asked Tarzan.

"No; I have no idea what the term means," replied the ape-man.

"We shall not tell you then, but shall let you see for yourself; then you will enjoy it the more. Of course you hunt much in your own country, I presume."

"I hunt for food only or for my enemies," replied the ape-man.

"You never hunt for pleasure?" demanded Pindes.

"I take no pleasure in killing."

"Well, you won't have to kill today," Pindes assured him; "the lions will do our killing; and I can promise you that you will enjoy the thrill of the chase, that reaches its highest point in the grand hunt."

Beyond the eastern gate an open, parklike plain stretched for a short distance to the forest. Near the gate four stalwart slaves held two lions in leash, while a fifth man, naked but for a dirty loincloth, squatted upon the ground a short distance away.

As the four hunters approached the party Xerstle explained to Tarzan that the leashed beasts were his hunting lions, and as the ape-man's observant eyes ran over the five men who were to accompany them on the hunt he recognized the stalwart black seated upon the ground apart as the man he had seen upon the auction block in the marketplace; then Xerstle approached the fellow and spoke briefly with him, evidently giving him orders. When Xerstle had finished, the native started off at a trot across the plain in the direction of the forest. Everyone watched his progress.

"Why is he running ahead?" asked Tarzan. "He will frighten away the quarry."

Pindes laughed. "He is the quarry."

"You mean—" demanded Tarzan with a scowl.

"That this is a grand hunt," cried Xerstle, "where we hunt man, the grandest quarry."

The ape-man's eyes narrowed. "I see," he said; "you are cannibals; you eat the flesh of men."

Gemnon turned away to hide a smile.

"No!" shouted Pindes and Xerstle in unison. "Of course not."

"Then why do you hunt him, if not to eat him?"

"For pleasure," explained Xerstle.

"Oh, yes; I forgot. And what happens if you do not get him? Is he free then?"

"I should say not; not if we can capture him again," cried Xerstle. "Slaves cost too much money to be lightly thrown away like that."

"Tell me more of the grand hunt," insisted Tarzan. "I think I am going to get much satisfaction from this one."

"I hope so," replied Xerstle. "When the quarry reaches the forest we loose the lions; then the sport commences."

"If the fellow takes to the trees," explained Pindes, "we leash the lions and drive him out with sticks and stones or with our spears; then we give him a little start and loose the lions again. Pretty soon they catch him; and it is the aim of the hunters to be in at the kill, for there is where the real thrills come. Have you ever seen two lions kill a man?"

When the black reached the forest, Xerstle spoke a word of command to the keepers and they unleashed the two great beasts. From their actions it was evident that they were trained to the sport. From the moment the native had started out toward the forest the lions had strained and tugged upon their leashes, so that it was only by the use of their spears that the keepers restrained the beasts from dragging them across the plain; and when they were at last set free they bounded away in pursuit of the unfortunate creature who had been chosen to give Xerstle and his guests a few hours of entertainment.

Halfway to the forest the lions settled down to a much slower gait, and the hunters commenced gradually to overhaul them. Xerstle and Pindes appeared excited, far more excited than the circumstances of the hunt warranted; Gemnon was silent and thoughtful; Tarzan was disgusted and bored. But before they reached the forest his interest was aroused, for a plan had occurred to him whereby he might derive some pleasure from the day's sport.

The wood, which the hunters presently entered a short distance behind the lions, was of extraordinary beauty; the trees were very old and gave evidence of having received the intelligent care of man, as did the floor of the forest. There was little or no deadwood in the trees and only occasional clumps of underbrush upon the ground between them. As far as Tarzan could see among the boles of the trees the aspect was that of a well-kept park rather than of a natural wood, and in answer to a comment he made upon this fact Gemnon explained that for ages his people had given regular attention to the conservation of this forest from the City of Gold to the Pass of the Warriors.

Heavy lianas swung in graceful loops from tree to tree; higher up toward the sunlight Tarzan caught glimpses of brilliant tropical blooms; there were monkeys in the trees and gaudy, screaming birds. The scene filled the ape-man with such a longing for the freedom that was his life that, for the moment, he almost forgot that Gemnon's life hinged upon his abandoning all thought of escape while the young noble was responsible to the Queen for his safekeeping.

Once within the forest Tarzan dropped gradually to the rear of the party, and then, when none was looking, swung to the branches of a tree. Plain to his nostrils had been the scent spoor of the quarry from the beginning of the chase, and now the ape-man knew, possibly even better than the lions, the direction of the hopeless flight of the doomed black.

Swinging through the trees in a slight detour that carried him around and beyond the hunters without revealing his desertion to them, Tarzan sped through the middle terraces of the forest as only the Lord of the Jungle can.

Stronger and stronger in his nostrils waxed the scent of the quarry; behind him came the lions and the hunters; and he knew that he must act quickly, for they were no great distance in his rear. A grim smile lighted his gray eyes as he considered the dénouement of the project he had undertaken.

Presently he saw the black running through the forest just ahead of him. The fellow was moving at a dogged trot, casting an occasional glance behind him. He was a splendidly muscled Galla, a perfect type of primitive manhood, who seemed bent upon giving the best account of himself that he might against the hopeless odds that must eventually win the game in which his life was the stake. There was neither fear nor panic in his flight, merely inflexible determination to surrender to the inevitable only as a last resort.

Tarzan was directly above the man now, and he spoke to him in the language of his people. "Take to the trees," he called down.

The native looked up, but he did not stop. "Who are you?" he demanded.

"An enemy of your master, who would help you escape," replied the ape-man.

"There is no escape; if I take to the trees they will stone me down."

"They will not find you; I will see to that."

"Why should you help me?" demanded the native, but he stopped now and looked up again, searching for the man whose voice came down to him in a tongue that gave him confidence in the speaker.

"I have told you that I am an enemy of your master."

Now the black saw the bronzed figure of the giant above him. "You are a white man!" he exclaimed. "You are trying to trick me. Why should a white man help me?"

"Hurry!" admonished Tarzan, "or it will be too late, and no one can help you."

For just an instant longer the African hesitated; then he leaped for a low-hanging branch and swung himself up into the trees as Tarzan came down to meet him.

"They will come soon and stone us both down," he said. There was no hope in his voice nor any fear, only dumb apathy.

15

The Plot that Failed

THROUGH THE TREES toward the east the ape-man carried the Galla slave who was to have been the victim of Xerstle's day of sport. At first the man had demurred; but as the growling of the hunting lions had increased in volume, denoting their close approach, he had resigned himself to what he may have considered the lesser of two evils.

Swiftly, the giant of the jungle bore the Galla toward the east where, beyond the forest, loomed the mountains that hemmed Onthar upon that side. For a mile he carried him through the trees and then swung lightly to the ground.

"If the lions pick up your trail now," he said, "it will not be until long after you have reached the mountains and safety. But do not delay—go now."

The native fell upon his knees and took the hand of his savior in his own. "I am Hafim," he said. "If I could serve you, I would die for you. Who are you?"

"I am Tarzan of the Apes. Now go your way and lose no time."

"One more favor," begged the black.

"What?"

"I have a brother. He, too, was captured by these people when they captured me. He is a slave in the gold mines south of Cathne. His name is Niaka. If you should ever go to the gold mines, tell him that Hafim has escaped. It will make him happier, and perhaps then he will try to escape."

"I shall tell him. Now go."

Silently the African disappeared among the boles of the forest trees, and Tarzan sprang again into the branches and swung rapidly back in the direction of the hunters. When he reached them, dropping to the ground and approaching them from behind, they were clustered near the spot at which Hafim had taken to the trees.

"Where have you been?" asked Xerstle. "We thought that you had become lost."

"I dropped behind," replied the ape-man; "but where is your quarry? I thought you would have had him by this time."

"We cannot understand it," admitted Xerstle. "It is evident that he climbed this tree, because the lions followed him to this very spot, where they stood looking up into the tree; but they did not growl as though they saw the man. Then we leashed them again and sent one of the keepers into the tree, but he saw no sign of the quarry."

"It is a mystery!" exclaimed Pindes.

"It is indeed," agreed Tarzan; "at least for those who do not know the secret."

"Who does know the secret?" demanded Xerstle.

"The black slave who has escaped you must know, if no other."

"He has not escaped me," snapped Xerstle. "He has but prolonged the hunt and increased its interest."

"It would add to the excitement of the day to lay some bets on that," said the ape-man. "I do not believe that your lions can again pick up the trail in time to bring down the quarry before dark."

"A thousand drachmas that they do!" cried Xerstle.

"Being a stranger who came naked into your country, I have no thousand drachmas," said Tarzan; "but perhaps Gemnon will cover your bet." He turned his face away from Xerstle and Pindes and, looking at Gemnon, slowly closed one eye.

"Done!" exclaimed Gemnon to Xerstle.

"I only demand the right to conduct the hunt in my own way," said the latter.

"Of course," agreed Gemnon, and Xerstle turned his face toward Pindes and slowly closed one eye.

"We shall separate, then," explained Xerstle, "and as you and Tarzan are betting against me, one of you must accompany me and the other go with Pindes so that all may be sure that the hunt is prosecuted with fairness and determination."

"Agreed," said Tarzan.

"But I am responsible to the Queen for the safe return of Tarzan," demurred Gemnon; "I do not like to have him out of my sight even for a short time."

"I promise that I shall not try to escape," the ape-man assured him.

"It was not that alone of which I was thinking," explained Gemnon.

"And I can assure you that I can take care of myself, if you feel fears for my safety," added Tarzan.

"Come, let us go," urged Xerstle. "I shall hunt with Gemnon and Pindes with Tarzan. We shall take one lion, they the other."

Reluctantly Gemnon assented to the arrangement, and presently the two parties separated, Xerstle and Gemnon going toward the northwest while Pindes and Tarzan took an easterly direction. The latter had proceeded but a short distance, the lion still upon its leash, when Pindes suggested that they separate, spreading out through the forest, and thus combing it more carefully.

"You go straight east," he said to Tarzan, "the keepers and the lion will go northeast, and I will go north. If any comes upon the trail he may shout to attract the others to his position. If we have not located the quarry in an hour let us all converge toward the mountains at the eastern side of the forest."

The ape-man nodded and started off in the direction assigned him, soon disappearing among the trees; but neither Pindes nor the keepers moved from where he had left them, the keepers held by a whispered word from Pindes. The leashed lion looked after the departing ape-man, and Pindes smiled. The keepers looked at him questioningly.

"Such sad accidents have happened many times before," said Pindes.

Tarzan moved steadily toward the east. He knew that he would not find the Negro and so he did not look for him. The forest interested him but not to the exclusion of all else; his keen faculties were always upon the alert. Presently he heard a noise behind him and glancing back was not surprised by what he saw. A lion was stalking him, a lion wearing the harness of a hunting lion of Cathne. It was one of Xerstle's lions; it was the same lion that had accompanied Pindes and Tarzan.

Instantly the ape-man guessed the truth, and a grim light glinted in his eyes; it was no light of anger, but there was disgust in it and the shadowy suggestion of a savage smile. The lion, realizing that its quarry had discovered it, began to roar. In the distance Pindes heard and smiled.

"Let us go now," he said to the keepers; "we must not find the remains too quickly; that might not look well." The three men moved slowly off toward the north.

From a distance Gemnon and Xerstle heard the roar of the hunting lion. "They have picked up the trail," said Gemnon, halting; "we had best join them."

"Not yet," demurred Xerstle. "It may be a false trail. The animal with them is not so good a hunter as ours; he is not so well trained. We will wait until we hear the hunters call." But Gemnon was troubled.

Tarzan stood waiting the coming of the lion. He could have taken to the trees and escaped, but a spirit of bravado prompted him to remain. He hated treachery, and exposing it gave him pleasure. He carried a Cathnean spear and his own hunting knife; his bow and arrows he had left behind.

The lion came nearer; it seemed vaguely disturbed. Perhaps it did not understand why the quarry stood and faced it instead of running away. Its tail twitched; its head was flattened; slowly it came on again, its wicked eyes gleaming angrily.

Tarzan waited. In his right hand was the sturdy Cathnean spear, in his left the hunting knife of the father he had never known. He measured the distance with a trained eye as the lion started its swift, level charge; then, when it was coming at full speed, his spear hand flew back and he launched the heavy weapon.

Deep beneath the left shoulder it drove, deep into the savage heart; but it checked the beast's charge for but an instant. Infuriated now, the carnivore rose upon its hind legs above the ape-man, its great, taloned paws reaching to drag him to the slavering jowls; but Tarzan, swift as Ara, the lightning, stooped and sprang beneath them, sprang to one side and then in again, closing with the lion, leaping upon its back.

With a hideous roar, the animal wheeled and sought to bury its great fangs in the bronzed body or reach it with those raking talons. It threw itself to right and left as the creature clinging to it drove a steel blade repeatedly into the already torn and bleeding heart.

The vitality and life tenacity of a lion are astounding; but even that mighty frame could not for long withstand the lethal wounds its adversary had inflicted, and presently it slumped to earth and, with a little quiver, died. Then the ape-man leaped to his feet. With one foot upon the carcass of his kill, Tarzan of the Apes raised his face to the leafy canopy of the Cathnean forest and from his great chest rolled the hideous victory cry of the bull ape which has killed.

As the uncanny challenge reverberated down the forest aisles, Pindes and the two keepers looked questioningly at one another and laid their hands upon their sword hilts.

"In the name of Thoos! what was that?" demanded one of the keepers.

"By the name of Thoos! I never heard a sound so horrible before," answered his companion, looking fearfully in the direction from which those weird notes had come.

"Silence!" admonished Pindes. "Do you want the thing to creep upon us unheard because of your jabbering!"

"What was it, master?" asked one of the men in a whisper.

"It may have been the death cry of the stranger," suggested Pindes, voicing the hope that was in his heart.

"It sounded not like a death cry, master," replied the black; "there was a note of strength and elation in it and none of weakness and defeat."

"Silence, fool!" grumbled Pindes.

At a little distance, Gemnon and Xerstle heard, too. "What was that?" demanded the latter.

Gemnon shook his head. "I do not know, but we had better go and find out. I did not like the sound of it."

Xerstle appeared nervous. "It was nothing, perhaps, but the wind in the trees; let us go on with our hunting."

"There is no wind," demurred Gemnon. "I am going to investigate. I am responsible for the safety of the stranger; but, even of more importance than that, I like him."

"Oh, so do I!" exclaimed Xerstle eagerly. "But nothing could have happened to him; Pindes is with him."

"That is precisely what I was thinking," observed Gemnon.

"That nothing could have happened to him?"

"That Pindes is with him!"

Xerstle shot a quick, suspicious look at the other, motioned to the keepers to follow with the leashed lion, and fell in behind Gemnon who had already started back toward the point at which they had separated from their companions.

In the meantime Pindes, unable to curb his curiosity, overcame his fears and started after Tarzan for the purpose of ascertaining what had befallen him as well as tracing the origin of the mysterious cry that had so filled him and his servants with wondering awe. Rather nervously, the two lion keepers followed him through the brooding silence of the forest, all three men keeping a careful lookout ahead and upon every side.

They had not gone far when Pindes, who was in the lead, halted suddenly and pointed straight ahead. "What is that?" he demanded.

The keepers pressed forward. "Mane of Thoos!" cried one, "it is the lion!"

They advanced slowly, watching the lion, looking to right and left. "It is dead!" exclaimed Pindes.

The three men examined the body of the dead beast, turning it over. "It has been stabbed to death," announced one of the keepers.

"The Galla slave had no weapons," said Pindes thoughtfully.

"The stranger carried a knife," a keeper reminded him.

"Whoever killed the lion must have fought it hand-to-hand," reflected Pindes aloud.

"Then he must be lying nearby dead or wounded, master."

"Search for him!" directed Pindes.

"He could have killed Phobeg with his bare hands that day that he threw him into the audience at the stadium," a keeper reminded the noble. "He carried him around as though Phobeg were a babe. He is very strong."

"What has that to do with the matter?" demanded Pindes irritably.

"I do not know, master; I was only thinking."

"I did not tell you to think," snapped Pindes; "I told you to hunt for the man that killed the lion; he must be dying or dead nearby."

While they hunted, Xerstle and Gemnon were drawing nearer. The latter was much concerned about the welfare of his charge. He trusted neither Xerstle nor Pindes, and now he commenced to suspect that he and Tarzan had been deliberately separated for sinister purposes. He was walking a little behind Xerstle at the time; the keepers, with the lion, were just ahead of them. He felt a hand upon his shoulder and wheeled about; there stood Tarzan, a smile upon his lips.

"Where did you drop from?" demanded Gemnon.

"We separated to search for the Galla, Pindes and I," explained the ape-man as Xerstle turned at the sound of Gemnon's voice and discovered him.

"Did you hear that terrible scream a while ago?" demanded Xerstle. "We thought it possible that one of you was hurt, and we were hurrying to investigate."

"Did someone scream?" inquired Tarzan innocently. "Perhaps it was Pindes, for I am not hurt."

Shortly after Tarzan had rejoined them Xerstle and Gemnon came upon Pindes and his two lion keepers searching the underbrush and the surrounding forest. As his eyes fell upon Tarzan, Pindes's eyes went wide in astonishment, and he paled a little.

"What has happened?" demanded Xerstle. "What are you looking for? Where is your lion?"

"He is dead," explained Pindes. "Someone or something stabbed him to death." He did not look at Tarzan; he feared to do so. "We have been looking for the man who did it, thinking that he must have been badly mauled and, doubtless, killed."

"Have you found him?" asked Tarzan.

'No."

"Shall I help you search for him? Suppose you and I, Pindes, go away alone and look for him!" suggested the ape-man.

For a moment Pindes seemed choking as he sought for a reply. "No!" he exclaimed presently. "It would be useless; we have searched carefully; there is not even a sign of blood to indicate that he was wounded."

"And you found no trace of the quarry?" asked Xerstle.

"None," replied Pindes. "He has escaped, and we might as well return to the city. I have had enough hunting for today."

Xerstle grumbled. It was getting late; he had lost his quarry and one of his lions; but there seemed no reason to continue the hunt and so he grudgingly acquiesced.

"So this is a grand hunt?" remarked Tarzan meditatively. "Perhaps it has not been thrilling; but I have enjoyed it greatly. However, Gemnon appears to be the only one who has profited by it; he has won a thousand drachmas."

Xerstle only grunted and strode on moodily toward the city. When the party separated before the house of Gemnon's father Tarzan stood close to Xerstle and whispered in a low voice. "My compliments to Erot, and may he have better luck next time!"

16

In the Temple of Thoos

As Tarzan sat with Gemnon and the latter's father and mother at dinner that evening a slave entered the room to announce that a messenger had come from the house of Thudos, the father of Doria, with an important communication for Gemnon.

"Fetch him here," directed the young noble, and a moment later a tall Negro was ushered into the apartment.

"Ah, Gemba!" exclaimed Gemnon in a kindly tone, "you have a message for me?"

"Yes, master," replied the slave, "but it is important—and secret."

"You may speak before these others, Gemba," replied Gemnon. "What is it?"

"Doria, the daughter of Thudos, my master, has sent me to tell you that by a ruse the noble Erot gained entrance to her father's house and spoke with her today. What he said to her was of no importance; only the fact that he saw her is important."

"The jackal!" exclaimed Gemnon's father.

Gemnon paled. "That is all?" he enquired.

"That is all, master," replied Gemba.

Gemnon took a gold coin from his pocket pouch and handed it to the slave. "Return to your mistress, and tell her that I shall come and speak with her father tomorrow."

After the slave had withdrawn Gemnon looked hopelessly at

his father. "What can I do?" he asked. "What can Thudos do? What can anyone do? We are helpless."

"Perhaps I can do something," suggested Tarzan. "For the moment I seem to hold the confidence of your Queen; when I see her I shall question her, and if it is necessary I shall intercede in your behalf."

A new hope sprang to Gemnon's eyes. "If you will!" he cried. "She will listen to you. I believe that you alone might save Doria; but remember that the Queen must not see her, for should she, nothing can save her—she will be either disfigured or killed."

Early the next morning a messenger from the palace brought a command to Tarzan to visit the Queen at noon, with instructions to Gemnon to accompany Tarzan with a strong guard as she feared treachery on the part of Tarzan's enemies.

"They must be powerful enemies that dare attempt to thwart the wishes of Nemone," commented Gemnon's father.

"There is only one in all Cathne who dares do that," replied Gemnon.

The older man nodded. "The old she-devil! Would but that Thoos destroyed her! How shameful it is that Cathne should be ruled by a slave woman!"

"I have seen Nemone look at her as though she wished to kill her," said Tarzan.

"Yes, but she will never dare," prophesied Gemnon's father. "Between the old witch and Tomos a threat of some sort is held over the Queen's head so that she dares not destroy either one of them, yet I am sure she hates them both; and it is seldom that she permits one to live whom she hates."

"It is thought that they hold the secret of her birth, a secret that would destroy her if it were announced to the people," explained Gemnon; "but come, we have the morning to ourselves; I shall not visit Thudos until after you have talked with Nemone; what shall we do in the meantime?"

"I should like to visit the mines of Cathne," replied Tarzan; "shall we have time?"

"Yes, we shall," replied Gemnon; "the Mine of the Rising

Sun is not far; and as there is little to see after you get there, the trip will not take long."

On the road from Cathne to the nearer mine, Gemnon pointed out the breeding plant where the war and hunting lions of Cathne are bred; but they did not stop to visit the place, and presently they were winding up the short mountain road to the Gold Mine of the Rising Sun.

As Gemnon had warned him, there was little of interest for Tarzan to see. The workings were open, the mother lode lying practically upon the surface of the ground; and so rich was it that only a few slaves working with crude picks and bars were needed to supply the coffers of Cathne with vast quantities of the precious metal. But it was not the mines nor gold that had caused Tarzan to wish to visit the diggings. He had promised Hafim that he would carry a message to his brother, Niaka; and it was for this purpose that he had suggested the visit.

As he moved about among the slaves, ostensibly inspecting the lode, he finally succeeded in separating himself sufficiently from Gemnon and the warriors who guarded the workers to permit him to speak unnoticed to one of the slaves.

"Which is Niaka?" he asked in Galla, lowering his voice to a whisper.

The black looked up in surprise, but at a warning gesture from Tarzan bent his head again and answered in a whisper, "Niaka is the big man at my right. He is head man; you see that he does not work."

Tarzan moved then in the direction of Niaka, and when he was close stopped beside him and leaned as though inspecting the lode that was uncovered at his feet. "Listen," he whispered. "I bring you a message, but let no one know that I am talking to you. It is from your brother, Hafim. He has escaped."

"How?" whispered Niaka.

Briefly, Tarzan explained.

"It was you, then, who saved him?"

The ape-man nodded.

"I am only a poor slave," said Niaka, "and you are a powerful noble, no doubt; so I can never repay you. But should you ever need any service that Niaka can render, you have but to command; with my life I would serve you. In that little hut below the diggings I live with my woman; because I am a head man I am trusted and live thus alone. If you ever want me you will find me there."

"I ask no return for what I did," replied Tarzan, "but I shall remember where you live; one never knows what the future holds."

He moved away then and joined Gemnon; and presently the two turned back toward the city, while in the palace of the Queen Tomos entered the apartment of Nemone and knelt.

"What now?" she demanded. "Is the affair so urgent that I must be interrupted at my toilet?"

"It is, majesty," replied the councillor, "and I beg that you send your slaves away. What I have to say is for your ears alone."

There were four Negro girls working on Nemone's nails, one at each foot and one at each hand, and a white girl arranging her hair. To the last the Queen spoke, "Take the slaves away, Maluma, and send them to their quarters; you may wait in the adjoining room."

Then she turned to the councillor, who had arisen. "Well, what is it?"

"Your majesty has long had reason to suspect the loyalty of Thudos," Tomos reminded her, "and in the interest of your majesty's welfare and the safety of the throne, I am constantly watchful of the activities of this powerful enemy. Spurred on by love and loyalty, the noble Erot has been my most faithful agent and ally; and it is really to him that we owe the information that I bring you."

Nemone tapped her sandaled foot impatiently upon the mosaic floor. "Have done with the self-serving preamble, and tell me what you have to tell me," she snapped, for she did not like Tomos and made no effort to hide her feelings.

"Briefly, then, it is this; Gemnon conspires also with Thudos, hoping, doubtless, that his reward will be the beautiful daughter of his chief."

"That hollow-cheeked strumpet!" exclaimed Nemone. "Who said she was beautiful?"

"Erot tells me that Gemnon and Thudos believe her the most beautiful woman in the world," replied Tomos.

"Impossible! Did Erot see her?"

"Yes, majesty, he saw her."

"What does Erot say?" demanded the Queen.

"That she is indeed beautiful," replied the councillor. "There are others who think so too," he added.

"What others?"

"One who has been drawn into the conspiracy with Gemnon and Thudos by the beauty of Doria, the daughter of Thudos."

"Whom do you mean? Speak out! I know you have something unpleasant in your mind that you are suffering to tell me, hoping that it will make me unhappy."

"Oh, majesty, you wrong me!" cried Tomos. "My only thoughts are for the happiness of my beloved Queen."

"Your words stink with falseness," sneered Nemone. "But get to the point; I have other matters to occupy my time."

"I but hesitated to name the other for fear of wounding your majesty," said Tomos oilily; "but if you insist, it is the stranger called Tarzan."

Nemone sat up very straight. "What fabric of lies is this you and M'duze are weaving?" she demanded.

"It is no lie, majesty. Tarzan and Gemnon were seen coming from the house of Thudos late at night. Erot had followed them there; he saw them go in; they were there a long while; hiding in the shadows across the avenue, he saw them come out. He says that they were quarreling over Doria, and he believes that it was Gemnon who sought the life of Tarzan because of jealousy."

Nemone sat straight and stiff upon her couch; her face was pale and tense with fury. "Someone shall die for this," she said in a low voice. "Go!"

Tomos backed from the room. He was elated until he had time to reflect more fully upon her words; then he reflected that Nemone had not stated explicitly who should die. He had assumed that she meant Tarzan, because it was Tarzan whom he wished to die; but it presently occurred to him that she might have meant another, and he was less elated.

It was almost noon when Tarzan and Gemnon returned to the city, and time for the latter to conduct Tarzan to his audience with Nemone. With a guard of warriors they went to the palace, where the ape-man was immediately admitted alone into the presence of the Queen.

"Where have you been?" she demanded.

Tarzan looked at her in surprise; then he smiled. "I visited the Mine of the Rising Sun."

"Where were you last night?"

"At the house of Gemnon," he replied

"You were with Doria!" accused Nemone.

"No," said the ape-man; "that was the night before."

He had been surprised by the accusation and the knowledge that it connoted, but he did not let her see that he was surprised. He was not thinking of himself but of Doria and Gemnon, seeking a plan whereby he might protect them. It was evident that some enemy had turned informer and that Nemone already knew of the visit to the house of Thudos; therefore he felt that it would but have aroused the Queen's suspicions to have denied it; to admit it freely, to show that he sought to conceal nothing, would allay them. As a matter of fact Tarzan's frank and ready reply left Nemone rather flat.

"Why did you go to the house of Thudos?" she asked, but this time her tone was not accusing.

"You see, Gemnon does not dare to leave me alone for fear that I shall escape or that something may befall me; and so he is forced to take me wherever he goes. It is rather hard on him, Nemone, and I have been intending to ask you to make someone else responsible for me for at least a part of the time."

"We will speak of that later," replied the Queen. "Why does Gemnon go to the house of Thudos?" Nemone's eyes narrowed suspiciously.

The ape-man smiled. "What a foolish question for a woman to ask!" he exclaimed. "Gemnon is in love with Doria. I thought all Cathne knew that; he certainly takes enough pains to tell all his acquaintances."

"You are sure that it is not you who are in love with her?" demanded Nemone.

Tarzan looked at her with disgust he made no effort to conceal. "Do not be a fool, Nemone," he said. "I do not like foolish women."

The jaw of the Queen of Cathne dropped. In all her life no one had ever addressed her in words or tones like these. For a moment they left her speechless, but in that moment of speechlessness there came the sudden realization that the very things that shocked her also relieved her mind of gnawing suspicion and of jealousy—Tarzan did not love Doria. And, too, she was compelled to admit that his indifference to her position or her anger increased her respect for him and made him still more desirable in her eyes. She had never known such a man before; none had ever ruled her. Here was one who might if he wished, but she was troubled by the fear that he did not care enough about her to wish to rule her.

When she spoke again, she had regained her calm. "I was told that you loved her," she explained, "but I did not believe it. Is she very beautiful? I have heard that she is considered the most beautiful woman in Cathne."

"Perhaps Gemnon thinks so," replied Tarzan with a laugh, "but you know what love does to the eyes of youth."

"What do you think of her?" demanded the Queen.

The ape-man shrugged. "She is not bad looking," he said.

"Is she as beautiful as Nemone?" demanded the Queen.

"As the brilliance of a far star is to the brilliance of the sun."

The reply appeared to please Nemone. She arose and came closer to Tarzan. "You think me beautiful?" she asked in soft, insinuating tones.

"You are very beautiful, Nemone," he answered truthfully.

She pressed against him, caressing his shoulder with a smooth, warm palm. "Love me, Tarzan," she whispered, her voice husky with emotion.

There was a rattling of chains at the far end of the room, followed by a terrific roar as Belthar sprang to his feet. Nemone shrank suddenly away from the ape-man; a shudder ran through her body, and an expression half fright, half anger, suffused her face.

"It is always something," she said irritably, trembling a

little. "Belthar is jealous. There is a strange bond linking the life of that beast to my life. I do not know what it is; I wish I did." A light, almost of madness, glittered in her eyes. "I wish I knew! Sometimes I think he is the mate that Thoos intended for me; sometimes I think he is myself in another form; but this I know: When Belthar dies, I die!"

She looked up rather sadly at Tarzan as again her mood changed. "Come, my friend," she said; "we shall go to the temple together and perhaps Thoos may answer the questions that are in the heart of Nemone." She struck a bronze disc that depended from the ceiling, and as the brazen notes reverberated in the room a door opened and a noble bowed low upon the threshold.

"The guard!" commanded the Queen. "We are visiting Thoos in his temple."

The progress to the temple was in the nature of a pageant—marching warriors with pennons streaming from spear tips, nobles resplendent in gorgeous trappings, the Queen in a golden chariot drawn by lions. Tomos walked upon one side of the glittering car, Tarzan upon the other where Erot had previously walked.

The ape-man was as uneasy as a forest lion as he strode between the lines of gaping citizenry. Crowds annoyed and irritated him; formalities irked him; his thoughts were faraway in the distant jungle that he loved. He knew that Gemnon was nearby watching him; but whether he were nearby or not, Tarzan would not attempt to escape while this friend was responsible for him. His mind occupied with such thoughts, he spoke to the Queen.

"At the palace," he reminded her, "I spoke to you concerning the matter of relieving Gemnon of the irksome job of watching me."

"Gemnon has acquitted himself well," she replied. "I see no reason for changing."

"Relieve him then occasionally," suggested Tarzan. "Let Erot take his place."

Nemone looked at him in astonishment. "But Erot hates you!" she exclaimed.

"All the more reason that he would watch me carefully," argued Tarzan.

"He would probably kill you."

"He would not dare if he knew that he must pay for my death or escape with his own life," suggested Tarzan.

"You like Gemnon, do you not?" enquired Nemone innocently.

"Very much," the ape-man assured her.

"Then he is the man to watch you, for you would not imperil his life by escaping while he is responsible."

Tarzan smiled inwardly and said no more; it was evident that Nemone was no fool. He would have to devise some other plan of escape that would not jeopardize the safety of his friend.

They were approaching the temple now and his attention was distracted by the approach of a number of priests leading a slave girl in chains. They brought her to the chariot of Nemone, and while the procession halted the priests chanted in a strange gibberish that Tarzan could not understand. Later he learned that no one understood it, not even the priests; but when he asked why they recited something that they could not understand no one could tell him.

Gemnon thought that once the words had meant something, but they had been repeated mechanically for so many ages that at length the original pronunciation had been lost and the meaning of the words forgotten.

When the chant was completed the priests chained the girl to the rear of the Queen's chariot; and the march was resumed, the priests following behind the girl.

At the entrance to the temple Phobeg was on guard as a girl entered to worship. Recognizing the warrior, she greeted him and paused for a moment's conversation, the royal party having not yet entered the temple square.

"I have not seen you to talk with for a long time, Phobeg," she said. "I am glad that you are back again on the temple guard."

"Thanks to the stranger called Tarzan I am alive and here," replied Phobeg.

"I should think that you would hate him," exclaimed the girl.

"Not I," cried Phobeg. "I know a better man when I see one. I admire him. And did he not grant me my life when the crowd screamed for my death?"

"That is true," admitted the girl. "And now *he* needs a friend."

"What do you mean, Maluma?" demanded the warrior.

"I was in an adjoining room when Tomos visited the Queen this morning," explained the girl, "and I overheard him tell her that Thudos and Gemnon and Tarzan were conspiring against her and that Tarzan loved Doria, the daughter of Thudos."

"How did Tomos know these things?" asked Phobeg. "Did he offer proof?"

"He said that Erot had watched and had seen Gemnon and Tarzan visit the house of Thudos," explained Maluma. "He also told her that Erot had seen Doria and had reported that she was very beautiful."

Phobeg whistled. "That will be the end of the daughter of Thudos," he said.

"It will be the end of the stranger, too," prophesied Maluma; "and I am sorry, for I like him. He is not like the jackal, Erot, whom everyone hates."

"Here comes the Queen!" exclaimed Phobeg as the head of the procession debouched into the temple square. "Run along now and get a good place, for there will be something to see today; there always is when the Queen comes to worship god."

Before the temple, Nemone alighted from her chariot and walked up the broad stairway to the ornate entrance. Behind her were the priests with the slave girl, a frightened, wide-eyed girl with tears upon her cheeks. Following them came the nobles of the court, the warriors of the guard remaining in the temple square before the entrance.

The temple was a large three-storied building with a great central dome about the interior of which ran galleries at the second and third stories. The interior of the dome was of gold as were the pillars that supported the galleries, while the walls of the building were embellished with colorful mosaics. Directly opposite the main entrance, on a level with a raised dais, a great cage was built into a niche, and on either side of the cage was an altar supporting a lion carved from solid gold. Before the dais was a stone railing inside of which was a throne and a row of stone benches facing the cage in the niche.

Nemone advanced and seated herself upon the throne, while the nobles took their places upon the benches. No one paid any attention to Tarzan; so he remained outside the railing, a mildly interested spectator.

He had noticed a change come over Nemone the instant that she had entered the temple. She had shown signs of extreme nervousness, the expression of her face had changed; it was tense and eager; there was a light in her eyes that was like the mad light he had seen there occasionally before, yet different—the light of religious fanaticism.

Tarzan saw the priests lead the girl up onto the dais and then, beyond them, he saw something rise up in the cage. It was an old and mangy lion. The high priest began a meaningless, singsong chant, in which the others joined occasionally as though making responses. Nemone leaned forward eagerly; her eyes were fastened upon the old lion. Her breasts rose and fell to her excited breathing.

Suddenly the chanting ceased and the Queen arose. "O Thoos!" she cried, her hands outstretched toward the mangy old carnivore. "Nemone brings you greetings and an offering. Receive them from Nemone and bless her. Give her life and health and happiness; most of all Nemone prays for happiness. Preserve her friends and destroy her enemies. And, O Thoos, give her the one thing that she most desires—love, the love of the one man in all the world that Nemone has ever loved!" And the lion glared at her through the bars.

She spoke as though in a trance, as though oblivious to all else around her save the god to which she prayed. There were pathos and tragedy in her voice, and a great pity rose in the breast of the ape-man for this poor Queen who had never known love and who never might because of the warped brain that mistook passion for affection and lust for love.

As she sat down weakly upon her golden throne, the priests led the slave girl away through a doorway at one side of the cage; and, as she passed, the lion leaped for her, striking heavily against the bars that restrained him. His growls rolled through the temple, filling the chamber with thunderous sound, echoing and re-echoing from the golden dome.

Nemone sat, silent and rigid, upon her throne staring straight ahead at the lion in the cage; the priests and many of the nobles were reciting prayers in monotones. It was evident to Tarzan that they were praying to the lion, for every eye was upon the repulsive beast; and some of the questions that had puzzled him when he had first come to Cathne were answered. He understood now the strange oaths of Phobeg and his statement that he had stepped upon the tail of god.

Suddenly a beam of light shone down directly into the cage from above, flooding the beast-god with its golden rays. The lion, which had been pacing restlessly to and fro, stopped and looked up, his jaws parted, saliva dripping from his jowls. The audience burst in unison into a singsong chant. Tarzan, half guessing what was about to occur, arose from the rail upon which he had been sitting, and started forward.

But whatever his intention may have been, he was too late to prevent the tragedy that followed instantly. Even as he arose the body of the slave girl dropped from above into the clutches of the waiting lion. A single piercing scream mingled with the horrid roars of the maneater and then died as its author died.

Tarzan turned away in disgust and anger and walked from the temple out into the fresh air and the sunlight, and as he did so a warrior at the entrance hailed him by name in a whisper. There was a cautionary warning in the voice that prompted the ape-man to give no apparent sign of having heard as he turned his eyes casually in the direction from which the words had come, nor did he betray his interest when he discovered that it was Phobeg who had addressed him.

Turning slowly, so that his back was toward the warrior, Tarzan looked back into the temple as though expecting the return of the royal party; then he backed to the side of the entrance as one might who waits and stood so close to Phobeg that the latter might have touched him by moving his spear hand a couple of inches; but neither gave any sign of being aware of the identity or presence of the other.

In a low whisper, through lips that scarcely moved, Phobeg spoke. "I must speak to you! Come to the rear of the temple two hours after the sun has set. Do not answer, but if you hear and will come, turn your head to the right."

As Tarzan gave the assenting signal the royal party commenced to file from the temple, and he fell in behind Nemone. The Queen was quiet and moody, as she always was after the sight of torture and blood at the temple had aroused her to religious frenzy; the reaction left her weak and indifferent. At the palace, she dismissed her following, including Tarzan, and withdrew to the seclusion of her apartments.

17

The Secret of the Temple

AFTER THE ROYAL party left the temple Maluma came out and paused again to gossip with Phobeg. For some time they talked before she bid him goodbye and started back toward the palace. They spoke of many things—of the man in the secret prison behind a heavy golden door beneath the temple floor, of Erot and Tomos, of Nemone and Tarzan, of Gemnon and Doria, and of themselves. Being human, they talked mostly of themselves. It was late when Maluma returned to the palace. It was already the evening meal hour.

In the home of his father, Gemnon paced the floor of the patio as he awaited the summons to the evening meal. Tarzan half sat, half reclined upon a stone bench. He saw that his friend was worried; and it troubled him, troubled him most perhaps because he knew that there were grave causes for apprehension; and he was not certain that he could avert the disaster that threatened.

Seeking to divert Gemnon's mind from his troubles, Tarzan spoke of the ceremony at the temple, but principally of the temple itself, praising its beauty, commenting upon its magnificence. "It is splendid," he commented, "too splendid for the cruel rites we witnessed there today."

"The girl was only a slave," replied Gemnon, "and god must eat. It is no wrong to make offerings to Thoos; but the temple *does* hide a real wrong. Somewhere within it is hidden Alextar, the brother of Nemone; and while he rots there the corrupt

Tomos and the cruel M'duze rule Cathne through the mad Nemone.

"There are many who would have a change and place Alextar on the throne, but they fear the wrath of the terrible triumvirate. So we go on, and nothing is done. Victim after victim succumbs to the malignant jealousy and fear that constantly animate the throne.

"We have little hope today; we shall have no hope if the Queen carries out the plan she is believed to be contemplating and destroys Alextar. There are reasons why it would be to her advantage to do so, the most important being the right of Alextar to proclaim himself king should he ever succeed in reaching the palace.

"If Nemone should die Alextar would become king, and the populace would insist that he take his rightful place. For this reason Tomos and M'duze are anxious to destroy him. It is to Nemone's credit that she has withstood their importunities for all these years, steadfastly refusing to destroy Alextar; but if ever he seriously threatens her power, he is lost; and rumors that have reached her ears that a plot has been perfected to place him on the throne may already have sealed his doom."

During the meal that evening Tarzan considered plans for visiting Phobeg at the temple. He wished to go alone but knew that he would place Gemnon in an embarrassing position should he suggest such a plan, while to permit the noble to accompany him might not only seal Phobeg's lips but jeopardize his safety as well; therefore he decided to go secretly.

Following the stratagem he had adopted, he remained in conversation with Gemnon and his parents until almost two hours after the sun had set; then he excused himself, saying that he was tired, and went to the room that had been assigned him. But he did not tarry there. Instead, he merely crossed the room from the door to the window and stepped out into the patio upon which it faced. Here, as throughout the gardens and avenues of the section of the city occupied by the nobility, grew large, old trees; and a moment later the Lord of the Jungle was swinging through his native element toward the golden temple of Thoos.

He stopped at last in a tree near the rear of the temple where he saw the huge and familiar figure of Phobeg waiting in the shadows below. Soundlessly, the ape-man dropped to the ground in front of the astonished warrior.

"By the great fangs of Thoos!" ejaculated Phobeg, "but you gave me a start."

"You expected me," was Tarzan's only comment.

"But not from the skies," retorted Phobeg. "However, you are here and it is well; I have much more to tell you than when I asked you to come. I have learned more since."

"I am listening," said Tarzan.

"A girl in the service of the Queen overheard a conversation between Nemone and Tomos," commenced Phobeg. "Tomos accused you and Gemnon and Thudos of conspiring against her. Erot spied upon you and knew of your long visit at the home of Thudos a few nights since; he also managed to enter the house on some pretext the following night and saw Doria, the daughter of Thudos. Tomos told Nemone that Doria was very beautiful and that you were in love with her.

"Nemone is not yet convinced that you love Doria, but to be on the safe side she has ordered Tomos to have the girl abducted and brought to the temple where she will be imprisoned until Nemone decides upon her fate. She may destroy her, or she may be content to have her beauty disfigured.

"But what you must know is this: If you give Nemone the slightest reason to believe that you are conspiring against her or that you are fond of Doria she will have you killed. All that I can do is warn you."

"You warned me once before, did you not?" asked Tarzan, "the night that Gemnon and I went to the house of Thudos."

"Yes, that was I," replied Phobeg.

"Why have you done these things?" asked the ape-man.

"Because I owe my life to you," replied the warrior, "and because I know a man when I see one. If a man can pick Phobeg up and toss him around as though he were a baby, Phobeg is willing to be his slave."

"I can only thank you for what you have told me, Phobeg,"

said Tarzan. "Now tell me more. If Doria is brought to the temple where will she be imprisoned?"

"That is hard to say. Alextar is kept in rooms beneath the floor of the temple, but there are rooms upon the second and third floors where a prisoner might be safely confined, especially a woman."

"Could you get word to me if she is arrested?"

"I could try," replied Phobeg.

"Good! Is there anything further?"

"No."

"Then I shall return to Gemnon and warn him. Perhaps we shall find a way to pacify Nemone or outwit her."

"Either would be difficult," commented Phobeg, "but good-bye and good luck!"

Tarzan swung into the tree above the warrior's head and disappeared among the shadows of the night, while Phobeg shook his head in wonderment and returned to his quarters in the temple.

The ape-man made his way to his room by the same avenue he had left it and went immediately to the common living room where the family ordinarily congregated for the evenings. Here he found Gemnon's father and mother, but Gemnon was not there.

"You could not sleep?" enquired the mother.

"No," replied the ape-man. "Where is Gemnon?"

"He was summoned to the palace a short time after you went to your room," explained Gemnon's father.

Announcing that he would wait up until the son returned, Tarzan remained in the living room in conversation with the parents. He wondered a little that Gemnon should have been summoned to the palace at such an hour; and the things that Phobeg had told him made him a little apprehensive, but he kept his own council rather than frighten his host and hostess.

Scarcely an hour had passed when they heard a summons at the outer gate, and presently a slave came to announce that a warrior wished to speak to Tarzan upon a matter of urgent necessity.

The ape-man arose. "I will go outside and see him," he said.

"Be careful," cautioned Gemnon's father. "You have bitter enemies who would be glad to see you destroyed."

"I shall be careful," Tarzan assured him as he left the room behind the slave.

At the gate two warriors connected with the house were detaining a huge man whom Tarzan recognized even from a distance as Phobeg. "I must speak with you at once and alone," said the latter.

"This man is all right," Tarzan told the guards. "Let him enter and I will talk with him in the garden."

When they had walked a short distance from the guards Tarzan paused and faced his visitor. "What is it?" he asked. "You have brought me bad news?"

"Very bad," replied Phobeg. "Gemnon, Thudos, and many of their friends have been arrested and are now in the palace dungeons. Doria has been taken and is imprisoned in the temple. I did not expect to find you at liberty, but took the chance that Nemone's interest in you might have saved you temporarily. If you can escape from Cathne, do so at once; her mood may change at any moment; she is as mad as a monkey."

"Thank you, Phobeg," said the ape-man. "Now get back to your quarters before you become embroiled in this affair."

"And you will escape?" asked the warrior.

"I owe something to Gemnon," replied Tarzan, "for his kindness and his friendship; so I shall not go until I have done what I can to help him."

"No one can help him," stated Phobeg emphatically. "All that you will do is get yourself in trouble."

"I shall have to chance it, and now good-bye, my friend; but before you go tell me where Doria is imprisoned."

"On the third floor of the temple at the rear of the building just above the doorway where I awaited you this evening."

Tarzan accompanied Phobeg to the gate and out into the avenue. "Where are you going?" demanded the latter.

"To the palace."

"You, too, are mad," protested Phobeg, but already the ape-man had left him and was walking rapidly along the avenue in the direction of the palace.

It was late; but Tarzan was now a familiar figure to the palace guards; and when he told them that Nemone had summoned him they let him enter, nor was he stopped until he had reached the anteroom outside the Queen's apartments. Here a noble on guard protested that the hour was late and that the Queen had retired, but Tarzan insisted upon seeing her.

"Tell her it is Tarzan," he said.

"I do not dare disturb her," explained the noble nervously, fearful of Nemone's wrath should she be disturbed and almost equally fearful of it should he refuse to announce this new favorite who had replaced Erot.

"I dare," said Tarzan and stepped to the door leading to the ivory room where Nemone had been accustomed to receive him. The noble sought to interfere but the ape-man pushed him aside and attempted to open the door only to find it securely bolted upon the opposite side; then with his clenched fist he pounded loudly upon its carved surface.

Instantly from beyond it came the savage growls of Belthar and a moment later the frightened voice of a woman. "Who is there?" she demanded. "The Queen sleeps. Who dares disturb her?"

"Go and awaken her," shouted Tarzan through the door. "Tell her that Tarzan is here and wishes to see her at once."

"I am afraid," replied the girl. "The Queen will be angry. Go away, and come in the morning."

Then Tarzan heard another voice beyond the door demanding, "Who is it comes pounding on Nemone's door at such an hour?" and recognized it as the Queen's.

"It is the noble Tarzan," replied the slave girl.

"Draw the bolts and admit him," commanded Nemone, and as the door swung open Tarzan stepped into the ivory room, now so familiar to him.

The Queen stood halfway across the apartment, facing him. Her hair was disheveled, her face slightly flushed. She had evidently arisen from her bed in an adjoining room and thrown a light scarf about her before stepping into the ivory room. She was very beautiful. There was an eager, questioning light in her eyes. She directed the slave to rebolt the door and leave the apartment; then she turned and, walking to the couch, motioned Tarzan to approach. As she sank among the soft cushions she motioned Tarzan to her side.

"I am glad you came," she said. "I could not sleep. I have been thinking of you. But tell me! why did you come? Had you been thinking of me?"

"I have been thinking of you, Nemone," replied the ape-man; "I have been thinking that perhaps you will help me; that you can help me, I know."

"You have only to ask," replied the Queen softly. "There is no favor that you may not have from Nemone for the asking."

A single cresset shed a soft, flickering light that scarcely dispelled the darkness of the room, at the far end of which the yellow-green eyes of Belthar blazed like twin lamps of Hell. Mingling with the acrid scent of the carnivore and the languorous fumes of incense was the seductive aura of the scented body of the woman. Her warm breath was on Tarzan's cheek as she drew him down beside her.

"At last you have come to me of your own volition," she whispered. "Ah, Thoos! how I have hungered for this moment!"

Her soft, bare arms slipped quickly about his neck and drew him close. "Tarzan! My Tarzan!" she almost sobbed, and then that same fatal door at the far end of the apartment opened and the tapping of a metal-shod staff upon the stone floor brought them both erect to gaze into the snarling face of M'duze.

"You fool!" cried the old hag in a shrill falsetto. "Send the man away! unless you would see him killed here before your eyes. Send him away at once!"

Nemone sprang to her feet and faced the old woman who was now trembling with rage. "You have gone too far, M'duze," she said in a cold and level voice. "Go to your room, and remember that I am Queen."

"Queen! Queen!" cackled the hideous creature with a sharp, sarcastic laugh. "Send your lover away, or I'll tell him who and what you are."

Nemone glided quickly toward her, and as she passed a low stand she stooped and seized something that lay there. Suddenly the slave woman shrieked and shrank away, but before she could turn and flee Nemone was upon her and had seized her by the hair. M'duze raised her staff and struck at the Queen, but the blow only aroused the frenzied woman to still greater fury.

"Always you have ruined my life," cried Nemone, "you and your foul paramour, Tomos. You have robbed me of happiness, and for that, *this!*" and she drove the gleaming blade of a knife into the withered breast of the screaming woman, "and this, and this, and this!" and each time the blade sank deep to emphasize the venom in the words and the heart of Nemone, the queen.

Presently M'duze ceased shrieking and sank to the floor. Someone was pounding upon the door to the anteroom, and the terrified voices of nobles and guardsmen could be heard demanding entrance. In his corner Belthar tugged at his chains and roared. Nemone stood looking down upon the death struggles of M'duze with blazing eyes and snarling lip. "Curses upon your black soul!" she cried, and then she turned slowly toward the door upon which the pounding of her retainers' fists resounded. "Have done!" she called imperiously. "I, Nemone, the Queen, am safe. The screams that you heard were those of an impudent slave whom Nemone was correcting."

The voices beyond the door died away as the guardsmen returned to their posts; then Nemone faced Tarzan. She looked suddenly worn and very tired. "That favor," she said, "ask it another time; Nemone is unstrung."

"I must ask it now," replied Tarzan; "tomorrow may be too late."

"Very well," she said; "I am listening. What is it?"

"There is a noble in your court who has been very kind to me since I have been in Cathne," commenced Tarzan. "Now he is in trouble, and I have come to ask you to save him."

Nemone's brow clouded. "Who is he?" she demanded.

"Gemnon," replied the ape-man. "He has been arrested with Thudos and the daughter of Thudos and several of their friends. It is only a plot to destroy me."

"You dare come to me to intercede for traitors!" cried the

Queen, blazing with sudden fury. "But I know the reason; you love Doria!"

"I do not love her; I have seen her but once. Gemnon loves her. Let them be happy, Nemone."

"I am not happy," she replied; "why should they be happy? Tell me that you love me, Tarzan, and I shall be happy!" Her voice was vibrant with appeal. For a moment she forgot that she was queen.

"A flower does not bloom in the seed," he replied; "it grows gradually, and thus love grows. The other, that bursts forth spontaneously from its own heat, is not love; it is passion. I have not known you either long or well, Nemone; that is my answer."

She turned away and buried her face in her arms as she sank to the couch; he saw her shoulders shaken by sobs, and pity filled his heart. He drew nearer to console her, but he had no chance to speak before she wheeled upon him, her eyes flashing through tears. "The girl, Doria, dies!" she cried. "Xarator shall have her tomorrow!"

Tarzan shook his head sadly. "You have asked me to love you," he said. "Do you expect me to love one who ruthlessly destroys my friends?"

"If I save them will you love me?" demanded Nemone.

"That is a question that I cannot answer. The best that I may say is that I may then respect and admire you; whereas, if you kill them without reason there can be no chance that I shall ever love you."

She looked at him now out of dull, lowering eyes. "What difference does it make?" she almost growled. "No one loves me. Tomos wanted to be king, Erot wished riches and power, M'duze wished to exercise the majesty that she could never possess; if one of them felt any affection for me it was M'duze, and I have killed her." She paused, a wild light flamed in her eyes. "I hate them!" she screamed. "I hate them all! I shall kill them! I shall kill every one! I shall kill you!" Then, as swiftly, her mood changed. "Oh, what am I saying?" she cried. She put her palms to her temples. "My head! it hurts."

"And my friends!" asked Tarzan; "you will not harm them?"

"Perhaps not," she replied indifferently, and then, as quickly changing again, "The girl dies! If you intercede for her again her sufferings shall be greater; Xarator is merciful—more merciful than Nemone."

"When will she die?" asked Tarzan.

"She will be sewn into hides tonight and carried to Xarator tomorrow. You shall accompany us; do you understand?"

The ape-man nodded. "And my other friends?" he asked, "they will be saved?"

"You shall come to me tomorrow night," replied Nemone. "We shall see then how you have decided to treat Nemone; then she will know how to treat your friends."

18

Flaming Xarator

HER WRISTS AND ankles bound, Doria, the daughter of
Thudos, lay on a pile of skins in a room upon the third floor of
the Temple of Thoos. Diffused moonlight entered the single
window, relieving the darkness of the interior of her prison.
She had seen her father seized and dragged away; she was in
the power of one so ruthless that she knew she could expect no
mercy and that either death or cruel disfigurement awaited her,
yet she did not weep. Above her grief rose the pride of the
noble blood of the house of Thudos, the courage of a line of
warriors that stretched back into the forgotten ages; and she
was brave.

She thought of Gemnon; and then the tears almost came, not
for herself but for him because of the grief that would be his
when he learned of her fate. She did not know that he too had
fallen into the clutches of the enemies of her father.

Presently she heard the sound of footsteps approaching
along the corridor, heard them stop before the door behind
which she was locked. The door swung open and the room was
illuminated by the light of a torch held in the hand of a man
who entered and closed the door behind him.

The girl lying upon the pile of skins recognized Erot. She
saw him place the blazing torch in a wall socket designed for
the purpose and turn toward her.

"Ah, the lovely Doria!" he exclaimed. "What ill fate has
brought you here?"

"Doubtless the noble Erot could answer that question better than I," she replied.

"Yes, I believe that he could; in fact I know it. It was I who caused you to be brought here; it was I who caused your father to be imprisoned; it was I who sent Gemnon to the same cell with the noble Thudos."

"Gemnon imprisoned!" cried the girl.

"Yes, with many other conspirators against the throne. Behind his back they used to sneer at Erot because he was not a lion man; they will not sneer for long. Erot has answered them; now they know that Erot is more powerful than they."

"And what is to be done with me?" asked the girl.

"Nemone has decreed Xarator for you," replied Erot. "You are even now lying upon the skins in which you are to be sewn. It is for that purpose that I am here. My good friend Tomos, the councillor, sent me to sew you into the bag; but first let us enjoy together your last night on earth. Be generous, and perhaps I can avert the doom that Nemone will doubtless decree for your father and your lover. She is permitting them to live through tomorrow at least, that they may witness your destruction, for thus runs the kindly mind of sweet Nemone." He laughed harshly. "The hellcat! May the devil get her in the end!"

"You have not even the decency of gratitude," said Doria contemptuously. "The Queen has lavished favors upon you, given you power and riches; it is inconceivable that one can be so vile an ingrate as you."

Erot laughed. "Tomorrow you will be dead," he said; "so what difference does it make what you think of me? Tonight you shall give me love, though your heart be filled with hate. There is nothing in the world but love and hate, the two most pleasurable emotions that great Thoos has given us; let us enjoy them to the full!" He came and kneeled at her side and took her in his arms, covering her face and lips with kisses. She struggled to repulse him, but in her bonds she was helpless to protect herself.

He was panting with passion as he untied the thongs that

secured her ankles. "You are more beautiful than Nemone," he cried huskily as he strained her to him.

A low growl sounded from the direction of the window. Erot raised his face from the soft neck of Doria and looked. He went ashy white as he leaped to his feet and fled toward the door upon the opposite side of the room, his craven heart pounding in terror.

It was early in the morning as the cortège formed that was to accompany the doomed Doria to Xarator, for Xarator lies sixteen miles from the city of Cathne in the mountains at the far end of the valley of Onthar; and the procession could move no faster than the lions drawing the chariot of the Queen would walk, which was not fast. Bred for generations for this purpose, the lions of Cathne had far greater endurance than forest-bred lions, yet it would be well into the night before it could be hoped to make the long journey to Xarator and return; therefore hundreds of slaves bore torches with which to light the homeward journey after night had fallen.

Nemone entered her chariot. She was wrapped in woolen robes and the skins of animals, for the morning air was still chill. At her side walked Tomos, nervous and ill at ease. He knew that M'duze was dead and wondered if he would be next. The Queen's manner was curt and abrupt, filling him with dread, for now there was no M'duze to protect him from the easily aroused wrath of Nemone.

"Where is Tarzan?" she demanded.

"I do not know, majesty," replied Tomos. "I have not seen him."

She looked at him sharply. "Don't lie to me!" she snapped. "You do know where he is; and if any harm has befallen him, you go to the lion pit."

"But, majesty," cried Tomos, "I know nothing about him. I have not seen him since we left the temple yesterday."

"Produce him," commanded Nemone sullenly. "It grows late, and Nemone is not accustomed to wait upon any."

"But, majesty—" began Tomos again.

"Produce him!" interrupted Nemone.

"But—"

"Here he comes now!" exclaimed Nemone as Tarzan strode up the avenue toward her.

Tomos breathed a sigh of relief and wiped the perspiration from his forehead. He did not like Tarzan, but in all his life he had never before been so glad to see anyone alive and well.

"You are late," said Nemone as Tarzan stopped beside her chariot.

The Lord of the Jungle made no reply.

"We are not accustomed to being delayed," she continued a little sharply.

"Perhaps if you placed me in the custody of Erot, as I suggested, he would deliver me on time in future."

Nemone ignored this and turned to Tomos. "We are ready," she said.

At a word from the councillor a trumpeter at his side raised his instrument to his lips and sounded a call. Slowly the long procession began to move, and like a huge serpent crawled toward the Bridge of Gold. The citizens lining the avenue moved with it, men, women, and children. The women and children carried packages in which food was wrapped, the men bore arms. A journey to Xarator was an event; it took them the length of Onthar where wild lions roamed and where Athnean raiders might set upon them at any moment of the day or night, especially of the night; so the march took on something of the aspects of both a pageant and a military excursion.

Behind the golden chariot of the Queen rolled a second chariot on the floor of which lay a bundle sewn in the skins of lions. Chained to this chariot were Thudos and Gemnon. Following were a hundred chariots driven by nobles in gold and ivory, while other nobles on foot entirely surrounded the chariot of the Queen.

There were columns of marching warriors in the lead; and in the rear were the war lions of Cathne, the royal fighting lions of the Queen. Keepers held them on leashes of gold, and proud nobles of ancient families marched beside them—the lion men of Cathne.

The barbaric splendor of the scene impressed even the ape-man who cared little for display, though he gave no outward sign of interest as he strode at the wheel of Nemone's chariot drawn by its eight great lions held in leash by twenty-four powerful blacks in tunics of red and gold.

The comments of the crowd came to the ears of Tarzan as they marched through the city and out across the Bridge of Gold onto the road that runs north through the Field of the Lions. "There is the stranger who defeated Phobeg." "Yes, he has taken Erot's place in the council." "He is the Queen's favorite now." "Where is Erot?" "I hope he is dead; this other is better." "He will soon be as bad; they all get alike when they get rich and powerful." "Had you heard the rumor that M'duze is dead?" "She *is* dead; my cousin's husband is a palace guard. He told my cousin." "What is that?" "M'duze is dead!" "May Thoos be praised!" "Have you heard? M'duze is dead!" and so it ran through the two streams of citizens that hemmed the royal pageant on either side, and always above the other comment rose the half exultant cry, "M'duze is dead!"

Nemone appeared preoccupied; she sat staring straight ahead; if she heard the comments of her people she gave no sign. What was passing behind that beautiful mask that was her face? Chained to the chariot behind her were two enemies; others were in her prisons. A girl who dared vie with her in beauty lay insensible in a sack of skins jolting over the rough road in the dust of the Queen's chariot. Her Nemesis was dead. The man she loved walked at her side. Nemone should have been happy; but she was not.

The sun, climbing into the heavens, was bringing heat. Slaves carrying an umbrella over the Queen adjusted it to fend the hot rays from her; others waved lions' tails attached to the ends of long poles to and fro about her to drive the insects away; a gentle breeze carried the dust of the long column lazily toward the west.

Nemone sighed and turned to Tarzan. "Why were you late?" she asked.

"Would it be strange that I overslept?" he asked. "It was late when I left the palace, and there was no keeper to awaken me since you took Gemnon away."

"Had you wished to see me again as badly as I wished to see you, you would not have been late."

"I was as anxious to be here as you," he replied.

"You have never seen Xarator?" she asked.

"No."

"It is a holy mountain, created by Thoos for the enemies of the kings and queens of Cathne; in all the world there is nothing like it."

"I am going to enjoy seeing it," replied the ape-man grimly.

They were approaching a fork in the road. "That road leading to the right runs through the Pass of the Warriors into the valley of Thenar," she explained. "Someday I shall send you on a raid to Thenar, and you shall bring me back the head of one of Athne's greatest warriors."

Tarzan thought of Valthor and wondered if he had reached Athne in safety. He glanced back at Thudos and Gemnon. He had not spoken to them, but it was because of them that he was here. He might easily have escaped had he not determined to remain until he was certain that he could not aid these friends. Their case appeared hopeless, yet the ape-man had not given up hope.

At noon the procession stopped for lunch. The populace scattered about seeking the shade of the trees that dotted the plain and that had not already been selected by the Queen and the nobles. The lions were led into shade, where they lay down to rest. Warriors, always on the lookout for danger, stood guard about the temporary encampment. There was always danger on the Field of the Lions.

The halt was brief; in half an hour the cavalcade was on the march again. There was less talking now; silence and the great heat hung over the dusty column. The hills that bounded the valley upon the north were close, and soon they entered them, following a canyon upward to a winding mountain road that led into the hills above.

Presently the smell of sulphur fumes came plainly to the nostrils of the ape-man, and a little later the column turned the shoulder of a great mass of volcanic rock and came upon the edge of a huge crater. Far below, molten rock bubbled, sending up spurts of flame, geysers of steam, and columns of yellow smoke. The scene was impressive and awe-inspiring. Before Cathne, before Rome, before Athens, before Babylon, before Egypt Xarator had towered in lonely majesty above the lesser peaks. Beside that mighty cauldron queen and noble shrank to pitiful insignificance though perhaps there was but one in that great throng that realized this. Tarzan stood with folded arms and bent head gazing down into the seething inferno until the Queen touched him on the shoulder. "What do you think of Xarator?" she asked.

He shook his head. "There are some emotions," he answered slowly, "for which no words have yet been coined."

"It was created by Thoos for the kings of Cathne," she explained proudly.

Tarzan made no reply; perhaps he was thinking that here again the lexicographers had failed to furnish words adequate to the occasion.

On either side of the royal party the people crowded close to the edge of the crater that they might miss nothing of what was about to transpire. The children laughed and played, or teased their mothers for the food that was being saved for the evening meal upon the return journey to Cathne.

Tarzan saw Thudos and Gemnon standing beside the chariot in which lay the still form of the victim. Of what emotions were passing within their minds none appeared through the masks of stern pride that sat upon their countenances, yet Tarzan well knew the suffering of their torn and bleeding hearts. He had not spoken to them once this day, for he had not had an opportunity to speak to them except in the presence of others; and whatever he might have to say to them must be for their ears only. He had not given up the hope of helping them, but he could not conceive that open and unnecessary familiarity with them at this time might accomplish anything more than to still further arouse the suspicions of Nemone and increase the watchfulness of all their enemies.

If Gemnon or Thudos noticed the neglect of their former friend and guest they gave no sign, for neither gave him any greater attention as he walked beside the chariot of the Queen a few paces in advance of them than they gave to the lions drawing the car to which they were secured. Their thoughts were upon the poor, dumb thing jolting upon the hard planks that formed the floor of the springless chariot bearing it to its doom. Not once had they seen the girl move, not once had she uttered a sound; and they hoped that she was either insensible or dead, for thus would she be saved the anguish of these last moments and Nemone be robbed of the essence of her triumph.

The ceremony at Xarator, though it bore the authority of so-called justice, was of a semireligious nature that required the presence and active participation of priests, two of whom lifted the sack containing the victim from the chariot and placed it at the edge of the crater at the feet of the Queen.

About it, then, gathered a dozen priests, some of whom carried musical instruments; and as they chanted in unison, the beating of their drums rose and fell while the wailing notes of their wind instruments floated out across the inferno of the seething pit like the plaint of a lost soul.

Thudos and Gemnon had been brought nearer the spot that Nemone might enjoy their agony to the full, for this was not only a part of their punishment but a considerable portion of the pleasure of the Queen.

She saw that they were giving no evidences of grief, thus robbing her of much of the satisfaction she had hoped to derive from the destruction of the daughter of one, the sweetheart of the other; and she was vexed. But she was not entirely discouraged; a new plan to further try their fortitude had occurred to her.

As two of the priests lifted the body from the ground and were about to hurl it into the crater, she stopped them with a curt command. "Wait!" she cried. "We would look upon the too great beauty of Doria, the daughter of Thudos, the traitor; we would permit her father and her lover to see her once again that they may better visualize her anguish and appreciate their own; that all may long remember that it is not well to conspire against Nemone. Cut the bag, and expose the body of the sacrifice!"

All eyes were upon the priest who drew his dagger and

ripped open the bag along one loosely sewn seam. The eyes of
Thudos and Gemnon were fixed upon the still figure outlined
beneath the tawny skins of lions; beads of perspiration stood
upon their foreheads; their jaws and their fists were clenched.
The eyes of Tarzan turned from the activities of the priest to the
face of the Queen; between narrowed lids, from beneath stern
brows they watched her.

The priests, gathering the bag by one side, raised it and let
the body roll out upon the ground where all could see it. There
was a gasp of astonishment. Nemone cried out in a sudden fit
of rage. The body was that of Erot, and he was dead!

19

The Queen's Quarry

AFTER THE FIRST involuntary cries of surprise and rage an ominous silence fell upon the barbaric scene. Now all eyes were centered upon the Queen, whose ordinarily beautiful countenance was almost hideous from rage, a rage which, after her single angry cry, choked further utterance for the moment. But at length she found her voice and turned furiously upon Tomos.

"What means this?" she demanded, her voice now controlled and as cold as the steel in the sheath at her side.

Tomos, who was as much astounded as she, stammered as he trembled in his sandals of elephant hide. "There are traitors even in the temple of Thoos!" he cried. "I chose Erot to prepare the girl for the embraces of Xarator because I knew that his loyalty to his Queen would insure the work being well done. I did not know, O gracious Nemone, that this vile crime had been committed or that the body of Erot had been substituted for that of the daughter of Thudos until this very instant."

With an expression of disgust the Queen commanded the priests to hurl the body of Erot into the crater, and as it was swallowed by the fiery pit she ordered an immediate return to Cathne.

In morose and gloomy silence she rode down the winding mountain trail and out onto the Field of the Lions, and often her eyes were upon the bronzed giant striding beside her chariot.

At last she broke her silence. "Two of your enemies are gone now," she said. "I destroyed one; whom do you think destroyed the other?"

"Perhaps I did," suggested Tarzan with a smile.

"I had been thinking of that possibility," replied Nemone, but she did not smile.

"Whoever did it performed a service for Cathne."

"Perhaps," she half agreed, "but it is not the killing of Erot that annoys me; it is the effrontery that dared interfere with the plans of Nemone. Whoever did it has spoiled for me what would otherwise have been a happy day; nor have they accomplished anything in the interest of Thudos or his daughter or Gemnon. I shall find the girl, and her passing will be far more bitter than that from which she was saved today; she cannot escape me. Thudos and Gemnon will also pay more heavily because someone dared flout the Queen."

Tarzan shrugged his broad shoulders, but remained silent.

"Why do you not speak?" demanded the Queen.

"There is nothing to say," he replied; "I can only disagree with you without convincing you; I should only make you more angry than you are. I find no pleasure in making people angry or unhappy unless it is for some good purpose."

"You mean that I do?" she demanded.

"Obviously."

She shook her head angrily. "Why do I abide you!" she exclaimed.

"Possibly as a counterirritant to relieve other irritations," he suggested.

"Some day I shall lose my patience and have you thrown to the lions," she ejaculated sharply. "What will you do then?"

"Kill the lion," replied the ape-man.

"Not the lion that I shall throw you to," Nemone assured him.

The tedious journey back to Cathne ended at last, and with flaring torches lighting the way the Queen's cortège crossed the Bridge of Gold and entered the city. Here she immediately ordered a thorough search to be made for Doria.

Thudos and Gemnon, happy but mystified, were returned to their cell to await the new doom that Nemone would fix for them when the mood again seized her to be entertained. Tarzan was commanded to accompany Nemone into the palace and dine with her. Tomos had been dismissed with a curt injunction to find Doria or prepare for the worst!

Tarzan and the Queen ate alone in a small dining room attended only by slaves, and when the meal was over Nemone conducted him to the now all-too-familiar ivory room, where he was greeted by the angry growls of Belthar.

"Erot and M'duze are dead," said the Queen, "and I have sent Tomos away; there will be none to disturb us tonight." Again her voice was soft, her manner gentle.

The ape-man sat with his eyes fixed upon her, studying her. It seemed incredible that this sweet and lovely woman could be the cruel tyrant that was Nemone, the Queen. Every soft line and curving contour spoke of femininity and gentleness and love; and in those glorious eyes smoldered a dreamy light that exercised a strange hypnotic influence upon him, gently pushing the memories of her ruthlessness into the oblivion of forgetfulness.

She leaned closer to him. "Touch me, Tarzan," she whispered softly.

Drawn by a power that is greater than the will of man he placed a hand upon hers. She breathed a deep sigh of contentment and leaned her cheek against his breast; her warm breath caressed his naked skin; the perfume of her hair was in his nostrils. She spoke, but so low that he could not catch her words.

"What did you say?" he asked.

"Take me in your arms," she breathed faintly.

He passed a palm across his eyes as though to wipe away a mist, and in the moment of his hesitation she threw her arms about his neck and covered his face and lips with hot kisses.

"Love me, Tarzan!" she cried passionately. "Love me! Love me! Love me!"

She slipped to the floor until she knelt at his feet. "Oh, Thoos, god of gods!" she murmured, "how I love you!"

The Lord of the Jungle looked down at her, at a queen groveling at his feet, and the spell that had held him vanished; beneath the beautiful exterior he saw the crazed mind of a mad woman; he saw the creature that cast defenseless men to wild beasts, that disfigured or destroyed women who might be more beautiful than she; and all that was fine in him revolted.

With a half growl he arose to his feet, and as he did so Nemone slipped to the floor and lay there silent and rigid. He started toward the door, and then turned and coming back lifted her to the couch. As he did so, Belthar strained at his chains and the chamber shook to his roars.

Nemone opened her eyes and for a moment gazed questioningly at the man above her; then she seemed to realize what had happened, and the mad, cruel light of rage blazed in her eyes. Leaping to her feet she stood trembling before him.

"You refuse my love!" she screamed. "You spurn me? You dare spurn the love of a Queen! Thoos! and I knelt at your feet!" She sprang to one side of the room where a metal gong depended from the ceiling and seizing the striker smote it three times. The brazen notes rang through the chamber mingling with the roars of the infuriated lion.

Tarzan stood watching her; she seemed wholly irresponsible, quite mad. It would be useless to attempt to reason with her. He moved slowly toward the door; but before he reached it it swung open, and a score of warriors accompanied by two nobles rushed in.

"Take this man!" ordered Nemone. "Throw him into the cell with the other enemies of the Queen!"

Tarzan was unarmed. He had worn only a sword when he entered the ivory room and that he had unbuckled and laid upon a stand near the doorway. There were twenty spears leveled at him, twenty spears that entirely encircled him. With a shrug he surrendered. It was that or death. In prison he might find the means to escape; at least he would see Gemnon again, and there was something that he very much wished to tell Gemnon and Thudos.

As the soldiers conducted him from the room and the door closed behind them, Nemone threw herself among the cushions of her couch, her body wracked by choking sobs. The great lion grumbled in the dusky corner of the room. Suddenly Nemone sat erect and her eyes blazed into the blazing eyes of the lion. For a moment she sat there thus, and then she arose and a peal of maniacal laughter broke from her lips. Still laughing, she crossed the room and passed through the doorway that led to her bedchamber.

Thudos and Gemnon sitting in their cell heard the tramp of marching men approaching the prison in which they were confined. "Evidently Nemone cannot wait until tomorrow," said Thudos.

"You think she is sending for us now?" asked Gemnon.

"What else?" demanded the older man. "The lion pit can be illuminated."

As they waited and listened the steps stopped outside their cell, the door was pushed open, and a man entered. The warriors had carried no torches and neither Thudos nor Gemnon could discern the features of the newcomer, though in the diffused light that filtered in through the small window and the aperture in the door they noted that he was a large man.

None of them spoke until the guard had departed out of earshot. "Greetings, Thudos and Gemnon!" exclaimed the new prisoner cheerily.

"Tarzan!" exclaimed Gemnon.

"None other," admitted the ape-man.

"What brings you here?" demanded Thudos.

"Twenty warriors and the whim of a woman, an insane woman," replied Tarzan.

"So you have fallen from favor!" exclaimed Gemnon. "I am sorry."

"It was inevitable," said Tarzan.

"And what will your punishment be?"

"I do not know, but I suspect that it will be quite sufficient. However, that is something that need not concern any of us until it happens; maybe it won't happen."

"There is no room in the dungeon of Nemone for optimism," remarked Thudos with a grim laugh.

"Perhaps not," agreed the ape-man, "but I shall continue to indulge myself. Doubtless Doria felt hopeless in her prison in the temple last night, yet she escaped Xarator."

"That is a miracle that I cannot fathom," said Gemnon.

"It was quite simple," Tarzan assured him. "A loyal friend,

whose identity you may guess, came and told me that she was a prisoner in the temple. I went at once to find her. Fortunately the trees of Cathne are old and large and numerous; one of them grows close to the rear of the temple, its branches almost brushing the window of the room in which Doria was confined. When I arrived there, I found Erot annoying Doria; I also found the sack in which he had purposed tying her for the journey to Xarator. What was simpler? I let Erot take the ride that had been planned for Doria."

"You saved her! Where is she?" cried Thudos, his voice breaking in the first emotion he had displayed since he had learned of his daughter's plight.

"Come close," cautioned Tarzan, "lest the walls themselves be enemies." The two men pressed close to the speaker who continued in a low whisper, "Do you recall, Gemnon, that when we were at the gold mine I spoke aside to one of the slaves there?"

"I believe that I did notice it," replied Gemnon; "I thought you were asking questions about the operation of the mine."

"No; I was delivering a message from his brother, and so grateful was he that he begged that he be permitted to serve me if the opportunity arose. It was to arise much sooner than either of us could have expected; and so, when it was necessary to find a hiding place for Doria, I thought immediately of the isolated hut of Niaka, the head man of the black slaves at the gold mine.

"She is there now, and the man will protect her as long as is necessary. He has promised me that if he hears nothing from me for half a moon he is to understand that none of us three can come to her aid, and that then he will get word to the faithful slaves of the house of Thudos. He says that that will be difficult but not impossible."

"Doria safe!" whispered Gemnon. "Thudos and I may now die happy."

Thudos extended his hand through the darkness and laid it on the ape-man's shoulder. "There is no way in which I can express my gratitude," he said, "for there are no words in which to couch it."

For some time the three men sat in silence that was broken at last by Gemnon. "How did it happen that you knew the brother of a slave well enough to carry a message from one to the other?" he asked, a note of puzzlement in his voice.

"Do you recall Xerstle's grand hunt?" asked Tarzan with a laugh.

"Of course, but what has that to do with it?" demanded Gemnon.

"Do you remember the quarry, the man we saw on the slave block in the marketplace?"

"Yes."

"He is the brother of Niaka," explained Tarzan.

"But you never had an opportunity to speak to him," objected the young noble.

"Oh, but I did. It was I who helped him escape. That was why his brother was so grateful to me."

"I still do not understand," said Gemnon.

"There is probably much connected with Xerstle's grand hunt that you do not understand," suggested Tarzan. "In the first place, the purpose of the hunt was, primarily, to destroy me rather than the nominal quarry; the scheme was probably hatched between Xerstle and Erot. In the second place, I didn't approve of the ethics of the hunters; the poor devil they were chasing had no chance. I went ahead, therefore, through the trees until I overtook the black; then I carried him for a mile to throw the lions off the scent. You know how well the plan succeeded.

"When I came back and we laid the wager, that gave Xerstle and Pindes the opening they wished but which they would have found by some other means before the day was over; so Pindes took me with him; and after we were far enough away from you he suggested that we separate, whereupon he loosed his lion upon me."

"And it was you who killed the lion?"

"I should have much preferred to have killed Pindes and Xerstle, but I felt that the time was not yet ripe. Now, perhaps, I shall never have the opportunity to kill them," he added regretfully.

"Now I am doubly sorry that I must die," said Gemnon.

"Why moreso than before?" asked Thudos.

"I shall never have the opportunity to tell the story of Xerstle's grand hunt," he explained. "What a story *that* would make!"

The morning dawned bright and beautiful, just as though there was no misery or sorrow or cruelty in the world; but it did not change matters at all, other than to make the cell in which the three men were confined uncomfortably warm as the day progressed.

Shortly after noon a guard came and took Tarzan away. All three of the prisoners were acquainted with the officer who commanded it, a decent fellow who spoke sympathetically to them.

"Is he coming back?" asked Thudos, nodding toward Tarzan.

The officer shook his head. "No; the Queen hunts today."

Thudos and Gemnon pressed the ape-man's shoulder. No word was spoken, but that wordless farewell was more eloquent than words. They saw him go out, saw the door close behind him; but neither spoke, and so they sat for a long hour in silence.

In the guardroom, to which he had been conducted from his cell, Tarzan was heavily chained; a golden collar was placed about his neck, and a chain reaching from each side of it was held in the hands of a warrior.

"Why all the precautions?" demanded the ape-man.

"It is merely a custom," explained the officer; "it is always thus that the Queen's quarry is led to the Field of the Lions."

Once again Tarzan of the Apes walked near the chariot of the Queen of Cathne; but this time he walked behind it, a chained prisoner between two stalwart warriors and surrounded by a score of others. Once again he crossed the Bridge of Gold out onto the Field of the Lions in the valley of Onthar.

The procession did not go far, scarcely more than a mile from the city. A great concourse of people accompanied it, for Nemone had invited the entire city to witness the degradation and death of the man who had spurned her love. She was about to be avenged, but she was not happy. With scowling brows she sat brooding in her chariot as it stopped at last at the point she had selected for the start of the hunt. Not once had she turned to look at the chained man behind her. Perhaps she had been certain that she would have been rewarded by no indication of terror in his mien, or perhaps she did not dare to look at the man she had loved for fear that her determination might weaken.

But now that the time had come she cast her indecision aside, if any had been annoying her, and ordered the guard to fetch the prisoner to her. She was looking straight ahead as the ape-man halted by the wheel of her chariot.

"Send all away except the two warriors who hold him," commanded Nemone.

"You may send them, too, if you wish," said Tarzan; "I give you my word not to harm you or try to escape while they are away."

Nemone, still looking straight ahead, was silent for a moment; then, "You may all go; I would speak with the prisoner alone."

When the guard had departed a number of paces, the Queen turned her eyes toward Tarzan and found his smiling into her own. "You are going to be very happy, Nemone," he said in an easy, friendly voice.

"What do you mean?" she asked. "How am I going to be happy?"

"You are going to see me die; that is if the lion catches me," he laughed, "and you like to see people die."

"You think that will give me pleasure? Well, I thought so myself; but now I am wondering if it will. I never get quite the pleasure from death that I anticipate I shall; nothing in life is ever what I hope for."

"Possibly you don't hope for the right things," he suggested. "Did you ever try hoping for something that would bring pleasure and happiness to someone beside yourself?"

"Why should I?" she asked. "I hope for my own happiness; let others do the same. I strive for my own happiness—"

"And never have any," interrupted the ape-man good-naturedly.

"Probably I should have less if I strove only for the happiness of others," she insisted.

"There are people like that," he assented; "perhaps you are one of them; so you might as well go on striving for happiness in your own way. Of course you won't get it, but you will at least have the pleasures of anticipation, and that is something."

"I think I know myself and my own affairs well enough to determine for myself how to conduct my life," she said with a note of asperity in her voice.

Tarzan shrugged. "It was not in my thoughts to interfere," he said. "If you are determined to kill me and are quite sure that you will derive pleasure from it, why, I should be the last in the world to suggest that you abandon the idea."

"You do not amuse me," said Nemone haughtily; "I do not care for irony that is aimed at myself." She turned fiercely on him. "Men have died for less!" she cried, and the Lord of the Jungle laughed in her face.

"How many times?" he asked.

"A moment ago," said Nemone, "I was beginning to regret the thing that is about to happen. Had you been different, had you sought to conciliate me, I might have relented and returned you to favor; but you do everything to antagonize me. You affront me, you insult me, you laugh at me." Her voice was rising, a barometric indication, Tarzan had learned, of her mental state.

"And yet, Nemone, I am drawn to you," admitted the apeman. "I cannot understand it. You are attracted to me in spite of wounded pride and lacerated dignity; and I to you though I hold in contempt your principles, your ideals, and your methods. It is strange, isn't it?"

The woman nodded. "It is strange," she mused. "I never loved one as I loved you, and yet I am going to kill you notwithstanding the fact that I still love you."

"And you will go on killing people and being unhappy until it is your turn to be killed," he said sadly.

She shuddered. "Killed!" she repeated. "Yes, they are all killed, the kings and queens of Cathne; but it is not my turn yet. While Belthar lives Nemone lives." She was silent for a moment. "You may live too, Tarzan; there is something that I would rather see you do than see you die." She paused as though expecting him to ask her what it was, but he manifested no interest, and she continued, "Last night I knelt at your feet and begged for your love. Kneel here, before my people, kneel at my feet and beg for mercy, and you may live."

"Bring on your lion," said Tarzan; "his mercy might be kinder than Nemone's."

"You refuse?" she demanded angrily.

"You would kill me eventually," he replied; "there is a chance that the lion may not be able to."

"Not a chance!" she said. "Have you seen the lion?"

"No."

She turned and called a noble, "Have the hunting lion brought to scent the quarry!"

Behind them there was a scattering of troops and nobles as they made an avenue for the hunting lion and his keepers, and along the avenue Tarzan saw a great lion straining at the golden leashes to which eight men clung. Growling and roaring, the beast sprang from side to side in an effort to seize a keeper or lay hold upon one of the warriors or nobles that lined the way; so that it was all that four stalwart men on either side of him could do to prevent his accomplishing his design.

A flaming-eyed devil, he came toward the chariot of Nemone, but he was still afar when Tarzan saw the tuft of white hair in the center of his mane between his ears. It was Belthar!

Nemone was eyeing the man at her side as a cat might eye a mouse, but though the lion was close now she saw no change in the expression on Tarzan's face. "Do you not recognize him?" she demanded.

"Of course I do," he replied.

"And you are not afraid?"

"Of what?" he asked, looking at her wonderingly.

She stamped her foot in anger, thinking that he was trying to rob her of the satisfaction of witnessing his terror; for how could she know that Tarzan of the Apes could not understand the meaning of *fear*? "Prepare for the grand hunt!" she commanded, turning to a noble standing with the guard that had waited just out of earshot of her conversation with the quarry.

The warriors who had held Tarzan in leash ran forward and picked up the golden chains that were attached to the golden collar about his neck, the guard took posts about the chariot of the Queen, and Tarzan was led a few yards in advance of it. Then the keepers brought Belthar closer to him, holding him just out of reach but only with difficulty, for when the irascible beast recognized the ape-man he flew into a frenzy of rage that taxed the eight men to hold him at all.

Warriors were deploying on either side of a wide lane leading toward the north from the chariot of Nemone. In solid ranks they formed on either side of this avenue, facing toward its center, their spear points dropped to form a wall of steel against the lion should he desert the chase and break to right or left. Behind them, craning necks to see above the shoulders of the fighting men, the populace pushed and shoved for advantageous points from which to view the spectacle.

A noble approached Tarzan. He was Phordos, the father of Gemnon, hereditary captain of the hunt for the rulers of Cathne. He came quite close to Tarzan and spoke to him in a low whisper, "I am sorry that I must have a part in this," he said, "but my office requires it," and then aloud, "In the name of the Queen, silence! These are the rules of the grand hunt of Nemone, Queen of Cathne: The quarry shall move north down the center of the lane of warriors; when he has proceeded a hundred paces the keepers shall unleash the hunting lion, Belthar; let no man distract the lion from the chase or aid the quarry, under penalty of death. When the lion has killed and while he is feeding let the keepers, guarded by warriors, retake him."

Then he turned to Tarzan. "You will run straight north until Belthar overtakes you," he said.

"What if I elude him and escape?" demanded the ape-man. "Shall I have my freedom then?"

Phordos shook his head sadly. "You will not escape him," he said. Then he turned toward the Queen and knelt. "All is in readiness, your majesty. Shall the hunt commence?"

Nemone looked quickly about her. She saw that the guards were so disposed that she might be protected in the event that the lion turned back; she saw that slaves from her stables carried great nets with which Belthar was to be retaken after the hunt. She knew and they knew that not all of them would return alive to Cathne, but that would but add to the interest and excitement of the day. She nodded her head to Phordos. "Let the lion scent the quarry once more; then the hunt may start," she directed.

The keepers let Belthar move a little closer to the ape-man, but not before they had enlisted the aid of a dozen additional men to prevent his dragging the original eight until he was within reach of the quarry.

Nemone leaned forward eagerly, her eyes upon the savage beast that was the pride of her stable; the light of insanity gleamed in them now. "It is enough!" she cried. "Belthar knows him now, nor will he ever leave his trail until he has tracked him down and killed him, until he has reaped his reward and filled his belly with the flesh of his kill, for there is no better hunting lion in all Cathne than Belthar."

Along the gauntlet of warriors that the quarry and the lion were to run spears had been stuck into the ground at intervals, and floating from the hafts of these were different colored pennons. The populace, the nobles, and the Queen had laid wagers upon the color of the pennon nearest which they thought the kill would occur, and they were still betting when Phordos slipped the collar from Tarzan's neck.

In a hollow near the river that runs past Cathne a lion lay asleep in dense brush, a mighty beast with a yellow coat and a great black mane. Strange sounds coming to him from the plain disturbed him, and he rumbled complainingly in his throat; but as yet he seemed only half awake. His eyes were closed, but his half wakefulness was only seeming. Numa was awake, but he wanted to sleep and was angry with the men-things that were disturbing him. They were not too close as yet; but he knew that if they came closer he would have to get up and investigate, and that he did not want to do; he felt very lazy.

Out on the field Tarzan was striding along the spear-bound

lane. He counted his steps, knowing that at the hundredth Belthar would be loosed upon him. The ape-man had a plan. Across the river to the east was the forest in which he had hunted with Xerstle and Pindes and Gemnon; could he reach it, he would be safe. No lion or no man could hope ever to overtake the Lord of the Jungle once he swung to the branches of those trees.

But could he reach the wood before Belthar overtook him? Tarzan was swift, but there are few creatures as swift as Numa at the height of his charge. With a start of a hundred paces, the ape-man felt that he might outdistance an ordinary lion; but Belthar was no ordinary lion. He was the result of generations of breeding that had resulted in the power of sustaining great speed for a much longer time than would have been possible for a wild lion, and of all the hunting lions of Cathne Belthar was the best.

At the hundredth pace Tarzan leaped forward at top speed. Behind him he heard the frenzied roar of the hunting lion as his leashes were slipped and, mingling with it, the roar of the crowd.

Smoothly and low ran Belthar, the hunting lion, swiftly closing up the distance that separated him from the quarry. He looked neither to right nor to left; his fierce, blazing eyes remained fixed upon the fleeing man ahead.

Behind him rolled the chariot of the Queen, the drivers goading their lions to greater speed that Nemone might be in at the kill, yet Belthar outdistanced them as though they were rooted to the ground. The Queen, in her excitement, was standing erect, screaming encouragement to Belthar. Her eyes blazed scarcely less fiercely than those of the savage carnivore she cheered on; her bosom rose and fell to her excited breathing; her heart raced with the racing death ahead. The Queen of Cathne was consumed by the passion of love turned to hate.

The nobles, the warriors, and the crowd were streaming after the chariot of the Queen. Belthar was gaining on the quarry when Tarzan turned suddenly to the east toward the river after he had passed the end of the gauntlet that had held him to a straight path at the beginning of his flight.

A scream of rage burst from the lips of Nemone as she saw and realized the purpose of the quarry. A sullen roar rose from the pursuing crowd. They had not thought that the hunted man had a chance, but now they understood that he might yet reach the river and the forest. This, of course, did not mean to them that he would then escape, for they well knew that Belthar would pursue him across the river; what they feared was that they might be robbed of the thrills of witnessing the kill.

But presently their anger turned to relief as they saw that Belthar was gaining on the man so rapidly that there was no chance that the latter might reach the river before he was over-hauled and dragged down.

Tarzan, too, glancing back over a bronzed shoulder, realized that the end was near. The river was still two hundred yards away and the lion, steadily gaining on him, but fifty.

Then the ape-man turned and waited. He stood at ease, his arms hanging at his side; but he was alert and ready. He knew precisely what Belthar would do, and he knew what he would do. No amount of training would have changed the lion's instinctive method of attack; he would rush at Tarzan, rear upon his hind feet when close, seize him with his taloned paws and drive his great fangs through his head or neck or shoulder; then he would drag him down and devour him.

But Tarzan had met the charge of lions before. It would not be quite so easy for Belthar as Belthar and the screaming audience believed, yet the ape-man guessed that, without a knife, he could do no more than delay the inevitable. He would die fighting, however; and now, as Belthar charged growling upon him, he crouched slightly and answered the roaring challenge of the carnivore with a roar as savage as the lion's.

Suddenly he detected a new note in the voice of the crowd, a note of surprise and consternation. Belthar was almost upon him as a tawny body streaked past the ape-man, brushing his leg as it came from behind him; and as Belthar rose upon his hind feet fell upon him, a fury of talons and gleaming fangs, a great lion with a golden coat and a black mane—a mighty engine of rage and destruction.

Roaring and growling, the two great beasts rolled upon the ground as they tore at one another with teeth and claws while the astounded ape-man looked on and the chariot of the Queen approached, and the breathless crowd pressed forward.

The strange lion was larger than Belthar and more powerful, a giant of a lion in the full prime of his strength and ferocity; and he fought as one inspired by all the demons of Hell. Presently Belthar gave him an opening; and his great jaws closed upon the throat of the hunting lion of Nemone, jaws that drove mighty fangs through the thick mane of his adversary, through hide and flesh deep into the jugular of Belthar; then he braced his feet and shook Belthar as a cat might shake a mouse, breaking his neck.

Dropping the carcass to the ground, the victor faced the astonished Cathneans with snarling face; then he slowly backed to where the ape-man stood and stopped beside him, and Tarzan laid his hand upon the black mane of Jad-bal-ja, the Golden Lion.

For a long moment there was unbroken silence as the two faced the enemies of the Lord of the Jungle, and the awed Cathneans only stood and stared; then a woman's voice rose in a weird scream. It was Nemone. Slowly she stepped from her golden car and amidst utter silence walked toward the carcass of the dead Belthar while her people watched her, motionless and wondering.

She stopped with her sandaled feet touching the bloody mane of the hunting lion and gazed down upon the dead carnivore. She might have been in silent prayer for the minute that she stood there; then she raised her head suddenly and looked about her. There was a wild gleam in her eyes and she was very white, white as the ivory ornament in the hollow of her throat.

"Belthar is dead!" she screamed, and whipping her dagger from its sheath drove its glittering point deep into her own heart. Without a sound she sank to her knees and toppled forward across the body of the dead Belthar.

As the moon rose, Tarzan placed a final rock upon a mound

of earth beside the river that runs to Cathne through the valley of Onthar.

The warriors and the nobles and the people had followed Phordos to the city to empty the dungeons of Nemone and proclaim Alextar King, leaving their dead Queen lying at the edge of the Field of the Lions with the dead Belthar.

The human service they had neglected the beast-man had performed, and now beneath the soft radiance of an African moon he stood with bowed head beside the grave of a woman who had found happiness at last.

✏ FREE DRINKS ✏

Take the Del Rey® survey and get a free newsletter! Answer the questions below and we will send you complimentary copies of the DRINK (Del Rey® Ink) newsletter free for one year. Here's where you will find out all about upcoming books, read articles by top authors, artists, and editors, and get the inside scoop on your favorite books.

Age _____ Sex ❑ M ❑ F

Highest education level: ❑ high school ❑ college ❑ graduate degree

Annual income: ❑ $0-30,000 ❑ $30,001-60,000 ❑ over $60,000

Number of books you read per month: ❑ 0-2 ❑ 3-5 ❑ 6 or more

Preference: ❑ fantasy ❑ science fiction ❑ horror ❑ other fiction ❑ nonfiction

I buy books in hardcover: ❑ frequently ❑ sometimes ❑ rarely

I buy books at: ❑ superstores ❑ mall bookstores ❑ independent bookstores
    ❑ mail order

I read books by new authors: ❑ frequently ❑ sometimes ❑ rarely

I read comic books: ❑ frequently ❑ sometimes ❑ rarely

I watch the Sci-Fi cable TV channel: ❑ frequently ❑ sometimes ❑ rarely

I am interested in collector editions (signed by the author or illustrated):
    ❑ yes ❑ no ❑ maybe

I read Star Wars novels: ❑ frequently ❑ sometimes ❑ rarely

I read Star Trek novels: ❑ frequently ❑ sometimes ❑ rarely

I read the following newspapers and magazines:
    ❑ *Analog*   ❑ *Locus*   ❑ *Popular Science*
    ❑ *Asimov*   ❑ *Wired*   ❑ *USA Today*
    ❑ *SF Universe*   ❑ *Realms of Fantasy* ❑ *The New York Times*

Check the box if you do not want your name and address shared with qualified vendors ❑

Name _____

Address _____

City/State/Zip _____

E-mail _____

tarzan 2-in-1

PLEASE SEND TO: DEL REY®/The DRINK
201 EAST 50TH STREET NEW YORK NY 10022

DEL REY® ONLINE!

The Del Rey Internet Newsletter...
A monthly electronic publication, posted on the Internet, GEnie, CompuServe, BIX, various BBSs, and the Panix gopher (gopher.panix.com). It features hype-free descriptions of books that are new in the stores, a list of our upcoming books, special announcements, a signing/reading/convention-attendance schedule for Del Rey authors, "In Depth" essays in which professionals in the field (authors, artists, designers, salespeople, etc.) talk about their jobs in science fiction, a question-and-answer section, behind-the-scenes looks at sf publishing, and more!

Internet information source!
A lot of Del Rey material is available to the Internet on our Web site and on a gopher server: all back issues and the current issue of the Del Rey Internet Newsletter, sample chapters of upcoming or current books (readable or downloadable for free), submission requirements, mail-order information, and much more. We will be adding more items of all sorts (mostly new DRINs and sample chapters) regularly. The Web site is http://www.randomhouse.com/delrey/ and the address of the gopher is gopher.panix.com

Why?
We at Del Rey realize that the networks are the medium of the future. That's where you'll find us promoting our books, socializing with others in the sf field, and—most important—making contact and sharing information with sf readers.

Online editorial presence:
Many of the Del Rey editors are online, on the Internet, GEnie, CompuServe, America Online, and Delphi. There is a Del Rey topic on GEnie and a Del Rey folder on America Online.

Our official e-mail address
for Del Rey Books is delrey@randomhouse.com (though it sometimes takes us a while to answer).